Mary Gladding Wheeler Benjamin

The Missionary Sisters

Mary Gladding Wheeler Benjamin

The Missionary Sisters

ISBN/EAN: 9783742812513

Manufactured in Europe, USA, Canada, Australia, Japa

Cover: Foto ©Andreas Hilbeck / pixelio.de

Manufactured and distributed by brebook publishing software
(www.brebook.com)

Mary Gladding Wheeler Benjamin

The Missionary Sisters

THE MISSIONARY SISTERS:

A MEMORIAL OF

MRS. SERAPHINA HAYNES EVERETT,

AND

MRS. HARRIET MARTHA HAMLIN,

LATE MISSIONARIES OF THE A. B. C. F. M. AT CONSTANTINOPLE.

BY

MRS. M. G. BENJAMIN.

PUBLISHED BY THE
AMERICAN TRACT SOCIETY,

Printed by

GEO. C. RAND & AVERY, 3 CORNHILL, BOSTON.

PREFACE.

THE memoir of Mrs. Everett was the work originally intended and commenced; but after this had been partly prepared, letters were received from several missionary friends in Constantinople, urging the writer to combine with it a memorial of Mrs. Hamlin. As these two ladies had been so closely associated in their missionary life and work, a biography of one would necessarily involve much of that of the other, and it was thought better to present them together, and from their united letters give a history of the Armenian Female Seminary in Constantinople through the years of their connection with it, than to make two separate volumes.

The writer is not without fears that the friends of both ladies may be somewhat disappointed in the present arrangement, and regret the omission of some interesting portions of their correspondence; but she trusts they will consider the difficulty of compiling such a work in a way to meet the wishes of friends, and at the same time not be tedious to the general reader. She has felt often no little perplexity in selecting from the very full and rich materials in her hands; and if the main object had been to prepare an entertaining book, much more of personal incident and local description might have been introduced, which have been left out to make room for fuller details of the missionary work.

It is sometimes objected to memoirs, that they are partial, setting forth all the virtues of their subjects, and keeping out of sight all their defects. As "there is no perfection here below," it is assumed that those good people whose lives are recorded for our imitation, must have had prominent faults as well as great excellences. That they were imperfect is doubtless true of them as of others, and certainly none are more sensible of their imperfections than those who have made the highest attainments in the Christian life; but that these remains of human infirmity necessarily continue to manifest themselves in unamiable tempers, and in words and acts contrary to the pure and lovely spirit of the gospel, does not follow. If it does, what becomes of the efficacy of God's grace on the heart? The Bible, it is said, should be a model for biographers. But does the Bible give us no examples of characters outwardly blameless? And if Joseph and Samuel and Daniel became what they were by the grace of God, under all the imperfections of the old dispensation, why should it be "deemed a thing incredible" that such characters should be matured by the same rich and abounding grace under the gospel? Why then, when reading the records of the life and experience of Christ's eminent servants, should we search carefully for the mention of their faults, and lay down the book with some such ungracious remark as this: "It is all very beautiful, though it is not the original, but only a flattered likeness, for no person was ever so perfect in this world." Why not rather magnify the grace of God, and be stimulated to follow more earnestly them who, "through faith and patience," have acquired such control over their inward corruptions, as for a long course of years, and under all the trials and temptations of this evil world, to maintain a deportment above reproach, and be conspicuous in every thing that is "amiable, and lovely, and of good report?" Many such there have been and are, in whom their nearest friends and most intimate associates can scarcely perceive a fault, while they themselves are humble, mourning in secret over their unworthiness and many shortcomings, and ready even to acknowledge themselves, as did the great apostle, the chief of sinners, whose only hope is in the mercy of Christ. And many more such there might be, if instead of settling it to be an attainment impossible, Christians would more generally keep before them the same perfect standard at which they aimed. Such were the two lovely missionary sisters whose characters and abundant labors in the Saviour's cause it has been attempted in the following pages to delineate; and it is hoped that through the record they have left of themselves in their familiar correspondence, some glimpses may be obtained of the workings of their inner life, and the way in which they were enabled to reach a piety so elevated, and to perform so much in the service of their heavenly Master.

CONTENTS.

CHAPTER XXIV.

CHAPTER XXV.

CHAPTER XXVI.

CHAPTER XXVII.

CHAPTER XXVIII.

MEMOIR.

CHAPTER I.

SERAPHINA HAYNES EVERETT was born in Monson, Massachusetts, Dec. 29, 1823; but as her parents removed to Southbridge in the same State before she was two years old, she always spoke of that as her native place. She was the child of godly parents, who endeavored to train up their family of fourteen children in the "nurture and admonition of the Lord." Her father, Deacon Henry Haynes, has for many years been a highly respected officer in the Congregational church of Southbridge. Of her mother, her children are the highest eulogium. Two of the fourteen died in infancy; and five others, after having acted well their part in life, and left behind them memories fragrant with all womanly and Christian graces, have been called to join the blessed company above. Three lovely sisters preceded Mrs. Everett to the " better country," and one has since followed.

Of this large household band, Seraphina was the seventh in age. She was an interesting child, and very early evinced a fondness for study, and great quickness in the acquisition of knowledge. Her father still dwells with pleasure on her early attainments, such as spelling in words of two syllables before she was three years old, and

reciting geography at four. Many reminiscences of her
winning ways and unusual intelligence are treasured up
in her childhood's home.

When Seraphina was ten years old, she was invited to
spend some time with a relative in a neighboring town.
While there, her sweet face and attractive manners won
the affection of a lady who had recently lost a daughter
of the same age ; and she asked her to come and stay with
her a while, and go to school at her expense. She remained with this lady quite happily for more than two
years, and then returned to her father's house. When
about fourteen she commenced teaching a small school,
and continued with good success for several months, after
which she again attended school in the adjoining village
of Sturbridge. It was while she was at this school that
she experienced her first permanent religious impressions.
Some of the circumstances connected with this crisis in
her life are as follows : —

There was at the time a special religious interest in
Southbridge, and her sister Mary was among the number
of those who were rejoicing in the new experience of a
Saviour's love. She wrote immediately to Seraphina, to
communicate to her the joyful tidings. On receiving this
letter, the latter resolved to return home that same evening, though to do so she must walk a considerable part of
the way, and it was then quite late in the afternoon. She
seemed to have brought her energetic spirit at once to the
resolution that she would seek the Lord, and that no obstacles should prevent it. Though ever conscientious, and
frequently the subject of deep religious impressions, she
had for some time previous to this manifested no particular interest in this subject, but was apparently all absorbed
in her studies. It was Saturday evening when she returned to her home, and greeted the sister whose letter
had aroused such an earnest desire and purpose in her
soul to be numbered with the people of God. That even-

ing she attended a prayer meeting, and in joining with two of her sisters in prayer after the meeting, she, with affecting earnestness, sent up her petition for mercy. The next Tuesday morning, when she returned to school, it was with a trembling but joyful hope that she had become reconciled to God. From that period she dated the commencement of her Christian life. She was then fifteen.

The two or three years which followed her conversion were spent by her in teaching and attending school alternately, and were divided between her own home and Sturbridge, where her eldest brother resided. No letters written during this period are preserved. A paper, on which, copied in pencil, are some half-obliterated "Questions for self-examination," from President Edwards, affords the only glimpse into her inner life at that time. There is no date to this, but just below is written, also in pencil, and in the same hand, which is quite unformed and juvenile, unlike her writing a year later —

"Resolved, Saturday evening, Feb. 27, 1841, that I will not, the grace of God assisting me, hereafter be guilty of sleeping while in the sanctuary, or when apparently engaged in his worship."

Seraphina's temperament was lively, and from allusions in her later letters, it may be inferred that this was, during the early part of her Christian life, a source of some trouble to her. She seems indeed, in her mature piety, to have judged rather severely of her Christian character at this time; more severely than from the recollections of her friends it would seem she had reason to do. The sister who knew her most intimately, relates that she always maintained the habit of secret devotion, and was ever ready to join in meetings for prayer, whether public or social. Her piety was always of a cheerful cast, partaking doubtless of her buoyant temperament; though the following anecdote shows that this habit of prayer had

2

much to do with it. When she was sixteen, she had the charge of a district school, in which were sixty or more pupils. A friend, who was surprised to see her so uniformly cheerful with such a care, asked her how she could always look so pleasant and happy with such a school on her hands. "Oh! I could not, if I did not pray every morning for strength and patience," was the reply.

It was doubtless this habitual communion with God which enabled her to grow so rapidly in grace, and to overcome every obstacle, both in natural temperament and outward circumstances, which impeded her Christian race. Whatever may have been her difficulty from too great exuberance of spirits in her earlier years, nothing apparently remained of it after she assumed the duties and responsibilities of a missionary's wife. A beautiful cheerfulness only was retained, which added a charm to her manners and a sweet grace to her countenance; and which showed itself frequently in her letters in playful allusions and lively sallies, and, chastened as it always was by earnest piety, formed one of the chief attractions of her correspondence.

Her home attachments were strong. Neither her frequent absences in early life, nor her later wide separation, seemed to have weakened in the least her affection for each member of the family circle. Of this both her earlier and later letters give ample proof; and these letters also furnish pleasing testimony to the wise and kind parental influence, and the sweet brotherly and sisterly love, which united in such strong ties that large family band.

The following, one of her earliest letters preserved, was written while she was teaching in Charlton, a few miles from her home. One of the two sisters referred to had died the year previous, and the other had married and removed to Millbury.

"Charlton, June 8, 1842. You know I almost boasted of not crying all last summer; but just think of going home, and finding no Eleanor and *dear Mary*, who was always there, — who would not cry? You, I know, will not blame me if I do. But I do not mean to complain, and my temperament is such that if I am unhappy it does not last long, and if we are separated from our earthly friends,

'One there is above all others,
Well deserves the name of friend,'

in whom we can confide, and with whom we can hold communion at all times, without distrust or disappointment, if we are in the right frame of mind, and cherish right feelings; and this, you know, is every thing. My affections are so much fixed upon this world, and the things of it, and so swallowed up in self, that I sometimes wonder how I dare approach the throne of grace, and address it with so much coldness and indifference. I sometimes think that I have not even a desire that my will should be swallowed up in God's will, and I wish I could in sincerity say, — 'Here, Lord, I give myself away.' Is it not strange that we, and professing Christians every where, do not possess more of the spirit of our Master, when he said, — 'Wist ye not that I must be about my Father's business,'—living as we do in this day of light, and opportunities of doing good? Shall we not be without excuse, if the world is no better for our having lived in it?"

CHAPTER II.

First School Days at Andover — Prospect of a Missionary Life.

In the autumn of 1842 Miss Haynes entered the Abbott Female Seminary in Andover as a pupil. There was at that time no boarding department in connection with this school. Some of the pupils from abroad boarded in private families, while others joined together in a common boarding-house, doing their own work, with a matron to superintend. Miss H. became a member of this latter establishment, and with her domestic employments besides her studies, which were rather severe, found full occupation for all her time and powers. But she had learned to be a good economist of time, and with all her duties, managed to get spare moments enough to write long and frequent letters to her dear home friends. There is a journal of a few leaves, commenced during her first term at Andover, and continued, with occasional entries, through the next two years. From this, and from the correspondence of this period, a few brief extracts are presented.

To a sister, under date of Nov. 14, 1842, she writes: "Your letter was received rather unexpectedly, but if possible, the more gladly. Of my feelings on its reception you can judge, but if ever I had occasion to weep from mingled emotions of pain and pleasure, it was at that moment. Dear sister Eleanor's pale countenance has not, I can assure you, been out of my mind during any very long period, since hearing of her increased ill-health.

. . . While my heart was pained by the intelligence of her illness, I could not avoid weeping for joy at the news of L.'s conversion. It did seem to me yesterday as if I must be at home and spend the Sabbath with you, to hear from L.'s own mouth what God has done for her, and to hear also of many others, who, like her, are experiencing the joy of sins forgiven. You know better than I do what to tell L.; but do urge her from me to live near to her Saviour, and watch and pray that she may not be led into temptation. And dear sister, I wish you to offer the same prayer for me, knowing how easily I am led astray from my duty and my God."

In the next letter, after inquiring about various members of the family, she says: "I *affect* no ignorance. For a time after I came here, my imagination could picture the situation of each of you, — and this was a great consolation; but now it is all confused. How much do you suppose, dear mother, I thought of you all at the time of our annual feast? Then I think I imagined you just as you were each hour in the day. One was gone, *for ever* gone, from our family meetings here on earth, who one short year since enjoyed with us the happy gathering. She will not return to us, but may we all go and join her, a 'whole family in heaven.' Dear Mary! It seems to me that oftener than ever I think of her, — of the kind, cheerful letters she used to write; and often when I look about me to imagine the situations of my brothers and sisters, I think of that little spot in the lone burial-ground, where her earthly remains lie."

In her journal of Jan. 1, 1843, she writes: "Seeking the aid of him who is both able and willing to impart strength, I now resolve to act more according to the promptings of my own conscience, seeking thus more faithfully to perform my duties towards God and man. In particular I resolve not to say any thing to the injury of another, and in this respect more faithfully to keep the

2*

18 THE MISSIONARY SISTERS.

command, to do unto others as I would that they should do to me."

Her next letter, written from Andover, Jan. 3, 1843, contains the first mention of her future husband.

"And the Sabbath school I must mention, because we have such a dear, good teacher, Mr. Everett, of the Theological Seminary. He sometimes calls on us, and does not go without closing the interview with prayer. He is intending to go as a missionary to Persia, when his studies are completed, and is now studying the language with Mar Yohanan, who is learning our language of Mr. E. The Bishop finds our language difficult to acquire, and asks a great many strange questions. Mr. E. gave for one example, that he inquired what manhood meant. He said he knew what man meant, but what did *hood* mean?"

In the spring of this year she returned home, uncertain whether she should enjoy the privilege so earnestly desired, of resuming her studies in Andover. Shortly after a proposal was received, which decided some of her uncertainties, and opened a way for her to enter on a new sphere of usefulness,—a sphere for which she seemed eminently fitted by natural endowments and thorough cultivation, as well as elevated and earnest piety. Some of her feelings, in regard to these new prospects, are expressed in a letter to an absent sister, written at the time.

"Southbridge, May 27, 1845.

"We want you here now *very much indeed*, (I am speaking for myself,) which I presume you would not doubt if you knew how many times I have said it during the last week; and perhaps you would have wished the same when I tell you, that if you had been here you would have formed an acquaintance with the gentleman in whom you say you are so much interested. When I wrote to you last, I did not suppose that he would be here

before the 1st of June, and knew nothing to the contrary
until a week ago last Monday, when I received a letter,
stating that he would be in Southbridge Tuesday evening.
My first impulse was to write immediately to you, but
March said the end of the world had not come yet;
and not knowing how long Mr. E. would be here, I thought
it best not to write. I assure you, the opinion I had previously formed of him was not changed. . . . Do not say
that I am under the influence of the *blind boy* entirely,
— will you? for the impression I first had of him when
in Andover was, that he was entirely devoted to the cause
of our heavenly Master, and I still think I never met
with a person who felt more for the advancement of
Christ's kingdom. How unworthy am I, dear sister, of
the regard of such a person, and how unfit to *think* even,
of ever being engaged in a work which requires so much
holiness and self-consecration, so much self-denial and
devotion to the cause which I have professed to love, and
yet neglected and dishonored. Do pray for me, dear sister,
that all my motives, actions, thoughts, and feelings may
be right in the sight of him who looks at the heart, and
knows all. I have prayed that I might not be permitted
to act wrong in this matter, which it seems to me is of
almost infinite importance; but my heart is so deceitful
and so little known to myself, that perhaps I have felt it
but little. What a consolation to think that all our ways
are in the hands of one who is able to guide them in
mercy!"

She spent the next summer in teaching in Sturbridge,
and in close application to reading and study during all
the intervals she could obtain from her school duties.

The following letter, and a few entries in her journal,
furnish the only record of her Christian experience and
her occupations during this summer, which she often afterwards referred to as one of the most pleasant portions
of her life.

"You know how delightful all nature is, robed in her mantle of green, and the flowers

'Every where about us are they glowing;'

and the birds, catching the inspiration, swell their notes of praise to the God of nature; and we, how can we resist the impulse we feel to join in the general chorus, and praise him too! I enjoy myself very much. The greatest difficulty I have is that I can not accomplish half enough; the days and weeks fly. Six are already gone since I came here; whether any good has been done by my labors in my school, or not, they will not return."

In her journal, July 14, she writes: —

"Lest my attention and prayers should be too exclusively devoted to one object, to the neglect of others equally important, it may be well to conform to a system by which each day some particular department of the great work of the world's salvation shall claim my attention. For the present I will adopt the following plan, seeking the Holy Spirit to guide me by his influences, that my soul may be filled with love to the whole human race, and that I may be exercised with a holy zeal for the interests of the cause of God in the world.

"Sunday, the church in our own land; Monday, the cause of education; Tuesday, the Bible cause; Wednesday, foreign missions; Thursday, home missions: Friday, seamen and temperance; Saturday, the Sabbath and Sabbath schools."

July 21. "I have reason to thank the Lord that he condescends to meet me with a blessing when I seek to draw near to him in prayer. I do trust that I feel a willingness and a desire to do or suffer any thing which will be for his glory."

July 31. "This day I close my school, and take perhaps a final leave of many of those with whom I have been associated. Have I done my duty to them? is a question which causes me anxiety. But regrets are now useless, and I pray God to bless what has been done in accordance with his will, and counteract any influence that may have been exerted, of a contrary tendency. May I meet all these dear children in heaven!

"And I must bid farewell to this my little room, where I have spent so many happy hours,— hours which I trust have not been wholly unprofitable;— where I have felt in some degree my unworthiness and sinfulness, and have been led to draw near to God, pleading his promises, until I humbly hope that in his infinite compassion he has drawn near to me. Now may his Spirit attend me to my home, and there restrain me that I wander not from him, but preserve me from the power of temptation, and help me to live devoted to his service."

CHAPTER III.

In the earliest letter of the next year, we find Miss H. again at her beloved studies in Andover.

ANDOVER, January 13, 1844.

DEAR SISTER: It is now the evening of the holy Sabbath. Clear and beautiful the day has been, fit emblem of the eternal rest which we hope to enjoy when the tempests of life have all subsided, and we enter upon a new, a heavenly existence, where no sinful thoughts will ever intrude, with nothing to divert from the celestial employment, which will engage our whole souls. "O glorious hour! O blest abode!"

Mr. Taylor has preached two excellent sermons to-day. He has been sick, and did not preach his new-year sermon until last Sabbath. It was very good; from the text "Redeeming the time, because the days are evil." He showed us the importance of laboring for God *now*. In the afternoon was the communion service. In the evening, at the Sabbath-school Concert, we were addressed by Mr. Green, Secretary of the American Board. He was in town during Saturday, spoke to the students in the evening, and has preached through the day at the chapel of the Theological Seminary. He is filled with the spirit of missions. It seems to be his life, his breath. I think he infused some of this feeling into the hearts of those who heard him. The work is to be done; and why not labor now, as well as after millions on millions have passed from the shades of heathenism into eternal darkness in the world of woe. Why do we not arise in the strength of Christ, with Paul for our example, and in obedience to the same commands, stimulated by the same promises, and anticipating the same blessed reward, why do we not *act?*

Filled with a holy zeal, he boldly preached the unsearchable riches of Christ in every direction where his name had not been named, enduring every peril to which a mortal can be exposed, yet, nothing daunted, he presses on in his good fight until his course is finished and he goes to receive his crown of righteousness. Are our lives more valuable than Paul's, that we should not lay them down in this glorious work?

You expect by this time to know the destination of your friends, if the Lord shall see fit to send us, who are so unworthy, to the heathen; but it is not yet decided; how soon it will be, I do not know. Tell father it is possible we may go to China; if not, it is probable to India, which we most earnestly hope will be approved by him and all our dear friends, because wherever there is a work for us to do, there the Lord will send us, and there I trust we shall delight to go.

Is it possible, dear sister, ere another short year has passed, that I shall have bidden a final adieu to those so dear to me? It may be so, but it is only an earthly separation, which is momentary. You would not detain us; we would not stay; but seeking to be clad with the whole gospel armor, go and carry the glad news of a Saviour's love to the perishing heathen. Oh, forget us not when daily you bow before the throne of Almighty grace, — *then pray for us.* . . . . . .

The following to her parents, dated Andover, January 28, 1844, beautifully exhibits the contending emotions which agitated her heart in view of circumstances which were beginning now to give greater definiteness to her prospect of a missionary life.

MY VERY DEAR PARENTS: It is Sabbath evening, and after having attended church twice, and spent some time in reading, meditation, and prayer, I yield to a strong desire to write to you, — to you, who in my early infancy dedicated me to God; who early instructed me, before closing my eyes in sleep, to say "Our Father," to one above; and taught me all the truths of our religion as revealed in the word of God; who have watched over me from year to year, ministering most kindly to all my wants when with you, and never failing to remember me at the throne of grace, whether present or absent. Much more than all this received at your hands, calls for my deepest gratitude and affection; which I fondly hope is not without a response, and a most hearty one, from my inmost soul. Often, very often, when separated from you and the society of brothers and sisters, my thoughts revert to my own dear home, and the circle of loved ones there; and then how I long to join you, to mingle my petitions with yours at the hours of devotion, and my voice in songs of praise. Those happy days when so many of us were assembled under the paternal roof, are passed. Two have firesides of their own to gladden and bless; one is far away from his youthful home; one dear one is in heaven; others away, though not far; one has a home in the sunny South; and only three from the large band daily meet around our own domestic hearth. Yet, dear parents, you murmur not that you are denied the happiness you might receive if more were permitted to be with you to cheer your way down the declivity of life. You have sought to train them up for usefulness in the world, and you have the unspeakable pleasure of feeling that most of those whom God committed to you, and whom you dedicated to him, have ratified the covenant " by surnaming themselves by the name of Israel; " so that, wherever they are, you can feel that they are in the service and under the protection of Israel's God. And one of your children seems called to labor in the cause of God on heathen ground, even your unworthy Seraphina; and more and more unworthy do I seem as I am led to a nearer view of the work as a stern reality.

Mr. Everett received a letter from Mr. Green, in behalf of the A. B. C. F. M., last week, stating that his papers had been laid before the Committee, and were accepted. No formal appointment was made, as they wished to confer with him further in regard to the field of labor, before his designation, when the two could be made together; requesting to see him as soon as convenient. He went to Boston yesterday, expecting to return to-morrow. Then, it is probable, the portion of the Lord's vineyard in which we are destined to labor will be assigned; that dark corner of the earth where we may be the humble instruments of scattering light and knowledge will be pointed out.

Oh, why am I called to contemplate this great and glorious employment, when there are so many in every respect far more worthy, and better fitted for the work! Often I fear that I may " run and not be sent; " but my earnest prayer is, " Forbid it, Lord, and consecrate me wholly to thee; fit me to be an acceptable laborer for thee, and send me to the heathen. Let me tell of a Saviour's love to the benighted, and, by pointing to Calvary, soothe some troubled spirit that had never heard the story of the Cross." And wherever the Lord may send me, there may I delight to go, even if it be to India's torrid clime.

You, my dear parents, as well as myself, are aware that

3

one of so ardent a temperament as mine is in peculiar danger of yielding to the influence of wrong motives. It may be possible that a strong attachment to an earthly friend will have an undue influence; against this I pray, and trust that my petitions are not in vain, and that the consecration to God of all my powers of body and mind, my highest love and best services, will be accepted. And as I endeavor daily to renew it, will not you, my parents, join me in my requests that I may have a purer heart, a more holy love, stronger faith, and every other grace necessary to make me an acceptable offering on the altar of missions? Your petitions will avail much in my behalf.

Mr. Everett will write you soon, if his designation is made. Dear father, you will not shrink to send, with your blessing, those whom you love to India, if such seems to be the appointment of Providence. I dare not think that, ere the months of this year have passed, I may be called to bid a last farewell to my *dear, dear* home and *much-loved friends.* But it is the *Lord* who says, "As thy day is so shall thy strength be."

Your very affectionate daughter,

SERAPHINA.

It seemed quite probable for a time that Mr. Everett and Miss H. would be appointed to join a company of missionaries to sail in a few weeks for India, and their minds were somewhat agitated respecting it, as they both felt themselves unprepared to engage so soon in the work before them. Mr. E. needed yet a half year to finish his theological course, and Miss Haynes wished also to continue another six months at her studies. But she writes in a sweetly submissive spirit, willing to go or stay, as the Lord should direct, and to go where he should appoint. The following passage from one of these letters shows how entirely she had consecrated herself to the missionary work: —

"I have been called to look at the near prospect of a home among degraded heathen, to a wide separation from you, my precious sister, from my dear parents, and all those to whom I am so closely and tenderly bound. But, by the grace of God, I have not felt the least shrinking, only as far as my unworthiness for the service is concerned. This, with the excitement occasioned by the suddenness with which it seemed, for a few days past, that we must engage in the missionary work, led me unguardedly to make an expression in my last letter which has since troubled me, lest you should interpret it differently from what I intended. My head and heart do ache when I think of the thousands of poor starving heathen, perishing for want of the bread of life, and so few ready to break it to them; but not when I think the blessed privilege may be mine, of denying myself a few of the pleasures and comforts of life, that I may hasten to them, and spend my days in seeking to lead to Calvary some of those benighted ones."

A single entry in her journal during her last two terms at Andover describes so fully her missionary feelings that it is introduced entire.

"A year has quickly flown since I was called to decide the important question whether I would share the joys and sorrows, the toils and trials of a missionary life. To this cause of God I have sought to consecrate myself; but the Searcher of hearts only knows whether the consecration is sincere. I trust I am his, to be used in whatever way will best honor his name; but have I the devotedness to him necessary to make me an acceptable laborer among the ignorant and degraded heathen?

"A year this subject has been almost constantly before my mind, and yet how cold is my heart! Often indeed have I wept bitter tears when I have considered the darkness that pervades so many millions of souls, and longed to be the means of dispelling the cloud from even one of these sin-darkened minds; of whispering pardon and peace to a soul just emerging from the thick shades of pagan idolatry; of pointing some self-tortured Hindoo to the cross of Christ, that he may hear the Saviour say, 'Take my yoke upon you, which is easy, and my burden, which is light.'

"What are all the sacrifices I may make in this work when I contemplate the scene on Calvary, where the Lord of glory bowed his head to purchase man's redemption? Or what the sufferings that may fall to my lot, compared with those of a *soul lost for ever?*

"Oh, why are my feelings so languid! My soul should rather burn with love for the perishing, so that my thanksgivings would daily be offered to God for the prospect he has given me of participating in the glorious work.

"Within the last few weeks, the period for a time seemed short that I might enjoy the blessings of a Christian land, of my own dear home, and the society of the loved ones wont to gather around that sacred spot. But the Lord made me willing, and enabled me to rejoice even in the anticipation of flying to the heathen. Yet it was with much trembling lest I should run and not be sent, that I have been led to call earnestly upon him who hears the young ravens when *they* cry.

"But God's time had not come, and it is that for which we wait, earnestly seeking to be better prepared to go whenever he shall call; to be clad in the whole gospel armor, ready for the trying conflict."

After spending her spring vacation at home, she returned for her last term to Andover. In a letter written May 13, after speaking with lively interest of a work of the Holy Spirit then in progress at A., she describes a visit she had recently made to Boston, to be present at the departure of Messrs. Hoisington, Scudder, and Taylor, with their wives, the company with whom they had expected to sail for India. After attending the public religious exercises of the evening previous, she went "on board the ship that was to bear them, perhaps for ever, from the scenes and friends they loved," and adds, "I trust it was by means of strength from God that I was kept calm, although my faith (I must confess it) had been severely tried in more quiet hours, when my poor weak nature called loudly for sympathy; then I felt how little was my confidence in God, how little my love for the poor heathen."

To her mother, a little later, she writes: "The future is not dark; it is the call of God which I seek to obey, and it is his voice that says, 'Lo! I am with you alway.' And is not this enough to dissipate all clouds of distrust and unbelief? Oh that it did work this in me at all times! But a voice within sometimes tells me, 'You are unworthy, you are not sent of God, and can not call the promise yours.' Perhaps it is so; and then is it not possible that these are temptations of our great adversary, designed to weaken my confidence in my heavenly Master? I do long to be entirely submissive in his hands, to trust him fully, confidently. I am weak, but he is almighty. My soul earnestly longs to be engaged in his work among the heathen, and I pray that I may go with my *whole* heart where he guides." . . . .

To one of her sisters she writes, July 8: "How good, how kind is my heavenly Father! I do pray that my life and health may be spared and grace given me to labor long in his service. Why do we live for any thing short of this? Why do we not count all else but loss, and feel that to win Christ ourselves, and lead others to him, is the only object worth living for? Yes; let us give all, it is not too much; it is nothing. It may cost a few tears, some pangs of grief; but what are they compared with the redemption of souls?"

Shortly after the above was written, her last term at Andover closed, and she returned to spend a little time at home before leaving it to return no more.

3*

It was finally decided by the Prudential Committee that Mr. Everett should join the Armenian mission in Western Asia. Of the reasons for this change in their destination there is no mention in any of Miss Haynes's letters. The only allusion to it is found in the following to one of her brothers, dated Nov. 9 : —

"The future is all uncertain. A long time we waited to know where the Lord would have us labor. He has now, in his own time, directed us to a most important and deeply interesting portion of his vineyard. Now the time when he wishes us to occupy this field is in his hand, and we hope to be ready whenever called for; ready to go, trusting in the arm of Heaven for strength and wisdom to fight the battles of the Lord amid the darkness of superstition. Oh for a more entire consecration to this glorious work, — more living faith, glowing zeal, and warmer love !"

In September Miss Haynes made her first and last visit to Mr. Everett's paternal home in Halifax, Vermont. Some of the incidents of this little journey, and the family meeting, are pleasantly described by her in several letters, which we are compelled entirely to omit, excepting a single sentence in a letter dated from the "loved old home," of which she writes : —

"All the family spent the Sabbath at home, save the brother at Barre, and the sister at Peru. S—— has told you how on Saturday after all had arrived, we visited the spot where the loved mother sleeps. It was a sad but precious time. My thoughts flew back to my own dear mother, and I thanked God that she still lives to bless me by her precious counsels and prayers."

The following to her sister Eleanor was written just on the eve of her marriage and departure from her childhood's home : —

"I did not think, when I wrote you last, that you would hear from us again so soon : that so soon I should be called hastily to pen my *last epistle* to you from my own dear home; probably the last in the land of my birth, my own loved America.

"The Stamboul arrived on Wednesday last. Mr. Everett received a letter from Dr. Anderson this afternoon, stating that the day appointed for her to sail for Smyrna is the 20th of this month, and we are to be in Boston on the 17th. So you see we have but one week here. Oh that we might spend that chiefly in attending to our spiritual interests, — in seeking entire consecration of soul and body to the great and holy work on which we are about to enter! Oh that worldly things might shrink into comparative insignificance, and Christ fill our souls! Do, dear brother and sister, be much in prayer for us, that we may be prepared by God's grace for every event that awaits us."

Miss Haynes's marriage to the Rev. Joel Sumner Everett took place Feb. 12, 1845. Five days later she bade a final adieu to her beloved parents, and the home and its pleasant surroundings so dear to her heart. The following brief extracts are some of her last words from her native land: —

Boston, Feb. 20, 1845.

MY DEAR, VERY DEAR PARENTS: Are you thinking of us to-day as embarking for our future home? You should have been informed to the contrary, before this, that your tender sympathies might be spared the pain a few days longer of seeing us in imagination commit ourselves to a passage across the wide, treacherous sea. . . .

I need not tell you that you are scarcely at all absent from my thoughts, and have not been since I looked upon your faces, and heard your voices for the last time on earth. I have prayed, and do pray God to be with and comfort, cheer, and bless you abundantly, continually fill your souls with peace, and spare your lives long to bless your family and the world. Pray much for us, that the promises of our Saviour may be verified to us, that we may be prepared for eminent usefulness.

BOSTON HARBOR, Bark Stamboul, Feb. 25, 1845.

MY VERY DEAR PARENTS: I can not forbear writing a word to you this evening, since all is so calm and quiet here, and we have nothing to keep our thoughts from turning to those with whom from henceforth we can communicate only in this way.

I have bade adieu to you, dear father and mother, and all the dear friends to whom my heart has been wont so fondly to cling, and from whom, even now, I am departed only in body, and I am not unhappy; no, *far from it.* The Saviour, to whose service I have given myself, is near me. He has sustained me amid the trying scenes of this day, and will not forsake me while I, at his bidding, "go far hence." . . . . .

Our captain talks very well about missionaries who have sailed with him, and is very favorable toward religious exercises on board, — prayers in the cabin and preaching on the Sabbath. Mr. E. heard him forbid a man who took an oath, to do the like again on board the vessel. . .

Love, love to all, from Sumner and myself. 6½ o'clock, and here we are just losing sight of our native hills at the rate of six knots an hour. The vessel turns a little on one side. I do not mean to be sick. Pilot leaving. Good-by.

SERAPHINA.

CHAPTER IV.

IT was a small missionary company that embarked in The Stamboul, Capt. Kenrick, for Smyrna, Feb. 25, 1845; Mr. and Mrs. Everett appointed to Smyrna, and Miss Harriet Martha Lovell (afterwards Mrs. Hamlen) to take charge of the proposed Female Seminary at Constantinople. But in earnest, whole-hearted consecration to the Saviour's cause, and fitness in every respect for the missionary work, these three were a host.

While they are passing their first days at sea, making acquaintance with each other and with the new world around them, we may appropriately introduce to the reader Miss Lovell, whose future life and missionary labors in connection with Mrs. Everett's, will make up a large part of the following pages.

The particulars that have been obtained of her early life are few, and in regard to dates and places, not very definite. Her father, Ovid Lovell, Esq., was a native of Charlestown, N. H., who married Miss Harriet Deming, only daugher of Benjamin Deming, Esq., of Danville, Vt., a very lovely and amiable lady. He had three children, two sons and his daughter Martha. He subsequently removed to Rockingham, on the opposite side of the Connecticut, where he had the misfortune to lose his wife, and Martha to be deprived early in life of a mother so

well fitted to guide and educate her young mind. She
found, however, an excellent home in the family of her
maternal grandfather, and one who almost supplied to her
the place of a mother, in Mrs. Deming, the second wife of
her grandfather, a woman of uncommon piety. It is
thought that to the influence of this good grandmother
may be traced the foundation of Martha's lovely character, and especially her early and devoted attachment to
the missionary cause, as that was a prominent characteristic of Mrs. Deming's piety.

When Martha was thirteen, her father was again married, and she found a home once more under the paternal
roof, in Palmyra, N. Y. The excellent lady who faithfully and affectionately filled her own mother's place, and
whom she seems always to have regarded with a daughter's love, writes of her: "When I entered her father's
family, I found her an amiable, conscientious child, lovely
in all her intercourse with her parents and brothers,
and always a great favorite with her young companions.
She was remarkably affectionate and kind in her disposition, and I can not remember ever hearing her speak an
unkind or hasty word."

But though so amiable, and evincing from early childhood an unusual reverence for sacred things, she did not
give evidence of piety until two years later. When she
was fifteen, the church in Palmyra, then under the pastoral
care of the Rev. Mr. Shumway, was blessed with a revival,
and she was among the first to partake of its blessings.
The following year she united by a public profession of
her faith with the people of God.

But the morning of Martha's life, which had been so
early clouded by a mother's death, was destined to be
again and again overcast. She was blessed with a most
tender and excellent father, whom she devotedly loved.
A brother-in-law writes of him: "He possessed a well-
balanced mind, sterling integrity, kindness of disposition,

and an urbane deportment that made him beloved and respected. In the culture and training of his children he spared neither expense nor effort." This good father was taken away when she was just at an age to feel such a loss most keenly.

Another affliction which threw a deep shadow over her young spirit, was the loss of her brother Frank at sea. Very frequent and touching allusions to this event are found in her letters. To these early sorrows, which seem to have left so lasting an impression on her affectionate heart, may perhaps be ascribed, in part, the habitual seriousness of her countenance and manner, though her natural temperament was reserved, and rather timid and retiring.

After her father's death Miss Lovell spent some years with her eldest brother in Wisconsin, and did not return to her mother in Palmyra until a year previous to the commencement of her missionary life.

Miss Lovell's mind seems to have been led quite early to the missionary work, with a desire to engage in it personally. Mr. R. G. Pardee, who was Superintendent of the Sabbath school with which she was connected for some years in Palmyra, and was also an intimate and valued friend of hers, writes of her: "The first feature of her character or actions which impressed me, was her constant attendance at the teachers' meeting, and her deep and unusual interest, shown in her very quiet way, in the truths of God's word. Next, I noticed her increasing interest in the monthly concert of prayer for the conversion of the world. We often took sweet counsel together in regard to the great cause of missions at home and abroad, and her eye, I could see, delighted to roam over the whitening fields of the American Board. She sent to me for all my books on the missionary work, and particularly the Missionary Herald for many years previous."

The result of all this thought and investigation was,

that she came to the calm, yet earnest conviction, that it was her duty to go herself to impart the knowledge of Christ and salvation to the benighted of her own sex in some dark part of the world. While her mind was still agitated on this important subject, she addressed the following letter to her former pastor, then settled in Newark, N. J.: —

PALMYRA, Sept. 13, 1844.

My dear Mr. Shumway: The importance of my errand will, I trust, be a sufficient apology for thus addressing you. I have for many weeks been wishing the advice of some Christian friend on a subject which lies near my heart, and I know of no one I can look to for counsel upon such a subject with more confidence than yourself. For several months the subject of foreign missions has dwelt much upon my mind, and I have scarcely at any time been released from other cares, but my mind has instantly reverted to it, and the thought has forced itself upon me, — perhaps it is *my* duty to devote myself to this cause. The thought of my small attainments, and of my piety, which I fear is still less, for a time checked this idea; but it is still ever returning. It would be difficult for me to tell you all the workings of my mind on this subject. That God should choose one so unworthy as I to engage in this great enterprise seems impossible, while I remember how many thousands there are every way better qualified, of eminent piety, and greater love for souls; and then I remember that many of these have strong ties to bind them to their homes and friends, while there are but few to detain me here; one after another has been removed, and but very few remain. Then a remembrance of my past religious course, of my many backslidings, of the many wounds I have brought upon my Saviour's cause, and the fear lest I should in future be guilty of the same, — all these make me to doubt. And again I find myself asking, What will the world say? I have never done my duty to those around me *here*, and will they not wonder at my presumption in thinking to teach others? I am deeply sensible of my past unfaithfulness, and I think nothing would give me greater pain than the idea of spending the remainder of my life, either here or elsewhere, so profitless, so unfruitful. When I review my past life, I am amazed at the long-suffering of God; and when I look around, and see how much there is to be done in the world before the earth shall be filled with the glory of God, and how indifferent the great mass of professing Christians appear to be, I wonder that God does not come out in judgment against his people.

And what can *I* do? That there is great need of missionary laborers of the right kind, we all know. If I had money, with my present feelings, I would give it to send such. Can I do any good by going myself? If so, shall I not say, "Here am I, Lord,—what wilt thou have me to do?" Oh! let me beg your prayers that I may be guided aright in a decision of this question; that if my heavenly Father sees that I shall only prove a dishonor to his cause, and shall not glorify him, I may not be encouraged to think more of this; but if I can in any way by this act be the means of saving one soul, or promote his cause, that . my duty may be made plain.

This matter has been thus far communicated to no one except my mother. I have felt much diffidence in speaking of it but to Him who seeth in secret. I will say no more, only to ask your counsels and your prayers.

This letter shows, besides her earnest inquiry in regard to her own duty, and her deep interest in the missionary work, her humility, and severity in judging herself. While she thus accuses herself of unfaithfulness and backslidings, she was looked upon by her friends as a pattern of consistent and devoted piety. This trait of humility

4

was always a prominent one in her character. She was ever ready, in lowliness of mind, to esteem others better than herself.

When Miss Lovell decided to offer herself as a missionary teacher to the American Board, it was with an unreserved consecration of herself to the Saviour's cause, and a willingness to go to any part of his wide vineyard which he might appoint. She replied to the question,—"Which of the stations of the Board would you prefer?"—"I *have no choice.*" "But surely you have a choice whether to go to the deadly clime of Africa, or some pleasanter field of labor, if the Lord will?" "As the Lord will," she said; "I really have not turned my mind to any place in preference, but leave it all to the Board."

On making her wishes known to the officers of the Board, she was told that they were just then looking for a lady to take charge of a proposed seminary for Armenian females in Constantinople, and were at that time in correspondence with two, one of whom would probably fill the post. She was, however, requested to give, in writing, her views of a missionary life, in compliance with which request, she addressed the following communication to Dr. Anderson: —

PALMYRA, Dec. 24, 1844.

DEAR SIR: Your letter of the 18th to Mr. Fisher was handed to me this morning, and in compliance with your request I hasten to reply to it, and to endeavor to make you in some measure acquainted with my desires and motives in relation to the work of missions. It would be difficult to say what first led my thoughts to this subject. From a child I have at times thought much of it; but it was not until a few months since that I began seriously to inquire what might be *my* duty. I had long felt a conviction that, as a professed disciple of Christ, I was not fulfilling his will while living for myself, forgetful of the

salvation of others; that his service required a more entire
consecration of myself than I had ever made. I asked,
"Lord, what wilt thou have me to do?" Fields for usefulness were not wanting on every hand, and while seeking for a suitable opportunity to engage in teaching at
home, I was led almost imperceptibly to think more and
more of the millions who are perishing in other lands for
want of the bread of life. I thought too that while here
every Christian may labor, but few are willing to leave all
and go to the destitute in other lands. I had received
many lessons in the school of affliction which had taught
me that my home is not here, and there were not as many
obstacles in the way of my going as in the case of many
much better qualified. I thought of it much, and made it
the subject of prayer long, before mentioning my wishes
to any one, until I *dared* no longer keep silence. I felt
that I could not enjoy the blessing of God, should I
neglect what seemed so plainly my duty. I had no
preference for any particular field of labor. My only wish
was that in some humble way I might be made useful,
and, if I could be more useful at home than abroad, that I
might not be permitted to go.

When the proposal of a station at Constantinople was
made known to me, I was almost overwhelmed under a
sense of my own incompetence and insufficiency for so
responsible a place. I felt that as I had no experience in
teaching, which might be requisite, I might perhaps be
more useful in some humbler sphere. Still, as I had committed the case entirely to God, I knew that if he designed
I should go there, his grace could qualify me. I trust I
have no wish to go where I could not be useful, or where
by my own inefficiency I might embarrass the efforts of
others; and it will be with trembling that I shall assume
this responsibility, should it finally be so determined.
That God may guide you in your counsels and decision is
my most earnest prayer.

Should it be thought best that I should go to Constantinople, perhaps you, sir, could inform me what means I should adopt, if any, preparatory to going; whether in the short time remaining any knowledge which I might gain further of the mode of teaching here in our best seminaries would be of service there. This, and any other suggestion which you might make, would be most gratefully received.

I presume it is not necessary to beg that your decision may be made known to me as speedily as possible, the time is so limited. In the mean time I remain most respectfully yours,

H. M. LOVELL.

REV. RUFUS ANDERSON, D. D.,
Missionary House, Boston.

Very soon after this letter was sent, she received intelligence of her appointment to Constantinople, with the request to hold herself in readiness to sail in eight or ten weeks. Soon after her sending application to the Board, she wrote to her brother in Wisconsin: "And now, my dear brother, I have that to communicate which I fear will hardly meet your full approbation, though I trust you will not oppose it. For a long time I have been satisfied that I was not answering the end of my existence in my present situation, and that I ought to endeavor to render myself useful in some way, by teaching or otherwise. It would be needless, and I fear you would hardly understand me, were I to tell you *all* that has led me at length to the determination to be a missionary. Should I tell you that for months past I have scarcely had any other desire but to be thus engaged,—that the love of Christ constraining me, as I trust, I am willing to leave my home and friends if I can be made the means of good to others,—you will not, I hope, accuse me of Quixotism or fanaticism.

"I have offered myself to the American Board. Should

my services be accepted, it remains with them to direct my future destination.

"Now let me beg of you to offer no opposition to this step, as it will only add to the pain of separation. I believe Providence has marked this course for me. I firmly believe it to be my duty, and trust that his presence will go with me. Do you remember I told you, my dear Fred, I sadly feared we should never meet again? Oh! must it be so? Never, never did I realize half the love I have for you, until since this decision has been made, of self-exile from you. My brother, a separation for this life is painful,—but must this parting be a final one? Shall we meet, after the short parting in this life, at the right hand of God? Oh! shall we both, with the sainted ones who are there, sit down with all the blood-washed throng above? What *can* I say to you, my dear brother, to express half the love I have for you, and the anxiety of my heart that you may no longer live a stranger to God and true religion? My heart can not rest satisfied till you and M. are brought to the feet of Jesus, and till there is a prospect that your little one shall be given to God. For this I will not cease to pray; and the hope and belief that this prayer will be answered, will cheer me when we shall be separated still farther. May God ever bless you!"

After receiving notice of her appointment by the Board, she wrote to the same brother, Jan. 6, 1845: "Now that the sentence of self-banishment from home and friends has gone forth, no words can describe the mingled emotions which fill my heart, especially at the thought of never, never seeing your faces again this side the grave. Not that for a moment I have ever regretted the decision, but oh, the thought that this parting may be for eternity! and how do thoughts of my own unfaithfulness, and apparent indifference to these things while with you, now distress and humble me! God knows I have ever felt a deep desire for your salvation; but I have been too prone to suffer a foolish and wicked reserve and diffidence to close my mouth when my heart was full. Could I but have the assurance that we should meet, an unbroken family, at the right hand of God, the parting but for this short life would be robbed of its sting." . . . . . .

When the time arrived for Miss Lovell to take leave of her friends and home, her pastor, the Rev. Mr. Fisher, kindly accompanied her to Boston, and remained with her until she had taken her last look at her native land. His society and kind attentions were a great comfort to her at this trying time.

She thus mentions Mr. and Mrs. Everett, whom she now met for the first time: " I am *very* much pleased with them, have no doubt I shall love them much; indeed, I do already. She has a sweet, pale face, and looks rather sad; but she has just parted from a large circle of friends, and it is not strange she should look sad."

The following is a part of her last letter from her native land : —

BOSTON, Monday morning, Feb. 24, 1845.

MY DEAREST MOTHER : I can not close my packet of letters this morning, without adding one word more, as I have a moment's time before dinner.

I am increasingly happy in the prospect before me. Trials and sorrows I expect, and I do not wish to be free from them. God will give me grace to bear them; and he will give *you* grace and wisdom according to your need, if you do but look to him for them. It is my constant prayer that you may be abundantly blessed, that H. and C. may be very, very soon converted and made children of God.

Will Clarissa be so kind as to ask Mr. Pardee what disposition he has made of my Sabbath-school class,—who is their teacher, etc. and give them, next Sabbath, my best love, and an assurance of my remembrance every Sabbath, and my prayers that they may all become heirs of glory.

Dear Henry, one word to you. My darling brother, you know not how your sister loves you; but God loves you better, even, than I do; and he is calling you to give your heart to him. I saw a little boy six years old, son of Mr. Champion, who died in Africa, who is anxiously wishing to be a man, that he may go and tell the poor Africans about the Saviour. He will not be called an American, because he was born in Africa, and means to go there a missionary. It is my prayer that God by his grace will give you a new heart to love and serve him, and make *you* a missionary.

Give my love, dear Clarissa, to all the girls, [mentioning several by name,] and all I have not mentioned. God bless you all! I am almost glad that none of you will be here, to-morrow. My serenity and peace would be disturbed. The parting with my dear pastor will be the trying moment.

Farewell for a little! We shall soon hear from each other, and if *faithful,* shall soon meet.

Affectionately your daughter,

MARTHA.

This beloved pastor has also been called to his rest and reward, and was, perhaps, one of the first to meet and welcome her to the blissful shores of her celestial home, as he was one of the last to bid her Godspeed as she sailed away from the shores of her earthly home, on her mission of love and mercy to a far-distant land.

CHAPTER V

WE left the little missionary company in The Stamboul, making acquaintance with each other, and with the novelties and wonders of their strange "life on the ocean wave." It required no long time for two persons like Mrs. Everett and Miss Lovell to become acquainted with and love each other. Their characters were in all respects congenial. Their hopes and aims for the advancement of the Saviour's kingdom and the welfare of their benighted Armenian sisters, were the same; and there sprung up between them, at once, an ardent friendship, resembling in devotion and constancy that which knit together in such strong bonds the souls of David and Jonathan.

Both ladies kept a journal of their sea life for their home friends. Mrs. Everett's is very full, and describes minutely and graphically the sights and incidents of their voyage. Miss Lovell's records more of feeling and reflection than of incident. We are compelled to limit ourselves to a few brief extracts: —

Mrs. E. writes, March 3. "Two weeks have passed since I bade farewell to you, my much loved father and mother, and my dear, *dear* home. These weeks have been busy, exciting, deeply trying, yet joyful. Christ has been near, and very precious to my soul.

"The morning of the 27th brought us a snow-storm, with a heavy sea, and consequently a rolling, tumbling vessel, yet we were quite comfortable during the day, and took some light food. Mr. E. was on deck part of the time, and, with his aid, I crawled to the door, and for the first time saw the majesty of the ocean. The storm of snow and rain continued, with some wind, and the whole broad expanse of dark blue waters seemed wrought into a fury. The scene was fraught with awful grandeur. The sea truly 'mounted to the heavens, and went down again to the deep.' Now the crested wave would approach in silent majesty to the side of our frail bark, dash upon it a torrent of its briny waters, or perhaps only sprinkle us with the white foam and spray it bore on its bosom, then retire slowly and suddenly, till it lost itself in the multitude hurrying on to take its place." . . . March 5. "Here, if possible, more emphatically than on the land, we are constantly made sensible of the omnipresence of the Deity. The winds, the mountain waves, the whirling spray, and the deep abyss of waters beneath and around us, unite their voices, and as with ten thousand tongues, proclaim, 'There is a God.' But the most precious manifestations of his presence are made in our own souls. He is to us an ever-present friend. He has thus far protected and blessed us, and we will not for a moment remove our confidence from his almighty arm. Dear father and mother, I wish you knew how calm and happy I have been since my home has been on the roaring deep." . . .

10.   "We are all as contented and happy as you could expect — perhaps wish us to be. We exercise as much as we can, with the constant danger of receiving thumps and bruises, and eat as much as we can, — at least, I do. We doze, talk, laugh, read, sing, think, and — how precious the privilege — *pray*. Although languid feelings and wandering thoughts are by no means strangers to us here, still we have much to drive us near the throne of grace; and the peace and joy there afforded seem doubly precious to us."

18.   "How rapidly are the days and weeks gliding by!

But my sympathies for my dear friends at home, be assured, are no less real, or my affections less ardent, because thousands of long, weary miles stretch themselves between us."

Miss Lovell writes, March 20: "I am now writing on deck. Mrs. E. sits at a little distance reading aloud to her husband, — the sailors all around us, mending sails, Capt. Kenrick at work carpentering, and in fine spirits in consequence of our rapid progress. I love to sit on deck and watch the movements of the sailors, — their prompt and cheerful obedience, with their ready 'aye aye, sir!' and oh, how often do thoughts of my poor lost brother come up before me, and fill my eye with tears, and my heart with sadness! I see enough of the life of a sailor before the mast to convince me that the life of our dear brother Frank at sea, with his previous habits and education, must have been a sad one; and I doubt not that he often most bitterly lamented having left us. Oh, how mysterious the providence which thus removed him, just as he was returning to us! But what we know not now, we shall know hereafter."

Mrs. Everett, — March 21. "Our last day on the Atlantic, and a finer one we could not have wished. The morning was delightful, and of additional interest for us from the discovery of land,— the coast of Portugal, thirty or forty miles distant. The breeze has been quite cool to-day, but we have spent the most of the time on deck, watching the course of the vessel through the comparatively quiet sea, and the brilliant reflection of the sunlight upon the gently moving surface of the water. Besides, we have had the company of four or five sails, and about sunset a large number of vessels were in sight at once. The enjoyment of such a day as this amply compensates for the trials we experienced during so many days. *And such a close!* After tea we went on deck, and saw land on either side,— Cape Trafalgar on the Spanish, and Cape

Spartel on the African coast. It appeared but a shade in the distance, but it was land. Then the sunset, — not a cloud was to be seen in the blue vault above, the sun had run his race, and for the last time we saw him sink beneath the dark waters of the Atlantic, leaving one of the richest, most perfectly beautiful skies I ever beheld. Half the circle of the horizon was most brilliantly lighted up by the rays of his departing glory. First, the deep orange rested upon the dark waters, which was mellowed into the full, clear yellow, and this gradually faded into the most delicate straw color, and finally lost itself in the pure blue above. You may think this was nothing remarkable, but it was beautiful, exquisitely beautiful. I lingered long, gazed and admired, admired and gazed. I had some thoughts of you all, at my own dear home, which I had left far in the west, where the sun was still high in the sky above it. But I did not long to be there. No, I believe the language of my heart was, —

> Jerusalem, my glorious home,
> My soul still pants for thee.'

"Glorious city! no shades of darkness envelop thee, for there is no night there, neither need of the sun, for the Lamb is the light of it. Oh, may the Lord enable us *all* to reach those heavenly fields, and walk the golden streets!"

Mrs. Everett, — March 22. "We were on deck at 4 o'clock this morning, and saw, by the light of the pale, full moon, the shores of Africa and Europe, — Morocco and Spain. We could see only the dark, irregular outline on the clear sky, although not more than fifteen miles from one to the other. Soon the moon majestically sunk into its ocean bed, and the same glorious sun whose fading radiance had delighted us so much last evening, rose in full splendor from his watery couch, and threw new life and beauty over the scene; and all the morning we have been feasting our eyes, and souls, too, by viewing on the one hand, hills jagged and broken, rising one above another, some through openings far in the distance, all of which, by their rocky, barren appearance, reminded us of barbarous Africa;—on the other hand, two high, rocky hills; but this is not all. Towers and castles, gray and crumbling, are to be seen, and ruined fortifications, intermingled with little white cottages; and these too, are scattered over the undulating declivity to the shore, amid the now verdant fields, and vineyards clad in heavy foliage. And we have seen *men*,—not men as trees walking, but a whole line of soldiers parading on the beach. This is with the aid of a glass, for we are distant two or three miles from the coast. But I can tell you nothing about it, nor of our feelings on viewing it. I only wish you were here, but that should be after a voyage across the Atlantic.

March 25. "A lovely day,—the thermometer almost at summer heat. The mountains of Spain still in view. I must tell you that on Sabbath afternoon, about the time of your morning service, we had religious exercises on deck. The day was fine, with but a slight motion of the vessel, and Mr. E. stood beside the work-bench, over which the Captain's cloak was thrown, and preached his sermon on the 'tenderness of Jesus,' to a congregation of fifteen. Such a presentation seemed well adapted to the wants of these sons of Neptune, wanderers on the treacherous deep. May they all be inclined to accept Christ as their friend and Saviour.

"Our simple, but I trust sincere acts of devotion, were performed in sight of a land which has long been crushed beneath the cruel reign of the Man of Sin. The town of Malaga was in full view, in the center of which the dome of an immense cathedral rises to the height of 270 feet. To this magnificent edifice multitudes of Rome's deluded votaries daily resort, and by means of holy water, confes-

sional, masses, and prayers to saints, prepare themselves,—
for what? Deluded mortals! The last great day will
show for what." . . .

"Unless detained here by a calm, we shall probably
to-day bid adieu to the shores of Spain, with whose
history is associated so much that is sad, dark, cruel,—
the seat of the Inquisition, the theater of bloody wars
and persecutions. But it is a sunny land of fruitful vineyards, and sweet orange groves. Oh that it might soon
be a truly Christian land!"

Miss Lovell, — March 29. "I have not told you how
attentive and polite Capt. Kenrick is to us. We like him
and his officers much. The crew are very orderly; no
profanity or drinking is allowed. Two sweet little land
birds visited us this afternoon; one flew into my window, and sat there panting and weary with his long flight
from the shores of Africa. He soon flew away, or attempted to do so, but fell exhausted into the water. His
mate still sits aloft in the rigging, giving us occasionally a
note like the canary bird. Last night we stood on deck
a long time, watching the beautiful phosphorescence which
lit up the waters. Wherever the surface of the sea was
broken, showers of living sparkles seemed to fly in every
direction. Mr. Everett took a rope, and with it struck the
water, producing an appearance rivaling in beauty any
artificial fireworks."

Under the same date Mrs. E. gives such a pretty picture, that we can not refrain from introducing it:—

"May you, dear parents, have as quiet, as lovely a Saturday evening as we have enjoyed. This has been a
beautiful day, but the sunset and twilight were *passing*
beautiful. Not a breath ruffled the gently swelling surface of the glassy sea, as it lay like one broad mirror, re-
flecting the mellow light thrown upon it by a perfect sky.
As the sun was hidden from our view beneath the blue
waters, its glory lingered, shedding beauty on both sky

2

and sea, and the stillness that reigned was the sacred, solemn stillness of the twilight hour. We seemed not to dare, certainly we cared not to speak, and the silence was unbroken save by the twitter of a little wanderer from the green-wood that had taken refuge among our sails, and the plunge of a porpoise, as in sport it threw itself high in the air, and then sunk in its native element. But these drew not our thoughts from him who is their maker as well as ours. We remained gazing and musing until the bright stars were twinkling above our heads, and then Sumner and I came down to our little room, and in that sweet, still hour, united our hearts in a season of communion with our kind heavenly Father, calling on our souls and all within us to bless his name for all the goodness and mercy that crown our days. We prayed for you and our dear friends, that the holy Sabbath, which is now approaching, may advance us all towards our heavenly rest, our blissful reunion in the skies."

Miss Lovell, — April 9. "Last night was a night of incessant tossing and pitching. The wind commenced blowing in the evening, and increased to a gale, what the captain called a regular Levanter. . . . Early in the night I was awakened by the song of the sailors above me. The chorus of 'cheerily ho!' was at first very pleasing, till something in the air, or the voices, suddenly reminded me so forcibly of Frank as to open the fountain of tears at once, and for a moment it seemed as though my heart would break. It was but for a moment; I was enabled to feel that it was God who had taken him, and could say, his will be done.

"Mrs. Everett is sick to-day, so that I have been obliged to go to the table without her. Charlotte Elizabeth says, in one of her works, that there are two classes of people in the world, those who are *sea-sick* and those who *are not*. She and I belong to the latter class."

In a letter to her brother, dated April 14, Miss Lovell writes : —

"We yesterday entered the Archipelago, and are now in sight of the shores of classic Greece. The islands which stud this sea so beautifully are around us on every side. A bright and clear sun is shining above us to-day, and the very air seems to breathe of joy and gladness. Yet this very air is bearing me far, far away from all the scenes I love so well; far from you, my dear brother, — and this thought somewhat checks the delight I am inclined to feel in the prospect of reaching my journey's end." . .

The same date she writes in her journal: "Passed to-day the islands of Milo, Siphanto, Paros, Serpho, and Thermia. The sun went down to-night behind the Grecian hills, bathing them in a flood of glory, and tinging the clouds around them with the most gorgeous tints imaginable. Altogether it was the most magnificent sunset I ever beheld, and fully realized my conceptions of Italian and Grecian sunsets. The evening which followed was scarcely less beautiful, and I remained on deck till a late hour, and thought of home and distant friends."

Their pleasant voyage was now drawing to a close. April 17, Mrs. Everett writes: —

"This morning we found ourselves slowly proceeding up the Gulf of Smyrna, land, upon each side, appearing at a very short distance from us. Olive and cypress trees cover some of the hills, others are rocky and barren, and upon the sides of others still, and here and there all along the shore, are spots of the most delightful verdure. About noon we just discerned, in the smoky distance, at the base of a high hill, and close by the sea-shore, the long-looked-and-wished-for Smyrna, our future home. What my feelings are I can hardly tell you, only that there is a mingling of joy and sadness, of hope and trembling. I am sure we feel truly grateful to our kind Preserver through the perils of our voyage, and an earnest desire for the continued guidance and grace of the same Almighty friend.

"When I look on the strange land that lies before us, a voice seems to sound in my ears, 'What doest thou here?' And when I see the magnitude and importance of the work to be done, my soul cries as never before, 'Lord, who is sufficient for these things?' Our only strength and hope is in the might of him whom we have come to serve. May we be enabled to do something for the honor of Christ!"

But their hopes were not to be so soon realized. It was not until the morning of the 19th that they were permitted to set foot in the city, which for two days had tantalized their eyes with its near prospect. Miss L. says: "Mr. Van Lennep and Mr. Johnston came out in a caique to the vessel, and accompanied us to Mr. Adger's house, in the Frank quarter. They gave us a warm welcome, and made us feel at once as though we had long known and loved them."

Soon after their arrival in Smyrna, they visited Bournabat, a beautiful village seven or eight miles from the city, where one of the missionary families was residing. Of the ride to this place she says:—

"The road to this village is delightful, passing through groves of olive and fig. These and the vineyards, the orange-trees covered with fruit and flowers, the burying-grounds, with their tall, dark cypresses, all remind me that I am in a strange land; but more than all, the thronging multitudes of bearded and turbaned Turks, Armenians and Jews, who crowd the narrow streets, many of them scarcely wide enough for three persons to walk or ride abreast, and the unknown tongues which salute my ear on every side, tell me that I am in a land of darkness and ignorance, and not in my own happy country."

But they did not allow the novel and interesting scenes around them to divert their minds, even for a few days, from the great object which had led them to this strange

land. They immediately obtained a teacher, and in one
or two days after their arrival, commenced taking daily
lessons in Armenian. Four days after their arrival,
Miss Lovell writes: "I have learned the alphabet, which
has thirty-eight letters, some of them extremely difficult
to sound, and am now reading in words of two syllables."

Mrs. Everett thus describes her first visit to an Armenian church: "In the afternoon of Thursday, Mrs. Adger
took us to call upon Mrs. Johnston, and on our return we
passed through some streets in the Armenian quarter of
the town. Seeing a collection of people before the door
of what seemed to be a chapel, we looked in and found it
was a congregation of Armenian females, this being the
last week of Lent. Oh that every Christian could for once
look upon such a scene as was presented to us in this
house of worship! The few feeble prayers and efforts
now put forth in behalf of those who sit in darkness,
would then be exchanged for fervent, importunate supplications, and diligent, untiring efforts for their salvation.

"The body of the church was filled with ladies neatly
dressed in the Armenian costume, which is quite graceful,
being, for the street, a sheet, or very large square piece of
white cloth, one side of which is held together under the
chin, after being thrown over the head, while the opposite
side falls behind, extending to the bottom of the dress.
These women were all standing with their faces towards
the altar where the services were performed. When we
approached the door of the church, several priests with
their long rich robes and flowing gray beards were standing, with crosses in one hand and lighted wax candles in
the other, over the Bible, from which they were chanting,
in an unknown tongue, in a loud, incoherent manner; after
which, one read the Scriptures by the light of two large
wax candles, held on each side of him by two boys dressed
in white. At this time a large number of candles, arranged
in a row behind the altar, were lighted. Oh, how spirit-

5*

ually dark!—and the light of the candles seemed only
to render the darkness more awfully visible. Chanting
followed, the books of the priests being held in napkins;
then the ceremony of washing one another's feet. A large
chair was placed, in which one sat down and bared his
foot, and another, kneeling before him, washed it in a pan
of water placed for the purpose, and anointed it from a
cup carefully held in a napkin by a boy, who was also
dressed in white like the others. Two others successively
took their places in the chair, to whom the same service
was performed, and who expressed their gratitude by kiss-
ing the hand of him who had performed the ceremony.
Our hearts were pierced, and we turned away, praying
that this darkness might soon be dispelled."

CHAPTER VI

THE annual meeting of the Armenian mission was to be held in Constantinople the last week in April. It was thought best for Mr. and Mrs. Everett to attend the meeting, as the knowledge of the missionary work they would thus gain at the outset of their missionary life would be very valuable to them. They accordingly left Smyrna, with Miss Lovell and the two missionaries going as delegates to the meeting, in the Austrian steamer, for Constantinople, April 26.

Of the incidents connected with this visit, the meeting, and the impressions produced on their minds by a first sight of the beauties and wonders of the great Turkish capital, Mrs. Everett must be the chronicler, as the letters written at that time by Miss Lovell have been irrecoverably lost. From Mrs. E.'s very full and graphic descriptions we make the following extracts: —

"PERA, CONSTANTINOPLE, April 29, 1845.

"Our accommodations on board the steamer were very good, our company the best we could desire. When I say this, I refer to the company of the missionaries; for such a crowd as surrounded us you can hardly imagine. There were persons from no less than twelve different nations, with their characteristic languages, customs, and religions, if such their superstitious faith and worship could be called. It was a painful sight—the Jesuit priests with their strings of beads, and the Mussulman repeating what are to him unmeaning words, and prostrating himself five times a day toward the tomb of the false prophet. . . . .

"We speedily and pleasantly passed through the waters, leaving the plains of Troy, Mount Ida, and the tomb of Achilles on our right hand, and on the left the islands Tenedos, Imbros, Samothracia, and others.

"Then came the passage through the Dardanelles, the shores of which were covered with delightful verdure, especially the little plains between and at the foot of high hills, rising a little back from the water. The castles on both the European and Asiatic sides, and the little villages here and there, made the scenery very fine. Oh if we could forget that 'man is vile!' This thought is continually present, and we would not have it obliterated, or absent from our minds, until the glory of the Lord shall fill the earth, as the waters fill the sea.

"On the second morning after leaving Smyrna, we looked upon the great city of Constantinople. The view of it from the sea is very beautiful, although we saw it at a great disadvantage, — a heavy fog resting upon it. The situation of the city is the finest possible. Constantinople itself, with its vast domes and almost countless minarets towering towards the sky, is on the European side of the Bosphorus, and the left of the Golden Horn; Pera on the right, (of the Golden Horn;) and upon the Asiatic shore of the Bosphorus is Scutari, itself as large as Smyrna. We anchored in the Golden Horn, and soon our one hundred and fifty passengers were scattered here and there in the caiques that dotted the water. Mr. Dwight came on board and took Mr. E., Miss Lovell, and myself, to his house, where we had a warm reception from Mrs. Dwight, and I seemed at once to be with an old friend.

"Mr. D. took us out, the morning we arrived, to see a

little of the celebration of Easter. It is a three days' festival, succeeding a forty days' fast. Thousands of people were gathered together, and, by feasting, music, and dancing, riding, swinging, and I know not what beside, were celebrating the resurrection of our Saviour.

"At one o'clock, Monday afternoon, the first session of the general meeting was held. You know the missionaries here, — Messrs. Dwight, Goodell, Schauffler, Homes, and their families; the ladies, of course, do not attend the business meetings. From Bebek, the site of the seminary for young men, are Messrs. Hamlin and Wood; — from Broosa, Mr. Schneider and wife. Mr. Benjamin and his family, recently from Trebizond, were here; but have since taken a steamer for Smyrna, and from there are to sail for America, on account of the ill health of Mrs. B. Mrs. Bliss is here, from Trebizond; and Dr. Smith, who calls himself a circulating missionary. He was sent to the mountain Nestorians, and now belongs to the Turkey mission; he has no family, and has hitherto been from one station to another, as his services were required. He is a preacher as well as physician, and so devoted to his work that he is willing to labor any where, and in any way, — seeming to covet self-denial. Monday evening all the mission families met socially at Mr. Homes's. It was a delightful visit, — all, all are so good. I wish I could tell you about all of them, so that you might love them too. Tuesday morning there was a prayer-meeting at Mr. Goodell's. There we first met Mrs. Hamlin, from Bebek. She is a lovely woman.

"Wednesday morning we — that is, Mr. Dwight, Miss Lovell, Mr. E., and myself — took a caique for Bebek, which is situated on the Bosphorus, six miles up. A description of the scenery on both shores of these straits I would gladly give, but its beauty passes my powers of description. It is far more beautiful than any thing I ever before beheld. Hills rise on either hand, covered with

verdure, in all the freshness of spring. Here, as everywhere, the dark cypress contrasting with the brighter
green around is very fine. There are villages and palaces
near the water's edge, through the whole distance, from
the Marmora almost to the very entrance of the Black Sea.
The palace of the Sultan, in which he now resides, is
directly on the shore, and our boatmen took us near, that
we might have a good view of it; the gardens, in the
rear of it, extending even to the top of the terraced hills,
with a variety of ornamental trees, some of which are in
full bloom, make the scene most enchanting.

"We reached Mr. Hamlin's, after our delightful sail,
where the brethren of the mission held their session.
Miss Lovell and I went directly to see Mrs. Wood and
Mrs. Benjamin, who was to leave for Smyrna in the afternoon. It was a sad hour, the last we spent with these
dear friends. Mr. Benjamin spoke of it as one of the most
trying in their lives. But it was good to hear the words
of wisdom and comfort as they fell from the lips of the
beloved patriarch, Mr. Goodell. He then commended all
to God, and we separated, we hope to meet again here, if
such be the will of God; if not, in a world where sin, sorrow, sickness, and death are unknown."

A large number of American and English travelers
were at this time in Constantinople, and the newly-arrived
missionaries were invited to accompany them in a visit to
the mosks, an invitation which they gladly accepted, as
such a privilege was then obtained with much more difficulty than now. Describing the magnificent structure of
St. Sophia, with its verd-antique columns, spacious gal-
leries, marble floors, and ivy-hung walls, Mrs. E. says:
"Is it impossible that again these massive walls and this
spacious dome will look down upon the humble worship-
ers of the living God, and resound with the praises of
the great Jehovah? All things are possible with God;—
let us continually beseech him to hasten the day when
this thick darkness shall be dispelled by gospel light."

After visiting the mosks and the seraglio, they left the party, as the gentlemen wished to be at home for their session. "In the evening we had at Mr. Dwight's a very interesting prayer meeting. So many good men together, — can you imagine how delightful it is? Yesterday morning we had a female prayer-meeting at Mrs. Schauffler's."

Writing to her sister from Pera, Constantinople, May 7, she says : —

"I must tell you how our hearts are rejoiced and encouraged to see the progress of truth in this city. I mentioned perhaps in another letter, that it was found necessary to enlarge the chapel for the Armenian service. It is in this house, Mr. Dwight's, and is now very commodious. The man who did the work, and who had not long attended preaching, would receive no compensation for his labor. Mr. D. then thought to make him a present of a fine copy of the Pilgrim's Progress, but found that he had been to the repository and purchased every book the Mission had published. There is a great call among the Armenians for the Scriptures, and any thing closely connected with them. A concordance is longed for, and one is in preparation. A sermon is published monthly, and three or four hundred copies are demanded for circulation among the different stations. To the last one was annexed the hymn, 'Rock of Ages.' Some other hymns have also been translated into the Armenian, and they are much interested in learning to sing. Mr. Dwight is preparing a small work on the science of music, or a system of rules, for their instruction. Some of the missionaries go over to the city two or three times a week, and meet sometimes a large number of Americans in a khan, with whom they familiarly discuss the doctrines of the gospel, and the subject is one of common conversation in the coffee shops of the city. The Sabbaths we have spent here have been delightful. In the morning, at 9 o'clock,

Mr. Schauffler, as usual, preached in the German language, after which Mr. Adger preached to a congregation of about a hundred Armenian *men*, who heard as for their lives; with their eyes intently fixed on the preacher, they sat motionless. We then had a precious sacramental season. Quite a large company was assembled, consisting of all the American missionaries now here, and five or six Scotch missionaries. In the afternoon there was preaching in Armenian, (it was our English service in the morning, sermon by Mr. Schneider,) which was followed by a sermon in Turkish, by Mr. Johnston, to the same congregation. In the evening, Mr. Schauffler preached in English at Mr. Goodell's.

"There is not much open opposition to the truth here at present, but in Trebizond, Mr. Bliss writes, the native brethren are suffering violent persecution; they can not go into the street without meeting every kind of insult and abuse. It is a fiery trial to these young disciples. May the Lord give them strength to stand in this evil day, and soon deliver them from their distresses.

"All the ladies, with the exception of one or two, are more or less feeble. It is the general opinion, I believe, among the missionaries, that if each could have a sister, aunt, or cousin with her, as is so common in America, to share her cares, labors, and trials, this premature breaking down of missionaries' wives might in a great measure be prevented. And now who has a better sister for this than I, in my dear M.?"

.   .   .   .

Mrs. Everett's journal contains interesting accounts of their visits to the city proper, the "Valley of Sweet Waters," and other places in its vicinity, with which the remainder of their stay was partly occupied. All these we must pass over. On the eve of their return to Smyrna, she writes as follows to her parents: —

PERA, CONSTANTINOPLE, May 22, 1845.

My very dear Father and Mother: You will see we have not yet returned to Smyrna, but we expect to take a steamer for that place this evening, and as there is a possibility of our finding the Stamboul there, I can not refrain from writing you a short letter, that you may have the latest news from us.

Dear, dear parents, do you know it is three months to-day since we have heard one word of your welfare? I then looked upon your faces, and heard your voices probably for the last time before we shall meet in the "spirit land." I think of you more and more each day, and sometimes realize the vast distance that separates me from you and a band of much loved brothers and sisters, when my heart is ill prepared for such thoughts, and it swells and throbs with involuntary grief; then tears are a sweet relief.

I have cause each day and hour to call upon my soul and all within me, to bless the Lord for calling me, so insignificant, so weak, to engage in such a glorious work as this among the Armenians, and for the prospect of usefulness my dear husband has among them. It is through him that I expect to do any work in this field; would that I were more worthy to be a helpmeet to one of God's servants in his arduous labors! May the grace of God enable me to cheer him on his way, make happy his home, and by my prayers and feeble efforts, aid his usefulness. I mentioned in my letter to M. the persecution at Trebizond. The fury of the enemies of the truth has since been more openly manifested. As the steamer for this place was about to leave there two weeks since, a man who has embraced the truth was seized in a coffee shop, and without the privilege of returning for a moment to his family, was hurried on board, and taken to this city. This was probably done by order of the Pasha of Trebizond. Here he was put in confinement in a lunatic

asylum. Some of the Armenian brethren having heard
these facts, went to his prison, and found him with a
heavy chain about his neck, fastened to the wall of his
room. He was weak and pale. They went a day or two
after to inquire for him, but did not find him. You may
be sure our hearts were all sad, and much prayer was
offered for the deliverance of this brother in bonds for
the gospel's sake. And the Lord heard. Last Sabbath,
to the great surprise and joy of all, T. entered the chapel
at the hour of Mr. Dwight's Armenian service. Measures
had been taken by the missionaries and Armenian brethren, to influence the English embassador to act in his
behalf. On Friday night there was an extensive fire
in the part of the city where he was confined, and the
sufferers from it were temporarily placed in the hospital;
and by this means the hypocritical patriarch, by whose
order T. had suffered during eight days and nights, gave
orders for his release, with the tardy acknowledgment
that he was innocent in the whole matter. The same
steamer that brought T. from Trebizond, brought also
intelligence from Mr. Bliss that his house had been
stoned, and windows broken by a large mob.

Can you imagine how much we think of and long to
see you? Ah! I know you can, for you, I dare say, are
no less anxious to hear of our welfare. Mrs. D. said to
me, thinking I was inclined to be sad, "Live one day at
a time." So let us ever trust in God, and go cheerfully
on. Write me letters *very* often. It may prolong my
days. . . . . . With the most ardent love,

Your daughter,

SERAPHINA.

CHAPTER VII

Return to Smyrna — Letters describing the Mode of Life, and Scenes and Incidents of Missionary Work in Smyrna.

Mr. and Mrs. Everett returned to their home, and preparation for their missionary work in Smyrna, — leaving Miss Lovell to commence her labors in Constantinople. The parting between these two friends, who had now been more than three months constantly together, was attended with much regret on both sides. It has been said that there are no circumstances more likely to bring out peculiarities of temperament and character, especially unamiable ones, than a long sea-voyage, taken in the way it usually is by missionaries. Thrown together in close, and sometimes very uncomfortable proximity, — shut out from all the rest of the world, and confined to each other's society for so many weary, sea-sick weeks, it would not be strange if persons thus meeting for the first time, entirely ignorant of each other's antecedents, and unacquainted with each other's tastes, and habits, and peculiarities, should sometimes find it necessary to call into requisition their whole stock of Christian forbearance and charity to obey the "new commandment" to love one another. Our two friends had passed through this severe ordeal with their mutual esteem and affection greatly increased, as their most confidential letters testify. Mrs. E. wrote to her parents just on the eve of parting with her friend, expressing her sorrow in the prospect of separation, and summing up her estimate of her virtues with this high eulogium, — "She is *almost perfect*." And Miss L. writes

to her mother not long after: "Have I ever told you
how much I love Mrs. Everett? She is a dear sister. I
never formed a stronger attachment for any one than for
her. Could our lot have been cast in the same city, I
should have been quite happy." But their separation was
not a very wide one, and they promised themselves the
pleasure of a weekly correspondence, which the missionary
letter-box* between the two cities would enable them to
maintain without any additional expense.

Mrs. Everett's letters, which during this and the following year were very frequent and particular, furnish a complete history of her own and her husband's employments,
as also of the missionary work in Smyrna, with its trials
and encouragements; while, at the same time, they give
graphic delineations of oriental life, and the corruptions
of the oriental churches. Some extracts only can be
given in these pages

"BOURNABAT, (near Smyrna,) June 12.

"After we arrived in Smyrna we remained a few days
in Mr. Adger's family, and then came to this village,
where we now are in a united and most happy family,
composed of the Riggses, Adgers, and Everetts. Mrs.
Riggs keeps house, and the rest of us board. The house
we occupy is surrounded by a wall, twelve or fifteen feet
high, with ivy creeping up its sides and hanging from the
top. The yard is large, and filled with trees,—acacia,
pomegranate, fig, orange, oleander, and mulberry,—and
the myrtle borders a walk to a jessamine bower at the
farther end of the garden. But you must not think of
vegetation here as in all the freshness of your opening
summer. The earth is parched and cracked with dryness
and heat; the grass is no longer green; the harvests are
being gathered, and we shall have no rain before Septem-

* By an arrangement with the Austrian post-office department, the missionaries in Smyrna and Constantinople had the privilege of sending back and
forth, once a week, a small tin box, containing their letters, proof-sheets, &c.

ber; so the trees are rather dusty, but green, and afford a refreshing shade; some of them are still in bloom.

"Of our house I can not say much that is interesting. For three families, it is not very commodious; but we are comfortable. We have two small rooms. The one in which we sleep and study has a common-sized window, stone floor, and high whitewashed walls. The other, of which we make a dressing and store room, has a window with two panes of glass near the ceiling, and a brick floor. In these rooms we have things of our own, so that we can look about us with more of a *home* feeling than we have been able to do for a long time.

"June 19. Just in the still twilight hour, last evening, my dear husband and myself having returned from our daily walk, were resting upon a swing, suspended from one of the trees at the end of our garden, when we heard the voices of Mr. and Mrs. Adger eagerly shouting our names, as they rushed from the house, and almost contending between themselves,—and for what? The privilege of presenting our *first letters from America.*

. . . .

"Shall I tell you, dear sister, how our days pass in this foreign land? I have described our situation here in a former letter. We rise usually about five o'clock; at seven the prayer-bell rings,—and then comes breakfast. Two mornings in the week we have a Bible-class directly after breakfast; on other mornings we commence our study at eight o'clock, and devote ourselves for five hours,—until dinner, at one,—to our Armenian: and we do this with our whole hearts,—it is not a task. Our great anxiety is to have our tongues loosed, and we are willing to toil for it. We read and translate a chapter in the Testament each day, attend to the grammar with Mr. Riggs, and are about to commence reading either Pilgrim's Progress or Robinson Crusoe, in Armenian. We write with the Armenian character every day, and are

6*

continually using words and phrases. I could now repeat to you the Lord's Prayer, and should like to do so, that you might know the sound of the language we hope ere long to be familiar with. It is not a very pleasant one to the ear, on account of the multiplicity of consonants, and the frequent recurrence of gutturals; it is rather difficult to speak.

"Our helps for getting the language, so far as books are concerned, are poor, — no grammar in the modern language, and the dictionary is for the ancient Armenian; so we have to pick up a great deal, and it is rather *up-hill* work. Miss Lovell has not so good teachers as we, and has some dark hours. We are highly favored in this respect; and to this, and excellent health, I attribute my uninterrupted courage. I pray that our zeal may not abate, but continually increase, until we can speak the words of eternal life to the multitudes perishing around us."

From Smyrna, whither they had gone to spend a day, (June 27,) Mr. E. writes, noticing the following among other objects on the way: —

"In coming from Bournabat, very often in the fields we see wells. They are dug quite deep, and walled, as at home; at the mouth is a stone curb, made by boring or chiseling a hole through the rock, as large as the well. These are frequently worn by the rope used in drawing, so much that the interior surface of the stone seems fluted. Near by the well stands another rock, with its upper side excavated, leaving a large basin for watering animals.

"Another thing we notice by the way, is a small piece of ground, level and smooth, walled around, and a large stone, or something of the kind, set up within, or rather at its edge, showing in which direction Mecca lies. These places are arranged for the accommodation of Mohammedans, who may be on the way at the hour of prayer, and here they bow themselves towards the tomb of the false prophet. How grateful should we be, that our God is omnipresent, and that worship any where is acceptable to him, if from the heart.

"Do you remember any thing in the Old Testament about *gleaning?* This morning we saw two poor black women gleaning a field of grain, — going over the field and picking up, one by one, the heads of wheat left by the reapers. Gleaning is still an Eastern custom.

"The green figs are now very conspicuous among the heavy foliage of the tree; and the olives, too, are getting their size. I love to look at the venerable olive-trees, their trunks broken and hollow with age, yet bearing an abundance of fruit, and exceedingly valuable. The olives themselves are much eaten, and the oil made from them is used in a variety of ways in cooking by the people of the country. They burn it also for lights." . . .

July 4. Mrs. E. writes to her parents a description of a terrible fire which was then raging in Smyrna, and which, in its fearful progress, laid waste a large part of the city. She says: "You can not conceive of the confusion and distress. Almost the whole of the Armenian quarter is swept away. Of their *nine hundred* houses, only *thirty-seven* remain. Their church, which was very rich, and the seminary for females, are gone; and thousands of their people are homeless, and without means of obtaining their bread." A day or two later she says: "It is estimated that between four and five thousand houses were consumed." In this time of distress, the missionaries exerted themselves to the utmost for the poor sufferers, and while trying to relieve their physical wants, embraced the opportunity thus offered to tell them of the Saviour who could relieve their greater spiritual need.

In a letter written soon after to one of her sisters, Mrs. E. says: —

"I will just tell you, M., how I spend an hour or two

in the afternoon. A mother, whose house was burned by the recent fire in Smyrna, came here this week and wished her little boy to be instructed, so I have commenced teaching him his A, B, C, in Armenian. I can not, of course, talk much to him, but I hope in this way to learn to speak some, and also to do the little fellow some good. I might have had two little girls to teach also, if I had known enough of this language, which I hope soon to be able to use a little."

To her parents she writes from Bournabat, Aug. 12: " Do you know, my dear parents, that this is the semi-annual anniversary of the wedding day of your children Samuel and Seraphina? And a solemn day it was that witnessed the girding on of ' that harness, which the ministry of death alone unlooseth, but whose fearful power may stamp the sentence of eternity.' And increasingly solemn does it seem, as each day I am led to feel the great grace and wisdom, strength, holiness, and prayerfulness, necessary to enable me to discharge aright my duties, simply *as a wife*. How unequal am I to the responsibilities which rest upon me now, while comparatively free from the trials and cares of married life. This I feel more and more daily, as I seek to lose myself in a spirit and practice of self-sacrifice; so much the more I discover the prevailing sin of my life,— *selfishness*. Oh for a purer spirit, a holier heart, — more fitness for life and death! Let me tell you, dear father and mother, that your children in this distant land are well, contented, and increasing in happiness continually. While we bless our heavenly Father, and you, that we have been permitted to unite our hearts and hands for life, — and that life to be spent in the glorious work of missions, — our daily prayer is, that the blessing of Heaven may rest upon our union, and our united labors in this land, and that you may never have cause to repent bidding Godspeed, to a far-off and strange land, one of the objects of your love and care. May the Lord hear the supplications which you mingle with ours for our usefulness here."

"September 9. This month the Mohammedans have their fast Ramazan. They neither eat, drink, nor smoke, from sunrise until sunset. The days at this season, you know, are long, and for those of the Turks who labor hard it is rather a severe penance, and their tempers sometimes become so soured before the signal of the close of the day, (the firing of a cannon,) that it is almost dangerous to have any thing to do with them in the latter part of the day. One might be inclined to think, from this fasting, that the Turks are very pious; but what are their notions in so doing? The Koran commands it, their laws enforce it, and they dare not do otherwise. Poor, ignorant, deluded Turks! They dare *lie*, and *steal*, and *murder*. How fatally they are bound in the chains of error, bigotry, and sin!

"The dress and general appearance of the Turks are such as would lead one to suppose they possessed much gravity, sobriety, and dignity. Their heavy turban, long beard, and slow, dignified step, all give this impression. But so many things I have heard, things continually taking place, which show what great and glaring guilt they can incur, that I fear almost the sight of them."

"September 18. It is now just five months since our arrival in this land. Truly, the Lord has been very good to us. His mercies are infinite. Our lives and health are spared, while others have been called into eternity. In the last night one near to us was called to his home above. Oh, how good that we can feel that he has gone to the home of his heavenly Father! The person I speak of is Alfred Van Lennep, a brother of the missionary. One week ago to-day, from the midst of health and activity, he was laid prostrate on a sick-bed, and last night he peacefully left this world for a mansion above. He was a young man of great promise, devotedly pious, and quite talented.   A mother, six brothers, and two sisters will deeply mourn his early removal."

" SMYRNA, September 26.

"This is a great religious holiday with the Greeks. It comes on Friday, so it is both *fast* and *feast*, — how inconsistent! What would you have thought if you could have been set down in this city this afternoon? Everybody in the streets, or thronging the doors and windows of the houses, dressed in their richest and gayest attire! Such a noise! And this is not the worst of it; wild, perhaps dissipated, Greeks going through the streets making the air ring with their awful singing, is something beyond my talent for description. This is the *Feast of the Cross*, and I shall describe the chief ceremony of the day from an account by Mr. Riggs: A multitude of people assemble near the seaside, at some appointed place, to witness the *baptism* of the Cross. A Turkish guard is present to preserve order. The people are kept back at a little distance, the priest stands near the shore with the cross in his hand, and arranged near him are some half dozen nearly naked men: the cross is thrown at some distance into the sea, and these practiced men dive for it, and honored, rewarded, and happy is he who bears out the baptized cross. Sometimes persons are drowned in this heathenish ceremony. This is religion! And the Greeks wonder why missionaries come to labor among them? 'Why not go,' they say, 'to the heathen?' "

There is much truth in the following remarks on the importance of missionaries cultivating a cheerful spirit.

"Do you know, Eleanor, that your sister Seraphina has a reputation for being very sedate and discreet? Would you believe it? To tell you the truth, dear sister, I sometimes fear that I shall not sustain that cheerfulness and sprightliness of feeling which I think are necessary in a country like this, where every thing has a downward tendency upon the character and feelings. Vivacity of disposition seems to be a most important ingredient in the character of a missionary, who is in such circumstances as to be obliged to draw from his own resources in this respect, and if he has not a large fund, it will be too soon exhausted. Not in this respect alone, but in all, the character of a missionary should have a high tone. Strong and well-established Christian principles are, however, the all-important thing; and I often wish that mine had had two or three years more in the Christian land I have left, in which to become matured and more firmly established."

There had hitherto been little encouragement in the missionary work in Smyrna; but about this time a greater interest seemed to be awakened, and the hearts of the missionaries were cheered with new hopes. Mrs. E. thus writes, Oct. 12: —

"Smyrna, you already know, is a worldly, wicked city; and so little fruit has been seen from the many faithful efforts put forth here, and the fervent prayers offered, that it has been almost given up by *men* as a hopeless field, — but, we trust, not of God. . . . This morning sixteen Armenians were present to hear the preaching of the gospel, and they listened with fixed attention, and apparently with intense interest, to a long sermon from Mr. Adger. It stirred up my soul to look upon them. After this service, a Bible class was proposed to the congregation, the plan for which had been made at the suggestion of one of the Armenians not pious, — and to this all but one or two remained, and appeared deeply interested. Sixteen is not, perhaps, a quarter of the number that attend preaching at Constantinople; but it is in Smyrna, this desert place. Five weeks ago no one would have thought of this. Then three or four of those employed by the station came to Mr. A.'s religious service, and he became almost discouraged in preaching to so few, and held a prayer-meeting with them instead. We know not the motive that leads these persons here, (the number has been increasing during the last month;) perhaps it is worldly, perhaps merely curiosity, — the Searcher of hearts alone knows. Of this we are sure, if they come as sincere inquirers after the truth, it is all of the Lord, and on his almighty arm alone the work can depend if it is to go forward, not on the feebleness of man; but what a fearful responsibility rests upon those placed here as instruments by which the Great Master will carry on his own work. How carefully they need to walk, how prayerfully!

"In the afternoon of to-day we first had our Sabbath school, which is now struggling into existence. It is in the hands of Mr. Everett, and he is much interested for its success. Some children will be gathered in who otherwise would probably have no religious instruction, and those who come to the Sabbath school remain at the English service immediately following. This congregation is not large, but the promise of our Lord is sure to the few gathered together in his name. This evening the three families of the station met here for special conference and prayer, with reference to the present encouraging appearances among us. Pray for us, dear brother and sister, do pray much for us; and that the Spirit of the Lord may be poured out copiously upon this city.

"Time seems more precious to me as each night tells that the hours of one more day are numbered with the past. Perhaps one reason for this feeling is that there seems so much to be done here; and another, that people around us value time so little. They seem to know *nothing* of its worth. The ladies spend much time in walking leisurely through the streets; but more, perhaps, in a way which requires less exertion and is a more agreeable occupation, — it is gazing upon others as they pass by their doors or under their windows. All houses are constructed, if possible, so as to have windows overlooking the streets, even if the second story must be placed a little *askew* upon the first, to gain place for a small window at the corner, so that one can have a survey of the whole length of the street."

"SMYRNA, October 18, 1845.

"MY DEAR SISTER: It is Saturday evening, the hours of which always partake in my feelings of the holy day so soon to be ushered in. But a little weary as I am, and with the sound of Armenian ringing in my ears, I will have a little time of communing with my much-loved sister.

"To-day completes our first half year on missionary ground. Oh, how quickly it has flown! and what have I done? what report have these days and months borne to Heaven? I have had a fine opportunity to test my acquisitions in the Armenian language to-day, by a visit from the wife of Baron Harutûne. It is the first time she has visited me, and she spent the day, the whole responsibility of entertaining her devolving upon me. You can, perhaps, imagine me awkwardly stammering and laboring to communicate an idea, sometimes secretly rejoicing over a little success, then perhaps mortified, after listening with all my power of eyes and ears, at a failure to comprehend what some one had endeavored to beat into my willing but incapable brain. There is now here a book distributer, who knows no English, but is very social and full of zeal. He has visited us several times, and has been here two or three hours to-day; he does not spare at all, but pours upon us a torrent of rather harsh and unintelligible sounds. I am sure, if we were shut up to talk only with him, we should soon know how to speak some Armenian.

"The result of the day has brought me to this conclusion, so far as progress in Armenian is concerned, — that I have

7

advanced a little, made a beginning, and am encouraged to go on, trusting in our great Master for all the strength needed for so great a work.

"I am feeling more and more, each day, the preciousness of time. How much is to be done; how much for one's own mind and soul, besides the great responsibility of laboring for the souls of others, — and this in such a position as I am placed in. The thought of it startles me, and I feel that I must be up and doing; labor in season and out of season, early and late, saving not only the hours, but all the little precious minutes which go to make up this short, fleeting life of ours.

"Still, I do not wish to feel that too great things are depending upon what one unworthy, inefficient person like me can do. All is, and must be, *of the Lord;* we are his tools, just the instruments by which, if he wills, he can work; so I think, perhaps the way he will make use of me is not that to which I am looking, and for which I am striving, which is, to be prepared to do something for the spiritual good of my sex among the people to whom we are sent. I do try to commit my way to the Lord, that he may direct my steps, and often seek grace and strength to keep my resolutions to be more calm and moderate in my course; and seek, more than any thing, *to live well,* to have my spirit continually such as will be pleasing in the sight of that Holy Being who searches our hearts, and is fully acquainted with their inmost recesses. . . .

"Did you know that this was a land of *earthquakes?* I did not until I came here. Others have felt them slightly many times since we have been here; but I never had the fearful sensation until last week, when we had three shocks that made this great house in which we are tremble from its foundations to its top-stone. I never experienced any thing so fearful, so awful, showing forth so sensibly the omnipotence of our God. Seventy or eighty years ago Smyrna was visited by an earthquake which destroyed a considerable portion of the city, and I sometimes think that this more terrible judgment than fire may come upon this wicked city ere the people will repent and turn to God. There is a report that upon the island of Mitylene sixty or seventy houses were, last week, overthrown by the earthquake. Perhaps I should not have written things which might make you in any degree anxious for us. You need not be so. We are not, for we are in the hands of God; and would not feel otherwise than to say,

> " 'My times are in thy hands;
> My God, I wish them there.' "

To another sister she writes, October 31 : —

"We have a little hope for Smyrna. A few, ten or twelve, come to hear preaching, and the pious persons here seem to be anxious, more than heretofore, to awaken an interest in the minds of others. One of these pious men is Hadji A., very poor and ignorant, but devoted and zealous in the cause of Christ. I will tell you one or two things which will show you his spirit. At the time of our communion-service, on the week of the annual meeting of the Board, all were in the country. Among the number was an English clergyman, a stranger here, whom Mr. Adger met and took with him to his house. At the dinner-table, Hadji inquired (in Armenian) of Mr. A. if the stranger had heard, and if his people knew of the great work the Lord had begun among the Armenians. Having a negative reply, he seemed greatly astonished, and said: 'When you go home, will you not tell your people about it? but first you must require a present from them, (according to an eastern custom,) because it is such great and good news.' One of the other Armenians suggested that the present required should be the promise of their prayers, that not only a few, but the whole nation should be converted. The Englishman was much pleased.

"Afterwards, the same man met Hadji in the street, and having no language in common, they had no means of salutation except by a shake of the hand. Only poor Hadji, knowing a few words of English, selected the one most in accordance with his feelings, which was 'glory;' and this, I trust, will be the poor man's theme to all eternity, and that of many of his nation, redeemed by the blood of Jesus from all this darkness and sin."

Of the following playful reply to a letter from one of Mr. Everett's brothers, there is no explanation, except what is contained in itself.

"You see I have taken a *small* sheet, and can write you only a *short* letter, because I have but *little* time. After all these diminutives, you surely can not expect much from your distant sister.

"I beg pardon, dear brother, for not having acknowledged, ere this, your letter, in which I had so large a share, by way of hints, calculated to make me a better wife. You have my sincere thanks, and a promise to try to profit by them. They certainly were not written from a knowledge of my particular deficiencies, as you know little of me as a wife, unless you have been informed by a private letter from my husband, — neither am I willing to think you intended to portray any particular characteristics of your own wife; for that would not be the part of a husband, especially such a one as I suppose you to be.

"I can not attempt to respond now to the things mentioned in your letter; much more do I shrink from replying to you on this paper, by stating my views on the duties or deficiencies of husbands, except to refer to the very comprehensive and safe injunction from the inspired apostle, — '*Husbands, love your wives.*'" . . .

In the same letter she relates some further particulars respecting T., the persecuted Armenian from Trebizond, whose case she describes in one of her letters from Constantinople.

"You heard about the case of persecution last spring, at the time we were at Constantinople. A young man, on account of his evangelical principles, was seized at Trebizond and hurried on board a steamer, by which he was taken to Constantinople, where he was thrown into prison, and kept confined in chains eight days and nights. When he was released, he was forbidden to return to his family in Trebizond, and it is contrary to the laws for a man to remove his family from one city to another, except on certain conditions. The Patriarch, wishing to appear as a friend to this young man, in order to win him back to the church, asked him if they could not manage together in some way, so that he might take his family to Constantinople, proposing this and that thing, to which the young man replied: 'That would be deception, and I can not do that.' The answer of the Patriarch was: 'Christ deceived, and God can not carry on his government without sometimes practicing deception!' What blasphemous words to proceed from the lips of a religious teacher, or head of a church!"

In illustration of her genial temperament, it may not be improper to present a playful correspondence in rhyme, which she exchanged with the Rev. Mr. H. of the Nestorian mission. Mr. H. who was passing the winter in Smyrna with his family, for the benefit of their health, had undertaken to deliver a letter from Mrs. E. to a friend in Bournabat, but forgetting it, wrote the following apology.

BOURNABAT, Wed. eve., Dec. 31, 1845.

"Of all the hard efforts that duty demands,
  Which a friend or a foe may require at our hands,—
    To do it and let come the worst: —
A fault to confess,
And the wrong to redress,
  In my humble opinion's the first.

7*

" Of all the sweet graces on earth that reside,
The fairest, the nearest to heaven allied,
  (Saint and sinner the saying receive,)
Now is it not so ? —
Dear sister, you know,
  'T is the grace that a fault can forgive.

" The letter you wrote and entrusted to me,
Wrapt up in a napkin, I've kept, as you see,
  (It should have been first on my docket:)
Now can you believe it,
And kindly receive it ? —
  I've kept it a week in my pocket."

Mrs. Everett's reply to Mr. H.:—

" For the injury done
  You make such a return,
As leads me to hope, I confess it,
  If again there should be
  Such a wrong done to me,
That you will in like manner redress it.

" I do not dare try
  To shape a reply
To your frank, though uncalled-for confession;
  But your genius and skill,
  (As ever they will,)
Have made a most happy impression.

" That sweetest of graces,
  (And just are its praises,)
Dear brother, I hope may appear,
  When I pardon you freely;
  And now will add merely,—
I wish you a Happy New Year."

SMYRNA, Jan. 1, 1846.

CHAPTER VIII.

WHILE Mrs. Everett was thus earnestly engaged in studying the language in Smyrna, and taking advantage of every opportunity to use her imperfect knowledge of it for the benefit of the people around her, Miss Lovell was no less diligently employed in the same efforts in Constantinople. She had found a delightful home in the family of Dr. Goodell, where she was received as an elder daughter, and where she at once proved the truth of the promise to those who forsake father and mother, brothers and sisters, for the sake of Christ. There is scarcely a letter to her home friends, in which she does not speak in terms of the most affectionate gratitude of her happiness in this dear missionary family, and of the unvarying parental kindness of Dr. and Mrs. Goodell. Indeed, her letters, as well as Mrs. Everett's, are full of the breathings of love towards every member of the missionary circle. In the most confidential communications of both, in which their thoughts and feelings seem to be laid open with the most entire unreserve, there occurs not one expression respecting any brother or sister of the whole missionary circle, but of the most cordial esteem and love. And most warmly was the love, which they so freely gave, returned; so that it might be truly said of them, "None saw them but to love them." Wherever they went, they seemed to carry with them an atmosphere of love.

The first letter we find written by Miss L. from her missionary home is to Mrs. Everett, the commencement of the weekly notes which they exchanged almost uninterruptedly during the year of their separation.

"PERA, May 27, 1845.

"MY DEAR SERAPH: Your bit of a note was received yesterday, and though disappointed at not hearing more from you, yet I could not but consider the strawberries a valid excuse, and was happy to hear they were *doing well*. I wish you could step into my sanctum this eve, and see how pleasantly I am situated. I have got matters all arranged, my room in order, and yesterday commenced with Armaveni a systematic course of study. My table is covered with books, dictionaries, etc. My copy in Armenian writing lies before me, with my first attempt at these new characters, and altogether my room has quite a literary appearance, quite the air of a study. What are you going to read first? I am about commencing Robinson Crusoe. But, oh! when, *when* shall I be able to use these sounds so as to make myself understood, and useful to others? I feel, however, that my advantages in having Armaveni and Ermonia* with me will be very great. Do not forget to pray for us, that we may be blessed in our mutual intercourse, that I may be enabled to exert a happy influence over them.

"My dear S. I need your prayers, for I am sometimes almost ready to faint in view of the responsibilities I have taken upon me. Still, I know I am not called to bear them alone. If God has called me here, if it was *his* voice I heard, (and surely it was not like the voice of earthly friends,) I know he will not lay upon me any burden too heavy to bear. My greatest fear is that I may forget that in God is my only strength."

*Two Armenian girls who had been under missionary instruction, and had acquired some knowledge of English.

In a note added the next morning, she says: "With regard to our concert, — Saturday morning I join with a friend in America in remembering our brothers; would you like to join? It is especially that they may be converted. I had thought of Wednesday morning for ourselves, for each other. Would that time, five, or half-past five, suit you? If not, mention any other day or hour."

The materials furnished from her home correspondence during this and the following year are very scanty. She doubtless wrote much during these two years, and gave her friends in America all her first fresh impressions and experience of the strange world around her, and of missionary life, and it is to be regretted that more of these letters could not be obtained. She writes to her mother, June 9: "I rise at half past four usually, and retire at half past ten, — study from nine till twelve, then lunch, — study from one till three, then write Armenian a little while. The remainder of the day I spend in reading, writing, or walking. We dine at 5, P. M., and Mr. G. usually insists upon my taking a long walk with him and the children after dinner. What will you say when I tell you that last Saturday I walked more than *eight* miles, and was not more fatigued than I have been in walking to Uncle William's? So you see I do not want for exercise. I have not had a symptom of dyspepsia since I arrived here, and find my appetite quite equal to all the strange dishes I meet with here. On Wednesday afternoons we are to have a kind of sewing society, teaching the children needle-work, and listening to reading. On Saturday I do not study, but reserve it for writing letters, mending, etc. We have a Sabbath school at 9, A. M., of the missionary children, — Mrs. Hinsdale, who teaches the missionary school, being superintendent. . . . . .

"The streets here at evening, particularly on Sundays, are a perfect *Vanity Fair*. Such a display of dress and fashion I have nowhere else seen. It is one of the greatest

objections to this place, that the missionary *must* necessarily pay some attention to etiquette and form. What
Mrs. Smith said, in her memoirs, of dress, applies with
much greater force to those living in Constantinople. . .

"I love the missionary cause better day by day, and
may I but live to see a flourishing school established
among this interesting people, and some of them brought
into the fold of Christ, the desire of my heart will be
gratified. We have three scholars engaged, besides the
two now here who are my teachers, as well as my scholars
in English. We met one of those engaged, in the street,
the other day, — a dark, black-eyed girl, about twelve
years of age. She was dressed in the Armenian dress,
full yellow trowsers, and a gay-colored outside jacket. She
caught hold of my hand, pressed it to her bosom and her
forehead, and kissed it again and again. I do not know
whether she knew I was to be her teacher. You can
imagine how seriously I feel the responsibility of the situation in which I am placed. God grant I may feel it
more and more, and then it will drive me to him who
alone can enable me to discharge it to his glory. Shall I
live to see these girls the humble followers of Jesus?
Very few of the Armenian girls are taught even to read,
though they have good minds, and are glad to be instructed. Armaveni I love very much. She says she loves the
Americans, who are teaching her nation, and she prays
God to bless them. She hopes the time will come when
Armenian females, like the Americans, will all know how
to read about the Saviour, and will all love him. Her
nation, she says, however wealthy, are not happy here,
and they have no promise of the life to come. Her heart
is all engaged in the new school.

"The great business of my life, at this time, is the mastery of this very difficult language, and I feel that it is my
duty to devote as much time as my health will permit to
this. I have very little time for writing."

In the absence of letters to friends in America for the next two months, her weekly correspondence with Mrs. Everett must continue the history of her own life, and things about her in which she was interested. Her second letter to Mrs. E. commences with two lines in Armenian characters, which would hardly interest the uninitiated.

"It is, I know," she proceeds, "very rash in me thus to lay myself open to a comparison with you in this matter of writing; but you know it is sometimes so much *easier* to express one's self in a foreign tongue, albeit it *may* savor of affectation! I wish I could tell you of the rapid progress I am making in the language, which bids fair to be the all-absorbing topic of interest for some months to come, at least; but, alas! if there is any royal, rosy, down-hill road to this attainment, *I* have not discovered it, and am plodding slowly along the old track, picking out one step after another. I trust, however, I shall not be left entirely unaided in this matter. How happy are we that we need never enter upon any undertaking in our own strength, that no work is too trifling for the blessing and aid of God, if undertaken for his glory! I think you are highly favored with regard to teachers. Armaveni does very well, but she would do better if she understood English better; in translating she is sometimes at a loss. However, we get on pretty well. . . . .

"I teach Armaveni in geography, arithmetic, writing, and reading. How many hours in the day do you study? Armaveni laughs at my letter." [Armenian words and phrases scattered all through it.] "She says I must tell you, 'I will not next time write such a funny letter, but all Armenian.' I hope you won't think I was obliged to ask her how to express myself.

"Mr. G. says I must give you his love in Armenian. Next time, perhaps, I will."

In her next, June 16, she gives a brief description of the public ceremonies attending the marriage of one of the Sultan's sisters.

"Since I wrote you, the great wedding so much talked of has taken place, and I devoted two days to seeing what might be seen of the festivities. The first was the day of the dinner given to the Embassadors at Hyder Pasha, below Scutari. We succeeded in securing a good seat (Mr. Goodell, Mrs. Hinsdale, the children, and myself) on an elevated platform, from which we could see all that passed. We saw the entrance of all the Embassadors, with their ladies, into the field in which were their tents. Soon after, the chief dignitaries of the empire arrived on the field, the bridegroom among them, (happy man!) and directly afterward the Sultan himself, in a carriage and four. We saw rope-dancing, and all sorts of jugglery, and a very fine balloon ascension, and heard some good music. The next day Mr. Dwight sent for me to go with them up the Bosphorus, to witness the escorting of the bride to her palace and her lord. We went in the steamboat, which anchored just between the two palaces, the one from which she was to go, and the one *to* which she was going. There was a very long procession of boats, each with the Turkish flag. These preceded the two or three royal boats, in which were her highness, and her ladies and attendants. Two of these boats were carefully covered, so that no vulgar eyes might catch even a glimpse of her royal person, and were rowed by twenty-four men.

"The procession moved up the Bosphorus on one side, and came down on the other, amid the firing of guns and the music of the band, and were received at the door of the palace by a number of black slaves. A passage was constructed from the water's edge to the door, and covered with scarlet drapery. As she left the boat, these curtains were carefully drawn around the opening, and *this* was all we saw of her. But there was, of course, little opportunity for any display compared with what there might have been by land. We went out, also, one or two evenings, to see the fireworks and the illuminations on the Bosphorus, which were very fine. And all this display was merely to escort a poor girl across the Bosphorus, to a husband she had never seen! Let us be thankful we were not born Sultanas."

The following, to the same, will show the reader some of the difficulties and discouragements attending the acquisition of a language like the Armenian, and some of the desponding feelings with which missionaries must contend in so arduous a work. It will also suggest the importance of the first fresh energies of the missionary being devoted to the accomplishment of a work so necessary and so difficult as the mastery of the language he is to use.

"PERA, June 23.

"I fear, my dear sister S., I am doing a very *selfish* act in writing you this afternoon, but my heart and *eyes* are full, and you know what a comfort it is to pour out one's heart to a *sister*, and I have no one else to whom I can do this but to him who seeth in secret. I am sad and depressed in spirits to-day, — ungrateful as this may seem when I have just received another letter from Palmyra, telling me that all are well, and praying for unworthy me. Mother writes me that two monthly prayer-meetings have been formed since I left, which meet at our house, one of married and one of young ladies, to pray for the Turkey mission and for me. Ought I not to be encouraged to new faith and new zeal, instead of giving way to doubts and fears? Ermonia has arrived to-day, and the thought of this new responsibility thus coming upon me, and of my unfitness for the station of a guide and instructor, has affected me as it has never before done. It has, I trust, however, driven me to the throne of grace, and I am assured none ever apply there in vain. You tell me, in

8

your kind note just received, that you hope you are
making some progress in the language, and as every thing
in my present state of mind takes a wrong turn, I have
been envying you your superior advantages for learning
the grammar from such a teacher, and also from having
others to study with you. I fear I am very stupid and
dull. I certainly make very little, if any, progress in
speaking. I do most sincerely hope you will never be
visited with the same feelings of discouragement and
doubt which I have felt to-day. I do feel that I am guilty
of extreme selfishness in thus troubling you with my
troubles; but will it not induce you to pray for me, that
my faith may be increased, that my weakness may be
aided? I will write no more till I am in a better
frame.

"June 24. I am ashamed of what I wrote yesterday;
but I will send it, that you may see that though 'happy
as a queen,' queens have their troubles. Still, though the
depression of yesterday has passed away, I fear that I am
not making that progress in the language which I ought,
and which is expected of me. Tell me just *how much*
you can talk, will you? . . . .

"I spent last evening at Mr. Dwight's. How I do love
them! Would that I had more of their spirit, or more
of the spirit of Christ! Oh, how important that we watch
every moment, — watch unto prayer! How ready is the
adversary to attack us *when and where* we least expect
his approaches! I think I feel daily more and more the
value and importance of a spirit of prayer. How happy
are we when at every interval of thought or employment,
and *in all*, we find our hearts rising to God involuntarily.
Oh that this may be more frequently our experience!
Mr. Goodell says I must give you much love from your
parents here, and charge you that you take good care of
your health, and be *good* children.

"You ask what I am doing besides reading Armenian?

I study the grammar, an ancient and modern and Turkish grammar, by *picking out* the modern; but it is not, of course, very rapid work with me at present. I feel the want of a teacher who understands and can explain the grammar and philosophy of the language. I *try* to speak a little, but it is a *very* little; I can not yet form sentences, and I almost fear I never shall. I also write a little nearly every day; and as I have several lessons to hear from each of the young ladies, you may imagine I have not many unoccupied hours."

To the above, Mrs. Everett responds: —

"MY DEAR SISTER MARTHA: If I could have got access to your *sanctum* last Monday, what could I have done? If nothing more, to comfort you, I would have thrown my arm around you, and mingled my tears with yours, remembering the kindness, so sisterlike, *I* have received in this strange land. And would we not have mingled our prayers, too, before the throne of our Father, unitedly pleading, as we have often done, for strength and grace for the performance of every duty? But 'the darkest wave hath bright foam near it,' and was it not so in your case? I hope not only that a *solitary star* is cheering your cloudy night, but that the clear morning sunlight is resting upon you I doubt not that in *Armenian*, dear M., you are in many points, perhaps in all, beyond me; I would unhesitatingly say all, if I would not seem to undervalue the instruction we received from Mr. Riggs; and Baron Harûtune may be better able to teach than your young ladies, as he has a better knowledge of English. But you have those with you constantly who converse in Armenian, and here your advantages are superior to ours. . . . .

"As to the grammar of which you speak, I have not done so great a thing as to *attempt* to study it; and am sorry that you feel obliged to do so, for it must be very discouraging at this stage of your progress."

After some other encouraging suggestions, she says: "Now *do not* have an anxious thought about study. You are 'neither stupid, nor dull,' and, I will venture to say, are advancing rapidly in Armenian, although by the hardest way. Please write me more of the character. I think it will benefit us. Believe me your ever sympathizing sister,

"SERAPHINA."

In her next, Miss L. is able to say: "Everything goes on quietly and pleasantly just now. I study every day except Saturday. Wednesday afternoon we are going to devote to needle-work, drawing, reading, etc., and, in short, we are going to commence a family sewing circle. I wish you could join us. Our female prayer-meeting we hold after dinner, at six o'clock, in my room, on Wednesdays, — and on Wednesday mornings I think our spirits meet, our prayers mingle before the throne of our common Father."

In writing to Mrs. E. July 7, she takes in her turn the office of comforter.

"Am I mistaken, or were you not indulging a sad mood when you wrote? I do not think you should look upon Smyrna as so unpromising a field; I trust God has yet much people there, and that it will prove that you and your dear husband were raised up and sent for just this purpose, to call out and instruct such. While God is doing so much for this people, in such a wonderful manner causing the light to spring up here and there, surely it is no time to distrust him, or doubt his power and willingness to bless the faithful labors of his children for any portion of this people. Let us *believe*, and let us pray. Yesterday we were once more permitted to gather around the table of our dying Lord. It was a good day. In spirit, I met the dear church in Palmyra at the feast of love, for it was also their communion season. In the afternoon, at the Turkish service, was an old man, ninety years old, who had never been there before. His grandson has long been an attendant, and, having much dispute on the subject of this new way at home, he, though an *infidel*, determined to go and hear for himself. He came, heard Mr. Dwight, and stayed to hear Mr. Powers in Turkish. His attention was deeply engaged, so that several times he exclaimed aloud, 'That is true, that is true!' and, at length, 'I was Saul, but am changed to Paul!' God grant he may indeed become a Paul. It will probably not be the last time he will hear the gospel, though the first."

"July 14. Your description of the terrible fire in Smyrna is indeed a sad one, but we will hope and pray that God may make it a great blessing to many of the sufferers. We will pray that it may be overruled to their good, and the furtherance of the gospel among them. I do not wonder you wish for the power to *speak* more than ever. I am now occasionally placed in circumstances when I think I would give the world if I could make myself understood. A. and E. have, during the two or three weeks past, had many friends to see them. They wished to see me, and I was obliged to sit and listen to their animated conversation, scarcely understanding a word, and without the power of replying a word to them. Is it not a trial? How much more so when, as in your case, you hope you might be able to offer them some comfort, to do them some good.

"I went to Mr. Dwight's last Wednesday morning, to hear him discourse to the Armenian females. Owing to some misunderstanding with regard to the time, but two came beside ourselves, — A., E., and myself. But Mr. D. very kindly commenced with only us, read and explained a chapter, and prayed. I was glad to find I could understand here and there a short sentence. . . . .

"Give my kindest regards to your 'best of husbands.'

8*

Can he *almost* preach yet? Do tell me, if you can, with any kind of ease, form sentences in Armenian; yet if you *can, don't say so*, for I shall be quite discouraged."

July 1, 1846.

" I have now been here so long that all the strange sights and sounds that so bewildered me, have become quite familiar, and seem quite a matter of course. I no longer run to the window at every cry of the *muezzin*, calling to prayer from a neighboring minaret, and the thousand and one different cries in the streets, in almost as many different tongues, now pass unheeded. A noise in the street just called me to the window. I will try to describe to you what was passing, — which although occurring every day, I have not become accustomed to. It was a funeral procession of an Armenian lady, and the noise I heard was the chanting of the priests and little boys who led the procession. There were six or eight little boys, dressed in long green-satin robes, embroidered with gold and silver, carrying, one a large gilt cross, one a censer with burning incense, others large wax tapers, and all chanting in a most unmelodious voice. Next followed a number of priests, also in splendid robes, with large, square black caps, and long crape veils thrown over them; next came the body, carried by four men, not in a coffin, but in an open box, the whole figure being exposed to view. At the head and foot of the box were placed great wreaths of flowers, orange leaves, and tinsel; sometimes these wreaths are hung full of lemons. The corpse, excepting the face, was covered with a gay-colored shawl, and over this a profusion of gold and flowers. After this followed a great crowd of men, but there was no sign by which you might distinguish the mourners. A few days since a funeral procession passed, which exceeded in splendor any I had before seen. It was that of a wealthy

Armenian lady, — a young bride, — and as they passed directly under my window, I could distinctly see her face. It was very beautiful, — she did not seem more than seventeen. She was perfectly covered with flowers and gold ornaments. A cross lay upon her breast, and a splendid cashmere shawl was spread over her feet. It seems very shocking to us to see a dead body thus decorated as if for a ballroom, and borne along thus exposed to every eye."

In the same letter she describes an araba ride. "I wish I could describe the vehicle in which we rode. It was drawn by oxen, and without seats, but with cushions, and as gay as red and blue paint could make it. They are frequently covered entirely with scarlet cloth. Over the oxen are fixed two long poles or rods, fastened to the tip of the horn and the end of the tail, forming a great bow over their backs, to which are attached a great number of scarlet tassels, and all ornamented with shells and bits of looking-glass."

TO THE SAME.

Aug. 27.

"Last week I was invited to attend the marriage of one of the evangelicals, as they are called, — that is, one of the pious Armenians. Being on Sunday, and seven or eight miles distant, I did not go, but one of my pupils who was there described the affair to me. The lady wished much to be married *à la Frank*, but her mother was too much opposed to her marrying a Protestant, so she yielded in this matter, and was married in an Armenian dress, — red silk trowsers, green silk *astare* or outside jacket, open at the sides, and dragging on the floor half a yard behind, with loose sleeves much longer than the arm; on her head the fez, and an innumerable quantity of gold coins, — her *dowry ;* the weight of which, woven in her long braids of hair, must have been very disagreeable. As soon as she was married, however, she laid aside her Armenian dress, and appeared in a white silk dress, white satin shoes, etc. — all *à la Frank*. According to the strict Armenian way, the bride must sit three days after marriage, alone,— be seen by no person but the one who brings her food, and at the end of the third day, for the first time, she is seen by her husband, as when she is married she must wear a veil.

"A day or two since I attended Mr. Dwight's Armenian service for the females. The bride and groom were present, and no one would have dreamed that they were other than English or Americans, except from their language. She is very pretty and agreeable. The people of this country are very affable and frank with strangers; they treat you at once as though they had known you for years. I have wished it were possible to throw aside my American reserve, and be as easy and familiar as they. The females, especially, with their rich complexions, and full, dark eyes, are very interesting. I feel my desire daily strengthening to be able, by imparting instruction, to be useful to some of them."

TO HER MOTHER.

"CONSTANTINOPLE, Aug. 2, 1845.

"MY DEAR MOTHER: When I sit down to write to you, so many recollections of your kindness to me, and of all the pleasant associations of home, come crowding upon my mind, that I am often forced to stop and collect my thoughts, and endeavor to *forget* home for awhile before I can proceed. I see you all bending at morning and at night before the family altar, gathering around the table, and sometimes wishing that ' Martha was here to eat with us.' I hear Clarissa, just at evening, making the air melodious with the sweet sounds of her piano and guitar. Every bright moonlight evening, I imagine she is 'bathing' in the moon's pure light, as Mr. P. would say. Each Sabbath I follow you to the house of God, and Henry to the Sabbath school. I am with you at your prayer-meetings and monthly concerts. In short, there is not a day but I think often of you, and at night I dream of you, and often also of my dear father and Frank as still with you. But my thoughts of home are almost always pleasant ones. I think of you as happy, and under the watchful eye of him who never slumbers nor sleeps, and of myself as ere long to be united to you again, and am thankful that God has called me to make this small sacrifice to his cause.

"The summer is now more than half over, and as yet my health remains perfect. I am more free from headache than ever in America, and am quite free from dyspepsia. Perhaps this is owing in a great measure to my diet being more simple than formerly. But little meat is eaten here compared with America. Vegetables, fruits, and *bread*, are the chief food. Bread is indeed, here, the staff of life, and miserable bread it is compared with yours, though I believe it is more healthy than American bread; however, I would gladly exchange the best meal I have eaten here for a slice of your sweet bread and butter, or one of your *ginger nuts*. Fruits are plenty, and very fine; grapes and melons are now in market in abundance.

"Of myself or of the school, I have nothing new to tell you. I am still studying, morning, noon, and *night*, I was going to say, but this is not true. I do not allow myself to study at all during the evening, for fear of injuring my eyes, as the Armenian characters are more difficult to distinguish than the English. We have five pupils engaged, who are waiting till we can get a house; there is no doubt that there will be as many applicants as we can take. I am eagerly looking forward to the time when I shall be able to communicate instruction to them. I am not yet able to *speak* much Armenian, but can understand a little when I hear it spoken.

"Sabbath afternoon, Aug. 3. I was interrupted yesterday in my letter, and resume my pen this afternoon to add a few lines. I have attended church and Sabbath school, and now sit in my room contrasting the mingled sounds which fall upon my ear, with the peace and quietness which reigns this holy day in Palmyra. Every imaginable kind of business is going on in the streets, and I always think there is more noise on this day than any other. Oh that every Christian in America could spend one Sabbath in this, or in some heathen land! Surely they would pray as they have never before done; surely they would feel constrained to labor and sacrifice more than they ever yet have done, for the spread of the gospel in these dark lands. We have abundant reason to bless God for the work which he has wrought here, and which is still going on, — that *any*, that so many, have been led to forsake their errors and superstitions, and embrace the pure religion of Christ. But what are these in comparison with the thousands, the millions, in this empire, who do not know him, and who, in all probability, will die without knowing him. My heart aches when I think of these things, and painful as it is to witness so much sin and misery, I am thankful that God has brought me here, if he will only use me as an instrument of giving light to but one soul, or in any way of strengthening his cause here. Oh that I could induce some others to give themselves to the missionary work!"

September 22, Miss Lovell writes to Mrs. Everett, "in the midst of the confusion and noise of packing, pulling down, and tearing up," preparatory to moving the school and Mr. Goodell's family next day into a house adjoining the chapel house, then occupied by Mr. Dwight. A week later she writes: —

"I will tell you something of my whereabouts. The Armenian part of the establishment is confined to the third story. There are four rooms and a hall: one of these will be a schoolroom this winter, the others sleeping-rooms. Mine is a front room, overlooking, as you know, the English garden, and with a pleasant view of the city, and I am much pleased with my quarters. The room next to mine is occupied by A. and E., and the hall will be the school dining-room. We have not quite as much room as we could desire, but shall try to make it answer for the present. I think we shall not take more than six girls this winter, though we have the names of seven applicants. You say, you sometimes almost wish you were united with me in this work. How many, many times, have I wished it might have been so. . . . .

"This morning I enjoyed the precious privilege of sitting down to the table of our Saviour, and commemorating his death, with between twenty-five and thirty Armenians. There were three Armenian ladies, the wives of Barons Apisaghom and Mugerditch and Ammorvia. It was a sweet and refreshing season to me, and, I trust, to all. I was able to understand a good portion of the service, and it was a precious foretaste of that blessed day when all who love our Lord Jesus Christ will sit down together in his kingdom, and enjoy free and uninterrupted communion with him and with each other for ever. Oh for the coming of the time when not only thirty, but the whole of this nation shall unite in celebrating a Saviour's dying love!" . . . . .

TO THE SAME.

"October 6, 1845.

"MY DEAR SISTER SERAPHINA: . . . You ask for more information about the school. It is *not* to be an entirely separate establishment. The scholars will eat and sleep and study up stairs; but Mrs. Goodell is to be the *mother* of them all, and not poor, inefficient I. Quite enough of responsibility will, however, devolve upon me. Mr. and Mrs. G. have not yet been able to complete their arrangements so as to receive any; but when Soorpohee comes we shall be ready for others. Mrs. Dwight and I have a half hour's conversation in Armenian each day, (but do not tell Mr. Adger this, else he will expect me to be able to converse with him,) and, if the truth must be told, our conversation is nearly all upon one side. Dear Mrs. D. is, however, very patient with me.

Mr. Goodell wishes me to give his love to you, and congratulate you, in his name, on having made such attainments in Eastern life as to have become fond of olives. This is, I suppose, partly by way of a side-thrust at me; for, alas! to my shame be it said, I do not like them. Mr. G. each morning puts *one* on my plate, — sometimes it is eaten, sometimes not.

TO THE SAME.

October 13, past 10 o'clock, p. m.

Late as it is, I can not retire without thanking you, my dear sister, for your cheerful and delightful note, as I fear I shall not have time to do so in the morning. We have been spending the evening very pleasantly in the company of Mr. and Mrs. Holladay, Mr. Schauffler, and the Dwights. Most sincerely do I hope that we shall not soon again be called upon to bid farewell to *returning missionaries*. The longer I live here, and the more I see of the wants of the people, of the thick darkness which covers the land, and the great need there is of faithful labor, the more sad does it seem that instead of the number of laborers increasing, it should be diminishing, by their return home. God grant that the health of those who remain may be precious in his sight. Ah! who will supply their places when they are gone? But doubtless he whose cause it is will take care of it; and oh, how happy should we be that the men and the means are all in his hands, and that he loves the cause infinitely more than our weak minds can conceive. What but this assurance could support our faltering faith, when we look at the greatness of the work and the feebleness of the means?

You ask what you shall tell the brother-in-law, who wonders if I am not lonely, with no one to share my joys and sorrows. Tell him I have a beloved sister, who in this distant land has been friend, consoler, encourager, and sympathizer, and has almost made me forget that I had left far behind me all the friends of my early youth.

When you see Capt. Kenrick, remember me most kindly to him. How I should like to go on board the Stamboul again. My compliments to "my admirer," the kind steward; and assure poor Aleck of my sympathy in his affliction, and of my earnest prayers for his spiritual welfare. Salute for me that precious little state-room in the Stamboul. I wonder if any echo of our pleasant songs is there yet.

TO THE SAME.

October 20.

We had expected to commence school to-day with at least Soorpohee and one or two others, but no one has arrived. They tell me, however, that it would be a very strange thing if they should come at the appointed time, so we await their time. Why do you not report yourself as to your progress in Armenian? When Mr. Adger comes I shall find out all about it,—how much you know, and how much you speak. At our female service last Friday Mr. Dwight had an audience of thirty persons, twenty of them females. Mr. Goodell says I must describe to my sister Seraph my little room and its accommodations, and I will do so that you may know how pleasantly I am situated. I have told you that it is a front room, small, but large enough for me. I have in it a bed, sofa, a nice bureau and bookcase, two or three

9

chairs, carpet, table, and last, not least, a Boston rocking-chair, just from America. With all these comforts my room is very pleasantly filled, and here Mrs. Dwight comes daily for half an hour for our Armenian chat, and here every Saturday evening we have our female prayer meeting, and here I hope to enjoy many sweet seasons of communion with God. Some time I hope to have the pleasure of welcoming you to a seat in my rocking-chair.

The long-desired school at length had a beginning. October 27 she writes Mrs. Everett: —

"I sit down to answer your note with feelings such as I can not well describe. I am sitting in my *school-room*, surrounded by *seven* Armenian girls, including A. and E. As I have not yet reduced them to order, there is a continual buzzing of Armenian whispers in my ears. I am pleased with the appearance of all; but, oh! how am I to teach them? Now, indeed, I begin to feel the want of a tongue which they can understand. My heart is so full of my new duties and cares that you must expect nothing else from me to-day. Oh, would that you were here, dearest sister, to assist me with your counsels, to cheer me with your smiles, and join your prayers with mine, for that divine direction without which I shall be utterly unable to do aught aright!

"Your prayers, I am sure, I have now. . . . . Thanks, dear S., a thousand thanks for your precious loan, your *husband's* miniature. Thanks to him for sparing it; but he might well do that, so long as he has the still more precious original. Thank you, too, for the cologne. I will try to think I feel your hand bathing my forehead sometimes, as you used to do on the Stamboul. . . . .

"Oh! if you knew in what a whirl my poor head is, you would wonder that I can write at all. I have, and always had, too much of the spirit of Martha of old, 'careful, and troubled about many things.' I have not learned the happy art of casting all care upon Him who careth for me, and I am wondering how all these new, and unformed, and discordant materials, are to be brought into harmony and system, particularly since I can not speak with them. I must go to the throne of grace, and seek for wisdom and guidance there.

"Mr. Dwight has just been in to read and pray with us, which he promises to do every evening. What a favor is it to me in my work, that I have such friends and associates to aid with their prayers and their counsels. You can not tell how much I love them all, and how much I prize their counsels and their society, and how unworthy I feel of this and the thousand blessings God is bestowing upon me.

"I have just had a long conversation with A. I feared she might feel that too much care was thrown upon her, and that her own studies were too much encroached upon; but, instead of this, she seems delighted and grateful that she is able to do any thing in the school. It has, she says, ever been her most ardent prayer since she went to Mr. Dwight's, that she might be able to teach the girls of her nation, and she thanks God that he now gives her the opportunity."

"November 11.

"My dearest Mother: I am now writing in the school-room of the 'Armenian Female Seminary.' A sounding title, you would say, probably, were you to see our little school; but we will not 'despise the day of small things;' on the contrary, you will, I am sure, thank God that he has permitted me to make this small beginning. I sit now at my table surrounded by eight Armenian girls, including two who have been with us before, all just now engaged in writing. I commenced, two weeks ago, with six scholars. Two have come since, and we have had applications to receive several others; but were unable to do so for want of room, and because it is thought that this number is as many as I can do justice to. The six who have now joined the school are between the ages of eleven and thirteen. Their names are Soorpohee, Aroosiak, Tachoohee, Senim, and two Mariams. The girls all board with us, and Mrs. Goodell has the general superintendence of their clothing, &c. Amaveni assists in teaching. Only one of the new ones learns English. They learn reading, writing, and arithmetic. Wednesday afternoons I teach them sewing. We have prayers with them in the morning, by Mr. Goodell, in Turkish, — in the evening, by Mr. Dwight, in Armenian. Each one commits a portion of Scripture to memory every morning, and we use the Bible as a reading-book. Sabbath morning they join our Sabbath school, instructed by Amaveni; and in the afternoon I teach them the catechism, which has been translated into Armenian. We also attend Mr. Dwight's Armenian service; but sit in an adjoining room, with the door a little open, as custom will not admit of our sitting with the men at present. I find my scholars much more tractable and docile than I had anticipated. They have never been accustomed to the quiet and discipline of our schools, and I feared I should find it very difficult to reduce them to any thing like order, particularly as I speak so little of their language.

.   .   .   .

"It would be impossible to tell you, my dear mother, what my feelings have been since the commencement of my little school. I am sure you will daily remember us at the throne of grace. It is our earnest prayer that all who come here may speedily be brought into the fold of Christ, and you can not imagine how my heart longs to speak to them of the Saviour; but as yet I am tongue-tied, and can only *look* my love to them, and interest in them, and commend them to God in prayer. It is, I think, one of the missionary's greatest trials during the first year, that he is unable to *speak*. We have had several applications to take other scholars, but have been obliged to refuse them. One man wept when Mr. Goodell told him we could not take his daughter. It is hard to be obliged to say no to them.

"Five o'clock, Sabbath evening. The number of Armenian hearers continues, I think, to increase, notwithstanding the unceasing efforts which the enemies of the truth are making to oppose it. They have lately taken a new track. Instead of condemning the reading of the gospel, as heretofore, the Patriarch has proposed that they should have it read at the patriarchate, occasionally mixing with it the writings of the Fathers. In this way he hopes to call off many from Mr. Dwight's meeting. To-day, we understand, they commenced their meetings. They have an *infidel* to expound the Bible to them. It was feared that he might thus draw off some who were still strongly attached to their own church, under the specious pretext of hearing the gospel. But God will bring all their plans to nought, and I believe most of them will see through his motives."

Dec. 7, she thus commences one of her weekly notes to Mrs. Everett : —

"Poor Mrs. Homes! I can think of nothing but her, and her sorrow. I have just returned from the funeral of her sweet little Mary. You expressed the hope in your note that she is now well, and *well* she is, — far better, oh, how much happier, than when on earth, even with all that the love of the fondest parents could do for her. . . . . Oh that this sudden and solemn dispensation may be blessed to the children among us; I long to see the children of the missionaries made partakers of the great salvation."

In the same note she relates some of the proceedings of the Patriarch's meetings : " Yesterday at the meeting at the patriarchate, Broosalie, their great champion, was *missing*,—fairly driven off the field. Baron Stepan and Avedis, and another of Mr. Hamlin's scholars were there, and after some argument, they observed some one going in and out rather suspiciously, and soon Stepan went out. Fifteen or twenty persons of the 'baser sort' were collected about the door to give them a *drubbing*. He escaped; but when afterwards the others left, one of them received a severe beating. Fit arguments these to repel the truth!"

TO MRS. T.

PALMYRA, December 11, 1845.

MY VERY DEAR FRIEND: . . . . . This evening a violent rain has detained me from meeting, and I joyfully devote the time to you. You, I suppose, are enjoying all the delights of a northern winter, at this time, perhaps, shivering over the stove, and listening to the merry jingle of the sleigh bells, (a sound unknown here,) while I am sitting in my room, with scarcely any fire, the rain pouring down in torrents upon the roof. We have as yet had no really cold weather, and no snow. The last of December, and in January, there are usually a few snowstorms, but it never falls to any great depth, or remains many days. . . .

"I have now been long enough in Constantinople to feel quite at home. The narrow, crowded streets, the gloomy, dismal-looking houses, even the very tiles upon the roofs wear a familiar look, and the turbaned Turk, with his long, flowing robes and beard, seems quite an old acquaintance. There is to me nothing inviting in Constantinople as a residence. It is true it is delightfully situated, and the scenery of the Bosphorus is magnificent, but the city is dirty and irregular, although there are some splendid buildings. For one who is desirous of gayety, and very fond of society, in Pera there may be many attractions, as there are many Franks, and many families of wealth and rank, foreign ambassadors, &c.

As for me, my society is confined, from choice, almost exclusively to our missionary circle, and to the few other Americans here; with one or two English families I have some acquaintance. But kinder and more warm-hearted friends than I find in our circle, I could not desire, and I have no inclination to seek for other friends. They have received me as a sister and daughter, and their kindness tends greatly to lessen the pain of separation from the friends of my childhood. Even were it not so, I should, I think, be happy here, for I have the hope of being in some degree useful, of not living entirely in vain. I am happy in my employments; I like to teach, and though I may do but little good, and may see *no* good resulting from what I do, yet I shall feel that the way is opened for somebody else to do good. It is something to have such a school established. It will, in time, by the blessing of God, be a blessing to the Armenians."

CHAPTER IX.

Mrs. E.'s Visit to the Sufferers from the Fire — Letters from Miss Lovell — The Patriarch's Anathema — Its Effects in Constantinople and Smyrna.

THE new year opened pleasantly on the two friends. Though their hearts turned with fond recollections to their native land, and all the pleasures connected with the reunions of the festive season in their loved home circles, they looked back with no longing to return. They felt every day more strongly the privilege of having been called to forsake all these for the sake of Christ, and every day they were becoming more interested in the work they had commenced, and in the people around them. In a few leaves of journal, with which Mrs. Everett commenced the year, is the following, under date of January 5, 1846.

"The meetings we have enjoyed yesterday and to-day in our little circle have been very precious. And although my mind has been led back to the first Sabbath and succeeding Monday of the year just closed, — which were spent in my own dear land, in the midst of its Christian privileges, — still I have enjoyed these sweet seasons of communion and prayer none the less, but the more, in the hope that I may see the darkness receding from this land before the bright appearance of the Lord, as he comes to build up Zion here." And again, a few days later, after lamenting her "want of love and zeal, of watchfulness and prayerfulness," she writes: "O blessed Jesus! how sweet is the hope that the mantle of thy love will be thrown over all these shortcomings in the last day; but I would feel the duty of striving to live, feeling that every one of my sins pierces again thy sacred body."

One of the first works of the new year in which Mrs. Everett engaged, was visiting the poor Armenian sufferers from the fire, to distribute among them money which had been received from America for their relief. She writes to her sister January 15.

"Three hundred and sixty-eight dollars have been sent, the greater part of which was collected in the vicinity of Boston; and the request was made that the missionaries should attend personally to its distribution. This is the safest manner of distributing it, as the religion of these Oriental Christians does not manifest itself particularly in their honesty, and much injustice has been done to the poor sufferers, if we may credit reports, by their rulers, in whose hands moneys received have been placed. Some objections to our going among the people were made, and the advice to put the money into the hands of the rulers and priests given, but rejected. Last week, a visit was made to about a hundred *sheds*, in which Armenian families live. These dwellings are literally sheds, built of rough boards, very slightly, and all crowded into a small square, in rows, with a passage no more than four or five feet wide between them. Here are crowded together men, women, and children, the old and young, the sick and well, a family of six or eight persons in a room eight or ten feet square, and so barren of comforts your heart would ache to see them. . . . Just imagine the state of the children of so many families crowded into so small a space. They appear to have no care, but are dirty, ragged, and left to run wild in idleness and ignorance. The boys are usually sent to school when old enough, but the girls are of far less consequence in the parents' estimation; it is even considered a great affliction to have girls in a family. In a large proportion of these rooms, is an invalid, — an old, insane, foolish, or blind person, —

dependent on the family for support. In one room, lives a widow, with four children, and a deformed brother, whom she must support by the few cents she may be able to earn during the day. In another, we found a woman with a drunken husband and five children, — one a small infant. These children were more nearly naked than any I have seen in this country, where there is so much real poverty. Other cases I might describe, but, to understand it, you must yourself see, to some extent, the great destitution and distress of these poor people. In America, you know nothing of poverty; I did not until I came here. And there is nothing to alleviate the distress of the poor sufferers; the condition of their minds and souls is more pitiable than that of their bodies, — the comparison of which is as time to eternity. Oh, my dear sister, do not cease to pray for this people."

These details have been inserted at length, because they present a graphic picture of such scenes of destitution as missionaries in those lands are often obliged to witness without the power of alleviating. Many causes, besides the desolating fires, which, in Constantinople especially, produce so much misery, occasion to the poor people of those countries physical privations, which, except in one or two of our larger cities, perhaps, are unknown in our more favored country; and many missionaries in the Levant have felt and said, like Mrs. Everett, "We knew nothing of poverty till we came here."

In the same letter from which the above extracts are taken, Mrs. Everett speaks of a young Armenian girl she was teaching.

"The time I spend with T. gives me a great deal of pleasure. You can imagine how interesting it is to see truth reaching a mind to which so little light has penetrated; truths in regard to the existence of her own soul, its relations to God and Christ, and almost every thing connected with revealed religion, seem new to her. She repeats at night a prayer in ancient Armenian, which is wholly unintelligible to her. I have tried to show her the sin and folly of doing this, and to aid her, or show her, that she might pray in words which she understands. I wrote a prayer, and have once used it with her, having previously committed it to memory. You can hardly conceive of the darkness which reigns in the minds of a large part of the people of this country."

The missionary mail-box between Smyrna and Constantinople continued to be the bearer of weekly communications between Mrs. E. and Miss Lovell. Their correspondence was frequently in Armenian, and their full letters, written very neatly in its strange characters, show the zeal and success with which they were pursuing the attainment of that difficult language.

Miss Lovell dismissed her school for two or three weeks' vacation at Christmas. January 21, she writes to Mrs. Everett.

"Last Monday, I had again the privilege of communing with upwards of forty Armenians. But two females besides myself were present, but it was a most delightful meeting." A week later: "My girls have all returned except Armaveni, and seem highly delighted to be here again. The affection they manifest for me is, I assure you, quite gratifying. If I can only turn it to their good, I shall be happy. I suppose you will hear from other sources of the terrible *anathema* which was yesterday pronounced by the Patriarch against Priest Vartanes and all his adherents. He fled at daybreak last Friday morning to Mr. Dwight's for refuge from those who were seeking for him, and has been there since. He sat with us in the dining-room," (a room opening into the chapel,) "to hear the sermon yesterday, and told me he had been excommunicated. I said I was sorry. He replied that he rejoiced to be counted worthy to suffer for Christ."

Of this same anathema, Mrs. Everett writes to her sister, February 1, that "it had that day been pronounced in the Armenian church in Smyrna against Protestants, by order of the Patriarch at Constantinople." Miss Lovell writes to Mrs. Everett, February 9 —

"This day has been set apart by the brethren of this station as a day of fasting and prayer, in view of the persecuted state of the Armenian brethren, and, as I have no school to-day, I have a little time to give you before meeting this evening. Since meeting this morning, the schoolroom and my room have been thronged with Armenian visitors, and the last has just gone, and left me in quiet possession. We had this morning a prayer meeting of the missionaries and the Armenian brethren. There were also quite a number of females present. The body of the chapel was filled with Armenians; the services were partly in English, and partly in Armenian. It was a good meeting, and I trust prayer was offered which God, our only help, will hear and answer.

"I wish I could tell you the whole history of events for the last two or three weeks, and the many interesting cases of steadfastness and firmness under persecution which we every day hear of. I regret to say that Ermonia went home last week in consequence of the present troubles. She did not at all wish to go; but her mother wished it. Her sister, too, was sick, and sent word to her that *she* was the cause of her illness, because she persisted in staying here. So, it was at length decided that it would be well for her to go home a few weeks, and comfort her mother till the storm shall pass over. I am, for some reasons, however, sorry that she went. To-day, the mother of another of the girls came to take her home. She stayed all day, saying that she could not go without her, as the priest would be there to-night to see if she had brought her. Her brother (Baron Apsaghom) told her not to go, and at last the mother went without her.

I was affected at the feeling which A. manifested when she thought she must go. One beautiful bright-eyed girl was at meeting with her father, who wishes to enter the school. She is thirteen or fourteen years of age, and I was so much interested in her appearance that I could not refuse to take her. We have had three or four applications to receive pupils since the commencement of this persecution. Poor people! They suffer greatly; but it is gratifying to see their firmness and apparent faith. That God will overrule it all for the furtherance of his cause, I have no doubt, but it is a time when it becomes us to be deeply humble, and to pray without ceasing."

What the terrible *anathema* is, which is so justly the terror of all Oriental Christians, Miss Lovell relates more particularly in the following letter to her sister-in-law in Wisconsin.

CONSTANTINOPLE, Feb. 16, 1846.

I am now writing in my little schoolroom, surrounded by my little flock of Armenian girls. My teacher is giving them a lesson in ancient Armenian, and in the mean time I can give you a few moments. I am obliged to seize such moments for writing, as, with teaching and learning, my time is almost entirely taken up. I have now eight scholars, and soon expect two more. Two are at home in consequence of a bitter persecution now raging against the evangelical Armenians. Perhaps some particulars of this persecution may not be uninteresting to you. It is understood to be against the principles and policy of the Turkish government* to persecute on account of religious opinions. The Armenian Patriarch, however, having been accused of being a Protestant, has taken this means to wipe off the reproach, and prove that he is guiltless of such a crime. A few weeks since, a sentence of excommunication was published and read in all the churches against a priest who has long been a pious

* This must have reference merely to their Christian subjects.

man, and all his adherents, — all who read the gospel and attend the preaching of the missionaries. Since then, the sentence has been repeated against all the prominent evangelicals by name, and a terrible curse pronounced upon them, and upon all who shall have any intercourse with them, give bread or water, or in any way assist them, or show them any kindness. Such is the dread of this curse, that almost every one suspected of this sin has been turned out of house and home. Every tie is forgotten. Children have driven their parents, and parents their children, from them, and wives have turned their husbands out of doors. There is great suffering and distress. The missionaries have taken many of the homeless ones into their houses, and have also hired a house to accommodate them for awhile, after making a vain appeal to the great men of their own nation for protection and relief. They are now awaiting the result of an appeal to the Turkish council; should this prove unsuccessful, they will send in a petition to the Sultan himself. We hope and believe God will incline the hearts of these rulers to favor and relieve his suffering people. Now, they are thrown out of business, spit upon, and stoned in the streets, and no one is permitted to enter their houses, or have any dealings with them. All have been commanded to remove their children from our schools, but only two of mine have yet been taken, though great efforts have been made to get them all. Those who left, went weeping bitterly, and promising to return after awhile. From the boys' seminary, at Bebek, more than half—seventeen or eighteen — have gone home, and the school is nearly broken up.

On Smyrna, this fearful curse seemed to fall with a still more blighting influence. In that city, scarcely any fruit of the gospel had been brought to perfection. Many hopes were felt by the missionaries at the commencement of the year; a larger number than ever before, attended the Sabbath preaching, and, at their own request, a Bible-class had been formed; but the good seed had not found a good soil, as at Constantinople, and now, under this trial, those who had heard the word joyfully for a season, proved to be of that class who, in time of persecution, fall away. Mrs. Everett writes to one of her sisters, April 2.

"Darkness seems to rest upon Smyrna. Were not our hopes fixed on God, we should cast them all away now, and give up in despair of seeing any brought from this slavery to the world, superstition, and sin, into the free-dom with which Christ makes free. All the Armenians of Smyrna seem agreed as to one thing, — that no man here shall serve the Lord. The pious Armenians are anathematized, but they are Constantinopolitans. The Patriarch's idolatrous paper was signed by all those who had attended the preaching of the gospel, and seemed hopeful, excepting one, who resisted long. He was turned out of his father's house, abused by his brother and all his friends; he was in turn threatened and flattered by large promises, but he did not yield until a few days since, when all combined in such an onset on the poor young man as he had not power to resist; he signed the Patri-arch's confession of faith, and *Smyrna was free from this new sect.* So exult these deluded people; but is it so? We can not and will not believe that the Spirit is clean gone.

> "'God moves in a mysterious way,
> His wonders to perform;'

and perhaps this is the way in which he intends to arouse both his children and the consciences of some around us, whom he designs to be the trophies of his free grace here."

Speaking of the general corruption in Smyrna, and the way in which even religious offices were purchased with

money, Mrs. Everett, in one of her letters, relates the
following story.

"There is a Greek priest here, a very poor, illiterate
man, who was for a long time a servant in the family of
a missionary who was formerly here. Afterwards, he
worked at various things, as he could find employment,
and finally concluded that he would become a priest. At
the first application, he was told he must pay 2,000 piastres, but he at last succeeded in obtaining orders for 500;
and this man is one of the best of the priests. He tries
to preach the gospel."

Both ladies enjoyed highly their first winter in that
fine Eastern climate. Miss Lovell writes from Constantinople, in February.

"We have had a delightful winter, and I can not but
pity you poor shivering mortals in Wisconsin. To be
sure, the streets are much of the time wretchedly muddy,
and walking is any thing but pleasant; but we can sit in
our rooms with very little fire. There has been very
little snow, and almost every morning I hear the birds
singing in the English palace garden under my window.
I wish I could send you some roses plucked from this
garden in the middle of January. It is just the time
when oranges and lemons are beginning to be very
plenty, and I wish I could send you some in exchange for
apples or good butter, two articles I miss very much."

And Mrs. Everett writes about the same time from
Smyrna: "The country is now in its glory, having none
of the parched, barren appearance of last summer, but is
as verdant as our May. Grain is coming forward finely;
the crops are harvested, I think, in June. I will put in
some little flowers I found by the way-side in mid-winter;
there are many in the fields. The finest thing we have
seen is the almond-trees, now in full bloom, appearing, at
a distance, like our peach, when first the blossoms open;
when faded, like the apple. You know we have ever-

greens, — the olive, cypress, citron, orange, lemon, — the myrtle also. The large gardens, just at the edge of the city, are now beautiful, having orange and lemon trees, with the ripe fruit contrasting finely with the dark-green leaves; and many vegetables are now in their prime."

Writing, March 2, to her eldest brother, of whose pleasant home in Sturbridge she always retained such delightful recollections, Mrs. E. says : —

"Is spring opening with you? How much enjoyment I have had in gazing at those hills, and listening to those birds from my window in the little cottage. But New England *hills and birds*, and *friends*, too, are numbered among past joys; yet not past; my friends still live in my heart, and the loved scenes of my early days will remain as green spots in memory's record; they will not fade. Spring I have been speaking of, and intended to tell you that we have had spring since last November. There has been much rain, and snow has fallen twice, but soon melted. . . . 'Every prospect pleases, and only man is vile.' Such a contrast as is exhibited between the physical and moral aspect of things about us is most painful.

"Yesterday, I was made to feel more than ever before the perfect darkness which reigns in the minds of a large proportion of the people of this country. A pious Armenian, from ——, is here on a visit with his wife. This woman, although not from the lower class of people, is unable to read a syllable, and, as to religious knowledge, a child in America, four years old, knows far more. Her mind, as far as I could discover, is a perfect blank. All her thoughts seemed to begin and end in the adornment of her person with bracelets, rings, necklaces, &c. She wishes to send her daughter, eleven years of age, to us for training and instruction, and we have partly consented to take her when we commence housekeeping."

Lest the reader should receive the impression from the

10*

bright pictures given above that the shores of the Levant
are an elysium of perpetual sunshine and flowers, we
make the following extract from one of Mrs. Everett's
letters, which, though not so pleasing, is perhaps a more
truthful description of a Levantine winter.

"You speak, dear E., of coming to spend your winters
with us. We give you a most cordial invitation to come
and pass next winter in our anticipated house, which, I
assure you, if it is what I expect, will be warm and sun-
shiny all the year. But I forewarn you not to expect the
same comfort out of doors; the summer is the time for a
cloudless sky; the winter for damps, rains, and chills.
The weather is not cold in general. One can go about
the house and out, without that stiff, freezing sensation
our New England winters produce, and, when we have a
number of pleasant days in succession, we think this is
one of the finest climates in the world; but, when rain
falls for almost a fortnight incessantly, so that the air and
every thing else is full of dampness, and the streets intol-
erably muddy, we think with much favor of our clear,
bracing climate, the merry ring of sleigh-bells, and more
merry shouts of the coasters and skaters. But we put on
thick boots, and manage, as often as possible, to hobble
and slip over the rough, miry stones for exercise and fresh
air."

CHAPTER X.

Miss Lovell's Illness, and subsequent Visit to Smyrna.— Mr. and Mrs. Everett remove to Constantinople — Interesting Particulars respecting the School and General Missionary Work.

THE warm friendship existing between Mrs. Everett and Miss Lovell had led them always to wish that they might be associated together in their missionary life and work; and to this wish they frequently gave expression both in their letters to each other, and to other friends. Mrs. E., in her visit at Constantinople, had made on the minds of the missionaries of that station, a strong impression of her peculiar qualifications for exerting a happy influence in the department of female education, and many of them had expressed the desire to keep her at C., to be united with Miss L. in the charge of the Female Seminary; but, as Mr. E. had been designated by the Prudential Committee to Smyrna, to fill what was considered an important post there, no serious proposals of the kind were made. Providence, however, brought about the accomplishment of these wishes in a manner they could not have anticipated, and would not have chosen.

In the latter part of February, Miss Lovell was attacked with a prevailing influenza, which settled on her lungs, and brought her very low. After weeks of suffering and great prostration, she began to recover, but so slow was her improvement, that her friends became alarmed lest her naturally delicate constitution had been permanently affected, and they proposed, as soon as the weather and her strength should allow, that she should visit Smyrna, and try the influence of its milder air, and visiting the missionary friends there.

During the weeks she was unable to write, some one of the kind friends about her made a regular report to Mrs. Everett of her state, both of body and mind. Some of these notes are too interesting to be withheld. Mr. Goodell writes.

PERA, March 3, 1846.

DEAR SISTER IN CHRIST: Your faithful correspondent appears decidedly better this morning; but she has been quite ill,—has had a hard cough and a very bad headache, and some symptoms of pleurisy.

You will all remember us in your prayers, for we are brought very low. This is the hour of darkness.* But, with him who hears the groaning of the prisoner, and sees every tear, there is no darkness at all. All is plain, and all is easy of accomplishment. Two of the girls have been taken away by their parents, but their beds and books left as a pledge of their return when the indignation shall be past. In the mean time four new ones have come, so that we are more than full. May the Lord soon bring us all out into a wealthy place! Especially may he, in this time of rebuke and blasphemy, pour out his Holy Spirit, and bring low many a proud heart and lofty look!

March 17th, Mr. Goodell writes: "I intend to send our beloved friend to you as soon as she is able to go; but she is weak, and I fear will not be able to go for three weeks. She has been in great danger from pulmonary symptoms. We have now twelve scholars in school. Only one is absent, and she is expected to return next week. Our school has been increased more than one third by this persecution. How wonderful! Love to all. Tell them

"'The year of Jubilee is come.'"

On the 24th, Mrs. Hinsdale, the teacher of the mission-

* Mr G. alludes here to the persecution then raging.

ary school, who finished her lovely Christian course a little
before Miss Lovell, writes to Mrs. Everett : —

"I have the delightful pleasure of saying what you will,
doubtless, hear from many others, that our dearly beloved
Miss Lovell is in reality much better. She has seemed so
like her former self for the last three or four days, that it
does one's heart good to look at her. . . . But I will take
up your questions. 'Is she cast down?' In reply to this
I have a few precious words that escaped her lips on her
sick-bed. On stepping into her chamber, as I was wont
to do after school, almost the first words she uttered were,
'Oh, I have had such a precious season! I never before
knew *how* sweet it was to lie passive in his hands, and
know no will but his.' I have read passages of the Bible
to her at different times, and prayed with her at her request, and she would often make remarks which showed
her deep interest in the word of God. Mr. Goodell, I
should think, has been in the habit of reading the Bible
and praying with her every morning. . . .

"You see that in my notes I have only time to tell you
how Miss Lovell is. Had I time I would tell you how we
all love her, but you can judge by what you feel for her
yourself. Her valuable life we know how in some degree
to appreciate."

There is a little note in pencil from Miss Lovell to Mrs.
Everett, which is without date, but was probably written
about this time.

"My dear, warm-hearted sister: I am going to write
you just one line to show you I *can* write. I have had a
very sweet illness. The Lord has been very gracious and
merciful to me; he has made all my bed in my sickness.
I am now daily improving; yesterday sat up two hours,
but am still very weak. They talk of taking me to Bebek
on Friday, and, more than all, they talk of sending me to
Smyrna. Perhaps I may go next week. Mr. Goodell will
write. I can write no more. Love, love to *all*, and thanks

for their sympathy and prayers. Of the kindness of friends here I have no language to speak. May the Lord reward them!"

The following note by Mr. Goodell to Mrs. Everett, playfully introducing to her her long-loved missionary sister, gives also the names of the scholars in her school, and discloses the secret of the rich spiritual blessings with which that school has been visited from the beginning till now.

"PERA, April 6, 1846.

"DEAR SISTER IN CHRIST: I have much pleasure in introducing to your acquaintance, and recommending to your kind attention, a Miss Lovell from the western part of New York, who has been in my family nearly a year, and whose name I think I must have mentioned in some of our correspondence. You will see that she has five or six meals a day, and more if necessary; and that she does not speak more than one word for every ninety or a hundred words that are spoken to her. Will you be her spokesman, or see that one be chosen, to answer for her all the numerous questions which may be asked in reference to her health, happiness, and school? In fact, she goes to Smyrna not to be *used* up, but to be *raised* up, for the school; although she had put it in such excellent order, that it went on like clock-work for awhile, yet the wheels now begin to need oiling, and other parts of the machine require attention.

"You will hear of the very interesting state of things at Oroomiah. Why may we not hope that our own schools may be visited in a similar manner with refreshings from on high? Will you unite with us in praying for this object? I herewith give you the names of those in the Female Seminary in the order they entered, that you may begin next Thursday with the first on the list. And may our prayers for that one be united, fervent, and effectual. The next day we will pray for the second, and

so on. Armaveni, aged twenty; Ermonia, aged nineteen;
Sinem, aged eleven; Sourpouyi, aged thirteen; Mariam,
aged twelve, of Pera; Takouhi, aged twelve (now absent);
Aroosiah, aged thirteen; Mariam, aged twelve, of Constantinople; Yeubraksy, aged eleven; Mariam, aged six,
from Hass Keuy; Deuruki, aged fourteen; Takouhi, aged
fourteen, daughter of Arakyal; Takouhi, aged fifteen,—
she, with her mother, brothers and sisters, excommunicated. Indeed almost every child in school is a daughter
of the excommunicated. May they all belong to the
church of the first born!"

Miss Lovell writes to her mother, April 5. After
giving the particulars of her illness, she says:—

"Through the great mercy of God every medicine
seemed to have the desired effect. I fully expected to
die, yet death had no terrors; but I felt a sweet satisfaction in committing myself and my school into the hands
of God, trusting that if he took me to himself, he would
raise up another better qualified to take my place. Of
the kindness of the dear friends here during my illness, I
know not in what language to speak."

In reference to the persecution she says:—

"I intended to keep a full journal of all which occurred,
to send to you, as there were many interesting events
occurring each day which could not fail to interest you.
But I was almost immediately taken ill, so that I was
unable to do so. The most important events you will, in
time, see in the *Missionary Herald.* Four men were
imprisoned, one or two banished, great numbers excommunicated and thrown out of employment, but their firmness and steadfastness has astonished even those who
hoped the best of them. Mr. Hamlin's school was almost
broken up, but is now filling up again. I lost three of
mine for a time, but many new ones applied. I have now
twelve. I wish I had time and strength to tell you more
of the persecution, which still continues, though with not

quite so much severity as at first. The Armenian congregation is as large as ever, and many who were never
known before, are now discovered to be firm and consistent Christians."

Mrs. Everett, writing about this time to her sister,
relates the following incident: —

"To-day a man came from Beirut, with letters of recommendation from our brethren there, who has lately been
expelled from a convent in Jerusalem. He is an Armenian from the region beyond Erzeroom. The gospel
found its way to him there, — he was convinced of its
truths, and afterwards went to reside at this convent.
They wished to make him a deacon after he had been
there about two years; but, on his refusing to receive
orders on account of his evangelical sentiments, he was
expelled. While in the convent he translated the four gos-
pels into the Kurdish language, for those of his nation who
live in the region from which he came, and do not know
Armenian, not even the priests who read the service in
the church. The young man comes here wishing to print
his translation. How steadily and surely the leaven of
truth is working in the mass of error!"

Miss Lovell, writing from Smyrna, to a friend recently
married, and speaking of one and another of her "early
friends and schoolmates" who were soon to be married,
says: —

"And soon I shall be left the 'last leaf on the tree.' I
shall not mourn very bitterly, however, while I have so
delightful an employment as I feel mine to be, and so
dear a circle of friends as I find here. Delightful employment! What would more than half the world think of
the idea of delight in connection with six or seven hours'
daily confinement in a small room, with a dozen or more
poor Armenian girls! Yet *I* feel that my employment *is*
delightful. Some of my girls are exceedingly interesting;
and when I go into my school-room, and witness the

sparkling of their beautiful black eyes, as they express their joy at seeing me, if I have been absent a few hours, I feel that it is better, far better, than drawing out a useless life, even among loved friends at home."

After four weeks spent very pleasantly with the missionary friends in Smyrna, Miss Lovell returned with improved health to Constantinople. But though much better, she was not yet strong enough to take charge of the school without more assistance, and the Constantinople station voted to invite Mr. and Mrs. Everett to spend the summer at Constantinople for the purpose of rendering such assistance, with which invitation they cheerfully complied, although they had just taken and furnished two or three rooms in the country, and had commenced housekeeping for the summer.

Mrs. Everett's first letter from Constantinople gives many interesting details respecting the school, and general progress of the missionary work in that city.

"Constantinople, May 25, 1846.

"My very dear Parents: If you have not received my last letter by ship, you will be very much surprised to see this dated at Constantinople. 'It is not in man that walketh to direct his steps,' and we hope the Lord has been the guide of ours. . . . .

"We found Miss Lovell suffering from a hoarse cold, and unable to go into her school. We arrived on Saturday morning; and on Monday I took her place in school, happy to be able to do anything for the relief of my dear sister, and I need not say very happy to be in the midst of eleven Armenian girls, who, we hope, by the grace of God, may become enlightened pious women. There are thirteen belonging to the school; one is absent from sickness,— the other was removed at the commencement of the persecution, and has not returned. These girls are all bright and interesting; the school promises much. May the

11

divine blessing rest upon it, and all our hopes be realized!
Oh, do pray much that the Holy Spirit's influences may
incline the heart of each of these girls to seek that wisdom which cometh from above. Two of them, and perhaps three, are pious. The eldest, A., is a lovely Christian.
You will rejoice to know that these girls are very fond
of reading their Testaments, and often seem much affected
by what they read and hear. One was weeping a few
days since as she had her Testament, and, on being urged
to tell the cause of her tears, said she was reading about
Christ's sufferings and death for her sins, and she wept
that she was doing nothing for him.

"Wednesday, p. m., the Armenian females have a
prayer meeting. I went to the meeting last week. Six
or eight were present besides those belonging to the
school. One of the women told me that some of them
had wished for such a meeting for a long time, but they
lived at such long distances from each other that they
could not meet together; but the Lord had sent this persecution, and thus brought them together, and they were
very happy to meet and pray. Those present were from
families occupying the houses hired for those who had
been turned out of their houses.

"It is good to be here, and see the large congregation
of Armenians, eagerly listening to the words of life. The
females no longer sit in an adjoining room, listening
with the door ajar, but take their places in the back part
of the chapel. The day before we arrived, Friday, there
were thirty females present. On Friday, p. m. there was
formerly a service for females alone, but, since the
men have been deprived of business by the persecution,
it has been a meeting for prayer, and all attend. You
would be delighted to hear the singing in these Armenian
meetings. All join, and with full voices. The Armenians
seem to have an uncommon taste for singing. The girls
in the school sing already, and are quite independent.

They sing 'Mary at the Saviour's Tomb,' 'Old Hundred,' 'Illinois,' 'Islington,' &c.

"Those persons who have children in the school, come often to see them, especially the mothers and sisters, and often express the desire that they, too, might come and learn. On Friday, P. M. the girls sew, and their friends understand that they are at liberty to come in and visit after the meeting. Last Friday, about a dozen were here; one could understand only Turkish, and as she had come from a distance to the meeting, and heard only Armenian, she begged that Mr. Goodell would read and pray with her before she went away.

"You will hear and thank God that he has brought deliverance to the poor persecuted Armenians. The man who was the instrument in getting them expelled from their shops and houses, is turned out of his office, and the greater part of them have returned to their business, and some to their houses. All this persecution has been only a means of advancing the truth, and *establishing* it in this land. The Patriarch has made himself very unpopular, and can not retain his place long. He thought to clog the chariot-wheels of salvation; but his efforts have only tended to give them a tenfold impetus. But what can all the patriarchs, bishops, Satan, and all his hosts combined, do in a contest with Omnipotence? The stone that was cut out of the mountain shall fill the whole earth."

In the same letter, Mrs. Everett communicates the pleasing intelligence, just received from Smyrna, that two young men went every day to Mr. Adger for instruction in the Bible, and ten or twelve were at the service the previous Sabbath, — showing that light was beginning to shine out of the thick darkness that had seemed for a while to settle over that city. She also speaks of glad tidings concerning the missionary work in Syria and Persia.

Of the annual meeting of the mission, Mrs. Everett writes in her next letter. . . .

"It was a time of deep interest; on several accounts unusual; one was, that never before were so many together from the various stations of the Turkey mission; another, that so great progress in Christ's work there has not perhaps been in any previous year; and the business was of the highest importance, and full of the deepest interest, — the preparation of a covenant and confession of faith, rules and order for the formation of an evangelical, a *real New Testament church in Turkey.* Century after century has passed, and these countries have known nothing of a spiritual religion. There is scarcely a foot of soil in the vicinity of this great city that is not in all probability mingled with the dust of those who have passed into eternity from the darkness of formalism, idolatry, or Mohammedanism. But blessed be our God that light begins to shine! It is indeed but a beginning, a single ray, compared with the thick darkness that is spread far and wide; but he who has sent a single ray, can and will pour such a flood upon this whole region as will scatter the deepest shades. Jesus *shall* reign."

CHAPTER XI

THE history of themselves and the school, as well as of the interesting events transpiring around them for the next six months, must be gathered almost entirely from Mrs. Everett's letters, as only two letters written by Miss Lovell during that time have been obtained. The first of them was to her brother Frederic, dated

"CONSTANTINOPLE, June 10, 1846.

. . . "I lately received a letter from Medora, and since then how many changes may have taken place. Who can tell, if you are still living, that death has not entered your little family, — death, who, since I wrote you, has been very near me, so that I fancied I heard his call? Yet, thanks to my kind Father in heaven, I still live, and have the promise of returning health. Soon after I wrote to Medora, I was attacked with an influenza and inflammation of the lungs. For a week or so, my life was in danger, and I had but little hope of recovery. I had, however, a good physician, with the kindest care and attention from all my good friends here, and, by the blessing of God, I am now nearly well. . . .

"My scholars are all now in the next room, busily engaged in trying to learn English. They are not taught English in school, but they are all so anxious to learn that I have given them leave to learn what they can in the evenings, when they have finished their other lessons.

11*

"Yesterday, I rode on horseback for the first time in this country. I rode to Bebek in the morning, and returned in the evening, enjoying it exceedingly. To-day, I rode again to Bebek, where the annual meeting of the mission is in session, and attended the examination of the Armenian Young Men's Seminary. The young men all learn English as well as Armenian, ancient and modern. They were examined in algebra and geometry, history, &c., and acquitted themselves admirably. I should like to invite you to a similar examination of *my* school one of these days, though I must confess they have not made much progress in mathematics or meta-physics; yet the improvement they have made is by no means contemptible. But it is bedtime, and I must lay by my unfinished letter till another day."

"13. I have a bouquet of beautiful flowers before me, which came from the Sultan's garden, and fill the room with their fragrance. By the way, his majesty has been absent five or six weeks on a journey, and is expected to return next Tuesday. Most magnificent preparations are making to welcome his return. Poor man! He seldom leaves the city; and, when he left it this time, he started in a royal steamboat, attended by his fleet. When he had proceeded a few miles, through *fear* and sea-sickness, he ordered the boat to turn about, — out of compassion for his officers and suit, it was said, and performed the journey by land.

"Pray, did you ever read a book on Greece, — 'Lord Byron and His Last Days,' &c. — (I forget the title,) written by his lordship's attending physician? This same man, Dr. Millingen, was my physician, and has a great many interesting anecdotes to relate. He is also one of the Sultan's physicians, and spends one night a week at the palace." . . .

From Mrs. Everett.

"CONSTANTINOPLE, July 2, 1846.

"MY DEAR SISTER ELEANOR: . . . Let me tell you something about the organization of an evangelical church in the capital of the Turkish empire, — the seat of Mohammedism, superstition, and infidelity. It is wonderful. God has done it, and it is marvelous in our eyes. This very interesting and ever-memorable event took place yesterday, in the chapel in Mr. Dwight's house. You are aware that there was quite a large number of Armenians who have been considered fit subjects for receiving the sacrament, and secretly it has been administered to them. The Patriarch has, as you also know, during the recent persecution, cut off by anathema all the ' new sect,' or gospel-readers, from the Armenian church, and thus they were left free to form themselves into an independent church. They requested the missionaries, some time since, to prepare for them some form of church organization, and it was done at the recent general meeting of the mission, and presented at a meeting yesterday of those who had previously received the sacrament. All felt it to be a most solemn and interesting meeting; such a time as some of the brethren of the mission had for years labored, prayed, and longed for, and such a day as we, who have but recently come. felt to be too much for us to be permitted to witness.

"The meeting was opened by prayer and reading of the Scriptures. The confession of faith, covenant, and church laws were read and explained. You must think of these persons as not having had, until recently, any real spiritual ideas, and no proper conception of a church free from a yoke of bondage to the grossest superstitions. After a vote from the Armenians to accept what had been presented, all arose, and solemnly assented to the confession and covenant, which were again read. Their names were then recorded, and we looked upon the infant evangelical church of the Armenians of Turkey, — a church of forty members, taking the New Testament as the groundwork of their faith, built on Jesus Christ as the chief corner-stone, and arising out of the corrupt, yes, long *dead* mass which has for so many centuries rested on the face of this whole country.

"The new church then made unanimous choice of a pastor from among themselves, — one who was set apart some months since as a preacher. A special exhortation to prayer for him was made, the deacons chosen, and the committee of the church, and all unanimously, and satisfactorily to the missionaries, and we hope also to the great Head of the Church.

"Now, we have new arguments to plead before the Lord, that he will come and water this vine of his own right hand's planting. Do join us. There are many other persons who are considered truly pious, and will very soon unite with these. They were not invited at this formation of the church, because it was considered a simpler way to unite only those who had been formally received into fraternities existing before, and let the church receive others upon examination. The first child is to be baptized in the way of the Protestants to-morrow in the chapel. It is the first child of the new pastor, — Baron Apsoghom. He is to be ordained next Tuesday.

"6. I was sent home from the dinner-table just now to take off my dress, and hang it on the terrace to air, and you would be almost frightened to know the cause if you were near. Miss Lovell and I went out after school to see one of the little girls who is at home unwell. Seeing a younger brother of the girl lying asleep on the floor beside her bed, we asked if he was sick, and the reply was that he had the *smallpox*. This was said with perfect unconcern, and when we expressed some alarm, and told with what dread we regarded it in our country, the friends smiled, saying repeatedly, 'No matter; no harm will come from it.' We were off as soon as possible. For me, there is no danger if the child has the disease, for I have just been vaccinated with effect. In this country, the smallpox is not feared at all, but the deeply-pitted faces we often meet show that sometimes it is not a slight thing here.

"Peculiarly in this country, in the midst of life we are in death. Last week, our friends wrote from Smyrna that a fearful earthquake had visited that city. Mr. Adger wrote that in their house the lime fell in flakes from the walls of one room, things were thrown down, and in another room the wall of the house, which is of stone, was rent from top to bottom. Mrs. Johnston also wrote that the wall in their house was rent, and several persons were killed in the city.

"On Tuesday, the 7th of July, Baron Apsoghom was solemnly set apart by prayer, and the laying on of hands, to the work of the gospel ministry over the newly formed church. He is a young man of good talents, and as good an education as the ecclesiastics of the Armenian church usually possess. He has attended the theological lectures of Mr. Dwight in former years, understands well the doctrines of the Bible, having had the instructions of the Great Teacher. His examination previous to ordination gave satisfaction and pleasure to those present.

"Although the ordination was not intended to be public, the chapel, at an early hour, was crowded in every part. Mr. Homes read the order of exercises in Turkish; Mr. Wood read the Scriptures in Armenian; Mr. Homes offered the introductory prayer in Turkish; sermon by Mr. Dwight in Armenian, from 1 Tim. iii. 1,—the office of a bishop; consecrating prayer by Mr. Goodell. All the missionaries present laid their hands upon the head of the pastor. Mr. Hamlin gave the charge; address to the people by Mr. Goodell; hymn read by Mr. Van Lennep, and sung by all the congregation; concluding prayer by Mr. Wood, and benediction by the pastor. A more solemn and interesting scene I never witnessed. The exercises were throughout most appropriate. All felt that it was none other than the house of God, and that the great Head of the Church seemed especially present. One of the Armenians said to Mr. Everett, 'I trembled and felt afraid;' and one said to me, 'It was heaven, and I felt as though the angels were all around.' All seemed to find it difficult to express the great joy they felt in witnessing such a scene."

"July 27, 1846.

"MY DEAR FATHER AND MOTHER: . . . The pious Armenians continue to suffer much in various ways from the enemies of the truth, though the Patriarch begins to see that the gospel is not easily crushed, nor its followers in reality, though in name, annihilated by the curses thundered against them from his lips. He has been rather quiet for a few weeks, the bankers of the nation having expressed their disapprobation of his course. The result of it has been, as they said, to establish a new sect from their nation. Yesterday, however, he anathematized a widow and her son and daughter, — the latter a member of the school, and all, we hope, the servants of Jesus Christ.

"To show you the spirit of opposition to the gospel which reigns in this place, I will describe a scene which we witnessed yesterday, the Sabbath, in front of Messrs. Goodell and Dwight's houses, which stand side by side. Mr. D.'s family are all absent, himself at Trebizond, and the others at Bebek. The man-servant, a pious Armenian, remains in the house. It was open as usual on Sabbath morning for the English service, during which some rude boys, passing, or coming on purpose, threw stones into the hall, through the door, one of which hit an old Armenian who had come early to the service. Calling out 'Protestant!' they ran. In the P. M., about

the commencement of the **Armenian** service, quite a
company of these base boys came along in front of the
house ; one would step up and knock at the door, and, as
soon as the servant opened it, a dozen or more stones
were hurled towards it ; then all made their retreat as
soon as possible. A little before sunset, as we were
quietly reading, we heard a screaming below in front of
the house, and, as we ran to the window, we saw Hohannes upon the doorstep of Mr. Dwight's house, firmly
holding a dirty young urchin, who was struggling and
screaming at the top of his lungs; while another of the
same stamp was making his way off as fast as his feet
would take him, he, too, screaming with fright. Mr.
Goodell went down, and found that the servant, being a
little on the watch, saw the boys approaching the door,
and took his place near it, so, when the boy was in the
very act of knocking, he opened suddenly, and seized him
fast. Mr. Goodell told Hohannes to keep the boy, and
he would go and bring a cavass, (a Turkish police officer.)
The young culprit continued his efforts to regain his
liberty, screaming in his frenzy of fear and rage. Just at
this moment, three officers came up the street on patrol,
with swords at their sides, and one a whip in his hands.
They inquired into the matter, took the boy by the arm,
dispersed the crowd, and walked off. In a few moments,
a woman came running up the street in a most frantic
manner, asking the trouble, what the child had done,—
knocking furiously at the door, thinking he was within.
A cavass, who was near, tried to silence her, and send
her home, but she seemed every moment to grow more
wild ; running this way and that, beating her breast, and
furiously shaking her hands, she demanded the boy, saying, 'They shall not make him a Protestant!' All was
at length quiet. The boy was early this morning released
from his night's quarters, doubtless with some cautions ;
having learned a lesson in life.

132   THE MISSIONARY SISTERS.

"28. My dear parents, I have a little time this morning to finish my letter. Two Armenian girls came in as I was about to commence writing, members of the school, wishing me to fit a dress for one of them. My tact at dressmaking does not come amiss here, and Miss Lovell fortunately has the same, for there is plenty to be done in this line among twelve girls, who are not much accustomed to Frank dress. Two of the older girls already cut their own dresses; the others, who are old enough, sew them, and will learn to do the whole. They are not made dependent by coming to the school, but are put to do every thing for themselves, aside from washing their clothes and cooking their food. I do long to see them all seeking those things which relate to their eternal welfare. M., in one of her letters, supposes it is possible that Mr. Everett has commenced preaching, but you must not imagine that at present. To master a foreign tongue, is a work of years. Sumner has made very good progress; can speak with some ease in conversation, and hopes, when we return to Smyrna, to be able to take the Bible-class. He says he will preach after three years from the time he commenced studying. I hope he may a little sooner, but three years would be considered soon, — only one or two have preached after so short a time. I am very grateful for the opportunity I have had to get a good foundation in the language. Such freedom from cares, and so good health I had not expected."

To one of her younger sisters, Mrs. Everett writes.

"I am sure the reason why we do not come nearer to the fulfillment of the injunction, 'Rejoice always,' is, that we are not whole-hearted Christians. Surely, there is no lack of reasons why we should be joyful in God. If our sins weigh like a heavy load on our hearts, there is a fountain ever flowing, which can cleanse all away; if the burden of souls around us presses on our spirits, have we not a Friend who knows all, even that which we would shrink from revealing to the most intimate earthly friend, and this Blessed One sympathizes in all, and is ever ready to soothe every sorrow and lighten every care." . . .

The following extract describes the first burial that took place in the newly formed Protestant community.

"As this was the first instance, some difficulty was apprehended, as in some places such persons have been refused burial. Leave has to be obtained from the government. This was readily given yesterday, it having been requested in the name of the priest Apsoghom,— the new pastor. So he is acknowledged as the priest of the Protestants, (Armenians.) The procession formed at the house where the child died, the corpse being in a covered coffin, not exposed according to the custom of the country. Quite a large company followed, preceded by their pastor, and one of the deacons. When they arrived at the burial-ground belonging to Protestants, the coffin was placed on the ground, and the friends formed themselves in a circle around the open grave, while the minister opened his Testament, read a few verses, made appropriate remarks, offered prayer, then said, 'Let the coffin be placed in the ground.' It was soon covered with earth, when he gave a hymn, which was sung by all, after which he pronounced the benediction, and all withdrew. Every thing passed off to the entire satisfaction and great joy of the missionaries, some of whom were near the place. A crowd gathered around to witness the novel sight; they were astonished at what they heard and saw, and remained perfectly quiet. The Armenian brethren consider what has happened almost a miracle. They give praise to God. Excommunicated persons, if buried at all by their church, are treated with great indignity, perhaps thrown into the grave face downwards."

"Aug. 26. We are all quite impatient to have the school in wider quarters, so that some, who are anxiously wait-

12

ing, may be admitted. One new scholar was taken last
week. She is fifteen years old, and can only read her
letters, but, with the desire she manifests to learn, in a
month she will be reading the Testament. Another girl,
about the same age, will probably be received soon; more
can not be until a larger house is taken. I love these
girls much, and they manifest much affection for me, so
that it is a great pleasure to labor for them in any way.
I never felt more that all the temporal knowledge they
can acquire is of very little consequence compared with
that wisdom which cometh from God only."

In the same letter, she says they would probably not
return to Smyrna in the autumn, as they had expected,
and it was soon after decided that, as Mrs. Everett's services seemed so essential to the school, and there was also
more than work enough to engage all Mr. Everett's energies there, they should remain permanently at Constantinople.

CHAPTER XII

THOUGH the work of God among the Armenians had been so signally prospered the last few months, and all the efforts of the Patriarch and his party to crush it seemed only to turn out for its furtherance, the enemies of the truth still showed their bitter hatred to it by persecuting its adherents in every way in their power. In Constantinople, families were compelled to leave their homes by the enmity of their neighbors, or individuals were taken forcibly from their houses, and thrown into prison, through the same malignant influence. In Trebizond, as well as at Nicomedia and Ada Bazaar, the pious Armenians suffered still more, being thrust into prison, where they were put in the stocks and half starved, refused burial for their dead, mobbed and insulted in the streets; yet, notwithstanding all these sufferings for the truth's sake, they mostly remained firm, and evangelical churches were formed in all those places. The heads of the Armenian, Greek, and Catholic churches leagued to make common cause against what they felt to be their common foe; but the truth alone was more mighty than this threefold cord, and was not to be destroyed.

Mrs. Everett to one of her sisters.

"Sept. 10, Thursday, P. M.

"The day particularly devoted to religious exercises by those assembled at the Annual Meeting of the Board,—

the day for the administration of the sacrament. We have observed the day, and we trust our prayers, though offered in weakness, may mingle before the throne of God with the many supplications ascending from our own dear American churches, and from Christian hearts at the various missionary stations in different parts of the world.

> " 'Though sundered far, by faith we meet
> Around one common mercy-seat.'

"9 o'clock, P. M. I have not written you about an interesting season which we were permitted to enjoy last Sabbath. The occasion was the admission of the first members into the newly formed church. The number admitted was ten, — seven males and three females. The latter seemed much affected, weeping all the time. I wish you knew one of these Armenian sisters, Z—n. She is very interesting in her personal appearance, bright, intelligent, and a warm-hearted Christian. In the female prayer meetings, she takes her part with as much propriety as if she had been trained all her days in these things. Her remarks and prayers are strikingly appropriate and fervent, and yet she is desirous of *learning* of any one who can help her in the divine life. As I have told you so much of this person in whom I am so much interested, I will relate some incidents in her family history. She is young; married about a year; from a good family, according to the phraseology of the world. She was formerly a great favorite with her mother, who committed every thing valuable in the house to her hands, and bestowed on her particular favors. She became enlightened in the gospel, and received its truths. At once her position was changed in the family. Every thing valuable was removed from under her hand, and she became the object of her mother's displeasure. Since her marriage, she has been entirely separated from her mother, who has not been to see her since the birth of her child, if at all before.

"One of her brothers is a deacon in the church; one of her sisters wishes much to know and walk in the truth, and takes every opportunity to come and visit this sister, so as to attend meetings and be instructed, but it is usually without the knowledge of her husband, who is a bitter enemy of the gospel. When the persecution first commenced, he labored, with some priests, all one night to get his wife to sign the Patriarch's confession of faith, till at last the poor wornout woman took the pen and wrote, saying, 'You all bear witness that I do this with my hand, and not with my heart.' Another sister has been just the reverse of this, — a bitter opposer; so bitter that she compelled her husband, a pious man, to leave his home; fairly turned him out. This week, we have heard that Z—n has gone to spend some time with this sister, and so Mr. Goodell says, 'This raging woman has become a lamb.' God grant it may be so, and that our faith may be greatly strengthened to pray for all who are fighting against him.

"17. A week has passed since I have written a word in this letter. I have just returned from the weekly prayer meeting, — this time at Galata, at the house of the good Scotch missionary, Mr. Allan. The great fast of the Turks, Ramazan, is drawing to a close, and to-night they call candle-night, and have some very fine illuminations. The mosks present a splendid appearance, with their brilliantly lighted minarets, between some of which fanciful figures are suspended, and so covered with lights as to cause the figure to appear like one of burnished gold. Some vessels on the Bosphorus are also beautifully illuminated."

October 25, Mrs. E. writes. "The work of Christ is progressing continually; the congregation of Armenians is steadily increasing; their chapel is already too small. An addition of ten has been made to the church since its

12*

formation. An Armenian Sabbath school has been formed, and is quite well attended. In addition to the preaching service, every Friday P. M., and the regular monthly concert, another prayer meeting has been established on every third Monday in the month, by the Armenians, to pray particularly for their nation. The weekly female prayer meeting is attended by a very good number. Sometimes more than twenty are present. Another interesting fact is, that several women, wives of the brethren, are greatly desiring to learn to read, and, a teacher having been secured, they have actually commenced. A school is also established for the children of evangelical Armenians. *Our* female seminary is outwardly in a prosperous condition. The first year, which commenced with three or four pupils, is about closing with fourteen, and others are waiting to join as soon as the school is removed to a larger house. Do pray that all these dear girls may become truly wise."

The following, from Miss Lovell to Mr. Pardee, shows some of the vexations to which missionaries are subject, in business transactions, in such a land as Turkey.

" CONSTANTINOPLE, Nov. 5, 1846.

"MY DEAR FRIEND: After a week or two of unusual fatigue and confusion, I sit down to devote the few leisure moments of Saturday evening to the remembrance of distant friends. There is no time when I so long for *home* as when I contrast the quiet, peaceful hours of Saturday evening, and of the holy Sabbath, in my native land, with the unceasing toil, and noise, and bustle which reign here without intermission. Those precious hours! I love to remember them; and I love to think that, at such times, I am sometimes remembered when, after the toils of the day and the week are over, you bow before our common Father to implore the rich blessings of the Sabbath for yourselves and for the distant missionary. I said we had been in unusual confusion. We have long been wishing to find a house with more ample accommodations for the school, as well as for a chapel for the new Armenian church. A few weeks ago, we heard of a large house which seemed to be just the one we were in search of, and measures were immediately taken to secure it. The contract was made and signed, our school dispersed, our furniture was packed, and we were ready to go. But, in this land of freedom, a *teskeré*, or permission from government, must be obtained before a man can change his dwelling. The house is very near an Armenian Catholic church, and, perhaps through their means, the minister was informed that it was desired for a Protestant school, and a *teskeré* was refused. The Grand Vizier told Mr. Carr, who went over to the Porte to remonstrate, that the American missionaries had of late given the government great trouble, and their request could not be granted; and he advised them to remain quietly where they are for the present. So we were fain to follow his advice, making a virtue of necessity, and have just concluded the arrangement of our house once more. This is only a specimen of the thousand annoyances we are continually subject to. I regret it very much, as we are unable to receive several pupils who very much wish to enter the school, and, as I have Mrs. Everett's assistance this winter, it pains me to refuse those who are so desirous to be instructed. But he, to whom we have desired to commit the management of all our concerns, for wise reasons, sees best that thus it should be. His will be done!

"Sabbath evening. I have to-day been permitted the precious privilege of sitting down at the table of our crucified Redeemer to celebrate his dying love. In the morning, listened to an excellent sermon from the Rev. Mr. Allan, of the Scotch Free Church, on the words, 'If ye then be risen with Christ,' &c., and at noon, in an

upper room, the communion was administered by Mr.
Schauffler in a most solemn and impressive manner. In
the afternoon, at the Armenian service, a great number
were present, notwithstanding the rain, and listened to
an excellent sermon from Mr. Dwight, on the nature of
true repentance. We were disturbed, however, by a
number of young men, who came evidently with the purpose of creating a disturbance by talking and laughing,
going out and coming in, &c. When service was over, it
was found that some who left before meeting was out,
had stolen the *shoes* of many of the brethren, which were
left in the hall below, for you must know the people of
this country do not keep on their shoes which they wear
in the street in the house, but leave them at the door. It
is the first time we have been disturbed in this way.
Persons have frequently come to the chapel with the
intention of making a disturbance, but have usually been
awed into silence by the solemnity and stillness of the
congregation.

"In a letter which I wrote to Mr. Fisher not long since,
I mentioned the death of one of the brethren, Hoosep, in
consequence of a fright received from a wicked man who
threatened to stab him. This same bad man, not long
after, attended the funeral of Hoosep, not knowing whose
it was, but only with the intention of disturbing the
Protestant funeral. On his way home, it being the Sabbath, influenced by curiosity, or some worse motive, he
determined to go into the chapel, and hear what Mr.
Dwight had to say. He went in, was convicted of sin,
convinced of the truth of what he heard, and that what
he had all his life been taught by his priests was false.
Whether he is now a *true* Christian or not, remains to be
proved; but he has since suffered persecution himself for
having announced himself a Protestant.

"Several Catholic (Armenian) vartabeds have lately
confessed themselves wearied with the follies and vanities

of their church, and convinced that Protestantism is true. Indeed, there is little doubt that the Spirit of God is working upon the minds of great numbers of all classes, and only the fear of persecution prevents their openly avowing themselves Protestants. Last week, we were informed that the day of their freedom is at hand. They will soon be openly acknowledged by the Porte as a distinct sect with their own head. It is very interesting to hear the frequent testimony of the Turks to the godly walk of the 'new sect.' 'Here is a people,' they frequently say, 'who do not lie, nor steal, nor blaspheme.' As one rich Pasha said on board of a steamer, in presence of many others, 'I would trust my whole harem and household with one of these Protestants, but I would not trust them to one of your bishops or patriarchs.' May God give them grace so to walk as not to bring reproach upon that blessed name by which they are called. Had I time, I could tell you of most interesting circumstances occurring every day. I regret the want of time to keep a journal of them for the benefit of friends at home.

"My school still flourishes in spite of efforts to oppose it. It is a delightful employment. I bless God that he ever put it into my heart to give myself to this work. Oh, how unworthy am I of such an honor! May my weakness be made strong in his strength!" . . .

Their earnest desires and prayers for their dear charge were erelong answered, and the year, which had been one of so many blessings to the evangelical Armenians, closed with the special influences of the Holy Spirit on both the Seminaries. Of this gracious work, Mrs. Everett gives the following particulars in a letter to sister, dated December 25, 1846.

"The first indications of special thoughtfulness were manifested three weeks ago last Sabbath. The services of the day were unusually solemn. The sacrament was

administered, and eight received into the church.
Towards evening of that day, two of the girls went to
Miss Lovell's room, seeming to have something they
wished to say, but hardly dared. At length, they said
they wished to know what they could do to get new
hearts; that they had for one or two weeks felt that they
were great sinners, and had been praying to God, but
that he did not hear their prayers at all. They were
directed to the 'Lamb of God, who taketh away the sin
of the world.' This circumstance led us to look about us,
at once, to see if we were ready to receive the answer to
our too feeble prayers, feeling rebuked for our coldness
and want of faith. It soon became evident that the Lord
was indeed with us. Others began earnestly to inquire
what they must do to be saved. Great solemnity pervaded the whole school; it was frequently addressed with
much earnestness, and all listened with the most intense
interest as they were exhorted to seek the Lord while he
was near. The voice of prayer was constantly ascending
from hearts burdened with a sense of sin, and scarcely an
eye was tearless. The week did not pass without results
which we hope will be lasting as eternity, and how
blessed! Three were hoping that God had shown them
mercy, and washed their hearts in the blood of his dear
Son. The Sabbath following this memorable week was
solemn. The fact of manifestations of the Spirit's
presence was mentioned in the chapel, and the Thursday
succeeding appointed as a day of fasting and prayer.
On Tuesday, the Armenian female prayer meeting was
held at the usual time, but with unusual interest. All
seemed to think that a new state of things existed, and
some were so much affected by it that they could not go
to their homes after the meeting, but remained until a
late hour in the evening engaged in religious conversation and prayer. Thursday was one of the most solemn
days I ever saw, and will long be remembered by many

hearts. The most perfect quietness prevailed among the girls of the school; all were thoughtful, prayerful, and reading the word of God, a new book to some of their Spirit-taught souls. The exercises in the chapel, which was crowded to overflowing, were deeply solemn and interesting. Two or three others of the girls were now rejoicing in Christ. One, with a countenance beaming from the peace within, said, 'God showed me my sins, and my heart was filled with sorrow, but he has shown me my Saviour, too, and filled my soul with joy.' 'Now,' she says, 'I pray continually for my companions, that they may repent and come to Christ.' And this feeling is very striking in all who hope for themselves, — a great anxiety for unconverted friends and relatives.

"Friday morning, I called on the females of four or five families, and could not but bless God for permitting me, so unworthy, to be here to see and hear such proofs of his goodness and power. In every house, new interest and deep feeling seemed to prevail in regard to the most important of all subjects. Those who are members of the church, with tears expressed their earnest longings for their friends out of Christ.

"Many interesting particulars in regard to the scholars and others, I have not time to write. Six of the girls give good evidence that they have become new creatures in Christ, and two others express hope. Oh the thought, that any may allow Jesus to pass by without blessing them !

"There are already evidences of the special presence of the Spirit in the Seminary at Bebek; for a week or two, unusual solemnity has pervaded the school, two are hoping that they have recently been born again. To-morrow is set apart as a day of fasting and prayer at the school. . . .

"Oh, my dear sister ! do you not think that my heart, if at all warm with love for Christ, and the souls for whom he died, must rejoice to be in scenes like these? I hope I have some gratitude that I have been permitted to make such progress in the Armenian language as to be able to speak with them at such times, however imperfectly, and unite in their prayers and praises. How many times have I said, 'Oh, I wish M. was here!' and 'How my mother's soul would rejoice in this!'"

CHAPTER XIII.

JANUARY 15, 1847, Mrs. Everett writes to her sister in Millbury, Mass.

"The school was dismissed on Monday for a fortnight's vacation. We felt sorry to have the girls dispersed just at this time, lest some of them might yield to the temptations to which they will be exposed; but we can commend them to the same merciful One who has, as we trust, led nearly all of them into his own fold. How sweet is the confidence that the Good Shepherd carries the tender lambs in his bosom. The state of feeling remained to the last very interesting, and the girls seemed to feel, when they left, that they must be particularly watchful and prayerful. Oh, dear sister, can you imagine how happy I am to have been permitted to see this work of the Spirit in this little school? There are still three or four for whom we have no hope. Do join us in praying that not one may be left out of Christ, and that not one may rest on a false foundation.

"The general state of religious feeling in the Armenian congregation is interesting. Some of the members of the church are much revived, new persons are coming to hear the truth, and, recently, preaching services have been established in Constantinople (proper) and Hass Keuy.

"You know the Protestants have already had their own baptisms and funerals. This week, what they supposed would be most difficult to accomplish has been

13

done. Permission has been obtained, and the first marriage taken place among them."

Miss Lovell to Mrs. Thayer.

"CONSTANTINOPLE, Feb. 10, 1847.

"Your kind and affectionate letter was received yesterday. . . . For all the news it contained, I thank you most sincerely. It is not often that my friends remember to tell me what is going on from day to day in my old home. I hope no one fancies that, because oceans roll between me and the land of my birth, I have ceased to feel interested in what takes place there. That can never be. While I have breath, I am sure my heart will ever cling to America as the home of its best earthly affections. . . .

"I am obliged to leave my writing every few minutes to look after the sick, so you must not wonder if my letter should seem somewhat disconnected. A few weeks since, during our Christmas vacation, Mr. Goodell's children were all seized with the scarlet fever. Since the return of the girls, two of them have been attacked with it, and sent home, and now two more are sick, but not with the scarlet fever. Owing to this sickness, the school is again partially broken up. Our Armenian teacher, too, was seized last week, and put in prison, upon a false accusation. Another instance of the ceaseless efforts of the enemies of pure religion to persecute and distress its friends. This man had just opened his house in the city for Protestant preaching, which so exasperated the Patriarch and his priests that they were glad to seize upon the first pretext that presented itself for punishing him. A priest visited his house, and severely threatened his wife, because she, though *not* a Protestant, had signed away her portion of the house, giving it into her husband's hands, that he might use it, as he wished, for a chapel. The husband, the next day, went to the priest's house,

and reproved him for thus threatening and frightening
his wife. A charge was then made out, stating that
Stepan, the teacher, had visited the priest's house, and
severely *beaten him*, a great crime among the Turks.
For this he is in prison; and as there is no one to swear
that he did not beat the man, though every one *knows* he
did not, and many Armenians can be found who will, for
a few piastres, swear they *saw* him beat him, I fear it will
be difficult to procure his release.

" You say you wish to know all about my school. You
have heard of the interesting revival we have enjoyed.
Our hearts have indeed been made glad in the work
which God has wrought here. Surely, what I have been
permitted to see, during the last few months, would have
repaid me for years of separation from those I love. We
hope that many of the girls have become true Christians.
Oh that *all* may become such; and that thousands may
have reason to bless God for the opening of this school!
I wish to feel, and I wish my friends to feel, when they
remember and pray for the school, that the primary
object should be the *conversion of every one* who enters
it; that every other thing should be secondary to this."

Speaking in the same letter of two of the missionary
children who were soon to leave for America, she
says:—

" *This* is one of the severest trials of missionary life,
that parents must part with their children just when they
arrive at an age to be a comfort and assistance to them,
that they may get an education, for it is impossible here
to give them an education which will fit them for future
usefulness."

Under the same date, Miss Lovell writes to another
Palmyra friend, Mrs. Louisa F. Aldrich.

" I find myself almost unconsciously looking forward,
sometimes, to the pleasure of seeing my old friends once
more; of seeing my brother's two daughters; but such

thoughts I quickly check as a thing out of the limit of probabilities. I have chosen my lot, or, rather, I trust God has chosen it for me, and I see no reason to regret it, although it involves with it a separation from those I hold most dear on earth. The last two years have been happy, very happy years. My employment I *delight* in. The climate I like, my health is now good, and kinder, warmer, more intelligent and refined friends than I have found in the missionaries I could not find the world over. They have received and welcomed me as a sister and daughter, and, in sickness and health, their kindness and affection have been unceasing. . . .

"You express an interest in my school. I have fifteen scholars, as many as our limited room will accommodate. They are many of them interesting girls, and I already love them much. . . . All but two or three of my pupils express the hope that they are Christians. That the change in some cases may prove not a genuine one, is possible, but we have seen enough in several of them to fill our hearts with wonder and gratitude for what God has wrought. When I remember how ignorant and unenlightened many of them were little more than a year ago, and then look upon their faces radiant with intelligence and love, when Christ and his cross are the theme, I can only say, 'It is the Lord's doing, and it is marvelous in our eyes.' "

Referring to the imprisonment of the teacher, mentioned above, she says : " When will the day come when freedom and peace shall dawn upon poor Turkey ? By the way, though, let me give you, as one of the signs of the times, the fact that our enlightened Sultan has declared the abolition of the *Constantinople slave-market* in a most philanthropic speech, made in person at the Porte the other day. Let it be published in *free* America. . . .

"Fires are very frequent. There are continual alarms,

and it is said to be the work of incendiaries. It is said
to be a common thing here when there is any dissatisfaction with the government, when a change of officers is
desired, to encourage these incendiaries, till the desired
change is granted! A few years ago this occurred. All
Pera was destroyed by fire, and finally a notice was
issued that there would be no more fires, and there *were*
no more. Some great officers were thrown out, and the
people were satisfied! Happy country! But, do you
know, with all their faults, I like the Turks. I am learning the Turkish language, and admire it exceedingly. I
do trust the day is not far distant, though now, humanly
speaking, it seems almost impossible, when the door will
be opened for the gospel to be preached to the Turks."

This desire, which seemed, so few years ago, to be so
distant in its accomplishment, Miss Lovell lived to see in
part fulfilled. She was permitted to rejoice in seeing
Turks, openly professing themselves Christians, allowed
to go at large in Constantinople, even within the walls of
the city proper; and now the day seems near when the
"truth, as it is in Jesus," shall permeate the whole
Mohammedan population of Turkey, as it has the Armenian, and this strongest hold of the false prophet shall be
shaken to its foundations.

Two days later, Miss Lovell thus describes her Sabbaths in a letter to her mother.

"My Sabbaths are generally very much occupied. At
nine in the morning, we have an Armenian Sabbath
school, which is now attended by a large number, both
old and young. At eleven, we have the English service,
the missionaries preaching in turn, aided by the missionaries of the Scotch church occasionally, and we are always
sure of having a good sermon. At twelve, we lunch; at
half past one, we go to the Turkish service, conducted
by Mr. Goodell, of which I begin to understand a little.
Immediately after he closes, Mr. Dwight, or the pastor,

13*

preaches in Armenian till half past three. At four, I
hear the girls say a lesson in the catechism, giving all the
references from Scripture. At five, we dine; at six, evening prayers, and at half past seven, an English Bible
class, attended by all the missionaries, and some few
others. This has been continued for many years. I
believe they commenced the Bible, and we are now in
the Psalms; having finished Job since I have been here.
Mr. Schauffler conducts it, and, by his intimate knowledge of the original languages, makes it very interesting.
What a precious, wonderful book is the Bible! The
more I become acquainted with it, the more do I love,
and admire, and wonder, and the more do I feel my
ignorance. What a study will this book be to us through
all eternity! I long to hear that Henry is studying and
loving his Bible." . . .

From Mrs. Everett to her mother, February 26.

"*Six* Armenian visitors have interrupted my writing
for a little time, — three of the good sisters, and three of
the schoolgirls. I feel happy in such interruptions, and
should be glad to tell you something about their visit.
The work of the Lord is making progress, sure and constant. The pious females have commenced a mother's
prayer meeting. . . . I have not been in school these
last days, not because I have not strength and heart for
it, but because all my time is necessary for myself. It
has been a great struggle for me to yield my place in
school, for I love it, and my dear sister, Miss Lovell, is
not really equal to the cares and labors which fall upon
her. My dear husband will probably relieve her by going
into the school an hour in the day at least. . . ."

Miss Lovell to her mother, February 28.

"Day before yesterday, it was *two years* since I left the
shores of America. . . . These two years, Mr. Goodell
last night remarked, have been two most eventful years
to the Armenian mission, — years of trial and persecution,

and of relief and hope. Many have been severely tried, and have come forth as gold purified from the furnace. God has prospered us in *our* undertaking of establishing a school, far, *far* beyond our expectations. We *expected* persecution, and that many obstacles would be thrown in our way; but the persecution only added to its numbers, and nothing has interrupted its prosperity but the sickness of several of the pupils at present; and this, I trust may prove to be for *their* good, for their growth in grace.

"I am now almost alone in teaching. Week before last, A. was sent for to attend the bed of her dying father. He died a few days since, and she is, I hear, grieving bitterly, and will probably not return for a few weeks. Her father was not a Protestant, and had left his wife's house for the house of a daughter, also not a Protestant, that his business might not suffer. But, when he was taken sick, he removed, and died in his wife's house. When it was known that he was dead, a great crowd collected, determined, if he was buried by the Protestants, to make a great disturbance. As he was not himself a Protestant, however, it was thought best that his own people should bury him. But, a few days after, another opportunity occurred for the Patriarch's faithful followers to execute their designs. A child died, whose father is a Protestant Armenian, though his mother is not. The father sent for Baron Apsaghom, the pastor, to bury him. He, with some other of the brethren, was proceeding on horseback to the house, (it being over in the city,) when they saw a great multitude approaching them of the hostile party; but, being on horseback, they escaped. Two of the brethren were, however, already at the house. These they seized and beat most unmercifully. One of the rioters was seized, and is in prison, and has given the names of several of his companions. In their haste to bury the child, the Patriarch sent two or three priests, who buried it without a license, which is an offense against Turkish law, and thus the probability is, that, instead of greatly injuring the Protestants, as they desired, the thing will turn against themselves. Thus it has been in almost every instance. God has made use of his enemies to advance his own cause, and has turned their own weapons against them.

"March 5, Saturday evening. On my way to my room, I was stopped by two or three of the girls, with some question they had to ask, and found it difficult to get away from them. One of the pleasantest things connected with my situation, is the affection with which they seem to regard me. If I go out for a day, or half a day, they gather around me, and seem as delighted at my return as though I had been gone a month. They are very good girls, and I very seldom have occasion to reprove them. I do love them very much; often when I go in to evening prayers, and look from one face to another, I feel my heart overflowing with love to each one of them, and with gratitude to God who directed my steps hither, and who has given me the lines in such pleasant places. And then the question comes, Can it be that one of these lambs shall finally be lost? Oh, dear mother! do pray for me that I may be *faithful* to them; that I may have grace to direct me in all my ways, and that I may be permitted the joy of seeing *every one* of my dear scholars sitting at the feet of Jesus. Some of them give delightful evidence that they are learning of him. One of them to-day said to me, 'I can not tell how *sweet* the thought of Jesus is to me. When I am in meeting, the time seems so short, I wish they might continue much longer.' Dear girl! Her course as a Christian, thus far, has seemed very bright and happy. I trust she may be a blessing to many.

"One of the girls is in great distress to-day on account of the sickness of her brother, the pastor of the church. He was taken ill a few days since, and has been deranged for two or three days. It is brought on entirely, the physicians say, by mental application. His studies, and cares, and anxieties have been very great and pressing since he was placed over the new church. I trust, however, God will spare him to labor long among them.

"He is a man of a very devoted spirit, and calculated to be very useful to the people of his charge."

The pastor's illness proved to be "unto death." To the great grief of his people, and of the missionaries, after a few days of suffering, he was called to "rest from his labors." His memory is still precious.

March 14, Miss Lovell wrote to her mother, with a few curiosities she was sending to her friends in Palmyra, among which were two dolls, dressed by the girls in the school. Miss L. writes some particulars about Oriental costume which may interest the curious in such matters.

"One of the dolls is in the costume of an Armenian bride, as she is dressed two days previous to the ceremony. She is then *entirely* enveloped in a thick veil, and carried to the church. Formerly,— and in some families it is now the case,— the bride was not for *a year* permitted to speak in the presence of her new father and mother without special permission. The long wax candle is borne before the bride when she goes to church. The other doll is dressed in the ordinary home dress, covered by the *ferajee*, or mantle, and *yashmak*, or veil, worn by all Turkish and Armenian females in the street. The ferajee is often of bright red, green, or blue, which gives a very brilliant appearance to a company of women. The veil is always white. The ferajee and yashmak you can take off, but, as you do so, observe carefully how they are put on, as the adjusting of the yashmak is one of the niceties of Turkish dress; they spend a great deal of time before the glass in arranging the folds of the veil, and always carry a little mirror with them in case of need. The full trousers (sometimes made of bright calico, or in summer of thin muslin) are called the *shalvar*. The long trailing garment, which is tied up under the ferajee in the street, is called the *entaree*. You would find it hard to believe that any person should ever rig out in so many different pieces of finery as do the females of this land."

CHAPTER XIV.

THE spring brought an important addition to Mrs. Everett's cares and joys in the birth of a little daughter, on the 11th of March. She gave expression to some of the overflowings of her grateful joy in the following letter : —

"March 27, 1847.

"MY VERY DEAR MOTHER : My own precious little babe is sweetly sleeping on her pillow, and as I have sufficient strength to write you a few words, in some sort, I can not forbear, though what to say I hardly know, except to tell you how good is our God, — *supremely good* to us, to me, deserving only his chastening. 'Oh, bless the Lord, my soul! Let all within me bless his holy name!' I often ask myself, Why all this mercy and goodness? and my thoughts turn to you, my dear parents, and brothers, and sisters, and I feel that it must be in answer to your prayers. I know that you are asking these blessings for your distant child. Is it not all of the free rich grace and mercy of God that we are so blessed; and is he not in this way calling upon us to consecrate ourselves entirely to his service? May his goodness not lie 'forgotten in unthankfulness, and without praises die!'" . . .

"When I look upon the little one in my arms, I must

exclaim, 'Who is sufficient for these things? But will not he who has placed her in our hands give us all needed grace and strength? If we feel our utter weakness and entire dependence, he surely will. In our dear, sweet Mary, we are very happy. A new fountain is opened in our hearts, which, as yet, wells forth only joy and gratitude. Do pray much for us, that, from the first, we may consider this little one as a lent treasure; that she may be a link to bind us to God and heaven, and not attach our hearts more strongly to this uncertain world." . . .

Miss Lovell to Mr. R. G. Pardee.

"CONSTANTINOPLE, April 7, 1847.

"MY DEAR FRIEND: I wish I could transfer to paper the busy and curious scene I have just witnessed. It being the last of the three Easter holidays, I went out this morning to recall, if possible, the sensations with which, two years ago, the day after my arrival at Constantinople, I witnessed the same sight. Perhaps I then described it to you, and, lest I may have done so, I will not now repeat it, only to say that several thousands, Greeks and Armenians, were assembled in what is known as the 'Grand Champ de Mort;' dancing, swinging, singing, begging, cooking, and eating in the city of the dead, each one striving to the utmost of his power, apparently, to make himself as little like man, and as much like a brute, as possible, and all in commemoration of the resurrection of our blessed Saviour! Many of them were, doubtless, dancing upon the very graves of their fathers, brothers, and sisters! Troops of soldiers are continually parading the streets to preserve order among these *Christians.* The whole city seems turned out of doors, ladies and children in their gayest apparel, and the stately, solemn Turk walks through the midst, smiling at their folly, no doubt, and with no high opinion of a religion which produces such effects.

"Last Thursday, which was with the Armenians the beginning of their holy days, witnessed a most interesting scene in the little chapel of the despised and persecuted Protestant Armenians. It was the day set apart for the ordination of Simon, brother to the late lamented pastor, of whose death you have heard. It was an interesting and affecting scene, and the circumstance of his being so soon and suddenly called to take his brother's place, added to the solemnity of the occasion. On the Sabbath after, (Easter Sabbath,) he, assisted by Mr. Dwight, administered the communion, and four persons were received into the church. There have been additions to the church at every communion season, and the chapel will soon be too small to contain all the communicants.

"We have now visiting us Dr. Glen, of the London Missionary Society, I believe, who, at the advanced age of *seventy*, is on his way to Persia, with his son, as missionaries. The father has been a missionary many years, has translated the whole Bible into Persian, has been home to attend to its publication, and is now on his return to put it in circulation. I could not but look upon it as an interesting sight, — this old man returning to the scene of his labors with his son, himself advanced in age, that with his own hands he may assist in scattering the word of God which he has translated, and thus, in some measure, reap the fruit of the labor of his life."

Miss Lovell wrote again to the same friend, May 15.

"We feel very much the want of a larger house, and in a more airy situation. The scholars suffer much in health from being confined in such close quarters. Poor girls! they can not, like the happy children in America, go out and enjoy a run over the green hills after the studies of the day are completed. Here there are no green fields to run over, and, if there were, no young girl can go out in the street without her mother, or some elderly friend or

14

servant. Oh that some rich man in America, some John Jacob Astor, who wishes to lay up treasure in heaven, would send us a few thousands to build us such a house, and furnish us such grounds as we need! We often amuse ourselves, as we pass some of the Sultan's empty palaces, with their beautiful gardens, with anticipating the day when the Crescent shall give way to the Cross, and some of these fine buildings shall be devoted to the Redeemer's service; when the name of Christian shall not be a by-word and reproach in the land; when the mosks shall be converted into Christian churches, and I and my flock be established in some one of these beautiful situations. But though all this seems wild and improbable enough; though, when we look at the strong hold which ignorance, and superstition, and error have taken in the land, these things seem impossible with man, yet faith bids us hope, yea *believe*, that the day will come when 'holiness to the Lord' shall be written upon every dwelling and every heart. . . .

"I bless God that we are permitted to see the good influence of this school in other ways than merely upon those gathered under our roof. It is creating a desire among the whole Protestant female community to read, and, stimulated by the example and encouragement of those who have learned, all, old and young, are lisping their a b c's. There is not a female in the church but can read. There are, among the congregation who occasionally attend at the chapel, seven or eight *grandmothers* learning to read, that they may for themselves feed upon the word of God. Not long ago, a little girl, four years of age, came to see her sister in my school. At evening prayers, we observed that she held a Testament in her hand, and what was our surprise, when it came her turn, to see that she had not only found and kept her place, but could read in an audible and distinct manner, although she was hardly old enough to speak plain. What is more, this little girl is *teaching her mother* to read, who is to be received into the church at the next communion, at the same time with her daughter Mariam. one of my scholars, eleven years old."

Mrs. Everett was soon able to resume her duties in the school, which she did with undiminished interest. In May, Mr. Dwight's family went to Bebek for the summer, and Mr. and Mrs. Everett commenced housekeeping in the house they had left, known as the Mission Chapel House. Of this change, Mrs. Everett writes to one of her brothers.

"We now have a home of our own, but not an American home. You know what kind of ideas a young enthusiast would have of a New England home; shall I describe 'the house we live in?' As you enter the door, you step upon a brick floor, with a kitchen on one side, (and such a one, constructed only for a cook's shop!) on the other, a room for wood or coal. Then, as you advance, you come upon a marble-paved court, with servants' room, magazine, &c. Then you begin to go *up stairs*, and these houses are almost all up stairs; — on the first floor, is the chapel and four rooms; then up again, and you would find a large schoolroom and five rooms more; the attic completes the house. . . . Mr. Goodell's house adjoins this. Now that Mr. Dwight's family has left, the schoolroom is in here, and one sleeping room for the girls. Mr. Dwight has his study here; Mr. Homes also. The English service is held in the chapel, and, besides a congregation of 150 or 200 Armenians on the Sabbath, they have meetings during the week. So you see what a public place it is."

In another letter, she speaks of all her romantic ideas of housekeeping having taken flight before these realities, so different from what her imagination had pictured, though she was enjoying a great deal notwithstanding; very happy in her own little family, and in being able

still to do so much for the people in whose welfare her
heart was so warmly enlisted.

On the first Sabbath in June, seventeen were received
into the church; among them, four of the pupils of their
school. Mrs. Everett, in reference to this, says: —

"Do you think it strange that our hearts were filled
with emotions of the deepest gratitude to him who has,
as we trust, called them to be lambs of his own fold?
Oh, may he ever lead, and guide, and keep them, and
make them eminently holy, and entirely devoted to his
service. These dear girls have been very consistent in
their conduct since they were brought to receive Christ
as their Saviour. Among those admitted, were the
mother and sister of the late pastor, (and also of the
present;) the latter from the school, the former a fine,
noble-looking woman, and quite intelligent. A year
since, she was very indifferent to religion, but was often
at the service to hear her son preach, and spent some
time at his house. She was most tender in her affection
for Baron Apsoghom, and was deeply afflicted at his
death, but surprised all by her calmness, and herself, too.
She said, 'If this son had died some time ago, I should
have been distracted, tearing my hair, beating myself, &c.
But now I am quiet; the Holy Spirit strengthens me.'"

Mrs. Everett, under different dates, gives particulars of
the sickness and death of one of the pupils in their school,
the first of their precious charge removed to a better
world.

"June 5. One of the dear girls belonging to our school
is lying at the point of death. She has not been well for
some months. About six weeks she has been confined to
her room, and much of the time to her bed, having a
cough, pain in her side, swelling of her lower limbs, and
every appearance of consumption. She is an interesting
girl, very affectionate, open, and kind in disposition, and
has been very thoughtful in regard to her soul's concerns,

but was not among those most decidedly changed during the last winter. During her illness, she has seemed strongly to hope and desire that she might recover, — speaking much about her dear school, and saying that, if her feet were only well, she would take her things in her hand, and join her companions. At the same time, she appeared sad and disinclined to reply when any thing was said to her about leaving this world. During the last week or two, her disease has rapidly advanced, her whole body being bloated even to her neck; and dear Mariam has been obliged to give up all hope of living long here. She has wished much to have her teachers and school companions about her. Yesterday, she called for me many times in her distress, but I could not go to her. This morning, as soon as I could leave my babe, I went, and found her very weak, but she greeted me with a smile, and, in answer to my inquiry how she was, she said, 'I am very joyful.' Through the day, yesterday, she suffered much pain, and seemed to realize that she could not long endure. In the night, she became easy, and her sorrow and mourning were changed to joy and praise. She said, 'For two or three hours, I could not sleep for my joy.' 'Jesus is my Saviour; I am going to be with him.' 'Praise to God!' 'When will he come and take me.' When I asked her if she wished to remain longer in this world, she promptly replied, 'No!' and to the question, Which do you prefer, to live or die? she replied, 'I wish to die.'

"June 10. This afternoon, I went out to see dear Mariam stretched upon her bed, the spirit struggling to be free from its house of clay for, we trust, a home where is no more pain, sorrow, sin, or death. It seemed as though the poor girl could not long continue to be a sufferer. I thought I should watch the departing spirit as it quitted its earthly tenement for a new, a celestial abode. But not so. For nearly twenty-four hours, she

14*

has lain unconscious to every thing, unless it be her own
protracted sufferings. What scenes are just before this
dying girl, and how long ere we shall be called to stand
before the great white throne? Oh, may we have Jesus
for our friend in that trying hour!"

June 26, Miss Lovell writes of a remarkable preservation which the mission chapel and seminary had had
from fire.

"My dearest mother, I sit down in the midst of dust
and smoke, and with a trembling hand, to tell you that,
through the great mercy of our heavenly Father, we have
again been preserved from falling a prey to another of
those terrible fires which so often ravage this city. Last
night, at 12 o'clock, we were aroused from our slumbers
by the alarm of fire, and found, to our great terror, that
all the buildings around us were illuminated by the flames
of a raging fire very near us. We, of course, had no time
to lose, but all set to work to tear up every thing in the
two houses, and put them into the magazine. We worked
till between five and six, when the fire abated, and we
thought ourselves safe. Just as the fire was about extin-
guished, the *wind arose*, and just in the direction of our
houses, and the burning cinders and great masses of fire
fell around us thick and fast, but, by great exertions, we
were saved. Had the wind arisen half an hour sooner,
no human power could have saved our chapel and seminary. Thus the Lord has again and again, and yet again
appeared for us when, to all human appearance, there
was no hope. It is now noon, and we have worked from
six till now in getting the things back again into the
house. Of course, all this moving in such haste is always
accompanied with much loss and damage to furniture,
clothing, &c., but oh, what reason have we to be grateful
that our houses are spared, our place of worship not
broken up, and we, like thousands, left houseless and
homeless. It is thought that 600 or 800 houses were

burned. We hope we shall not be obliged to close school, though it will be many days before we shall get in order again. If we find we are not sick to-morrow, we shall continue."

Mrs. Everett writes, July 1.

"I have just come up from the chapel, where a meeting has been held in commemoration of the formation of the first evangelical church among the Armenians, it being one year to-day since that ever-memorable event took place. This moment, I hear them singing, —

"'Awake, my soul, to joyful lays;'

and wish to run back and join the song. I left as Mr. Goodell was speaking in Turkish, and the meeting nearly through. It has been a year of mercy to this little church, its original number having been more than doubled. The church has been afflicted by the death of a beloved pastor, but the Lord has not forsaken his people, although for a time they were cast down. May we see still greater things during the coming year!"

A few days later, Mrs. Everett thus speaks of the death of a very lovely missionary child.

"We can hardly believe that we shall never more see the sweet face of dear Mary Dwight. She was universally beloved, and by her parents most tenderly so, but the arm of the Almighty and All-merciful One is beneath them, and they are sustained. . . . She spoke once of dying; said she wished to die and go to Christ, and at another, 'Christ will receive me.' Is not the kingdom of heaven of *such?* Oh, these dear little ones! they get so near to our hearts that we are in danger of forgetting that they are born to die. As I look upon my own dear Mary now, I am forced to feel how frail the tie that binds her to this world. Earlier even than the lovely one to-day laid in her lowly bed, this flower may be

"'Transplanted to those everlasting gardens,
  Where angels walk, and seraphs are the Wardens.'

By this dispensation, how are we parents called upon to seek the early conversion of our children."

That which the mother's fond love thus deprecated she was called to experience. The tie which bound her first sweet flower to her, proved indeed a frail one, and of brief continuance, and the cherished little Mary Seraphina was the third of the *little Marys* to take her place in the Pera burying-ground. But this is anticipating.

CHAPTER XV.

THOUGH the young mother's heart might sometimes indulge a momentary foreboding as she looked on her first-born, and was reminded, by the bereavements of others, of the uncertain tenure by which she held her own treasure, the shadow was but a faint and quickly passing one. The little Mary was a healthy and happy babe, and Mrs. Everett's letters, for many months, are full of her, and of the joys and hopes she had called forth.

Mrs. Everett to Mrs. Fuller, Cambridge, Mass.

"Constantinople, July 26, 1847.

"MY VERY DEAR FRIEND MARY: About two years and a half have flown by since we parted, probably to meet no more until time is finished with us, and our eternity begun. On those blest shores where we hope to meet, farewell is a sound unknown. But these years; if we could meet, should we not have much to relate in regard to the way in which our God has led us? I am happy that we are not entirely ignorant of what has occupied the mind, heart, and time of each other during this period; still, my history for the past few months is yet to be told; and if you were now to enter my room, I suppose, after giving you some sensible proofs of my affection for yourself, I should lead you across the room to a little crib, in which, under a *charming little quilt,* sleeps the sweetest, most precious little babe *I* ever saw. (Oh, forgive me!) We call this darling *ours.* Her name is Mary Seraphina, and she is now four and a half months old. . . . She has already thrown closely around our hearts tendrils, which, if severed, must leave them sorely bleeding. We try to remember that she is lent, and may at any time be rightfully claimed by him who has committed her to our care. May she be indeed a lamb in the Saviour's fold; his here and for ever!

"I think I wrote you about the circle of pious Armenian females, their prayer meetings, their desire to learn, &c. Quite a large number have since united with the church, nearly thirty in all. You have learned with much interest, I am sure, of the precious and deeply interesting season in the girls' school last autumn and winter. Four who were subjects of the revival have already united with the church; two others are propounded, and one dear girl has, as we trust, joined the church above. What a precious hope, that this first one taken from our school has gone to that better world, where all is purity and joy, and she will live, learn, and praise for ever."

Miss Lovell to Mrs. Thayer, Palmyra.

"BEBEK, August 23, 1847.

"MY VERY DEAR FRIEND: It is the afternoon of the blessed Sabbath, and I presume *you* are just at this hour going up to the house of God to worship with the great congregation. All around you speaks of the quiet and stillness of an American Sabbath. I fancy I hear the sweet sound of the 'church-going bells,' and now the thrilling tones of the organ swell upon my delighted ear."

After dwelling at some length upon the painful contrast presented by the scenes around her, she adds: —

"But though all the outward influences are so unfavorable to the enjoyment of this holy day, we can and *do* have pleasant and profitable Sabbaths in our own houses. We are permitted to worship in our own chapel or houses unmolested, and, in the retirement of our own dwellings, we can meet and welcome the visits of the same God who makes glorious with his presence the sanctuaries of Christian lands. . . .

"Oh, this glorious hope, the rest that awaits the people of God! When will the glad hour come when we shall appear in his presence? For I sometimes feel that it will be a glad hour when this mortal shall put on immortality, this corruptible, incorruption; when this body of sin and death shall be laid aside, and I shall be 'like him,' for I 'shall see him as he is.' . . .

"I am now spending a week or two of my summer vacation with Mr. Goodell's family, at the house of one of our kind friends in Bebek. It is most delightfully situated, and I wish I could give you some idea of the enchanting prospect spread out before my eyes at this moment. The wind has gone down, and the Bosphorus is smooth as glass. The shadow of every rope and sail may be seen in the quiet waters; the setting sun is tinging the palaces and other buildings on the Asiatic side opposite us, the light and graceful caïques are darting swiftly over the waters, and the house where we are now staying is so situated upon the side of a hill, overlooking the village, the water, and the opposite side to a great distance, that at one glance the eye can take in the whole beautiful scene. Upon almost every hill around us, is some beautiful kiosk, or private summer house of the Sultan; for he is a man of taste, and selects and beautifies every choice and lovely spot for himself."

From a long and interesting letter written by Miss Lovell to her mother, September 13 we make the following extract.

"My dear mother, let us be more constant at this

throne of grace; let us at all times have a spirit of prayer. There *is* such a thing as that the heart, in whatever pursuit the body may be engaged, will be continually drawn towards God, and is no sooner released from other cares, than it will immediately fly heavenward, because its home, its best affections, are there. Blessed indeed are they whose *continued* experience is the enjoyment of this state! *Glimpses* of it I have enjoyed for weeks past. Prayer has never been so delightful to me, the thought of death and of heaven so sweet and desirable, as of late. Sometimes, indeed, I have felt a strong desire, if it might be the Lord's will, to depart and be with Christ, and yet, I pray that I may have *no will but his.* If it be his will that I should live many years, may he give me grace to spend them faithfully in his service, to do much for him; but oh! it will be a welcome summons that calls me to lay down this body of sin to go and serve him for ever, free from all imperfections. I have written so much about myself, but you will forgive me; I want you to know how much I enjoy. I often wish we could enjoy one more month, or week, or even day together, and talk together of heavenly things, and recount all the mercies of our Father to us both. But the day is drawing nigh, how near we know not, when we shall, I trust, meet with exceeding joy before our Father's throne. Oh! shall we meet *all* those we love there?" . . .

With such feelings, such habitual communion with God, can it be wondered that she was always meek, humble, self-denying, "always abounding in the work of the Lord," and that her most intimate associates should be able to discern in her scarcely a fault?

Let us now return to Mrs. Everett, who, while Miss Lovell was spending the weeks of their summer vacation with the Goodells so pleasantly in Bebek, and the other missionary families were also in the country, was left with her little family alone in the large chapel and schoolhouse in Pera. Though very unlike in many points of natural character and temperament, these two lovely missionary sisters were one in spirit. For them both, "to live was Christ," and they seemed always to cultivate that intimate communion with him which led them often to think with pleasure of the time when they should depart and be with him for ever.

In writing to one of her sisters-in-law, the day after Miss Lovell had written the letter from which the above extract is taken, Mrs. Everett says:—

"The work in which we are engaged is *one*, our Master is *one*, and, if we are faithful in his service, we shall at last have *one* home in those prepared mansions above. How glorious the prospect! We shall be 'near and like our God.' Our souls will then be purified, and our services also. Sin will not be mixed with all we do. Our hearts now so wavering, faith so weak, love so cold, will be established, purified, and flow forth pure and strong for ever."

Many pleasant glimpses we get through Mrs. Everett's familiar letters to her home-circle, of her domestic enjoyments, and many details, given with all a young mother's admiring fondness, of the baby Mary, and her pretty ways, and all her parents' delight in her. They made frequent visits to their friends in the country, to recruit their strength, during those warm weeks of August and September. But, even with her young babe and her household cares, which left her little time for rest, Mrs. E. would not allow the weeks of vacation to pass without doing something with reference to the work she had so deeply at heart. She wished much to be able to talk freely with the Greeks about her, servants and others, of the love of Jesus, and to point them to the Lamb of God; and, urged by this strong desire, she engaged a Greek teacher, and gave all the time she could, during these weeks of comparative leisure, to improving herself in this

15

language, of which she had already considerable knowledge.

Writing, September 1, she says:—

"We were at one of the villages on the Bosphorus last
week for an excursion, a little picnic, and saw the first
railroad in Turkey, a short way for carrying bricks from
a kiln. The car is moved by men, a clumsy little thing,
but runs quite easily on its iron way. Mr. and Mrs.
Goodell, who have been in this country about a quarter
of a century, had never seen a railroad. We helped them
into the car, and Mr. Everett, taking the place of *steam*,
gave them a ride.

"And, moreover, there has been in Turkey an exhibi-
tion of the wonderful power of the electro-magnetic telegraph, first to a company of missionaries in Mr. Hamlin's
study at Bebek, and then in the presence of the Sultan."

On the night of the 15th of September, the missionary houses in Pera were again threatened with
destruction by a large fire in the near neighborhood,
which was blown directly towards them by a violent
wind. But this time, as before, the Lord graciously
interposed, and the raging flames were stopped when
within a few doors of them.

In a letter written by Miss Lovell near the close of the
year, to Mr. Pardee, we have a concise history of the progress of the school, together with some of the encouraging
results they were already permitted to see of their unre-
mitting efforts and prayers for their beloved pupils.

"CONSTANTINOPLE, Dec. 6, 1847.

"MY DEAR FRIEND AND BROTHER: . . . Since I
last wrote, we have been able to increase our number of
pupils to twenty-three. The whole number who have
been connected with the school is twenty-six. *One* we
believe is with the redeemed above; one left on account
of ill-health, and one was, two or three weeks since, mar-

ried to a pious young man, a native helper and colporter. She is one who gives good evidence of piety, and we trust will prove a blessing, by her example and influence, to the females of Broosa, where her husband has gone to reside. In the course of four or five months, I shall also be called to part with my two assistant teachers, the first who came to the school. A——, you perhaps know by name. She has been to me a great assistance and a great comfort, and a great blessing to the school; and nothing but the belief that it is the Lord's will that she should go and carry the same blessings to others, reconciles me to the idea of parting with her. She will be married in three or four weeks to a native brother, who was to-day licensed to preach, and who will probably soon be ordained over the infant church at Trebizond. Thus, you see, I am losing my pupils one after another, but I trust they are going to sow the good seed, to be fountains of sweet waters to this thirsty land. Help us to thank God that we are so soon permitted thus to extend our influence.

"Of the twenty-three now in the school, seven are quite young, and the care of them is proportionally great. Pray that God may, by his Holy Spirit, early impress their young minds, and bring them to himself. We have frequent and encouraging evidences of the presence of the blessed Spirit with us. Two of the older girls, we hope, have, within two or three weeks past, found the Saviour, and two or three others, of whom we formerly had some doubts, give daily increasing evidence of a work of grace in their hearts. Of at least half of our number, we have a good hope that they are the lambs of the Saviour's flock. With all these encouragements, we are not without our trials. The wickedness of the heart sometimes shows itself, and, though always obedient to me in my presence, yet the force of evil habits is so strong in the case of one or two of the new-comers, that they are a continual source of anxiety to me. But grace divine can change the vilest heart, and make it a temple for the Holy Spirit, and I would not despair of any whom God may see fit to send to us."

At the close of this letter, written a week later, Miss L. says: "I enclose a copy of the paper given last week to Lord Cowley, by which the *Protestants are at length acknowledged*, and their freedom, civil and religious, guaranteed to them. This great thing has been obtained by Lord Cowley's perseverance and fidelity to the Protestant interests. The Armenian (Protestant) church observed last Thursday as a day of thanksgiving for this great mercy, and of prayer that they might henceforth walk worthy of their high vocation, and adorn the doctrine of God their Saviour, in all things."

Mrs. Everett, writing a similar account of the school, says, in reference to the two who were to be married:—

"The object for which we labor is accomplished when we see these dear girls going here and there as angels of light and mercy to their benighted sisters; and, while we are sad at parting with them, we rejoice that we can feel confidence that they go to spread the glad tidings of salvation among their people who are in darkness."

CHAPTER XVI.

THE first letter of the new year, written by Mrs. Everett, is so full of interest that, though long, it is inserted almost entire.

"CONSTANTINOPLE, Jan. 6, 1848.

"Father, mother, brothers, and sisters dear, I wish you all a happy new year, and may it be a year of rich blessings to each one of the loved circle. Grace, mercy, and peace, health, and happiness, abundantly be your portion! . . .

"You will be interested to hear of our meeting in concert with you on the first Monday of the new year, — a meeting long to be remembered by all those present as one of the richest foretastes of the happiness of the bright world above, the dawn of heaven below. Arrangements had been previously made for a general communion, and, as one remarked in the course of the exercises, 'The North gave up, and the South kept not back.' They came from the East and from the West, and sat down with Abraham, and with Isaac, and with Jacob, not really by sense and sight, but surely by faith. There were assembled in our chapel English, Americans, Scotch, Germans, Armenians, and Jews; and every man heard in his own tongue wherein he was born. The meeting was opened with prayer by Mr. Goodell in Turkish; hymns

15*

were then read in English, German, and Armenian, and
sung at the same time by the whole assembly, to the
tune of Old Hundred. The Scriptures were then read
in Turkish by Baron Harootun, the recently ordained
pastor of the churches at Nicomedia and Ada Bazaar.
Mr. Schauffler then made an address in German. Mr.
Allan, Scotch missionary to the Jews, followed in English,
Mr. Dwight in Armenian; then the bread was distributed,
and prayer offered in English by Mr. Wood, and the wine
administered by Baron Simon, pastor of the Armenian
church here; then a hymn was sung, as at the commencement of the services, in the three languages, to the tune
of Martyn. Mr. Goodell pronounced the benediction in
his peculiarly impressive manner in Turkish, and all
separated with, I venture to say, more earnest longings
for that blessed place where 'the assembly ne'er breaks
up.' Was it not good to be there in the midst of such a
company, every one of whose hearts had been touched by
Jesus' love, all sitting at his feet, remembering his death
in his own appointed way, and seeking to learn of him?
One must look up after such a season as this, and say:—

"'Oh, glorious home! oh, blest abode!
I shall be near and like my God.'

"One part of the exercises I had almost forgotten to
mention. Mr. Goodell, in Turkish, brought to mind the
state of things in Constantinople seventeen years ago,
when he first came here, and there was not one, or *only*
one, with whom he could have Christian communion,
and now what a goodly company, from so many different
nations, could sit down at the table of him who had
redeemed them with his own precious blood, and adore
the wonderful displays of God's power in this dark land!
Encouraged by the faithful promises of the Almighty, as
well as by what our eyes see and our ears hear, what
may we not expect in future years? There were present,

on this occasion, about one hundred and fifty persons, the majority Armenians.

"You will be glad to hear of the temporal prosperity of these poor persecuted Armenians. The Sultan has issued a proclamation, in which they are recognized as a distinct sect, under the name of Protestants, — their affairs being placed in the hands of the —— Pasha, with whom they are to communicate through an agent chosen from among themselves. An order was also issued at the same time, to the governors and pashas in the regions where there are Protestants found, that their rights and privileges in all respects be regarded and secured. Have we not all occasion to praise our God, who has wrought such wonders in this dark land?"

After speaking of special encouragement at that time in the Jewish work, Mrs. E. continues.

"We have been made glad also in our female seminary by indications of the Spirit's presence, so that, a few weeks since, at the request of some of the church members, a day of special prayer was observed, and we trust not in vain. The girls are now separated for a vacation of three weeks, but we trust they will not be left to wander from him to whose care we daily commend them. Since the school has increased in numbers, the majority are, we fear, out of Christ. Will you not remember them before God?

"Before dismissing the school, we had our first examination, inviting only a few friends for want of room. All expressed much satisfaction with what they saw and heard, and really, I think you would, any of you, have been pleased to see the bright, intelligent faces of these girls, and hear their ready answers in the various studies to which they have attended. I must say that I feel, from day to day, richly rewarded for all the time and strength I give to this dear school. May it be blessed more and more, and be made the means of spreading light and knowledge and truth through all this land!"

Miss Lovell's first letter of the new year is full of grateful recognition of all the kindness of the Lord. "If I were to attempt," she says, "to speak of the Lord's mercies to me, and to number them, where should I begin, or where end?" As usual, she places among her chief causes of gratitude the sweet society and tender affection of her missionary friends. Speaking of the family in which she enjoyed so delightful a home, she says: "I often think that this house is like that of Obed-Edom, upon which the blessing of God rested while the ark remained within it; for almost every one who enters here seems to receive a blessing."

Though Mrs. Everett's time and thoughts were so much given to the people around her, she was able to spare from both for her dear home-circle; and her younger brothers and sisters received many letters from her, filled with excellent advice respecting their studies, reading, &c., and earnest and affectionate entreaties to make religion their first concern. Some of these are so valuable that we regret that want of space obliges us to omit them.

January 26, Miss Lovell writes just as school was about to recommence. "Last week I received an application to take *one more*, so urgent that we could not refuse. These applications are frequent, and it is painful to refuse, especially when, as in this case, the friends are many of them opposed, and the probability is, that if she is not taken she will go back to the errors and falsehoods of her former belief."

Miss Lovell writes to her mother, March 10.

"My school goes on as usual, except that two have been obliged to go home on account of ill-health. Two or three weeks ago, one, who has been in school only a few weeks, begged permission to go home, saying she would return in two days. She is an orphan, and lives with two sisters, who are very much opposed to the gospel, and who burned her Testament and other good books, and, we have since heard, threatened violence to her if she came to the school. She, however, in spite of their threats, escaped secretly from them by the help of another sister who is friendly, and came to us. Since she went home, we have heard nothing of her, and we have no doubt she is forcibly detained by her sisters. Her reason for going home was that their house, &c. were going to be sold, and it was necessary that all the children should be present. This, quite likely, was a story invented by the sisters to get possession of her once more. I feel for her much, for we had begun to hope that she was seeking and learning the way of salvation. We hope, however, that the Lord will open a way for her return.

"We have had this term some indications of the presence of God's Spirit. One at least, perhaps more, will unite with the church at the next communion. Several are thoughtful and inquiring. The school was never pleasanter. . . .

"I received, not long since, two letters from Mrs. I. T., in the first of which she gives an account of her pleasant visit to you, of the village, the little cottage, &c. Oh, how vividly did her letter bring home and the scenes of my childhood before me! Those little rooms, the trees and flowers, witnesses of so many a childish sport, the scene of so many happy hours! How like yesterday does it seem when I was there listening to a father's gentle and affectionate tones! How does my brothers' merry laugh still ring in my ear!

"You remember my mentioning Dr. Millingen as one of the physicians of the Sultana Balida, (Queen Mother.) She has been very dangerously ill, and he spent several days at the palace. Upon her recovery according to

custom, alms were ordered to be distributed to the poor,
and to all the schools in the city. Of course, even the existence of our school is hardly known among the Turks.
When they mentioned to Dr. M. that they were giving
alms and presents to the schools, he told them they had
omitted the two Protestant schools in Pera and Bebek.
Some one immediately took down the names and places
in writing, and the next day an officer came with a bag
of money, and distributed to each of the girls, both in my
school and Mrs. Hinsdale's. So we are, thanks to Dr.
M., at least acknowledged as on a par with other schools.
Is it not a pleasant custom, this of the Turks, of giving
alms to the poor as a token of gratitude for any great
mercy received?

"Mrs. Millingen showed us, a day or two since, the
presents the doctor had received on this occasion, — two
gold snuff-boxes, and a coffee-cup richly ornamented with
diamonds."

In March, Mrs. Everett received the afflicting tidings
of the death of her eldest sister. She thus writes in
reference to this event, March 22.

"MY VERY DEAR SISTER M.: With what words shall
I commence my letter to you? My heart is full, over-
burdened, and it almost refuses to give utterance to the
grief which so oppresses it. You do not tremble to hear
the cause. For days and weeks and months your heart
has been bleeding, while, all unconscious of the sorrow
which was preying on your spirit, and on all our dear
family, I have been occupied, body and mind, with my
accustomed avocations.

"But the sad, the distressing tidings have reached us.
And it is indeed true that our dear, precious sister
Eleanor has bidden adieu to the scenes of earth, and
become an inhabitant of mansions in the skies. Oh! I
can hardly realize what my pen has traced. Is it so?
You were near; you saw her waste away under disease;

you watched by her side and administered to her wants;
you spoke words of comfort and hope to her sinking
spirit, and, as it struggled to be free from its tenement of
clay, you commended it to the Father of mercies; then
you closed those dear eyes from which the light of life
had faded; kissed the cold brow, and saw the precious
remains of our beloved sister committed to the cold earth
to await the coming of our Saviour on the resurrection
morn. You can realize that her loved voice is hushed
for ever to mortal ears; that her tender eyes will never
more rest on those who were her fellow-pilgrims here,
nor her affectionate heart flow out, as it was wont, in
deeds of love to all. . . .

"But I have been all this time indulging in nature's
sorrow, instead of looking, with the eye of faith, above
and beyond this vain, fleeting world. We feel the rod,
but it is from a Father's hand. He gave, and he has
taken. He does all things well." . . .

April 6, Miss Lovell writes to Mr. Pardee.

"Our meetings are unusually full, and there are some
cases of awakening in quarters of the city which have
been regarded as less hopeful than many others. At the
communion, last Sabbath, five persons were admitted to
the church, one of them a member of my school, who we
hope has lately been converted. Her brother was also
received at the same time, and was perhaps converted
through her instrumentality, though both *thought* themselves Christians before she entered the school, and read
the gospel; yet they are now convinced that they knew
nothing of the power of religion, — the *great change*
spoken of in the gospel had never taken place in their
hearts. Now all is new. That there is indeed a great
and blessed work of grace going on among this people,
no one can doubt, — a work which it is a privilege to
witness, and to be engaged in as a fellow-laborer with

Christ. Oh that our faith and zeal were only equal to the encouragements we have!"

Speaking of several of the missionaries who were in feeble health, Miss L. says: "I look forward with trembling to the day when these pillars of the work here will be removed. Who will fill their places? Oh that we could hear of a more and more active and widely diffused missionary spirit in America! Is this not, *ought* it not to be, the great enterprise of the age, — of the Christian world?"

Mrs. Everett, May 13.

"Sabbath eve. I have laid aside my book, dearest M., to tell you how happy I have been in teaching the little ones of our flock this evening. It is the first Sabbath of the term, and I have taken the small girls to instruct, while Mr. Everett gives the larger ones a lesson from the Assembly's Catechism. There were seven in the little company that surrounded me, and all listening with such eagerness that it was a feast *to feed them.* You would have been deeply interested to listen to their questions and answers, and the expression of their ideas on the subjects before us. I was pleased and pained by the mingling of correct, intelligent ideas with the grossest ignorance and superstition. How unworthy I am to be in such an interesting field of usefulness."

About the same time, she wrote to her mother.

"Sumner has told you that we expect to spend the long vacation at the islands.* For several reasons, we think this is important. Mary is getting her teeth; and for myself, also, although the good accounts of my health are true, still, with the confinement of three hours' teaching in addition to my family cares, I need a little change; and, in consideration of my having had colds coming upon me, and lingering so long, we shall go down occasionally before the middle of July, to stay from Friday

* The Princes' Islands, in the Sea of Marmora.

eve until Monday morning, for the sea air and baths. I sometimes feel that it is the part of wisdom to save strength for days to come, but we find it difficult always to do right in this respect."

CHAPTER XVII.

MISS LOVELL to Mrs. Thayer, Palmyra.

"CONSTANTINOPLE, June 3, 1848.

"MY VERY DEAR FRIEND: Your kind and truly welcome letter of Feb. 18 was received about two weeks since, and gave me, I assure you, great pleasure. What indeed should we do without these precious letters? You know something of what it is to be in a foreign land, far from home, but you do *not* know what it is to be separated from *all* the friends of your childhood, and that with no hope of again seeing their faces in this world, — and you can hardly know or realize the longing one has in such circumstances to hear from those friends, the fear that absence and the roll of *years* should rust, or perhaps sever, the chain of affection which once so closely bound fond hearts.

"June 8. I had written thus far several days ago, when I was interrupted, and obliged to lay aside my pen, which I have not found time to resume till now. . . . I have no news to communicate to you in return for all the news contained in yours. My *whole world*, with all its interests, is in these days confined to my school. I could tell you of each new scholar, — how many yesterday had *perfect lessons*, how many have left, and how many are wish-

ing to come, &c. — but all this, though it might be *news*,
would not be very interesting to you. But it will, I am
sure, be interesting to you to know that from time to
time one and another are giving evidence of a saving
change, — are coming out of darkness, such as you in
America can scarcely conceive of, into the glorious light
of the gospel. Last Sabbath, one of the former pupils of
the school was received into the church, and we hope
next communion three or four more will unite with them.
I have seven or eight little girls, between the ages of
seven and nine, whom I long to see becoming Christians
also."

On the 17th of June, another dreadful fire occurred in
Pera. Mrs. Everett's description of it is so graphic, and
pictures so vividly the terror, confusion, and labor, caused
by those fearful conflagrations in a Turkish city, that,
though long, we give it unabridged.

"ISLE OF PROTE, July, 1848.

"MY DEAR DISTANT PARENTS : I have at last found
a few moments, while baby is sleeping, to sit down and
commence a letter to you ; but the fatigue and excitement
of the last week will not allow me to write an account of
its scenes and changes with a very steady hand.

"Another terrible conflagration has laid in ashes fifteen
hundred or two thousand houses in the very heart of
Pera ; and although we as a family have only to speak of
mercies, and an almost miraculous preservation from the
raging flames, still, some of our circle have suffered
deeply. Mr. Dwight, especially, has lost nearly all his
house contained. He and his family are at this island,
but as they were intending to return to their house in
Pera soon, they brought only a few odds and ends with
them, leaving there every thing valuable. Their keys
were at our house. The day of the fire we went to
Bebek ; as we returned, towards evening, we saw a smoke

rising from Pera. Mr. Everett hastened our carriage,
and people were just beginning to 'run to and fro as we
entered the city. Sumner jumped from the carriage,
and ran through the streets to learn the situation of the
fire, and coming up soon, said it was just below Mr.
Dwight's house ; at the same moment we saw in the
crowd our man-servant hurrying by with the keys. They
were soon in the house ; but, alas ! no porters were at
hand to take the things ; a few were at length obtained,—
but in the streets confusion was every moment becoming
more confused. Mr. Goodell started from the house with
three men loaded, for our magazine, but found it impossible to keep them with him, and reached the house with
only two, afraid to return lest he should be trodden under
foot in the streets. The other man afterwards found his
way to the house. Some other things were removed, and
all perhaps might have been, could porters have been
obtained. Sumner several times started from the house
with things in his hands, and meeting persons whom he
knew, disposed of them and returned, — and finally left
with what he could carry, amid a shower of fire, having
succeeded in saving a mere handful of what the house
contained,— perhaps a fourth of Mr. D.'s valuable library,
with his study table and its contents, his cloth suit, a few
of Mrs. D.'s dresses, their carpets, and I do not know
what few things beside.

"Mr. Everett went on to Mr. Homes's house, a little
farther up in the same street, which contained his library
and many mission books, but comparatively few of his
household goods, the greater part being at Bebek. One
part of the library was in boxes, in the hall near the door,
and Mr. Everett offered a man two hundred piasters —
about ten dollars — to take it away, but to no purpose.
Those books were, however, saved, but nothing else was
taken from the house.

"During this time I was walking up and down our

house with little Mary, in the greatest anxiety about my
dear husband, who I knew would put no bounds to his
exertions till his strength was all exhausted; at the same
time trying to quiet the school-girls, who were at the
highest pitch of fear and excitement.   They at once
packed up all their clothes, and with their bonnets on
their heads, they ran to and fro, watching the flames,
some of them weeping, trembling, and almost distracted.

"Sumner made his appearance, and *I* was frightened.
You would not have known him.   Almost his first words
were, 'We shall have the work to do here,'—and the
flames were rushing on frightfully;—but I had hope, and
continued to have so much, that for two or three hours I
did little but follow Mrs. Goodell's example, and put in
readiness to take with us each two or three changes of
clothes, in case we must flee, and leave all the rest buried
up in the magazine under a pile of ruins.   Under our
house is a large fire-proof magazine, lined with stone, and
closed from the top by iron doors.   This Sumner made
ready.

"The raging element came nearer and nearer, and we
commenced in earnest taking down our things.   Every
article of clothing, every curtain, beds, crockery, books,
&c., &c.   Can you imagine what a time?   Some Armenian brethren came to the rescue; but the weight must be
on ourselves.   Then, besides our own, from the schoolroom and chapel, seats, books, maps, &c.   The girls were
sent away about ten o'clock.   Mrs. Goodell with her children left at eleven.   Strength and calmness were given
me for the occasion, and I stayed by and worked until
midnight, when we had disposed of nearly all that was in
the house, excepting chapel seats, school desks, &c.   The
flames were just upon Mr. Schauffler's house, one street
from us.   Still I prayed, and faintly hoped that the Lord,
as he had twice previously done, would deliver his own
house of worship and a place for the school.

16*

"Mr. Wood and Mr. Bliss had come from Bebek. Other friends had come to our assistance, and a person being in readiness to take me away, I took up our precious babe, who had slept through the whole, and left the house, not expecting to enter it again. We were most kindly received, with Mr. Goodell's family, at the house of an English friend. After an hour or two, the gentlemen joined us there, and we tried to get a little rest for our weary bodies; but excitement did not allow much sleep.

"At the dawn of day, to our surprise and great joy, we learned that our houses were standing, and again we were called upon to praise the Lord for his wonderful goodness in sparing the house for prayer and school, and abodes for ourselves. It was Sabbath morning, and a mercy to us that it was a day of rest. Notwithstanding the confusion in the house, the chapel was opened, and service held both in English and Armenian.

"We remained under the hospitable roof of our kind friends until Monday morning, then with grateful hearts returned to our home. Oh, what a scene of desolation was spread before us! A vast bed of smouldering ruins, — only naked chimneys standing to mark the recent abodes of thousands of now destitute people. It seems almost a miracle that our houses were saved. The owners came at the eleventh hour, and caused little engines to be worked from a terrace just back of the house, and thus it was saved, ours having caught once or twice on the roof.

"These conflagrations are awful judgments. Oh that the people would learn righteousness! Thousands are reduced to want, and thousands who had set their hearts on houses, gold, and diamonds, saw them perish in an hour, and yet take no thought to lay up treasure in heaven, but give themselves more entirely to perishing vanities."

Miss Lovell, after giving a brief description of the same fire, writes.

"Would you like to know how the fire was stopped? It is said that in the course of the night the Sultan, learning that the fire was still burning, ordered *three* guns to be fired, (which is known to be a mark of his signal displeasure.) As soon as these guns were heard in the city, the Pasha understood it at once. The fire *must go no farther.* Men were immediately stationed in places most threatened, water poured upon them, and they commanded to let it go no farther, and *it was stopped.* Happy for us that the Sultan waked when he did!"

Mrs. Everett's letters during the summer make frequent mention of the illness of her babe; but, as it seemed to proceed from teething, no special apprehension was felt by the parents until the latter part of August, when they took her back to their house in Pera, for the purpose of having medical aid nearer at hand. The little sufferer, however, lived but a few days after their return. The bereaved mother thus writes under this great sorrow.

"MY DEAR, DEAR PARENTS: How shall I write it! 'The Lord gave, and the Lord hath taken away; blessed be the name of the Lord.' Our precious child, our darling Mary, is in heaven. Yesterday (Sabbath) we committed all that remained to us of this loved one to the dust. The day preceding, September 2, her freed spirit took its flight to Jesus' arms, and this our first-born child, on whom we had lavished untold love, is no longer with us, to be the delight of our eyes and the joy of our hearts. Our house is left unto us desolate, our hearts are wrung with grief while we drink the bitter cup poured out for us; but there is sweetness mingled in the cup. We have the most precious consolations, — they are abundant, *divine.* She was one of those little ones of whom Jesus himself said, 'Suffer them to come unto me, for of *such*

is the kingdom of heaven;' and we can not doubt that
this little one is one of the lambs folded in the arms of
'Israel's gentle Shepherd.' Another hand is to heaven's
harp-strings given, another sweet voice has joined the
infant choir in that blessed world above. Can we wish
our loved one back in this dark world of sin and sorrow?
No; we will leave her there, where we hope soon to join
her. We loved her here, oh! how tenderly, and I trust
gratefully, striving to cherish the feeling that the treasure
committed to us might at any time be called for by him
who placed it in our hands. We acknowledged his right
to it, and he has come and taken his own, and we have
nothing to say. 'I was dumb, I opened not my mouth,
because thou didst it.' 'I know, O Lord, that thy judgments are right, and that in faithfulness thou hast afflicted
me.' *My* soul needed chastening from the Lord. I have
felt it, and sometimes trembled. God spoke loudly to us
in removing our dear sister Eleanor, but I needed more
stripes still,—again to feel the smarting rod. Oh, pray
that this may be truly a sanctified affliction to our souls;
that we may be eternally profited; that it may yield the
peaceable fruits of righteousness, for which we shall bless
God for ever."

After some account of little Mary's illness, she continues.

"She drooped like a lovely, fading flower, which no
earthly power could save; but

> "'Not in anger, not in wrath,
> *The reaper* came that day,
> 'Twas an angel visited the green earth,
> And took the flower away!'"

"Oh, how her little form was wasted away! Nothing
remained but the frame of our precious child, and for several
days it seemed strange that her active little spirit could
be holden of it, but it was bright to the very last,—until
within an hour of its release."

Of her dear child's place of burial, she says, in a later letter: —

"The remains of our precious child are placed by the side of dear Mary Dwight, to await the resurrection morn. The place where they lie is an open ground for general rendezvous on all occasions, *nothing* of sacredness being associated with it, except by the bereaved hearts of a few individuals. Not long since, from the Armenian part of the ground, stones were collected for building a church, having multiplied till they were lying one upon another. What a host will rise up here in the last great day!"

About a fortnight after Mrs. Everett had committed the lifeless remains of her first-born to the earth, her stricken heart was comforted by the gift of another little daughter. She writes in her journal a month after her birth: —

"O thou covenant-keeping God! make her entirely, for ever thine. Write her name in the Lamb's book of life, and, whether she lives or dies, may she from her *infancy* be a subject of renewing and sanctifying grace, and may we, to whom thou hast committed this immortal being, never cease praying and laboring for her salvation until she is safe, — a lamb in Jesus' fold, relying wholly upon thee for grace and strength to fulfill our high trust."

While Mrs. Everett had been passing through these varied experiences in her domestic life, Miss Lovell had resumed her accustomed duties with renewed health and interest after her long vacation. September 16, she writes to Mr. Pardee

"We returned from the island where my last was dated, about three weeks ago, and opened school last week. We feel that we have the greatest reason for gratitude that, amid all the sickness that has prevailed for the last few months, none of our pupils have been called away. One of Mr. Hamlin's most promising and pious young men died of the cholera while we were at Protè, and another brother, a member of the church, also died about the same time of the same disease; perhaps I have written you of this before. Since we returned to the city, death has again entered our circle, and snatched a darling lamb from the embrace of its parents, we fondly believe to join the fold above. Little Mary Everett, then the only child of her fond parents, a sweet little girl of seventeen months, after several weeks of suffering, was taken from us two weeks ago to-day. . . .

"Fires have of late been so frequent as to keep us in a constant state of alarm. Almost every night there is one. One took place in the city proper a few weeks since, which, it is said, consumed *two thirds* of the wealth of Constantinople. I hardly ever retire at night without feeling how more than *possible*, how *probable* it is, that I shall be awakened by the flames of our own dwelling. The terrible cry, 'Yan gun var!' (there is fire!) sends a chill and a feeling of dread over me, such as no other sound awakens; and well it may. When you look out upon one of these terrible conflagrations, consuming its hundreds of buildings, while it seems that no mortal power can stop its progress, and think of the thousands who will be houseless and homeless, and who have *no* comfort, *no* consolation, one may well tremble. We have been most signally and providentially preserved, while the fires have burned all around us. These fires have, of course, raised the rent of houses and the price of provisions enormously, and our friends who lost their houses in the late fire are unable to get houses in Pera, and will probably remain in Bebek this winter. We shall feel the want of their society much. There will be only our family, and Mr. Everett's, with Mrs. Hinsdale, in town. . .

"I am at present teaching without any assistance, Mrs. Everett's health not allowing her to teach. My number will probably be somewhat smaller than last winter. The trustees of the school have decided that it is not expedient to receive those under ten or eleven years of age; and as these little ones were a great responsibility to me while without assistance, and not old enough to reap the full benefits of the school, it was decided to send four or five of the youngest home. It is, I assure you, a sore trial to part with these little ones, to whom I have become strongly attached, but I hope when they are a little older they will all return. Two of the older ones have also left to be married. My present number is seventeen.

"September 23. Yesterday was observed in the school as a day of fasting and prayer. It is our custom always to observe such a day as soon as possible after the commencement of each term, and we have always found them to be good and profitable days; strengthening to our own souls, and happy in their effects upon the minds of the girls. Yesterday, although I trust the Holy Spirit was with us, yet there was not that deep solemnity which we have witnessed at former times. We need, oh, how greatly we need, the special and powerful influences of the Spirit! Many things *seem* to be against us as a church and mission. So many of the missionaries are in feeble health, the pastor is at present away, the absence of Mr. Dwight, which is a loss almost irreparable, and the cold state of the native church, — all lead us to feel that our help must be from God. Will you not — I am sure you *do* — pray for us, that we may experience a reviving from on high? And let me commend my school especially to the prayers of the Sabbath school. Will not those of them who love to pray remember the Armenian seminaries, that we may again hear the inquiry, 'What must I do to be saved?' and see these precious youth turning to God."

It was not long before Mrs. Everett was again able to resume her place in the school, from which her own pri-

vate joys and trials never long withdrew her interest.
The following letter makes us pleasantly acquainted with
some of their employments, and social as well as religious
pleasures, at this time.

"CONSTANTINOPLE, Nov. 25, 1848.

"MY DEAR SISTER M.: I am going to tell you how
this day has been spent, that you may see how we pass
all our Sabbaths for the present. At eight and a half
o'clock, A. M., is the Armenian Sabbath school, now confined almost entirely to the girls of the school; so it is
held in the schoolroom. The girls repeat seven verses of
Scripture to Mr. Everett and Miss Lovell; then Mr. E.
gives an exposition of the lesson, commencing and closing with prayer. At nine o'clock, Mrs. Hinsdale attends
to the Sabbath school in English, in which Mrs. Goodell
now assists her. It consists of the missionary children,
and a few others who attend the day school. At ten and
a half, is the English service in the chapel; preaching
by the missionaries in turn; and we have excellent sermons. At half past one, Mr. Goodell gives an exposition
in Turkish, following which is a sermon in Armenian by
one of the missionaries; after this, the girls go to the
schoolroom, and Baron Simon, the pastor, questions them
upon the sermon. Dinner comes between four and five.
After this, Mr. Goodell has prayers with the scholars,
while the children of our families, either in our parlor or
Mr. Goodell's, repeat hymns, sing one, and have prayers.
This is beautiful. Then Sumner hears the older Armenian girls in the Assembly's Catechism, and I hear the
younger ones repeat Scripture and hymns, and tell or
translate some story to them. At eight o'clock, Miss
Lovell reads with them from the Old Testament. You
will see that the intervals for reading are not long. I do
not read half I wish to do, but, as you say, I try to
improve the snatches of time here and there."

"December 9.

"DEAREST M. : We have had to-day one of our monthly meetings, and I must tell you about it. Since our families are so scattered, it has been thought desirable that we meet as often as once a month; and the Saturday following the first Monday has been appointed. The meeting is to be held at the houses of the different families alternately. In the forenoon, the gentlemen have a meeting for business, and the ladies one at the same hour for prayer, while one of the gentlemen meets the children. After this, a half hour is devoted to singing; then dinner or lunch; and in the afternoon a meeting for conference and prayer is held, and all return to their homes well pleased with the monthly meeting. To-day, Mrs. Goodell and I (for we join hands in almost every thing) set tables for thirty-two persons, which is the number belonging to all our families, excluding three babies; but the Bebekians did not turn out to a man, as we Peraites do, and there were some vacant seats. Our dinner is a picnic, each lady furnishing cold meat, bread and butter and cake, or something equivalent. Is not this a happy plan of getting together to keep up a social feeling, as well as to unite our prayers before the mercy-seat, seeking for ourselves and those around us a quickening in the spiritual life? We feel it to be good. You must know, dear sister, that we kept Thanksgiving in concert with our dear friends in old Massachusetts. In this, we joined with our good neighbors, furnishing the table jointly. Besides our two families, we had Mr. Schneider, the papa of our dear Susan and Eliza, and Mr. and Mrs. Homes.

"It is time for me to lay down my pen, as I am in a cold room, and suffering from a cold. Dear Martha has been confined to her room, for a day or two, by a very severe cold. It is unfortunate for her to have a cold and cough just as we are planning for an examination. Needle-work, plain and ornamental, is to be examined as well

17

as studies. We are losing our scholars, one after another, to become wives for some of our good young men. We regret to have any one leave before finishing her four years' course. But so it must be. A nice little girl of fourteen is soon to be married to the pastor of the church. She is a good girl, but all too young, according to our opinion."

CHAPTER XVIII.

MRS. EVERETT writes in her journal, January 14, 1849.

"I am resolved from this time to make new and persevering efforts to be prepared to lead the devotions of the Armenian girls in a more edifying manner than I am now able to do. Do thou, Lord, give the *spirit*, without which the words of prayer are abomination before thee.

"Oh for a deeper interest in the spiritual concerns of these dear girls! May I not increase my desires for their salvation by seeking opportunities of personal religious conversation with them? Is not the beginning of the year a good time to commence anew the performance of a duty in which, for months past, I have been sadly remiss?"

Little of special interest occurred in the missionary work, or in the missionary families, during the winter. All went on quietly, with much outward prosperity, but with a lack of those reviving spiritual influences which they had previously enjoyed so richly. Early in the spring, they had the pleasure of welcoming a number of newly arrived missionaries, and helping them on their way to their various destinations, as also of receiving a visit from Mr. and Mrs. Schneider, on their way from their first missionary home in Broosa to Aintab. Writing while they were in Constantinople, Mrs. Everett says: —

"Is not the removal of Mr. Schneider and family from

their home of fifteen years to an uncivilized city, leaving their daughters, aged twelve and fourteen years, behind,[*] an instance of Christian heroism? They are devoted servants of our Lord, and consider no sacrifice too great if they may be the means of saving souls."

In the same letter, March 6, she writes.

"The church here is at present apparently in a very good state. Mr. Hohannes, who has recently returned from the United States, has been chosen co-pastor with Baron Simon, and will be ordained soon. There is now a regular preaching service at Hass Keuy, as well as in the city proper, here in Pera, and at Bebek.

"Our school is very pleasant; not as large as last term."

March 26, Mrs. Everett writes.

"It is a comfort to know that, into the home of the blest above, *nothing entereth that defileth.* This is one of my most cheering views of heaven, — there is no sin there, neither in thought, nor word, nor deed; and, when we are groaning under this body of death, it is a pleasant thought that many who were dear, very dear to us here, have already entered those mansions, and have begun that life which is love, — love pure, perfect, eternal. I have of late thought much of our dear sister Eleanor. It is one year ago that the intelligence of her death reached us."

The next day, she commences a letter to one of her sisters, with the delightful news that there were evidences of the special presence of God's Spirit again in their school, the immediate cause of which visitation seemed to be the tidings just received of a powerful revival in the Oroomiah mission. After speaking of this, she proceeds.

"Miss Lovell this moment came in to tell me that one of our dear pupils who was this morning borne down

* These daughters were left in Constantinople, to be under Mrs. Hinsdale's instruction, and reside in the mission families. They were much in Mrs. Everett's family.

with a sense of her sinfulness, and pleading that the day might be spent in fasting and prayer, is now rejoicing in hope; wishing all to join her in singing praises to God for his wonderful mercy to her soul, which was ready to be swallowed up and lost. We are going to commence school this afternoon with a season of prayer and thanksgiving. Another, who for some days has been very deeply impressed with her need of a new heart, feels that her prayers are heard, and that she is accepted of God, through Jesus Christ. She came to me yesterday, wishing to talk about her soul; said that in a hope she had formerly indulged she had been deceived, and she trembled, but knew that God was ready to save her. This morning, after conversing with Miss Lovell, she led in prayer, in a manner truly astonishing. Several others are very serious, and the members of the church manifest a very subdued feeling. Oh that I might send this intelligence to you upon the lightning's wings, that you might even now unite your prayers with ours that we may not grieve away this Blessed One! We need your prayers *always*. Pray for this native church, — it is in a heavy sleep; for the Bebek Seminary, — our hope of preachers from it will be cut off unless the Lord in mercy revive his work in it."

To her brother, April 23.

"I must tell you that just at present we are rejoicing in concert with the heavenly hosts, over new-born souls. You will have heard of the glorious revival in Oroomiah. When the news reached us that God was pouring out his Spirit there, we all felt that he was willing and able to bless us, and have found it even so. Although there has not been a general work of grace, we have had some precious mercy-drops in our school for Armenian girls, and in our own families. Six of the schoolgirls have found joy and peace in the Saviour, and appear to show as decided cases of conversion as we see in our own land.

17*

"Oh, how it rejoiced our hearts to see those who had been careless and thoughtless, on their knees, with crying and tears seeking mercy, and afterwards with beaming countenances speaking of the love of Jesus. One saying, 'I have found my Father, and I want no more;' another, 'Prayer is so sweet to me that I do not wish to leave the throne of grace to go this way or that;' 'Satan continually walks by our sides to turn us from the right way, but the Lord will deliver us,' &c. &c.

"When we saw such a state of feeling among the Armenian girls, we felt that those in our own families who have been nursed in the lap of piety, children of the covenant, and the subjects of so many prayers, must not be left out; and the Lord heard us. As there was more than usual interest among the members of the native church, it was thought best to have a series of meetings, which were held last week, and were very interesting.

"A young man was ordained last week as co-pastor with Baron Simon, of the church here. Baron Hohannes is to be ordained next week over the church at Ada Bazar. There will then be five ordained native pastors, and three churches still remain without pastors. There is much to encourage our faith in the good reports we are constantly receiving from different parts of the interior. At Aintab and vicinity, at Arabkir, Sivas, &c., the Lord is doing a great work. . . .

"Our days are flying swiftly by; we are now four years' old missionaries! I suppose if you were to see me, you would say I look 'a little worse for the wear,' but I am your sister still, and love you and your dear wife, and wish to hear from you oftener than once in a year. What a shame to send this hurried letter so far away, but if it only assures you that you are remembered and loved, it is enough. Sumner says, 'A little love, if you please.' *He can not love little*."

In May, Mrs. Everett visited the missionaries in Broosa.

This city, beautifully situated on a fertile plain at the foot
of Mt. Olympus, near the northern coast of Asia Minor, is
a place of considerable historic interest, having been the
first capital of the Ottoman empire. Mrs. E. made this
visit partly for health, and partly to take charge of an
Armenian girl from the seminary, who was going to reside
in one of the missionary families there. Of the incidents
of this little journey, she gives a sketch in a letter to her
husband. Taking with her, besides the Armenian girl,
her babe and Greek nurse, and accompanied by an American friend who had been some time with the missionaries
in Constantinople, and was desirous of visiting Broosa,
they proceeded to Gemlik, the nearest port of Broosa, a
pleasant steamer sail of six hours on the Marmora, at
which place arrangements had been made for them to
pass the night.

The residue of the journey, they performed the next
day, setting off at six o'clock in the morning, and reaching
Mr. Ladd's, in Broosa, about five, P. M., having, says Mrs.
E., "performed in the whole day the journey of six hours
a la Turk, and three *a la Américané*, (not by steam.) Of
the incidents of this visit, and the principal objects of interest in and about Broosa, she gives a graphic account
in several letters from the 17th to the 30th of this month.
These, for want of space, are omitted.

One of the objects of curiosity seen in the mosk called
Yuldurem, at Broosa, was " a huge copy of the Koran,
two and a half or three feet square when the book is shut.
It was the copy read by Bajazet, 500 years ago. It is
written upon parchment, in letters more than a half inch
in size, with the points and decorations put on with gilt
and colors, and *all with the hand*."

"In passing through these Turkish cities," says Mrs. E.,
in concluding her sketches of this excursion, " one is led to
cry in spirit, How long, Lord, how long shall the false
Prophet bear sway over such a multitude of souls, daily,

yearly hurrying in such numbers to the realities of that world for which they are all unprepared. But Jesus shall reign, and these mosks and churches will yet be consecrated to the worship of Christ, the Saviour of the world. Lord, hasten the happy day!"

June 26, Mrs. E. again writes of a fearful fire, from which, for the "fifth time," the chapel and seminary houses in Pera were in "imminent peril, yet preserved."

August 4, Mrs. Everett writes.

"We have enjoyed to-day a precious season. We have welcomed to the church of Christ *five* dear lambs, children of the mission families; the youngest is nine years of age, the eldest fourteen.

"I have told you of a new organization of a mission church here. There was formerly a Mediterranean church, composed of members of all the stations. This station has withdrawn, as here a distinct church is needed. Mr. Goodell acts as pastor; Mr. Schauffler and Mr. Everett as deacons.

"To-morrow, five of our Armenian girls are to unite with the church. The dear lambs are dispersed. May the Lord keep them! Three of them are to be married, and will not return."

From the same, October 5.

"My dear Sister: Did I not long exceedingly to send you all a message of love by the post to-day, I should not take my pen even for an hour, as the day has been set apart to be observed by our school for fasting and prayer, in accordance with our custom near the beginning of each term. Mr. Goodell is now holding a meeting with the girls in Turkish. We have many new scholars this term, and greatly need a visit from the Holy Spirit. Some of our older pupils having left, the majority of the present ones are, we fear, unconverted.

"How many, many things I have to say! You see I commenced this with the intention of making it a journal, but it has proved vain, my time for writing is so little, and my correspondents many. Besides all on the other side of the ocean, I have correspondents in Oroomiah, Erzeroom, Trebizond, Broosa, Salonica, Smyrna, and Aintab, and in some of these places two.

"Our family is now as last winter. Mrs. Hinsdale and Susan and Eliza S. have returned to us. We are very happy to receive them.

"I have so often told you of our very pleasant connection with Mr. Goodell's family, that you can imagine how we live from day to day. There are no other persons to come into our meetings now, but we hold them regularly on Thursday evening, sing together Friday evening, hold monthly concerts, and take up a collection, have a weekly female prayer meeting, and two meetings with the scholars aside from Sabbath exercises. A part of almost every evening we spend together, while one reads aloud. Our walks we usually take together. Truly, the 'lines have fallen to us in pleasant places.' May the Lord make us faithful stewards, determined to know nothing but Jesus Christ, and him crucified, and grant us his blessing, without which all our efforts will be vain.

"But how uncertain is all before us, and how unnecessary we are to the progress of God's will, we have been led to feel by a very mysterious and afflictive dispensation by which a dear missionary brother has been removed from the field of labor which he had hardly entered. Mr. Maynard, who came out so recently in company with Mr. Dodd, to labor among the Jews in Salonica, has been taken to a higher and holier sphere.

"You will remember that a Mr. Parker, from Boston, a graduate of Andover, was my fellow-traveler to Broosa. He remained among us till sometime in August. He then went to Salonica, and, in company with Mr. Maynard, took a few days' journey into the interior, after which he went to Athens, was attacked with the same fever, and died on the same day with Mr. Maynard, at Dr. King's house.   His passage was engaged for the United States.   Have we not heard the voice of the Lord saying, 'Be ye also ready?'"

CHAPTER XIX.

FROM Mrs. Everett to her sister M——.

January 1, 1850.

" WE had an examination of the school a week ago last Friday, and dismissed the dear girls for Christmas holidays, — two weeks. The examination was not 'got up,' but gave us a good deal of satisfaction and encouragement. The girls have been very quiet, well-behaved, and diligent, and made good progress in their studies. My Greek scholar, who only knew the alphabet when she entered the school, can read in the Testament, has committed to memory Watts's Catechism for Children, and finished Emerson's Arithmetic, (first part.) She comes now to a little Greek service with her father. Her mother is a Catholic.

" January 25. There has been a temperance meeting in the chapel to-day. The evangelical Armenians are generally on the right side. A Greek was present at the meeting, and joined the society, who has just been released from prison. He was seized, about a week since, by order of the Greek Patriarch, whose intention was to banish him; but efforts immediately made for his release, by the Protestants, proved successful. He is not a member of the evangelical church, but he has for months past been enrolled with them civilly, and has been anathematized by the Greek church."

Miss Lovell to Mr. Pardee.

"CONSTANTINOPLE, March 26, 1850.

"We have visiting us a Hungarian lady,—one of the refugees,—the Countess Dembinski. She is staying a day or two with us, awaiting the arrival of her husband. These poor Hungarians! Our sympathies are kept constantly alive in their behalf. God grant them a day of deliverance and freedom!

"Our school is going on prosperously and pleasantly this term. We shall receive three or four new ones next week. I was told last week that I might immediately have *forty* if we could receive them. We have two Greek girls. There is now apparently quite a spirit of inquiry among the Greeks, so that we have a regular service every Sabbath, attended often by twenty or more. Some appear really, and we hope savingly, interested in the truth.

"We are still mourning the absence of the special influences of the Holy Spirit in our church and congregation. New hearers are continually coming, our chapel is full, and we hear in all directions of new cases where persons are becoming enlightened, and convinced of the errors of their own church; but alas! we do not hear the inquiry, '*What must we do to be saved?*' I trust you will remember and pray for us, for, unless the Holy Spirit be given, and the church revived, 'all will come to desolation.'

"Have I ever mentioned to you the case of Priest Keoorh? You have read in the Herald of Priest Vertannes, who has long been a faithful helper and sort of evangelist in this city. *Der Keoorh*, as he is called, was a friend of Vertannes, but has now come out from his church. He is a prominent priest among them, respected and beloved. He is fully convinced of the errors of his church, reads the gospel, meets with Simon, the pastor,

and prays with him, but alas! has never yet brought his
mind to the point of breaking off and forsaking all for
Christ. He cherishes the idea that he may remain in his
church, and one by one break off all its superstitious
practices, and so carry all the people with him. We hope
he will be brought to see that this is a device of Satan to
prevent his openly espousing the truth, and obeying the
dictates of his conscience. He has a daughter whom he
wishes to send to our school; whether he will have
courage to do so, remains to be seen. Should he do so,
it will perhaps settle the matter at once, as he will then
be known to be a Protestant. It is a most interesting
case, and we all watch it with much interest, as, should
he come out openly and decidedly, he must exert a great
influence.

"We have three sisters, who are coming to school next
week, whose father, a man in good circumstances, has left
his family entirely, taking with him all the money and
valuables, silver and gold, in the house, leaving them to
find bread as best they can, because they are Protestants.
But, as he has left them, the girls are able to come to
school, which they could not do before."

Miss Lovell to Mrs. Thayer, May 3, 1850.

"You ask if I shall not some time come home. My
friends here laughingly tell me that when I have been
here *ten* years they will all vote for my going home; and
I think the feeling is now becoming more in favor of
missionaries revisiting their native land than formerly.
Indeed, it is oftentimes, I think, of the greatest advantage
both to the individual and to the cause generally. But,
as for myself, I have no expectation that I shall ever see
my native land again. When I bade it farewell, it was,
in my own mind, *for ever*, and, while my health remains,
my post is *here*. . . . But we truly know but little
of what is the mind and will of God. 'It is not in man

18

that walketh to direct his steps.' I desire to leave all my future in his hands, who has thus far ordered all my course so kindly and mercifully; only praying that while I live I may be employed in his service.

"My school is going on prosperously and pleasantly. We have had some interruption from illness among the girls, but they are now better. We are expecting to remove into the country in the course of a few months, when Mr. Goodell will relinquish his place to Mr. Everett, who will have charge of the school in future, — of the boarding department, I mean. I look forward with pain to the time when Mr. Goodell will no longer have any connection with the school. His prayers and efforts have been, I am sure, greatly blessed. But I trust God will still be with us. Mr. and Mrs. Everett I love as brother and sister, Mr. and Mrs. Goodell as father and mother. . .

"We like our new minister, Mr. Marsh,* and his family, exceedingly. Unhappily for us, they spend the summer in the country, so that we can not see them as much as we could wish. Have I told you that we had, not long ago, a present of a piano from a lady in Massachusetts, Mrs. Burgess, of Dedham? A most acceptable present I assure you, though I find scarcely any time to play upon it."

With the first days of summer, Mrs. Everett's heart was gladdened by the birth of a little son. In her first mention of this "new treasure" in a letter to her parents, she says: "May he live in the courts of the Lord for ever! We have, from the dawnings of his existence, sought to consecrate him to the Author of his life.

The intention of removing the female seminary to the country was accomplished this summer. A very pleasant

* Hon. George P. Marsh, United States Minister to Turkey.

house in Bebek,* which seemed to be just the one for the school, was secured, after the usual unpleasant preliminaries to such matters had been disposed of. The house had been occupied for some time by the families of Messrs. Wood and Homes, the former of which left about this time for the United States, on account of the severe and long protracted illness of Mrs. Wood. Miss Lovell thus represents the difficulties to be encountered in all business matters in Turkey.

"July 3. We are to go into the house which Mr. Wood and Mr. Homes have occupied in Bebek. After much trouble and vexation, Mr. Everett yesterday succeeded in getting the contract signed for six years. You have no idea of the difficulties in accomplishing such a business in this country. In the first place, you must lay it down as a settled point that you will *be cheated* in some way, and then that the business will be drawn out and prolonged to the utmost possible limits, and then you will always feel a suspicion that, after all, there is some crook or corner you have not seen, some hole to creep out of; in short, no one here has any confidence in another, and this is the principle upon which business must be done. In a matter involving so much as the taking of so large a house for so long a time, Mr. Everett has felt a great deal of anxiety, but we hope the matter is now happily arranged. It is a delightfully situated house overlooking the Bosphorus, but it is not large enough to accommodate the number of pupils we wish to take, so another wearisome and difficult piece of work must be accomplished,— the building of an addition. This we *calculate* to have done by the beginning of September, but I *presume* it will not be done before two or three months later, and

---

* Bebek is about six miles from the city, on the European side of the Bosphorus, delightfully situated, the houses rising one above another on the steep sides of a ravine, and commanding the most charming and varied prospects. It is the seat of the Young Men's Seminary.

thus I fear our vacation will be greatly prolonged. Our school will close with an examination next week, Friday."

On the 10th of the same month, Miss Lovell writes: "Mrs. Everett has just left us to take possession of our new house in Bebek, and thus our pleasant family, which for more than four years has dwelt together so pleasantly and happily, is broken up; and next I must go. It is like tearing away heart-strings to leave this dear family, where, like a cherished daughter, I have so long shared the love and prayers of those whose love and prayers are worth so much."

In another letter, Miss Lovell again refers to her feelings in the prospect of leaving the house where her five years of missionary life had been mostly spent.

"We have enjoyed so much happiness and prosperity in this house that my heart's affections cling to it as to a loved home. It was the beginning of our little school; it has been, I humbly trust, the birthplace of many souls. Here in my own little room, how often have I listened to the inquiry, 'What must I do to be saved?' and how often I have joined in the prayer of thanksgiving for mercy obtained and peace found! Every room and every closet seems hallowed and consecrated ground. Oh that the holy influence might remain to bless those who shall dwell here after us! Much, however, as we have enjoyed in this house, a change seemed necessary. It is very desirable that we should have country air, and a place of exercise for the girls, both of which we shall have, with plenty of water, in the place we have taken. But we feel like saying, 'If *thy* presence go not with us carry us not up!'"

In the same letter, she writes.

"From the interior, we continue to hear cheering news. Aintab seems to be a favored spot, and I sometimes almost long for *two bodies*, that one might labor there.

"One little incident I will relate, which shows the power of this work upon those interested. When Dr. Smith came on to the annual meeting, a poor man of Aintab came to him, and put into his hands 100 piastres, (all he possesses probably does not exceed four or five hundred piastres in value.) Give this to Mr. ——, of Constantinople, and tell him that ten or fifteen years ago I stole from him an article worth forty or fifty piastres. I wish to make restitution for my great sin. This money will repay him, with interest." Does not this show the power of the *gospel* as well as the power of *conscience?*

A few days later, Mrs. Everett writes to her sister from her new home.

"How I wish I could describe to you the situation which we have come to occupy. It is really indescribably beautiful. The house is but a very short distance from the shore of the Bosphorus, and, being in an elevated position, has a most charming prospect of the villages and palaces on both shores for some distance, the Heavenly Waters, so much resorted to on holidays and for excursions, on the opposite side, with high hills rising behind. A beautiful kiosh of the Sultan crowns the summit of the highest hill, which is directly in front of us on the other shore. The house, we think, with an addition now being made, will be very convenient.

"We hope now to be ready for school the 1st of September. I shrink from what is before us. The responsibility of this school is *very great.*

"September 1. It is the still hour of Sabbath evening, and oh, how refreshing it is to our weary spirits to pass the Sabbath here after five years in the noisy city, though here we are constantly reminded that we are not in our own Christian America. Here it is man's day, not the Lord's day."

Of a missionary brother at one of the interior stations,

18*

who had been very ill, from whom they had recently had a visit, she writes.

"Mr. —— said that often, when he walked out in E. for exercise, he returned home completely exhausted, unfit for any thing, from the overpowering anxiety he felt for the souls of perishing multitudes about him. Be thou astonished, O my soul, at thy deadness. Oh for a new baptism!

" September 3. Our dear sister Martha has come, and we are making plans for the future. May we be divinely directed, and a desire for the salvation of the souls of our dear pupils guide all our thoughts and acts! It rains to-day, so that we are prevented going to the little prayer meeting, but Martha and I pleaded together the promise to 'two or three.' Those daily seasons of prayer we had in her state-room on board the Stamboul are not forgotten, and I trust their influence on us has not ceased.

"Our female prayer meeting is on Tuesday, at 4, P. M. Three of the ladies of the Scotch mission, who are here for the summer, join us."

In a letter written to the brothers and sisters of her husband, about this date, she says : —

"Our house here has been taken for six years, and is just the place of places for our school, — so it seems to us, — and we feel that a kind Providence has favored us in obtaining it. The air is delightful, water abundant and good. There is a nice little garden, with a large grape-vine covering the porch over the door which opens towards the Bosphorus. Then there is a large terrace which will be a fine playground for the scholars ; higher up is *the hill*, which has some cultivated patches, a young vineyard, some fruit-trees, and a fine sitting-place under the shade of some pine-trees, commanding a view that your eyes would love to look upon. Have I given you my idea of our new home? Now, think of the cares and duties that come with it; twenty or more young girls to be clothed, fed, and instructed, &c."

From the same, September 28, 1850.

"MY DEAR SISTER M.: The messenger this morning brought a package of letters, forwarded from Pera by the hand of our dear Mr. Dwight. I shouted, 'Mr. Dwight has come!' and every part of the house seemed to echo the words, for they were caught up and repeated by the scholars, one after another, with the greatest delight. My letters, or a letter and note from your dear hand, were most joyfully seized, but how my heart sunk within me as I glanced at the contents. Oh! '*it is well;*' I prayed, Lord, help me to feel it in my inmost soul! Our Father can not do us an injury, though he cause our loved ones to suffer, and our hearts to bleed. Until I hear again from you, my hopes will prevail that our dear sister Maria's health may be restored. May her soul find sweet peace in trusting in Jesus, and her hopes be clear and bright as she looks forward and upward. I am so surprised and overcome by the suddenness of these tidings, that I can bring nothing else to mind."

"October 4. Dear sister, we have just returned from a prayer meeting, held in the place of our singing meeting, with reference to the departure of Mr. Hamlin's family to-morrow. Dear Mrs. H. is very, very feeble. Her case is not considered hopeless by the physicians, and they have ordered her immediate removal to the Island of Rhodes. We have all been doing what we could to assist in their hasty preparations. May it please our heavenly Father to restore our dear sister! Our station is under the cloud; Mr. Wood has gone; Mr. Hamlin will be absent for the winter at least; Mr. Goodell is going in the spring.

"Mrs. Dwight says mother felt anxiety about me. If she could come and make me a visit, she would be relieved, I am sure. My face she would find paler and thinner than it was once; and, besides our two babes, we have a large household, but the children are well and good, the house very cosey and delightful, and we have enough to eat, drink, and wear. Surely 'our cup runneth over.'"

Miss Lovell to Mrs. Thayer.

"BEBEK, Dec. 13, 1850.

"MY DEAR FRIEND: Having just bethought myself that to-morrow is post day, and that your kind letter of September 9 is unanswered, I hastily lay aside dress-making, books, and every thing else, that I may thank you for that most welcome letter, and pave the way for another. But, my dear friend, would that you would not always *wait* for an answer before writing, but give me a glad surprise some fine evening by an *unexpected* letter, a thing, by the way, I know very little about, as most of the letters I receive are watched for and expected, and longed for, many a weary day before they arrive. . . .

"One part of your letter affected me to tears. It was that in which you so kindly chide me for saying that I have no home in America. My heart goes out in love and warmest thanks to dear Mrs. Rogers and you for your affectionate offer. Oh, how it would delight me once more to sit down with you, to walk those streets I so often see in dreams, and hear the voices whose tones are still fresh in my memory! But this will probably never be. While my health remains good, I would not leave my loved employment here; should that fail, I must *then* see what the Lord would have me do. Much as I love America, and dearly as I prize the friends I have left there, *here* I wish to spend my days, and here I hope to die, and rise in the morning of the resurrection in company with some of my beloved flock. I often wonder that I am not removed, and some more efficient and useful person placed here in my stead, and, whenever God shall see fit to remove me, I can only thank him that I have so long been permitted to have a part in his work, while so many, eminently fitted for usefulness, are removed. . . .

"I have this week a vacation in school. Next Monday, we begin again with twenty-two pupils. We have applications for more, and shall probably receive them soon. In the mean time, the care of these fills up all my time. So many of them are quite young that the care of their clothing is no small matter. We received a few days since a box full of useful articles, calico, cotton, &c., from a little society in Andover. It came quite opportunely, as winter is beginning, and many of the poor girls were in need of clothing." . . .

CHAPTER XX

THE special influences of the Spirit of God, which had
so often blessed the school while it remained in Pera,
were not long withheld from it in its new retreat. Mrs.
Everett and Miss Lovell both give substantially the same
particulars of this new work of grace, under dates of
February 3 and 4. The following is Miss Lovell's, written
to Mr. Pardee.

" My last letter, you remarked, closed in what seemed
to be a crisis of peculiar interest. It *seemed* to be such,
and our hopes were indeed strong that the Lord was
about to bless us; but these appearances proved to be
but 'like the early dew,' and very soon those who were
weeping and praying were again careless and thoughtless. A season of coldness and carelessness succeeded,
when the heavens seemed to be brass over us, and the
earth iron under our feet; nothing appeared to produce
any impression upon any mind, until the death of Mrs.
Hamlin, and her triumphant experience, came upon us
with a voice too loud to pass unheeded. Soon after, the
death of one much beloved by all the pupils, a former
member of the school, who died very suddenly, but
peacefully, and rejoicing in her Saviour, seemed to produce a powerful effect upon all who knew her. A few
days after the death of the last mentioned, was the day

appointed for fasting and prayer in the school. It was likewise observed by all the missionary circle, and was a day of exceeding interest to us all. The Spirit of God seemed present in all our little meetings, and we could not but say, ' Truly God was in this place, and we knew it not.' One dear child for whom we have felt much anxiety, and for whom many prayers have been offered, was enabled that day to rejoice in the hope of pardoned sin. For three others, we have the same good hope, and two or three who before were doubting, are now clear, and rejoicing in hope of eternal life. Pray for this little band of converts. But we can not feel that the work is finished. We would not feel satisfied while *one* remains unconverted. The younger portion of the girls seem quite thoughtful, and are continually coming to my room, in the hours when they are out of school, that I may talk and pray with them. There are some indications of interest in the other seminary, and we would fain believe that the day to favor Zion has come, that the clouds are gathering over us which will erelong burst in floods of mercy upon this thirsty land.

"Our school now numbers but twenty-two. Two of our Greek girls were taken away by their mother, although the father was very desirous that they should remain. We have still two interesting Greek girls, one of whom hopes she is a Christian, and the other is deeply interested in religious truth. I have two little Italian girls, also in the Greek class, who come as day scholars. They are Catholics, and have attended the school of the Sisters of Charity, but, their mother finding they learned nothing good there, took them away, and begged admittance for them into our school. One of our pupils from Nicomedia was taken away last week to be married. She is only fourteen years old, and she is the third of the same age who has been married within a year, all from Nicomedia. The people are not yet ready to give up their long-cherished custom of early marriages. It is, however, a serious obstacle to the prosperity of the school, as almost invariably as soon as one begins to get interested in her studies, and gives promise of becoming a fine scholar, she is taken away. Still, we hope that, in the short time that many remain, they do receive lessons which will be of lasting benefit to them, and make them blessings to all around them. Twelve or fourteen have been married from the school, and I hope that *all* of them are pious Christian women. But I am most happy when I think of the two of our flock who are now *safe* in heaven. I think of them with delight, as so much fruit reaped and safely housed, and, were there no other, I could bless God that he sent us across the wide waters *for this.* But, blessed be his name, *this is not all.* We trust there will be a bright and precious band to join them, one after another, as the summons may come which calls them away."

Mrs. Everett writes, March 4: "Since my last letter, I do not know of any new cases of special religious interest among the scholars. Those who have recently obtained hope, appear well. We long to see others coming to Jesus."

Miss Lovell to her sister-in-law in Wisconsin.

"BEBEK, April 2, 1851.

"Several days have passed since this letter was commenced, but I will try this morning to bring it to a close. I spent yesterday in sight-seeing, in company with a part of Mr. Goodell's family, and a large company of American travelers. We visited the Royal Mosks, St. Sophia, &c. As I have, I presume, described all these before, I will not repeat. I will only mention the mausoleum of the late Sultan Mahmoud, which I have not visited before. It is a small, chaste, and beautiful building of white marble, containing the tombs of Mahmoud, some of his

wives and children, and two or three sisters. These
tombs are very large, and are covered with velvet embroidered with gold, and over this are thrown splendid
Cashmere shawls. I counted on the tomb of Mahmoud,
which is the largest, thirteen of these expensive shawls
folded and thrown over. Upon the turbaned head of the
tomb, is a splendid diamond decoration. There were
many objects of interest hanging around; a large sheet
covered with Arabic characters, — I presume from the
Koran, — written by his own hand; a beautifully embroidered praying-carpet from Mecca; in a cabinet, the gir-
dles which he had worn in his lifetime, glittering and
heavy with precious stones; I saw in one, three emeralds
nearly half as large as hens' eggs. I brought home from
the Seraglio Garden a bouquet of flowers, which are filling
my room with fragrance, and which I wish I could send
you. I may send you one or two pressed, as a memorial
of the day and place. Have you lost your fondness for
such trifles? We *used* to preserve such memorials in
days gone by. Perhaps the little ' olive plants ' around
your table take up now all your time and thoughts."

The following from the same pen, though written at a
later date, may be introduced in this connection.

"I returned yesterday, August 28, from Buyukdere and
Therapia, — the former the residence of Dr. Millingen.
His house is pleasantly situated on the Bosphorus; a
good walk brings one in full sight of the Black Sea, — a
most magnificent prospect. I enjoyed a visit of three
days there much; they did every thing to make my visit
pleasant, — showing me all the interesting spots in the
neighborhood.

" You may have heard of the great oak-tree under
which Godfrey de Bouillon encamped, with all his army,
when just about to set off for Jerusalem on a crusade.
It is at Buyukdere, and is a splendid tree, consisting of
seven trunks, all connected in one, and called the seven

19

brothers, — the largest tree I ever saw. I inclose you a leaf from it; also a sprig of ivy from the ruins of an old Genoese castle at the opening of the Black Sea, on the Asiatic side. The ruins are some 700 years old, and the view from them the finest imaginable. Also a sprig of cypress from a Turkish cemetery on the top of the mountain near the ruins. There we saw an old dervish, born in Candahar, in Affghanistan. He has been in Cashmere, Lahore, Cabul, and many other places, and had many stories to tell. He lives entirely alone at the top of the mountain, practicing the rites of his religion."

It is pleasant to see how warmly the affection between our two missionary friends continued to glow during all the years of their unrestrained and most intimate intercourse. After they had been six years almost uninterruptedly together, Miss Lovell writes to one of her most intimate friends: "You ask if I love Mrs. Everett as well as ever. Indeed I do. She is a sweet and precious sister; no one can look upon her sweet face without loving her at once, and that love increases daily as you see her in every relation of life."

One of the prominent traits in Mrs. Everett's character was filial gratitude and affection. She delighted to ascribe what she was, under God, chiefly to parental influence; and the warmth of her love for those who had so faithfully guided her childhood and youth in the ways of true wisdom, years and absence seemed never to abate. We take more pleasure in presenting her example in this respect, as filial piety can hardly be reckoned among the prominent virtues of our age or country. The blessing which accompanied the example and instruction of these parents, may also encourage other parents to similar faithfulness. She writes to her parents, April 8, 1851.

"It is with deep gratitude that we are permitted to hear of your comfortable health in your declining years, and it always calls forth the prayer that you may be long

spared, if it please our Father in heaven, to bless your
children by your prayers and counsels, and the world by
your efforts for the advancement of Christ's kingdom. I
often think that, next after my Saviour, I must strive, *for
your sakes*, to be a faithful laborer in the vineyard of the
Lord, as it is, under God, in consequence of the consecration which you made, and the prayers you have offered,
and the faithful instruction you have given, that one of
your children is permitted to occupy such a sphere of
usefulness. But your work is only begun in thus sending
forth your weak, unworthy child. It will be worse than
in vain, unless the Lord be with me to teach, guide,
strengthen, and bless. Oh, I beseech you, my dear father
and mother, never cease to remember your distant children before the mercy-seat, and may the blessing of many
ready to perish be upon your heads, and in the last day
may many rise up and call you blessed!"

Miss Lovell to Mr. Pardee, June 1.

"Since I last wrote you, there has been no new case
of special interest in the school, but those who had then
newly expressed a hope in Christ, continue to give increasing evidence of a saving change, and one other, for
whom I have long felt much anxiety, begins to give evidence of at least an increasing interest in spiritual things,
if not of actual conversion. We last week received two
new scholars from Tokat, the first we have ever received
from so great a distance. They are interesting and
promising girls, from one of the first families in that city,
but, living so far in the interior, their manners and appearance are very different from those of the girls brought
up here. They will, I hope, if they go through their
course here, be prepared to exert a great and good influence when they return to Tokat, where, I believe,
there is but one female who knows how to read, and that
an aunt of these girls.

"Our friends are now gathering in from the interior for

the annual meeting. Mr. Schneider is here, and it would do your heart good to hear him relate the wonderful work of the Lord in Aintab. I wish I could tell you half the interesting news which comes in to us, from day to day, from different places in this dark land. Little spots of light and hope begin to be seen in every direction. Oh, may the full flood of noonday brightness soon cover the land!

"I was yesterday counting the probable number of missionary children in Constantinople now under Protestant and religious influence. When I came here, six years ago, there were not in all more than sixty,—a little more than thirty in Mr. Hamlin's Seminary, and a little less in a Jewish missionary school. Now there are more than three hundred. May we not hope much from these three hundred children? Pray for these schools; and may their numbers be greatly increased, for, alas! there are thousands of children in this city who are growing up in almost Egyptian darkness."

Mrs. Everett, July 3.

"The general meeting of our mission has passed, and we are able to take a long breath again. There were more than usual present. We had friends constantly with us five weeks, besides all incidental company. The meeting was an unusually interesting and important one; the sessions continued two weeks. The reports from the different stations were exceedingly interesting, and the demand for more laborers in all parts of the field extremely urgent. Oh for a new baptism upon us who are here! our day for labor is short. What a loud call to do with our might what our hands find to do, in the unexpected removal of our good, devoted brother, Dr. Smith, of Aintab. The overwhelming intelligence of his decease reached us just in the midst of the meeting. He fell with his armor on; a more devoted, active soldier of the cross never was in the field. At the meeting last year, he was our guest, and we often remarked that he seemed to have lost a relish for all other topics of thought and conversation except the all-absorbing theme of the advancement of Christ's kingdom in this land.

"As more ladies were with us this year than usual, we had a meeting to compare notes, and devise ways and means for accomplishing more in our particular department of missionary labor. One plan was to have a circular letter written by a sister from each station quarterly, detailing all of special interest that has transpired in her work, or her want of success in effort, her encouragements and her trials. Mrs. Schauffler wrote the first as a report of our meeting."

This plan of a circular among the ladies was not long kept up, owing partly to the many engagements and often feeble health of the missionary ladies, which prevented their doing many things that their warm interest in the missionary work would have otherwise led them to do. But a circular of that kind, started by Dr. Smith, of Aintab, was for several years maintained quite regularly by the male members of the different stations of the Armenian mission, the youngest member of the station being the one to write it.

One subject of discussion brought up before the meeting of this year, was the removal of the school to the city again, or to some suburb where it would be in the midst of a large Armenian population. But, as this question was not settled until some time later, we will not enter into it here.

The departure of Mr. and Mrs. Goodell for America in the spring of this year, left a large void in the missionary circle, and especially in the hearts of the two missionary sisters, who had so long lived with them under the same roof, and had regarded them as father and mother in the land of their adoption. They left their three youngest children in Constantinople, the two boys in Mr. Van

19*

Lennep's family, and the daughter Emma in Miss Lovell's care, who performed faithfully a mother's part to her during her parents' absence. With those dear friends, Mrs. Everett and Miss Lovell corresponded frequently during their separation. The following from Miss Lovell, with no date but the month, appears to have been written directly after their departure, and while they were still in Smyrna.

"MY DEAR PAPA: How shall I address you? How commence a note to you? I am not used to this way of speaking to you. I would gladly throw by pen and paper, and grasp your hand, and then I should be at no loss for words. Time has been when I should have trembled at the idea of addressing a familiar note to *Mr. Goodell;* but if I venture now upon the act, and even commence with the familiar title, 'dear papa,' it is your indulgence and fatherly kindness which must bear the blame. I have been too long indulged the privilege, to readily relinquish it. I wonder what you are doing now. Oh for a telegraph, or a carrier-pigeon, or a pair of wings; but, as none of these are at hand, I suppose I must content myself with imagining. Of one thing I am sure,— you are *not* writing the commentary on your knees; you are *not* taking little Ellen 'upon it;' you are *not* climbing that steep hill under my guidance; you are *not* singing 'I would not live always,' or 'Oft in the stilly night,' with the piano; you are *not* taking your nap in the large easy-chair beside the stove in the next house ;* you are *not*— oh! I can think of a thousand things you are *not* doing —you are *not here!* Yet perhaps you *are* here in spirit; perhaps you are even now in prayer for the school which you so loved, and perhaps, while reading this, you will send up one petition for her who is now writing, and for those for whose spiritual welfare she desires to spend all her days. Sure I am that you will not forget us. Though

* Mr. Goodell's family had spent the previous winter in Bebek.

an ocean may separate us for a little season, you will often pray for us, and will, God willing, soon return to give us again the benefit of your counsels and your experience."

In another, written probably the next week, having no date but Thursday P. M., she says : —

"I have caught myself several times this week involuntarily listening for Papa Goodell's well-known step and voice at his usual time for visiting just after lunch, and once actually took my bonnet, and was just about to run over to your house, — alas ! *yours* no longer. . . .

"How shall we sing to-morrow evening without you ? You will think of us with our harps on the willows, will you not ?"

Mrs. Everett writes, August 2.

"In this city, light is being diffused, and we are expecting that erelong multitudes will come out from the darkness, and openly confess the truth. Mr. Dwight was saying last evening that he had received a message from the President of the great Armenian Council, through an Armenian, that this is the time for the Protestants to work; that nearly half of their number are, in heart, on our side. Where now there is one missionary, we ought to have ten; a chapel should be built in Pera, to give more character in appearance to the new sect, and it would soon be thronged. The Patriarch recently put out a tract holding forth the principles and doctrines of the church, and Mr. Hamlin has written and published a most thorough and convincing reply, which is read very extensively, and will do great good. Mr. Hamlin might have access to Armenian families of distinction, and discuss the great truths of the gospel, but he is confined with his school and motherless children."

Mrs. Everett to Mr. and Mrs. Goodell, September 11.

"Our family is again large. Mrs. Hinsdale is still with us, but will go to Pera next month; sister Martha and

Emma, as usual. At present, we have three of the dear
children of Mr. Hamlin. He has gone to Rhodes to
remove to the Pera burying-ground the remains of his
almost idolized wife. Henrietta and Susan, the two oldest,
and sweet baby Mary, with her nurse, are with us. Carrie and Abby are at Mr. Schauffler's. Mr. H. will come,
if prospered, after sixteen days more, and the dust of our
cherished sister will be deposited by the side of Mrs. Van
Lennep. How our bereaved brother is to go on with his
duties, and the care of his motherless ones, we can not
see. Probably he will permit Carrie and Abby to remain
in some of our families, though unwillingly.

"Vacation has passed, and the scholars are again with
us; but not all. Two have been married; one good girl
to a Christian brother in Nicomedia; making five of our
scholars married there; and one sweet young girl has
gone to Broosa as the wife of the new pastor, ordained
there on the removal of Mr. Ladd here. Two other
pious scholars have left, and we feel weakened. Some
little ones have come in, but the number does not yet
exceed twenty. Miss Lovell was counting our married
pupils a few days since. They are eighteen, and all but
one or two hopefully pious. Ought we not to thank God
and take courage? Miss L. has, during the vacation,
been copying the names of all the scholars from the commencement, one to a page, giving or leaving space for a
sketch of each one. She is also copying into the book
all the annual reports of the school. After a few years,
will it not be an interesting history, think you? May
dear Martha long be spared to the school!" . . .

The latter part of this year, Mrs. Everett was again
called to mourn the death of a dear sister. She thus
closes a letter written to another sister on this occasion.

"Precious sister, which of us shall first greet you above,
and join with you and the other sainted ones in your
ascriptions of praise to our adorable Redeemer? Let us

bear the cross faithfully, patiently, till the Master calls. Oh, then to be accepted in him, and receive a crown of life that fadeth not away! 'Let me die the death of the righteous.'

"The many things I had to write, I am wholly unfit for to-night. Oh that we could mingle our tears. 'There's no weeping there.'"

She was herself the next of that household band called to join the family above.

CHAPTER XXI.

Miss Lovell's Marriage — Continued History of the School — Letter from an Armenian Lady.

THE beginning of a new year found Mrs. Everett prostrated with a severe illness, from which, however, she was beginning to recover, and several other members of the family also ill. Writing to one of her sisters, January 23, after relating all they had just passed through, she says : —

"Now, dear sister, have we not cause to sing of mercy? Oh! shall we not, do we not, consecrate ourselves, our children, our *all*, anew to the Lord, seeking from on high the grace and strength we shall daily and hourly need to enable us to perform our vows? How I should love to sit down and talk with you, my dear, dear sister, and bow with you before the mercy-seat as in days gone by! But what changes, what scenes have I passed through since we parted! I *sometimes* feel that I am no more the same being."

An event was now about to take place of great import-ance in the history of the school. The reader shall have the first intimation of it in the "*whisper*" in which Mrs. Everett conveyed it to her sister across the Atlantic.

"It is evening; dear Ellie, Sumner, and papa are quietly sleeping; Emma has gone to her bed; sister Martha has gone to the singing meeting, and the scholars are at their evening studies; and now, dear M., I shall whisper to you something about this same sister Martha. Did you ever have a thought of the school without her as its head, its center, its *life* almost? It was her 'first love' from its first existence; she had nurtured it, and, by the blessing of God, she has seen the seed bring forth much fruit.

"But she is going to give her place to another, and she, *she* is to take the place of our dear departed sister, Mrs. Hamlin, to be a mother to those dear children for whom all our hearts have ached; and how well fitted she is to take that position, I can not begin to tell you, nor, in fact, to tell you my feelings in this matter in any way. I believe it is of the Lord." . . .

Miss Lovell, writing to her mother in reference to the same subject, thus expresses some of her feelings.

"But God's thoughts are not our thoughts, and I, who but a few weeks since looked forward to nothing but living and dying at my present post, now see the hand of God so plainly pointing me in another direction, that I have not a shadow of a doubt as to the line of duty. Yet *duty* seems here a cold word, where every feeling of my heart goes with it. . . .

"Do you not wonder, dear mother, that I can consent to leave this much-loved school? And do you not wonder at my presumption in assuming such responsibilities; in even thinking for a moment of occupying the place of one so lovely and beloved, so gifted with every virtue? Ah, mother, if you could know with what feelings I have consented to do this, you would at least not accuse me of rashness and thoughtlessness, but would, as I am sure you will, remember me unceasingly before the throne of grace, that I may have strength and wisdom from above to assist and guide me.

"With regard to this school, where I have spent nearly seven years so happily, and from which I thought nothing but death could separate me, I leave it, though

with feelings of the tenderest regret, yet in the full
assurance that it is my heavenly Father's will, and that
he will provide for all its wants, will continue to make it
the object of his tender care, will richly bless it as he has
done in days past; yea, perhaps far more abundantly
than he has done since it has been under my care. For
this I shall ever pray."

The marriage was solemnized the 18th of May. Mrs.
Everett's description of it is the most minute and
graphic.

"BEBEK, May 24, 1852.

"MY DEAR MOTHER: . . . Dear Miss Lovell has
left us. We had hoped she might remain until the close
of this term, but our judgment coincided with the judgment and feelings of the parties concerned, and the marriage took place on the 18th instant; and as a wedding
in our house was such an unlooked-for event, and, withal,
such a happy one, I must tell you all about it.

"Considering the peculiar circumstances of Mr. Hamlin,
and that it was in the middle of our school term, with
school in session, it was thought best to have a private
wedding, and there were only about *eighty-five* present.
These were our mission circle, with the families of our
embassy, Marshes, Browns, and Homeses. The missionary
children numbered twenty-five, and the scholars twenty-
five. The hall was hung with horse-chestnut boughs,
with the beautiful white cones, and the parlor adorned
with vases of flowers.

"The company assembled in the parlor, and at the
appointed hour, two, P. M., the bridal party entered, the
bride in white muslin, with a wreath of white flowers
around her hair. Miss Harris, who is going to Oroomiah,
was bridesmaid, and Henry Schauffler groomsman. Upon
their entering the room, our scholars came into the hall,
and stood as they had been previously directed, the
smallest in front, closing the entrance to the parlor with

a phalanx of heads. All in the room instinctively rose upon their feet, and stood during the very interesting and impressive service by Mr. Schauffler. Congratulations followed; first were the kisses from the five little daughters. Then the bride's loaf was brought in upon a waiter. This, and another very large loaf of fruit cake beautifully frosted, had been furnished by Mrs. Brown, wife of the Secretary and First Interpreter. -

"After the cake was passed, the hymn was sung, commencing, 'When all thy mercies, O my God,' and then the party was invited into the hall, where the table had been previously prepared.

"In our dining-room adjoining the hall, the scholars' table was set. After eating, the table was drawn one side, while the children marched in order to

"'Children, go,' &c.,

which Mr. Van Lennep played on the piano. It was a beautiful sight, and, altogether, it was a beautiful wedding, — all went well. When they were actually taking my sister away, my feelings quite overcame me; but the guests had nearly all dispersed, and I soon recovered myself, and went about to send home tumblers, plates, &c. put the house to rights, and actually went up with our Bebek families to take tea with the bride, and was up the next morning *about* as bright as though I had not passed through the fatigue and excitement of such a wedding.

"Many prayers accompany our dear sister to her new home; a happy one it will be if her physical strength is equal to her new cares and responsibilities. Emma Goodell went with her, making six girls, — the eldest thirteen, the youngest still a babe, hardly two years old."

Miss Lovell's removal from the seminary necessarily caused a greatly increased amount not only of care and responsibility, but of labor, to devolve on Mrs. Everett. She writes just after this event.

20

"The school never was so full as now; twenty-six is
the number. Mrs. Hinsdale is with us this summer as a
boarder, making a family of more than thirty to superintend, with some teaching, the Benevolent Society of the
school, little prayer meetings, &c. &c. The constant
watchfulness over all these young persons is the most
wearing. The Armenian teacher is an excellent one; the
assistant pupil does very well. Very seasonable help in
the way of clothing has just come from a seminary in
Bloomfield, N. J. Sumner does much for the school,
but goes to the city three days in the week. My health
never was better than now, and I hope in God, and take
courage.

"June 18. It is four weeks to-day since the wedding.
The school has gone on well, beyond our expectations.
Sumner relieves me of hearing classes whenever he can,
and although my cares and duties are neither few nor
small, and sometimes weigh heavily, still I am wonder-
fully well, and I hope grateful for the opportunity and
the strength to do something for our Master.

"Do not think of me as wearing out; my health never
was better than now, but we do hope that some one may
soon come to our aid. Pray, what have you and our dear
parents thought about my having a sister by my side? I
have not continued to write about it, because I supposed
before my letter to you on the subject should have
reached you, a person might have been secured; but
Dr. Anderson says, in a letter received to-day, that no
one is found. May the Lord guide! This is a blessed
work. Oh that I might accomplish more!"

Just before her marriage, Miss Lovell sent to Mr.
Goodell, then in America, a translated copy of a letter
written to her by Armaveni, her first pupil and assistant
teacher, afterwards married to pastor Muggerdich, who,
at the time this letter was written, was settled over the
little Protestant church in Rodosto. It will be read with

interest, as also the accompanying postscript by Miss Lovell.*

"Rodosto, April 5, 1852.

"Dear Sister in Christ: Your letter, full of love, sent by my brother, I received, for which I thank you very much. Although you wrote not having received the news of the death of my beloved child, it yet comforted me exceedingly, and it is a great kindness to comfort the afflicted.

"The death of my child has been to me a most heavy affliction. I did not think that in all the wide world any thing could console me, but my heavenly Father has granted me consolation and patience, and given me light to discover in his word great joy, for he does not suffer his servant to be entirely destroyed. 'He smites, and his hand heals.' Now I can plainly see that in love he has thus chastised me. He is too good and kind needlessly to chastise his children. Truly, 'whom the Lord *loveth*, he chasteneth, and scourgeth every *son* whom he receiveth;' and these light afflictions, which are but for a moment, are not worthy to be compared with the great blessings which we receive while under his chastening rod.

"Oh, how good is our heavenly Father, who does not suffer us to follow the desires of our hearts, but in love disciplines us, and uses all means to make us holy as he is holy, and to fit us to enter his eternal glory.

"I bless my Saviour that I have this consolation, that my beloved children, though belonging to a sinful race, through his mediation are received into the heavenly kingdom, and now enjoy its glory with innumerable saints, and standing before their God, they see his face full of inexpressible glory, and bless and praise his name.

* Miss L. remarks in an accompanying letter to Mr. Goodell, that Armaveni's letter had lost much of the sweetness of its expression by being translated.

Oh, blessed hope which the Saviour has given, that 'of
such is the kingdom of heaven!' Now heaven seems to
me more desirable than ever, and the thought of dying
and leaving this world is very sweet.

"I thank you and Mr. Everett that you allowed my
brother * to leave the school and come to me in my
affliction, which was to me a great comfort. . . .
"ARMAVENI."

"P. S. Since copying the accompanying letter, I have
learned with great pleasure that in Nicomedia a *Protestant girls' school* is to be opened, with *our Akabee* for a
teacher, and the prospect of at least *thirty* girls to begin
with, of course a good proportion from the old-church
Armenians. I feel more delighted at this than I can
express. Akabee is making a very good impression there,
and will, I think, do admirably. This I regard as indeed
good fruit from our school; and I trust that your prayers
will follow this offshoot of our beloved school. I could
write a great deal of the influence which those girls are
known to exert in Nicomedia, but have not now the time.
Did I ever write you of a letter which Armaveni Hanum
wrote from Rodosto to one of the females here, which
accidentally fell into the hands of one of the old-church
Armenians, who was so much delighted and astonished
at it, that he caused it to be extensively circulated among
the rich bankers as an astonishing specimen of what an
Armenian female could do? Thus our modest, retiring
Armaveni was permitted to preach the gospel to the
proud Armenians!"

Mrs. Everett, July 12.

"MY DEAR MOTHER: . . . Have you thought at
all about Kate's coming out here? I should have written
with more confidence and earnestness about it, had I supposed so long a time would have passed before a teacher
could be found. At the last date no one was secured,

Her brother was a teacher in the girls' school.

though Dr. Anderson and Mr. Goodell had two or three in view. But we are willing to leave all in the hands of him who is 'too wise to err.' We closed school for the summer vacation, July 2. The examination, and the company it brought, nearly exhausted the little store of strength I had; and I must say that a week and a half of comparative rest has not restored my courage, though my strength has been restored in a great measure. Do not think I have been ill,—it has only been a *worn-out* feeling that I do not remember to have had before. My dear husband has gone to Nicomedia and Ada Bazaar, on a missionary tour. He has been absent a week, and is expected to return to-morrow; but if he comes he must go back on Saturday, to attend a council at Nicomedia.

"Mrs. Hinsdale is a great comfort to us by her company morning and evening. She lunches at Mr. Hamlin's, where her school is. Mrs. Hamlin gets on finely with her little family. We should be sad to leave this charming Bebek, but glad if the Lord opens a wider door of usefulness elsewhere. We have had some very interesting visits from Armenian friends lately; and our school was never more prosperous than at its close."

The following extract from a note to a missionary sister in Marsovan, will show more fully the "labor and care" of an examination in such a school:— .

"My labors had all along been quite equal to my strength, and when the last week came, with all the preparations for examination in the way of work, classes, &c. &c. and the friends (of the scholars) began to come in even two days beforehand, I was poorly prepared for the excitement, labor, and care of an examination-day."

A letter, without date, but written near the close of the vacation, to the same missionary sister, is in a more cheerful strain.

"MY DEAR SISTER: It is too bad, really unsisterly, to delay so long writing to you; but you will judge me

20*

lightly, after the doleful account I gave of myself in my last little note. The vacation has nearly past, and it has been spent in a strange way for me, principally in running about, doing as little as possible either for myself or others. But it has been with a good conscience, and I think with the divine blessing; do not think me irreverent. My strength and courage have in a great measure been restored, and I am looking forward to the reopening of our school with hope and real pleasure, feeling still most deeply how much we shall need help from above. Pray for us.

"A teacher for our school has at length been found; Miss West, of Palmyra. She seems to be the right one. . . . Shall I tell you that the station have approved of sending for one of my sisters to come and live with me, in order to help in school, or more especially in the missionary work generally among the females? But how many things may prevent the accomplishment of the plan! If the Lord will. I hope tremblingly."

It was eight months from the time of Miss Lovell's marriage, before Mrs. Everett was permitted to greet the teacher who was to fill her place, and with her one of her own beloved sisters, — the one she had for years longed to have associated with her in her missionary life. Those were months of great care, and exertion beyond her physical strength. It was during this time that she first complained of weariness even to exhaustion, as in the letters above quoted; and though she seemed to have recovered much of her elasticity during the long vacation, and her letters after the commencement of the fall term are uniformly cheerful, it is believed her constitution never entirely regained its former vigor.

From Mrs. Everett, Sept. 7.

"My PRECIOUS SISTER: . . . Our school commenced yesterday. The scholars were unusually punctual,—twenty the first day. We had the house all ready for them, and they seem as happy to return as we are to welcome them. There will be several new scholars. Oh for the presence of the Good Spirit! Shall we not be visited? We can not be denied. You will remember us, and Miss West, though not here, will be praying for us. My health is quite good, and the children quite well, and very happy. Dear Mrs. Hinsdale is to be with us to comfort and aid a part of the day.* Sumner says I shall not hear any classes except it be necessary with the Greek girls; and surely, with the whole domestic concerns, clothing, and sewing, and religious exercises, I have enough. But I love it with all my heart, notwithstanding all the care and trial."

"Nov. 9. My time is all filled up, — divided among at least *thirty* in our own household; cold weather calls for many stitches. School is going on very pleasantly, and we are not without encouragement. Some are thinking on their ways. One sweet girl has a heart glowing with love to her Saviour, newly found; old things have passed away; all have become new. It is a privilege to labor for these dear girls, though an arduous and responsible work."

Mrs. Everett goes on to speak of several deaths in the mission circle, — Mrs. Morgan of Salonica, and Mr. Sutphen of Marsovan, both of whom were called away very early after entering the missionary field, and Judith Perkins, a daughter of Rev. Dr. Perkins, of Oroomiah.

"Nov. 23. Several of the scholars seem thoughtful. A few evenings since one came to tell me how she was distressed on account of her unfitness to die, — unable to sleep; others have wept over their sinfulness. Lord, increase our faith! It is now nearly three months since our term commenced, and we are going to give a recess

---

* Mrs. Hinsdale was not acquainted with the Armenian language, and could only assist by sitting in the school sometimes to maintain order, or in the sewing department.

of a few days next week. I spoke of fatigue in the first of my letter. My health is good, very good; but I sometimes get tired, and who does not, even in more quiet life than mine? We are going to observe Thanksgiving on Thursday 25th, (are you?) and I have been making pies. All the members of our circle are to meet at Mr. Dwight's, in Orta Keuy, (half-way between Bebek and Pera, on the Bosphorus,) and we are to have religious services in the morning, and then a *picnic* dinner. There will be forty-five persons, great and small."

To Mrs. Bliss, Marsovan : —

"BEBEK, Dec. 9, 1852.

"MY DEAR SISTER: If my poor notes were of any value to my dear sisters who have less society and less variety in their isolated homes than we, I should feel more pained at my inability to tell them how often and affectionately they are remembered. As it is, *I* become the loser in not hearing more frequently from those in whom I feel a constant interest. You, my dear sister, can not doubt my earnest wish to have a more regular correspondence with you. You know I love you, and always wish to hear of you, your husband, and dear children, and the work the Lord has given you to do among those around you; and we wish you, too, to tell us of our beloved sister, so sorely bereaved.* I am glad she is with you. . . .

"You ask about Propian. I have rather avoided speaking to her of her future prospects, because she is so young, and I wish her thoughts to be as little distracted as possible while she remains in school. I know that she anticipates leaving us next summer, and I hope she has a sincere desire to do good wherever she may go. She is womanly, and appears devoted as a Christian. She is interested in the spiritual welfare of her companions;

* Mrs. Sutphen.

one with whom she is intimate hopes that she has recently been born again, and several in school are in an interesting state of mind."

Mrs. Everett's affectionate heart cherished tenderly the memory of departed friends. She generally wrote to her parents on the anniversaries of her sisters' death. Dec. 12, of this year, she writes: —

"Eleven years ago, and on the evening of this holy day, the spirit of our dear sister, your precious daughter Mary, soared to the world of purity and blessedness above. All the scenes of those last days, and the final scene, have been very vividly in my mind to-day; the patience and calmness of dear Mary, — her saying at noon to Mr. C. that her faith increased as her strength failed, — her talking with father towards evening, expressing the feeling of her great sinfulness, but her trust in an all-sufficient Saviour, — I have been telling it all to Sumner and Mrs. Hinsdale this evening, and I could not refrain from mingling my remembrances and my tears, and prayers and praises with yours.

"How you have been stricken! The anniversary of dear Susie's 'going home' has just passed; Eleanor's will soon come. But what cause for gratitude and praise that these loved ones left such bright evidence of a preparation for the blest mansions above! I have many happy thoughts about them; and I trust that you, my dear father and mother, are comforted, and can *rejoice* even, in their eternal gain."

Referring to her sister whom she was expecting to assist her, she says: —

"And have you indeed given M. up at the call of her Master? In this, too, may you find comfort and joy! It is a sacrifice which has cost you much; but it has been made for him who has a right to all we are, and all we have, and whose service brings a rich reward. You, through your children, may scatter light in the paths of those who sit in darkness, and may many in the last day rise up and call *you* blessed!

"My thoughts are often with you by day, and in my dreams I visit you. May the good Comforter ever grant you his presence!"

"Dec. 29. My dear Sister K: A pile of pressing sewing lies by my side. I have been distracted all day with preparing work for a seamstress whom I employ a few days, — hearing Greek lessons, making ready sewing for our school sewing society, and sitting in the midst of the twenty-five girls for three hours, attending to their work, and above all this, having the ordinary duties of my family of thirty-five persons. We have help in all our work; but my *head* gets very weary as well as my hands.

"Is not this a poor beginning for a birthday letter, for I am twenty-nine years old this 29th day of December, and I can say, 'Surely goodness and mercy have followed me all the days of my life.' Shall I not make a new consecration of all my powers and my blessings to the Author of all? How much unfaithfulness *I* have to mourn over! I do hope, dearest sister, that you will accomplish far more for our Master than I have done, if you are spared ten years to labor on earth."

Before closing this chapter, and the record of this year, we will look for a moment at Mrs. Hamlin in her new home, and new and most interesting duties. These first months of her married life, though very happy, were not unclouded. The youngest of the little group whom she had taken to her heart with almost a mother's love, the sweet babe who was the pet and joy of all, was taken from her fond care early in September. She writes with much tenderness of this event, and of her own disappointment in not being permitted to train up this dear child, as she had fondly hoped to do. From the several inter-

esting letters written during these months, we will make
only one extract.

"BEBEK, October 29, 1852.

"I should like to introduce to you in person my dear
husband and our four daughters; but I will not begin
upon this theme. Suffice it to say that I can now fully
understand and appreciate the sincerity and meaning of
your warm congratulations, and that I do find our sweet
girls a 'great treasure.' The 'responsibility' I am surely
not unmindful of, and at times it has seemed almost
crushing; but I have taken refuge in the promise, 'My
grace is sufficient.' As I write, dear Louisa, my heart is
full; too full for pen and ink. Would that we could sit
side by side for a few hours. You alluded to a subject in
yours which has long been to me one of great interest,
and now doubly so. It is, the duty of parents — yes,
and their *privilege*, — to train up their children to fulfill
the last command of our Saviour, 'Go ye into all the
world,' &c. I am glad, dearest L., that you have felt it a
privilege to consecrate yours 'with the first sight of their
infant faces' to this work. Be sure the consecration will
be accepted, and you will be blessed in it, and, though
God may choose his own way of glorifying his name in
your beloved children, all will be well. But oh that all
parents did but feel — especially all Christian *mothers* —
the obligation resting upon them in this respect! It is
my most earnest prayer that all our dear children may be
called of God to this work. I would not wish them a
happier work, a happier life, than that of the faithful
missionary, though it may be a life of toil and self-denial."

CHAPTER XXII.

Removal of the Seminary from Bebek to Hass Keuy — Description of the
New Seminary Building — Interesting Letters — Commencement of War.

WE will now leave Mrs. Hamlin in the retirement of
her new home, and follow the history of Mrs. Everett, in
connection with that of the Seminary, during the short
remainder of her life.

The question of removing the Female Seminary to
another locality, which had been so long under discussion
by the mission, had at length been decided. In many
respects, the house it occupied in Bebek possessed advantages that could hardly be looked for in any other position. It was quiet and retired, and in one of the most
delightful and healthful situations on the Bosphorus.
The building was also, in its internal arrangements,
admirably adapted to the wants of such an institution,
and, while comprising all the needed room, was more
compact and convenient than houses in Constantinople
are usually found.

But, with all these advantages, it was thought, as the
work among the Armenians advanced, and opportunities
for intercourse with them were opening and extending
continually, that the situation of the Seminary was too
isolated. The Armenians, in Bebek and its immediate
vicinity, were few, and though the friends of the pupils
visited them from time to time, often remaining over
night, or longer, it was not exerting exactly the influence
which it might do if in the midst of an Armenian popula-

tion. Although Mrs. Everett's duties in the school were now such as to prevent her visiting to any extent among Armenian families, it was hoped that when the new teacher should arrive, and she should also have one of her sisters to relieve her in some measure in her family cares, she would be at liberty to visit more; a work for which, by her winning manners and great readiness in speaking the language, she was peculiarly fitted. It was therefore decided that, as soon as a suitable house could be obtained, the school should be removed to Hass Keuy, one of the large suburbs of Constantinople, lying on the Golden Horn, where many of the most wealthy and influential Armenian families reside.

It was very trying to Mrs. Everett to leave Bebek. The moving of such an establishment from Pera had been very laborious; and all the changes and improvements they had found it necessary to make, and which they would probably find no less needed in any other house to which they might remove, made the labor appear still more formidable. They would leave, too, the small but delightful missionary circle in that village, to take up their residence quite distant from all the missionary families, and this, besides withdrawing them from the social intercourse they had enjoyed so highly, would place them at a distance from the religious meetings which they so much valued for themselves and their children. But, as soon as they were convinced that such a removal would be for the promotion of the cause which they "preferred above their chief joy," they cheerfully acquiesced.

It was not till after much negotiation and many delays, that they succeeded in obtaining a house in Hass Keuy. The unfriendly Armenians looked with jealousy on the proposed settlement of a missionary family and school right in the midst of them, and laid many obstacles in the way. But their efforts proved in vain. The Lord

21

had a work for them to do there, and they at length succeeded, in February, 1853, in securing a house very well adapted to their wants, though it lacked the convenience of arrangement which had so much lightened the labor of housekeeping in their Bebek home. One who has lived only in the well-arranged houses of our own country, where every thing is planned on the labor-saving principle, can hardly form an idea of the weariness of keeping one of those Constantinople houses in order. No thought of convenience or saving of work seems ever to have entered into the minds of their architects; but only the securing of as much space and fresh air as possible; and as the price of labor is cheap, and they are accustomed to employ many servants, the native housekeepers do not feel the inconveniences of their large rooms, and the distances between them, as missionary ladies do.

The latter part of January, Miss West and Miss Haynes arrived in Constantinople, to the great joy and relief of Mrs. Everett, though, as they both had a *language* to learn before they could communicate with any of the Armenians in the family or in the school, it must necessarily be some time before they could relieve her very effectually in either department.

On the 18th of February, Mrs. Everett welcomed another little daughter to her home and heart, to whom the name of Susan Maria was given, and, as soon as the mother's strength was sufficiently restored, they began to make preparations for their removal, which was effected about the 1st of April.

From Mrs. Everett.

"HASS KEUY, April 12, 1853.

"MY VERY DEAR PARENTS: No longer from dear Bebek do we address you. We have taken our pilgrim staff in hand, and passed over the hills to this village, where we have, at the call of our Master, pitched our

tent for a season. It is more than a week since we left
our happy home of three years. Sumner had moved the
school furniture previously, but still we had *enough* to
do; our friends from Mr. Schauffler's and Mr. Hamlin's
came and *un*willingly helped us away. It was hard to
leave those dear friends and that charming spot, but we
were prepared for it by two years of discussion, looking
for houses, &c.; and then the securing of a house in this
village, in the midst of a very large Armenian population,
and the occupation of it without any disturbance, seemed
to indicate the will of him whom we wish to serve, and
we feel happy in following the indication of his providence.

"Hass Keuy is on the Golden Horn, the harbor of the
city. It is by land about seven miles from Bebek, and
two or three from Pera. We are now within a half
hour's row of the city, while before it was an hour and
more by caïque, a little less by steamer; so that Mr.
Everett is nearer his work at the book magazine. On the
Sabbath, we can attend English service at Pera, going by
boat, with a walk of five minutes here, and fifteen there.
You perhaps know that there is a distinct evangelical
Armenian church in this village, of from twelve to fifteen
members; the greater part of this large population are
Armenians, many of whom are intellectually convinced
of the truth, but are kept back, by fear of one another
and their church, from confessing it. Many were favorable to our coming among them with our school, and
they are families of the higher class in society. Our
landlord is an Armenian. He has an immense sum of
money due him from the Turkish government, and, because he has not succeeded in getting it, he is reduced to
the necessity of renting a part of his large house, in
which there are twenty-five or thirty rooms, and five
large halls. We have two of these halls, with the rooms
opening from one side of them. These rooms are high

and large, — not very old, but covered (the floors) with straw matting, and ah, *the fleas!* they have full possession, and how we are to be rid of them I do not know; and then their friends, called in this country *board* bugs; they, however, are manageable; *we hope* to exterminate them.

" We have, in addition to the rooms I have mentioned, a small house, into which a passage was opened through the wall from one of our rooms.

" Now, can you imagine the distance from one front door, opening on one street, to the other on another street? Our kitchen and water are in the lower floor of the small house, while our family rooms are on the upper floor of the large house. These have been chosen for health, as Hass Keuy, during three months in the summer, is excessively hot, being much exposed to the sun, and getting little of the north wind. There are accommodations in our house for he chapel, thirty boarding scholars, and a *day school,* which is to be opened under our supervision, and taught by one of our former pupils.

" We are hard at work still in the fitting up which such a change involves; we hope to get sufficiently in order to bring back our scholars next week. We shall have many visits from Armenian families, as well as from our little Protestant community. This will take time and strength, but we hope may not be in vain spiritually. ' Who is sufficient for these things?' There is not a more extensive and hopeful field of labor in all this vicinity than is before us. Under our own roof, what a work, — what care and responsibility! I often shrink back, and say, ' Why am *I* here?' Oh, my own dear parents, when you think of your distant children, let it be with fervent supplication for wisdom, grace, and strength, that we may each be found faithful to our high trust.

" Dear M. is an unspeakable comfort. How should I have gone through with all the toil of the past weeks

with a little infant in my arms, and two others at my
side, without her? She is very well, and making good
progress in Armenian; she goes on as fast as Miss West.
She uses words as fast as they are acquired, and that is
the secret of success in speaking. I long to have these
sisters actively employed in this most inviting work, and
in fact they are already, though a long time may elapse
before they can take their turn in conducting our little
meetings, or talk freely with those about us.

"The family of our landlord has two ladies. They are
still of the old church, but will be friendly with us, and
we hope to do them good. They send us bouquets of
flowers with salutations, and will visit us as soon as we
are in order. To such visitors sweetmeats must be given,
and to all Armenians *coffee.*

"Our house has a high situation, overlooking a large
part of the village, a part of the city, some beautiful hills
with mosks and cypress groves, and a part of the Golden
Horn. From our sleeping-room, which is large and has
a stove, we look down upon a beautiful garden. It is
laid out most tastefully with mosaic paved walks, grass
plats, flowers, and marble statues, quite a number with
high pedestals, surmounted by female figures eight or ten
feet high. It is owned by an Armenian banker, who got
enormous wealth into his possession by having the whole
charge of the Turkish custom-house. When his fraud
was discovered, he was thrown into prison, where he has
been lying for months; in the mean time, the Turks are
disposing of his property among themselves by sales
much below the value of the articles. The fall of this
man has helped us to come into Hass Keuy without
formal opposition. . . .

"Our Bebek friends could hardly be reconciled to our
leaving there. But they and we — and will not you? —
pray that it may be for the glory of God. Pray that this

21*

house may be filled with the presence of the Holy Spirit.
We held our first little prayer meeting last week."

After the arrival of her sister, Mrs. Everett left much
of the home correspondence to her, and as her letters
contain almost the only record of the very interesting
work among the Armenians of Hass Keuy which Mr. and
Mrs. Everett were permitted to accomplish during their
brief sojourn there, we shall draw freely from them.

Miss Haynes to her parents, May 1.

"The new chapel is fitted up in our house, and services
were held there all day yesterday. In the morning, an
exposition of Scripture; in the afternoon, regular preaching, in Armenian of course. After service, monthly concert. I attended the preaching service, but could not
understand enough to keep the thread of the discourse.
The preacher, Baron Simon, has a good countenance, and
his manner is unaffected and earnest. Seraphina said
that his sermon yesterday afternoon was one of the most
pungent, searching ones that she has heard from *any one*
since she has been in Turkey. Mr. Everett saw some of
the men weeping under it! Oh that it might arouse all
who heard it to cry unto God with supplications and
tears, 'until the Spirit be poured from on high;' this was
the text. The concert was very interesting. Some of
the native helpers are turning their eyes to the waste
places in the interior, willing to leave their kindred, and
many comforts which they enjoy here, to go and preach
the gospel to their countrymen who are pleading for the
bread of life."

She writes, May 14: "We get tired sometimes, particularly Seraphina. She does not spare herself in any
thing, and often undertakes too much for her strength."

Mrs. Everett to her brother in Indiana.

"May 11, 1853.

"We are now in the midst of Armenians, and hope
and pray that our removal may not be in vain. There

has been no open opposition to us, but not many have yet ventured to visit us. . . .

"Our situation is good for Hass Keuy; but the air is not as good as that of the Bosphorus. . . .

"The general meeting of our mission is to-day having its last session; it has been one of the deepest interest. The field white for the harvest has been represented; but the laborers are too few, — two missionaries have been taken from this city for other posts. *We* seem to be fixtures; but how unworthy of our position! Oh for more strength, more zeal, faith, and love! How often do I sigh for more talent, while, alas! the one committed to me is sadly misimproved. I wish you were a missionary, March.

"Now, just think, this work, so interesting, may be interrupted, — though we *hope* not. The rumor of war has no doubt reached you; and perhaps you have been more alarmed than we, — who have seen the Russian commissioner indignantly turn his back upon the overtures of the Turkish government; the Russian embassy follow-ing suit; the Turkish fleet made ready, and the crescent-formed batteries arranged at the mouth of the Black Sea; the troops reviewed, &c. &c. Yesterday the report came to our ears that war was declared by the Czar, and the Russian fleet within forty miles of the Bosphorus. It was also said that a messenger had come to the Porte with an *ultimatum*, and must have a decided answer in twenty-four hours. Greeks and Armenians are much alarmed; they say that the Turks are arming themselves with knives, &c. in their houses. What is before us, and poor Turkey, we know not; but the Lord of Hosts is our refuge, and will be 'a very present help in time of trouble.' Sumner has just come in, but brings nothing new about war. We rather expect that it will not come, as now the English fleet is on its way to assist the Turks, and the French fleet is at the Piræus, and Russia may draw back. The Lord reigns; the hearts of kings are in his hands. The Sultan has this week issued a firman, granting new privileges to all Christian subjects. The Protestants are now on an equality with Greeks, Armenians, and Catholics."

The following letter from Mrs. Everett, besides its own intrinsic excellence, exhibits so beautifully the principles which made her so lovely as a wife, that we need not apologize for introducing it even among so much of local and missionary interest.

"HASS KEUY, July 9, 1853.

"MY DEAR SISTER LUCY: . . . From something K. wrote I felt that if I ever addressed you as Lucy Haynes it must be soon, — perhaps I am even now too late; but never mind, we are going to have a private talk. Oh, how many times have I longed to speak to you, and more than ever since dear M. came, and we have talked about you so much.

"You appear before my imagination, the young, girlish (*thoughtless*, I *almost* said) creature you were eight years ago, and I can scarcely believe that you too have added such a period to your existence. Do you shrink from the unknown future? It is not strange, — well you may; a most solemn step you are taking, — a step which involves all life's interests, and whose consequences will stretch on from time to the remotest ages of eternity. Dearest sister, are you leaning upon an Almighty arm? You have found a dear earthly friend, one worthy of your love, judging from sister M.'s account of him. Give him your heart's affections in full, when the *supreme* place has been consecrated to your God. Oh, how can you enter upon a relation so fraught with holy responsibility, without first offering yourself upon the altar of God, and receiving that preparation which can only be granted by him who is the source and fountain of all wisdom and grace? Do you think this is not the time to urge you to

give your heart to your Saviour? that it is the time to
be merry, and that serious, solemn thoughts are inap-
propriate? Oh, do not be so mistaken! This is *the*
time to make a double consecration. 'As for *me and
my house*, we will serve the Lord.' You can not make
a true offering of yourself upon the marriage altar, if
it has not been purified by the grace of God; but let
the pure incense of a sanctified love burn there, and the
heart is a treasure *worth giving* and *worth receiving*.

"My dear sister, how many things I would say to you,
— *from experience*, you know, I can speak. You are
older than I was when I was married, and perhaps better
prepared; but *I* did not think half enough about being a
good wife; perhaps I was too confident, thought *of
course* I should be a good wife . . . True, pure love,
flowing from a pure heart, would be a source of pure
joy; but alas, what erring creatures are we! Make it
your study to please your husband, Lucy; never think
that he will *at any rate* love you, and that it is his *duty*
to cherish you, now that he has chosen you as the companion of his life, whether you are lovable or not. You
have *one* to please, *one* to live for; and the happiness of
your husband and yourself is in your own power to a great
extent. Set 'traps to catch sunbeams' all about your
house; and above all, let there be an altar upon which
the sacrifice of sincere hearts shall daily rise to God.

"'In this beginning of your journey, neglect not the favor of Heaven;
Let the day of hopes fulfilled be blest by many prayers.''

From Mrs. Everett to her parents: —

"HASS KEUY, Aug. 14.

"Shall I give you a sketch of to-day? Before breakfast I prepared the month's wash, assorting and counting
clothes; afterwards attended to the children and miscel-
laneous house matters, with six guests; received a note
from our good Scotch friends in the other part of Hass

Keuy, that they would spend the afternoon with us; they
are missionaries to the Jews, and most devoted and intelligent people. They came, — Mr. and Mrs. Thompson
and their three children. In the middle of the day I
stole away and visited two of our Protestant families, one
of which buried a little child yesterday.

"While we were at our supper-table, Miss West, who
has been at Bebek, came home, bringing Susie Hamlin.
The Thompsons have left; my three babes are sleeping
near me, and I am trying to write, but my pen does not
go smoothly. . . .

"It is our vacation. After the scholars left we had a
succession of guests, until we all ran away about two
weeks since, and spent ten days at our dear Bebek. It
was a busy but delightful time. There has been special
interest in the seminary at Bebek, — three or four hopeful
conversions. You learn through the papers of the prospect of war between Russia and Turkey. We see all
sorts of preparations, and hear all sorts of rumors, — sometimes start at the sound of a cannon, — but no war has
yet come, nor probably will. The prospect yesterday
and to-day is brighter than in six weeks past. We ought
to have kept a journal of politics the last two months.
It would run : —

"Change of ministry; repairing war ships; building
new ones; reviewing troops; towing war ships to the
entrance to the Black Sea; change of ministry twice in
one day; collecting troops in the interior; great distress
in families; outrages; unsafe to travel in the interior;
soldiers sent to the frontier; forty thousand crying for
bread and clamoring for war, — 'Better to fight than sit
still and starve!' they say; arrivals of steamships, English and French; the detention of an American frigate
for our safety in case of need, &c. &c.

"The present state of affairs seems to be this : — Two

days since a steamer came into port, bringing a treaty, in which the five European powers agree in asking what Russia alone had demanded, — that is, a kind of protectorate of the Christian subjects of the Ottoman government. To-day or to-morrow there was to be a great convocation for consultation. The Turks will probably *accede*, and so we shall have peace, and the protection, (that is, native Christian sects,) not only of England, but France! Prussia! Austria! and Russia! The Lord is *our* refuge; therefore will we not fear."

From Miss Haynes, Sept. 4.

" This is the day for the commencement of our Fall term. There are some dark clouds in our horizon. Mr. Dwight and Mr. Benjamin have come as a committee to talk with Baron H., our teacher, in reference to a change in his views and feelings, which he has recently declared without making known what they are. He says that he can not conduct a meeting, or devotions in school, as he has been in the habit of doing. It is feared that it will be necessary to discharge him entirely; and if so, it will probably be a difficult thing to supply his place. It is very trying and painful, as he has long been in the school, and a consistent member of the church; though his sister has often remarked, and Mr. E. the same, that there was a lack of spirituality about him. He is a licensed but not ordained preacher. How it will end we know not, and perhaps I ought not to have mentioned it in this stage of the affair. There seems to be an unusual degree of interest among the members of the church generally. A week ago to-day a special prayer meeting was held at Pera, and we heard that one of our older school-girls was distressed about her soul. Our congregation is increasing in numbers. Yesterday more than fifty were present in the afternoon, including but two of the school. Seraphina attended all the services in the chapel, helped in

the care of the children, and heard the little Armenian
girls recite their Scripture lessons and hymns; this, too,
when she had been sick all the week, — (mercury at 84°,
3 P. M.)   You can not imagine how much she resembles
her mother.   She looks tired and worn to-day."

CHAPTER XXIII.

IN September they had the happiness to welcome Mr. and Mrs. Goodell back to their missionary home. Soon after their return it was decided that they should make Hass Keuy their residence; and Mr. and Mrs. Everett found themselves, to their great delight, again closely associated with the dear family with whom they had spent their first four years in Constantinople so happily. Mrs. Everett communicates the following cheering news respecting the school to one of her sisters: —

"September 22.

"You will rejoice to hear that a new song has been put in the mouths of several of the pupils. Ever since the term commenced, there has been a good state of feeling manifested. One of the girls, during the vacation, had deep convictions of sin. Her feelings were deep and tender when she returned, and others soon joined her in seeking the Saviour; six think they have found him. One, a girl from Tokat, who was almost in despair for three or four days before she found comfort, came with a beaming face and said, 'I have laid all my sins on Christ.' That is the secret, dear Maria, is it not? We must come directly to Christ, and lay our souls on him

" ' Just as I am, I come, I come.'

22

"How can we praise the Lord sufficiently for such unspeakable blessings? It seems to me that we are indebted in great measure to the earnest pleading in our behalf of a good countryman of ours, — a Mr. Roberts, from the State of New York. He is a whole-souled Christian. He was a very worldly man, — was prostrated by the measles, — lay upon his back five years, — during which time he vowed to the Lord to serve him as faithfully as he had done the world. As soon as he recovered he commenced his work, laboring for the county poor in his own State; then going west as a colporter; then among the Indians; then to Panama to labor for the souls and bodies of the sick; then in California; then at the Five Points, New York. He at length formed the plan of distributing the Scriptures in Rome. He earned passage money to England; when he had remained there sometime, a friend gave him a passage to Italy. His principle is to take no money except as presents. He lives in the most simple manner, and dresses in coarse cloth. When he was driven out of Rome, he went to Malta, where he sold many Bibles to Italians; and when the heat there became oppressive, a friend gave him a free passage to Constantinople. Here he has sold very many books, — on board vessels and among seamen especially.

"What the poor Turks are coming to, is a question for time to decide; all events are under the control of Infinite Wisdom. There is now no help for it; war is inevitable. The Turks are mad for a fight, and the government, *nolens volens*, must submit to the will of the people. Good preparations have been made, so say good judges, who have been to examine the fleet and the fortifications on the frontier. They are still collecting soldiers. Mr. Everett says two were taken from our vicinity yesterday. What distress all over the country in the families of those taken off!

"In case of war, and it is virtually declared, we may remain undisturbed here in the city. The fighting will probably be in the provinces. We have no war ships in the harbor at present, but there are several of the French and English, and we could at any time find protection under the English flag. If the decision had been for peace, there would have been great disturbance here in Constantinople, arising from the dissatisfaction of the people,— *i. e.* the common people,— who have a hope that their condition will be bettered by a war. But it will probably be, — 'change the place and keep the pain.'

"My dear M——, perhaps you are not pleased with all this talk about war; neither do we like it, and we go about our work as though the foundation of God stood sure, as indeed it does. He is Lord over all

"Mr. Goodell has engaged a house very near us. Will it not be delightful to us to have them as associates again? They say they must send for one of their daughters to come and teach the children here. Mr. G. and Mrs. G. too, tell us many things about America,—*changes in every thing.* They think girls in our country are very delicate. Mr. Goodell is quite alarmed at the prospect of the race running out, and there is a surplus of young ladies in New England, so they are forming societies for sending them West. I am glad we get a small share at the East; more are needed.

"There are girls here, such as they are, but not enough good ones, — not educated, cultivated, intelligent ones. Will it not surprise you to know that one of the native Armenian pastors has married a girl *who could not read?* 'Tell it not in Gath.' His mother could not find one among our educated girls who suited her, and so she chose this one. It was a great risk; but she has learned to read, and is well disposed to religious things. You know, among the Orientals, the mother finds a wife for her sons, and usually the brothers seek husbands for their sisters, or engage them when they are sought. It is not the custom for a son to marry until the daughters are disposed of.

"One of our first scholars is married to a man in Broosa. The brother of her husband lost his wife, — she was an unenlightened woman; he is a pious man, and in seeking a second companion, resolved to take one who should be pious and educated, as well as good-looking. As the brothers own a house together, and the bride would be a companion to our pupil, *her* mother was deeply interested to find one suited to her tastes and disposition; but among our Protestant girls, those they wished, they could not get one, and they *must* have somebody.

"The person seeking a wife is in the city, and the mother of the brother's wife. They wished to go to Broosa next week, if they can finish their business. So the mother makes it known among the Armenians of the old church, that a wife is wanted for a young Protestant, one who will go to Broosa to live, attend Protestant service, &c., and lo! eight or ten are offered. The selection is made, on the recommendation of friends, of course, — a young girl of seventeen, for the widower with a child of four years. The mother of the brother's wife went to see the girl, was pleased, but thought a Protestant should see the person he was going to marry, and so arranged for their meeting. She told me the story last evening with great satisfaction, — '*I made her open her own mouth, and say she was willing to go!*' Another innovation upon Oriental custom.

"You see, dear Maria, what a large letter I have written to you. . . .

"May the presence of the blessed Comforter ever be with you, and if the world is sometimes dark, may the brightness of the future compensate for all. You must look above and beyond."

From Miss Haynes.

"Mr. Dwight came over and attended the Thursday evening meeting. Three persons came from the family of our landlord, who have never been present at a Protestant service before. Two others of the family have been in a few times. One Tuesday evening two of the family came in with a man who is one of the most intelligent and influential in the village. He has been to England, and speaks English. Mr. Everett had much religious conversation with them, and had family prayers before they left. The woman appeared much affected, weeping during the whole prayer. She is fifty years old, and probably never heard an extempore prayer before. Mr. Dwight spent the night, and the next morning went into the other part of the house with Mr. Everett, and again conversed a long time with them and another partially enlightened man who came in.

.   .   .   .

"October 10. Seraphina has been to call on some Armenian families this afternoon. One woman she found in a very serious state of mind. Mr. Everett saw her on Saturday evening, and she told him that she was so much troubled about her sins that she could not sleep. She is the mother of the young man who united with the church soon after we came here. Annah and Horopsima, our Tokat girls, spend their vacations there, and are much beloved by the family. About three weeks ago, sister and I called there, and Seraphina told her something of Horopsima's experience, — her great distress on account of her sins, which almost overpowered her for several days, and her exceeding joy after she had laid all her sins on Christ. The woman listened attentively but said little, although she told her son to bring the Testament for Seraphina to read. She read a portion, and remarked on

22*

it, and what was quite gratifying to us, two young ladies were there on a visit, and heard it all. They seemed glad to meet us, and I saw their eyes moisten while Seraphina was talking to Horopsima. They have never been to Protestant service. The woman has been many times, and has heard enough to know her duty. We hope the Spirit of God is now showing her what she ought to do.

"There has been a very interesting conversion at Pera recently; a man who has heard the gospel for four years. The Lord showed him his sins, and he was in such agony that he could do nothing but cry for mercy. Then he says, 'God gave me the Saviour.' Such cases show that the Lord has not entirely withdrawn his Spirit. Seraphina said the other day, after conversing with one of the girls, 'I do not see how any one can doubt the reality of the new birth.' Six of these dear ones give evidence of a work of grace upon their hearts; several others are quite serious, and seem to be seeking new hearts. It has been a great pleasure to me to be able to say even a few words to them, and to understand something of their feelings from their own lips.

"Eubrakse's sister, Mahkteki, who was one of the five who went to talk with Seraphina on our fast day, said to me, on Friday morning, that she was happy; Christ was near to her, and she was near to him; that she loved to pray, &c., and, on the evening of the same day, she went to the door of the room where sister was talking with one or two of the girls, and said, 'Mayn't I come, too?' and, when sister asked her of her feelings, she was quite ready to give a reason for the hope that was in her, yet with meekness and fear. She is a very lovable girl, and now doubly so. A few days since, she came to Mr. Everett, and with tears asked him some questions about grieving the Holy Spirit, alluding to a sermon which he preached two weeks before. She asked several questions showing that she was becoming acquainted with the Christian warfare.

"With all our rejoicing, we are made very sad by the defection of Baron Hechadoor. I wrote mother about him, and now that we have learned his views more fully, our worst fears are realized. He is not far from infidelity, though we have a faint hope that he is not confirmed. He is capable of doing much harm, but the Lord can take care of his own truth, and vindicate his own cause. He is our trust. ' Though *wars* should rise up against us, we will not fear.' "

From Mrs. Everett.

"November 24. *Thanksgiving* it has been with us, and we suppose with you, too, though our last papers give us no information on the subject. There was a plan made for all our American families to meet to-day at Mr. Hamlin's for a sermon and picnic dinner, but the notice was too late, and the distance too great, and the weather too unsettled, for us in Hass Keuy to join, so we, the Everetts, went home to papa Goodell's, taking our goose and pies along with us; and we have had a very pleasant day. After tea, I came home and put my three weary chicks to bed. Mr. E. and Mr. Goodell came for the Thursday evening meeting.

"How much have we experienced of the loving kindness of God during the past year in special blessings, — the arrival of our dear sister and a teacher, the precious loan of darling Susie coming to this village where our school has been so richly blessed, and so wide a door of usefulness has been opened to us. . . .

"You are doubtless looking with more than usual interest for tidings from us. Hostilities you knew had commenced. The Turkish forces crossed the Danube. Several battles have been fought, in which, from accounts, the Turks have done well. The last two days, the reports say that there is an armistice; the king of Belgium is going to mediate.

"You will be glad to hear that we have encouragement in our missionary work, especially here in Hass Keuy. The Sabbath services are well attended. Thursday evening, we have a meeting. Tuesday afternoon, sewing circle and meeting for the females. Saturday evening, school prayer meeting. Friday evening, singing. We have now not only a good number of Protestant families to visit, but several families of the higher class of Armenians — bankers — are seeking intercourse with us for the purpose of religious inquiry. Several evenings, we have been invited to their houses, and Mr. Everett has had opportunities of speaking fully and freely upon the most spiritual and practical points of Christian doctrine. Several persons seem to be earnestly seeking the narrow way; they have laid aside their fear to so great an extent as to go through the streets with us in the evening, having lanterns with two or three candles carried before us. Oh for the Holy Spirit, to convince them of sin, and lead them to Christ!

"Our school is increasing in numbers. We have thirty boarders; six day-scholars. Miss West and Melvina are making good progress in Armenian, and are much beloved by all. I should love to have you come and see us as we are. How much we could *tell* you that we can never write. My moments for writing are *very* few. My three children take *so* much of my time, — one about as much as another. *To train them,* — what a work!"

From Miss Haynes.

"November 15. Mr. Everett and Seraphina have gone to visit at the house of an Armenian whom we met last week in the other part of our house. The family of our landlord called, and went with them. The visit was planned beforehand, and Mr. E. invited for the sake of having a conversation about the gospel. There are some half dozen or more of the relatives and particular friends of our landlord, who are interested in the truth, and wish to talk and inquire, but are not ready to declare themselves Protestants. Nicodemus-like, they will come by night, plan these evening visits, and invite Mr. Everett.

"One evening last week, our landlord sent for Mr. E. and Seraphina, and I went too. We found five persons from other families, and four generations of that family, assembled. The old grandmother over ninety years old, her son, Hohannes Agha, and his wife, their eldest son, Gurel Agha, his wife and two youngest children, and the brother next in age, Hampartsoon Agha. These are the members of the family whom we usually see. The younger brothers, the ones who annoyed Mr. E. when he was taking the house, do not make their appearance; Mr. Everett sees them at times, and says he intends to go into their rooms, and make their acquaintance. We are treated very politely and ceremoniously, coffee and sweetmeats served in Turkish style. By the way, I have learned to drink the Turkish coffee, so that I can dispose of my little cup very easily, without milk, thick and black! The little girl, three years old, went round and took the cups from the guests, and I can not describe the grace with which she did it. In the act of taking the cup, she took hold of the hand, and touched it to her lips, then released the hand, and retained the cup in her own. Thus early are these children trained in their manners.

"One of the guests was the finest Armenian lady I have seen. She had a handsome face, fair and fresh, also bright and intelligent in expression. In conversing with her, Seraphina found her more intelligent than any Armenian woman she has before known. She reads the Bible and other books, which is very uncommon for a woman who has not been instructed by the missionaries. The women of our landlord's family can not read a word.

Even Gurel Agha's wife, the bride, does not know her letters, although she owns diamonds and precious stones to the value of four or five hundred dollars, which she had brushed up to wear to a wedding a few weeks ago, and expended forty or fifty dollars for new dresses to wear on the occasion. But I have wandered from my main subject, — the visit.

"Mr. Everett talked much with the men, and they asked questions, not in a caviling spirit, but as though they really wished to find out truth and duty.

"Last evening Hampartsoom Agha came in, and by asking a question, brought forward the subject of the new birth, and continued in earnest consultation with Mr. E. and Baron Sarkis, who happened to be here, until half past ten o'clock. Mr. E. preached to him faithfully the gospel way of salvation, while he sat with his eyes fixed upon him, almost breathless, at one pause saying, 'It is a difficult thing,'—at another, 'If one does not believe, he will be lost.' He seemed like the young man in the gospel, not far from the kingdom of heaven. Mr. E. says he will yet be brought in. It will be a great blessing to the family if he is, as he is the best educated, and most intelligent, —amiable and obliging: he is their favorite.

"Last evening Mr. Everett and Seraphina came home delighted with their visit. There were there eight men of high rank in the village, and about the same number of women. At first they talked of the news of the day, war, &c. The woman of the house said she did not wish to hear about the war. The other females being seated near her, she said, 'We will talk by ourselves, and let the men talk together.' But soon she perceived a change in the conversation. Mr. E. was answering some question on a religious subject. She instantly exclaimed, 'Ah, there is preaching, let us attend,' and she sat with her head stretched forward, to catch every word that Mr. Everett said about the gospel way of salvation. Hampart-

soom was there; and by asking questions and making remarks, led Mr. E. to go over the same ground that he did
with him on Tuesday evening. Three or four times in the
course of the evening, they all laid down their pipes, and
listened with the most serious attention, while Mr. E.
preached to them repentance and faith in Christ, in the
most plain and pointed manner. Seraphina said she could
hardly refrain from weeping at the sight. She felt that
the truth was really affecting the hearts of at least one or
two of this interesting group. The woman of the house
she has never seen before, and she was much pleased with
her. She is anxious to come to the preaching service
in the chapel. The matter was discussed among them in
the course of the evening, and Seraphina encouraged
them to come. One said, 'Who attends? Are there
many?' Another said, 'Well, how shall we go? Shall
we put on yashmak and Ferequ?' 'Yes,' sister said,
'put on your yashmak, &c.' Another woman wished to
send three children to our school, and one to Mr. Hamlin's, if they could be admitted."

From Mrs. Everett.

" HASS KEUY, Dec. 13, 1853.

"MY DEAR SISTER K.: We have all of us mercies
to sing of, — we are not in the midst of the horrors
of war, though it has come near. A very disastrous
naval battle was fought last week in the harbor of
Sinope, on the Black Sea. You may get accurate information of the battle, and may not, from the news-
papers. If you should see a letter in the 'Tronler,'
from Constantinople, it would probably be from Mr.
Dwight, and of course, reliable. Steamers have been sent
to Sinope, from the English and French fleets, and the
report is like this: —

"'A part of the Turkish fleet, eleven ships, but none of
the largest, were anchored in the bay of Sinope. Three
Russian ships of war saw them there, and anchored out-

side, in the mean time, sending a small brig across the sea
for the fleet. Under the cover of the fog, the Russian
fleet came on strong,—three three-deckers, and two two-
deckers were placed in a line opposite the poor, helpless,
devoted Turks, awaiting the dispersion of the fog. Who
can imagine the dismay that fell upon those hopeless souls,
as the curtain was lifted up! The Russians immediately
gave a broadside, pouring, as some say, 'red-hot shot'
directly into the Turkish ships. Any other people would
have cut their cables, and drifted ashore, that all might
not be lost; so says an English officer. But the Turks
are mad for a fight, and fought like tigers. The 'Bear'
had the advantage. Every one of the vessels (frigates,
corvettes, &c.) was lost, and *four thousand* men are
missing,— some, perhaps 150, are taken prisoners,— some
were drowned in attempting to swim on shore, but the
greater part were hurled into eternity, either by the blowing up or sinking of the ships. The Turkish quarter of
Sinope was nearly destroyed by fire. The people of the
town fled, from fear, into the interior, and while they
were absent, robbers came in from the mountains, and
pillaged their homes. This is war! Oh, how awful!
How many widows and fatherless ones cry for food, and
mourn their dead!'

"As Mr. Goodell was going to Pera, on Saturday, as
many as 150 women had assembled near the barracks,
and were screaming and wringing their hands.

" The Russian ships remained a day or two at Sinope,
for repairs, and then returned to their own port.

"Dec. 14. Melvina must have told you what encouragement we have in our new field of labor. 'How
hardly shall a rich man enter into the kingdom. All
things are possible with God.' Some of these Nicode-
muses may still sit at the feet of Jesus, and permit others
to come and listen to his blessed teachings. A few
days since, two young ladies spoke to our assistant teach-

ers, as they were passing, and asked them to visit them. 'But you do not come to us,' was the reply. 'No, we can not,' they said, 'the rich go and tell many things that they have heard, but if we were to go we should be persecuted.'

"There is a lady near us, who seems not far from the kingdom. She and her husband have long been partially enlightened, but still attended the old church. Their son was converted in Mr. Hamlin's seminary, and has been the means of establishing family worhip at home, and is very anxious for the conversion of his mother. She feels her sinfulness, and sometimes is distressed. She knows she is lost in her present state, notwithstanding she has reformed her outward life in many respects. For example, she does not mean to say what is not true. 'Oh,' she says, 'we are brought up to think it is no sin to tell lies sometimes; it can not be avoided; *alas! it runs in our veins.*' And so it does.

"Our scholars are almost daily increasing. The 'Board' give us an appropriation for twenty-five boarders the coming year. We have thirty now, and eight day-scholars."

23

CHAPTER XXIV.

IT has been remarked that Mrs. Everett's letters were
fewer and shorter the last two or three years of her life;
but one who knew her many cares and duties during those
last years, wonders that she found time to write so much.
"Haste not,— rest not," seemed to be her motto. There
was no mark of negligence or hasty performance on anything to which she put her hand. Perfect neatness and
order reigned in her household; her children were always
fondly watched, and no children could be more neatly and
properly clothed, though all their garments, as well as
most, if not all of her own, she cut and prepared herself,
besides cutting and fitting those of many of the scholars,
and taking a large share in the preparation and direction
of fancy work done in the school, and sewing for the
poor. Though Miss West was now able to take the principal charge of the school, Mrs. Everett still instructed
the Greek class; besides which, she continued to talk and
pray almost daily with the pupils in turn, to visit the sick
and the poor, as also to make many visits, both among the
Protestant Armenians, and those who still adhered to the
old church, for the purpose of religious conversation.
The relief which her sister was able to afford in her domestic cares, instead of being used for rest, which she
really needed, was turned to the account of visiting, and

in this way she accomplished much — more than can now be known — for the Redeemer's cause, after their removal to Hass Keuy. She was seldom absent from a meeting, either English or Armenian, held at their station, and she entered, with all her soul, into every prayer meeting held, either by the missionary or Armenian sisters, whenever she was where she could join them. Yet it was difficult, in seeing her, and in visiting her, to realize how much she was doing. She was always social, so happy to welcome her friends, so ready to return their visits, and her lovely countenance always wore an expression so cheerful and amiable, that one not intimately acquainted with her, and with the missionary work in Constantinople, would hardly have suspected that a larger than usual share of care and responsibility was borne by her, but might rather have supposed that a less than ordinary amount had fallen to her lot.

Mrs. Everett to Mrs. Clark, Framingham, Mass.

HASS KEUY, Jan. 16, 1854.

"The books you sent, dear cousin, have given us very great pleasure. What interest hovers over 'The Last Leaf.' The bereaved husband has done well in the delineation of a peculiar, but lovely character.

"Have you seen 'Light on the Dark River'? We are reading it with tender interest. The subject of it was very dear to us. How many bright examples we have of true, fervent, living piety, and best of all, a perfect example in Christ, our Saviour, — but oh, we follow him 'afar off,' and so get little of the joy and peace a *close walk* with him would secure. Cares distract, the world allures, and our souls grovel in the dust.

"Dear cousin, I was very weary last evening, having just returned from our dear Bebek, where we had spent a few days of our vacation. The last term of our school was one of unusual prosperity. Miss West is taking her place as teacher. . . . . .

"The best of Heaven's blessings has been granted us in the outpouring of the Divine Spirit upon our pupils. I could give you many interesting particulars, had I time. We have much to encourage us in our work in this village. The doors of Armenian houses have been opened to us, — even those of the richest and most aristocratic families, — and some persons have manifested a real interest in the truth, as pressed upon their hearts and consciences by Mr. Everett. We feel most grateful that our steps were directed to this place.

"The prejudices of Armenians seem to be softened. Some days since, a child died in a family where the parents are convinced of the gospel truths, but still have a connection with *the* church. They called the priest to bury the child, but exceptionable parts of the service were omitted. The son, a youth of seventeen, a member of Mr. Hamlin's Seminary, formerly, and very pious, preached a little sermon after they had performed their part. The child was then carried to the grove, in a *covered* coffin, *without candles and the cross* preceding. Last Sabbath a Protestant child was buried in the Armenian burying-ground, with the permission of the Church Session. . . .

"Our work is not at all interrupted by the very unsettled and uncertain state of this empire. We do not know what may be in store for us, but can trust Infinite Wisdom to direct in all things. Much as we wish to see you all, we do not wish to go home."

From Miss Haynes.

"It was a matter of great wonder that the Protestants could bury their dead in peace, in the Armenian burying-ground. I saw the little band from my window, as they left the grave. A number of boys and young men collected about the place, and threw a few stones at the grave, but committed no other violence. We hear that they threaten to dig up the body if another is buried there. The Armenian Christmas, and other great feast days, have just passed, and the church hierarchies, in their zealous vigilance over their people, have created quite a panic among them in reference to us, so there seems to be something of a reaction just at present. They are more shy of us; but it may not last long. The work will doubtless go forward, if we labor in faith. Mr. E. has had interesting evening visits, even during the past week. The young man of whom I wrote, who came to service, and was so much affected as to go home with Baron Sarkis, continues in the good way, — conducts worship in the family in the presence of boarders and guests, and comes to the morning prayer meeting and prays there. He is a silk merchant, having a shop in the city, and, being a man of considerable learning and natural ability, and moreover bold to speak his mind, he can exert much influence among his associates.

"Another thing that gives us joy, is Baron Hachadoor's return to the truth. He wishes to come to the communion, and is ready to confess his great sin in falling into such errors, — and does confess, in personal conversation, that he has been doing wrong, and that he found no peace when he was in that condition. He came to the morning prayer meeting on Monday.

"In looking back to the time of our coming here, I think we can see great progress. This morning meeting has increased from one or two, to six or eight, — and the Thursday evening meeting from six or eight (from without) to twenty and twenty-five."

From Mrs. Everett.

"March 20, 1854.

"MY DEAR PARENTS: You will pardon me if I commence my letter to you by giving an extract from one written by Dr. Anderson to this mission.

"'It is better to trust in the Lord than to put confidence in princes.' Whatever comes, dear brethren, we pray you do nothing rashly. Stand at your posts till the last moment. If you must flee, let it be to the nearest point, and only till you can return again. If you can not labor at Erzeroom, or at Trebizond, you can, it may be, at Erzenyan, Arabkir, Divrik, Sivas, Diarbeker, or a dozen other places. If driven from one city or post, you may find refuge in another. We can sustain you easier on a full salary in Turkey, or in its neighborhood, than on half the sum, or even less, at home. Were you all broken up for the time, yet, if you nobly lay siege to the country, while not able to enter it, the spirit of the churches at home will be sustained, and will even gain activity and energy. The powers of darkness are struggling, it may be, in the *great battle*, to recover ground they have lost in these lands of sacred associations, and to drive you all away. That, I take it, is the grand point at issue, and not the questions debated by the 'Four Powers.'

" ' Therefore, dear brethren, hold your ground at all hazards. Guard yourselves, your wives, and your little ones by all proper means, but don't be driven away. The heavenly intelligences are interested in the effect of these impending conflicts of great nations, chiefly as they relate to you. Stand firm in the strength of the Most High, and he will give you the victory. I need not suggest to you how important to your infant churches, and to the Reformation and the Protestant community in Turkey it is, that not one of you show any signs of fear or faintness. It is even more important to them than to the churches at home. Nor is it unimportant to your brethren at the Missionary House, and to your brethren of the Pruden- tial Committee ; 'For now we live, if ye stand fast in the Lord,' and our prayer is, that the Lord Jesus will be with you in whatever storm he may allow to break upon you, and that he will make all things conduce to your happiness, and to the furtherance of the work he has given you to do.'

"Is not this noble? worthy of one who holds a high

position under our Great Captain ? But you must not think because I have written this, that any of our number have been inclined to faint or flee, or that there has been any cause for such a course. Although great preparations for a great war are going forward, still there have been no disturbances here, and may be none, unless the Greeks should make some demonstrations as partisans of Russia, which they will by no means dare to do, as they would thus run the risk of being massacred *en masse.* The Turks here had a great trial in submitting to the recent requisitions of the English and French. A special conference was requested. Reschid Pasha was made Minister Plenipotentiary for the business. At his palace the Sultan met the English and French embassadors, the head of the Moslem priesthood, &c. The ultimatum was presented; that they sign a treaty guaranteeing to the Christian subjects of the Ottoman government right to give evidence in court against Turks, — that they (the Christians) hold property in the same manner as Turks, — that the capitation tax should be removed, &c. The Sultan and his party remonstrated, — it was against their religion.

"The embassadors gave as a consequence of refusal that in eighteen hours the Russian fleet would be in the Bosphorus. There was no escape. The Sultan gave assent, from which there was no appeal, as he is considered a successor of Mahomet. The paper was signed, after a whole night's conference. The following day it was flying on the wings of steam toward England, and not even the Prime Minister knew a breath of the affair. But all things have moved on quietly since it is known.

"Barracks are being prepared for English troops here, and the English ships here are to bring stone and lime for fortifying themselves in the *Crimea.* Is not this bold ? But they will doubtless succeed in planting themselves on the shores of the Black Sea.

Oh, but the horrors of war!—one shudders!

"Famine will undoubtedly accompany war, and then if disease should be added, how much distress, how many souls rushing into eternity! You must not be anxious about us, except so far as to lead you to offer supplication in our behalf to him who is our only refuge and hope.

"Our work continues interesting and promising. The school is full,—thirty-five boarders,—and many of them are large girls, and serious. They love prayer, and try to act as become followers of Jesus, but they need constant advice and instruction. Several small girls are in all respects quite dependent upon us. We all have our hands, heads, and hearts full. Our *heads* get weary,—alas for me! I do wish I possessed a quiet spirit. Imagine yourself, dear mother, with your disposition to care for everybody and every thing, in my place, and you will understand how difficult it is always to be quiet, cheerful, kind, patient, and all that is 'lovely, and of good report.'

"What should I do without our good, quiet, patient sister M. in this house, with forty-five persons, my three little ones, and other missionary work! I venture to say we should not, could not have endured,—but the Lord provides. Miss West is doing nobly, but the educational department is enough for her.

.   .   .   .   .   .

"We have had a visit from Rev. Mr. Granger, a Baptist clergyman from Providence, R. I. He is returning from a visit to the missions in Burmah, &c. Last Sabbath evening he gave an account of the work of the Lord there, in our chapel, and it was translated into Armenian. Mrs. Everett to Mrs. Fuller, Cambridgeport, Mass.

HASS KEUY, April 14, 1854.

"'Surely, goodness and mercy have followed me *all* the days of my life;' but the last year has been peculiarly

one of blessing. I wrote you, did I not, that one of my
dear sisters might come and join me in this foreign land,
and in the good work of our Master here ? And, in great
goodness, she was brought hither, and is now sitting by
my side.

. . . .

" Our house here is very commodious, and our family very
large. We have thirty-five boarding scholars, and twelve
day scholars. You can imagine, to some extent, what a
care such a school, house, and family involve ; but you
will not compare it with a boarding-school in America.
We have to attend a good deal to the clothing of our
girls. They do various kinds of needle-work, which we
dispose of for their benefit. I could write very much, but
time fails me.

" The blessing of God has been granted to us most
graciously. You, perhaps, have seen a notice of the
revival in our school, which Mr. Everett copied from my
notes. It was published in the Journal of Missions,
New York Observer, &c.

" Three of the dear girls united with the church last
Sabbath. Three others have been accepted, and we have
hope that three or four more are the children of God.

. . . . . .

" You will be pleased to know that our dear father, Mr.
Goodell, is our neighbor; it is so pleasant to have such
associates. They come and take supper with us one
evening in the week, and one we go to them. We have
our singing and prayer meetings together. We occasionally visit and receive visits from our dear friends in Pera
and Bebek. All are in health and quietness at present,
but what a fearful prospect is before this land and all
Europe! *War*, and not merely the rumor of war, reaches
our ears. In this city we do not expect to be disturbed,
though much excitement, irregularities, and distress, particularly for food, are already experienced. The Greeks,

who are not subjects of the Turkish government, to the number of thirty or forty thousand, have been ordered to leave for their country. Houses and business must be given up,—servants, all, all must go.

"Soldiers are collecting from all parts of the country. English and French ships of war are gathering here, and going to the Black Sea. The Russian army has crossed the Danube, and is remaining there for reinforcement; and what a host they will present! A fearful struggle is coming on. The English think to enter the Crimea, and at the same time fighting has commenced in the Baltic.

"Oh, if we could not fall back on an Almighty arm that rules and governs all, would not our hearts fail with the heart-rending events transpiring around us, though the roar of battle should not reach our ears! If Russia should gain domination here, the progress of truth and light might be arrested, but we do not, *can not* believe that God will permit such an event. The present seems to be a time for sowing the good seed broadcast. The British and Foreign Bible Society is sending out a large supply of the Scriptures, to be distributed among their own, and also foreign soldiers.

"I must mention a most interesting prayer meeting that was held this week in Pera, with reference to the present state of this country. There was a large attendance of the Protestant residents, American, English, Scotch, and an humble, confiding trust in the King of kings was manifested, while prayer was made for kings and rulers, the army, and ourselves."

From the same.

"HASS KEUY, June 7, 1854.

"MY VERY DEAR PARENTS: The days and weeks will slip by, and leave my earnest purpose to write 'home' all unfulfilled. Ah! the truth is, your childish child has *another* home, and one that not only demands or calls forth her heart's strongest affections, but also requires all her mental energy and physical strength. Who would have thought that Providence ever would call me to act in such a sphere? It is a comfort and support, when sometimes I am ready to faint, that the All-Wise *did* ordain what has come to pass, and that he will still strengthen and bless even one so unworthy.

"Miss West and Malvina are every day becoming more established in their respective departments, and we, who have been just able to bear up under our burden, feel it greatly lightened. Our life is any thing but a quiet one, — in a sense we are public property. 'No man liveth to himself,' or should; *we could not*, if we tried. At the same time we have personal comforts and enjoyments innumerable. *One* more we long for, namely, tidings from home, from *you* and our dear brothers and sisters. Why are our hearts left to faint within us? Two months you have been in your new home, and no word of remembrance has come from thence to us. . . .

"We are in the midst of General Meeting. There are from abroad, Messrs. Ladd and Morgan from Smyrna, Mr. Schneider from Aintab, Mr. Powers from Marsovan, and Mr. Bliss and family from Trebizond; the latter came some time since for health; they have been our guests for a few weeks. What a trial, to be feeble and laid aside from one's work! I do pity them, as I do all such, even those who have their faces set towards our own dear native land. You must pray that we may not be obliged to go home.

"The meeting, thus far, has been a quiet one. The reports from the different stations were full of interest. Yesterday was held the semiannual meeting of the Auxiliary Bible Society. It was deeply interesting, — held in the large saloon of the English Hotel. The audience was worthy of a Christian land, — highly refined and literary. Twenty or more clergymen sat in a large semicircle in front of the assembly, — American, English

Scotch, Irish, &c. missionaries, chaplain to embassy, and
chaplain to the army. Mr. Spence, our minister, has been
elected President of the Society, and was in the chair.
Mr. Goodell opened the meeting with prayer; Mr. Spence
made a finished speech; the report was read, and then
followed resolutions and speeches. Mr. Schneider spoke
most effectively, portraying the wonderful things God has
wrought by means of his word and Spirit in Aintab and
vicinity. One of the chaplains literally poured out his
Irish heart, and Mr. Schauffler soared, and bore his hearers with him, far above the earth. And then, how interesting! an officer in the army, in his red jacket, and leaning on his sword, spoke from the depths of his pious soul.
The hours flew by, and all seemed equally unconscious of
fatigue and heat. I have made my story all too short to
convey any idea of the interest of the meeting. May its
fruits be plenteous!

"To-day the meeting of the Mission was in our parlor,
and the question there decided which was discussed last
year, Mr. Van Lennep's going to Tokat. They go as
soon as they can make preparations. It is a trial to them,
and we are very sorry to have them leave us. Mr.
Dwight expects to remove his family into the city proper,
to a house that has been bought for a chapel.

"Our school is increasing in numbers and interest.
The general missionary work continues interesting. Our
chapel was *full* last Sabbath. What we shall do by and
by we *think*, but can not tell."

June 21, Miss Haynes writes : —

"One girl left the school to be married last week. A
widower came on from Broosa, and chose this girl of fifteen, and her mother gave her consent and took the girl
home from school before the subject was lisped to *her*.
Poor thing. I pitied her from the bottom of my heart.
Her cousins went over to see her after she was informed
of the engagement; on their return I asked them how

she felt; if she wished to go. They looked very sad, and said, no, she did not wish it. The man is pious, and I hope will be kind. The girl is large and womanly in her appearance, and very good-tempered, but I fear has not self-reliance enough to have the care of housekeeping.

"The school will be filled up with new scholars, and consequently will be harder to manage. Ten have already been received from Armenian families, — that is, from families who have not become Protestant. Some of these come entirely uninstructed in reading, and even in the common rules of morality. It is therefore no small affair to indoctrinate them into a regard for truth, honesty, unselfishness, &c. The girl who has just left to be married is the one who said, when reproved for lying, that 'she did not know that it was contrary to the rules of the school!'

"One, two, or three new scholars drop into the day school occasionally; one seeing his neighbor not afraid to send, says he will send his, too. Seraphina called this week to see the woman who by her opposition kept her children so long from the school. She went in the evening with Mr. Everett, and the woman kept herself in the other room until Seraphina took a light and went to find her. She was sitting in the midst of the beds of eight sleeping children spread out upon the floor. (They roll the beds up in the morning, and put them in closets.) She received Seraphina very pleasantly, and talked for some time about sending the little girls to school, &c., the three little boys come regularly. She will send two girls if we will take them both as boarders. Seraphina consents to take the elder, but thinks the second still too young to come except as a day scholar. Seraphina told her if her children came and learned to read, and became interested in it, she would herself wish to learn, and *would* learn. She expressed the greatest astonishment,

24

saying, 'What! *I* learn to read!' and laughed at the idea.

"Kevosk, the youth who preached at the funeral of his little brother, has been given up by his father to the work of preaching the gospel. He has been an interested attendant of the Monday morning prayer meeting from its commencement. . . .

"One woman who has not been to our service or conversed with a missionary, somehow obtained a translation of Doddridge's 'Rise and Progress,' and read it. The priests were in the habit of calling frequently at the house of this woman. One day, after she had been reading Doddridge and become much interested, she told the priest that he did no good by his visits; that he came and talked about the war a little, then always called for his *brandy*, and left. That was the way he always did. Then she produced her book, and told him to read *that;* that would show him his duty. The priest took the book, read a little, and laid it down, looking ashamed and condemned. Mr. E. learned this fact through the family of Partiko, who has lately come over to our side. When I went to the female meeting last week, the woman of the house where it was held told me of an interesting conversation which she had with a Jew. He listened to her attentively, while she talked to him of salvation by Christ alone. She was quite delighted about it. She feels that there is encouragement to pray if there are but two or three to unite."

Mrs. Everett to Mrs. Clark.

"HASS KEUY, July 17, 1854.

"MY DEAR COUSIN: . . . When distracted, weary, and worn, I do sometimes long to be a child again, and, free as a bird, hie to the home nest. Desponding thoughts and feelings are quite unnatural to me; but I actually cried this morning, and told Malvina I did wish I could go somewhere, and be *taken care of* a while; pardon me, do. . . .

"Strength, health, in an unusual measure have been given me, and precious opportunities to labor in our Master's vineyard, and I would call upon my soul and all that is within me to praise the Lord. The summer vacation of our school has commenced, and our dear pupils are dispersed.

"The good work in this village has progressed much in the last year, but our desires are by no means filled. Lord, increase our faith! I should love to give you particulars in regard to our labors here, but alas! my pen almost *rusts* in my desk, while my heart burns to commune with the distant loved ones. . . .

"Miss West is doing admirably as a teacher, and M. takes a good share in the care of the house and needlework; and still, if we could each double our capacity to do and bear, *all*, *all* would be most fully employed. My dear children are requiring more and more attention. Ellie is nearly six; Sumner, four; and baby, Susie, seventeen months. . . .

"The sad tidings from the war reaches you through the public prints. Our work is not interrupted by it, nor our peace disturbed, save by mental excitement and sympathy. Our expenses are increased, as all provisions are very dear. The poor suffer; our door is knocked at many times a day by those who take a piece of bread thankfully. . . .

"How I should love to see your dear children, and to show you mine. Oh! let us train them for heaven, and then we may meet."

To Mrs. Fuller, Cambridgeport.

"July 28.

"MY DEAR FRIEND MARY: If I tell you that my dear husband has to-day returned from Broosa, after a week's absence, you will not anticipate a long letter from me this evening; yet I fear to postpone it till to-morrow, lest I fail entirely. The ship by which this is to go leaves port the day after.

"We are *enjoying* a vacation in our school, and although we follow our dear pupils to their homes with anxious interest, still we rejoice in the short freedom from care and labor which such a school brings upon us. Our examination would have interested even you, I am sure. They sang beautifully, and their recitations in geography, arithmetic, and English would have been intelligible to you, and the various specimens of needlework you would have appreciated. Several of the pupils are not to return to us; but all hope they are the children of God, and we can commit them to him who is able to keep them from straying.

"Mr. E. went to Broosa, hoping to be invigorated by a short respite from his many duties, but he has suffered from hoarseness and slight fever, though better now. My health is good, but the warm weather makes me a little languid this summer, which is quite unusual. . . .

"You should have been with us this P. M., as we visited a large Armenian house. We walked in the extensive garden, the lady of the house with us, in native costume. Then we went into the house, sat upon the divan covered with crimson and yellow damask, — partook of sweetmeats and coffee in native style, — then went over the mansion, containing thirty rooms, beside large halls. We sat down again in a lower room, drank sherbet made from gooseberry syrup, — made our salaams, after much pleasant conversation, and left. The ladies in this house were married, one at eleven and one at twelve years of age. The young woman, or *bride*, as they call her, though she has been married eighteen years, can read, and I am going to send her a Testament and a copy of Pilgrim's Progress." . . .

From Miss Haynes.

"August 8.

"Yesterday P. M. I made some calls at the houses of some of our girls and other natives. The sick woman, in whose narrow room we held the little meeting last winter, is very feeble, and yesterday morning she thought herself dying. She said she was not only ready, but *wished* to go. She said that she prayed thus, — 'O Lord, if it be thy will, take me now to thyself, — *to-day* take me to thy heavenly kingdom, and *to-day* let me see thy glory. Yet, let thy will be done!' Another woman, when I asked her how she did, exclaimed, 'I am joyful, I am very joyful with Christ. He is exceeding merciful to me, and I praise him for his goodness.' I felt greatly refreshed to witness the spirituality of these simple-hearted people, as I do when I visit such here, and hear them express their gratitude and joy for the blessings of the gospel. It is a much greater pleasure to me to go to a house where there is not a chair or table, and only an apology for a sofa, but where Christ is the light of the house, than to go to the most splendidly furnished house in the village where Christ is not loved and honored. One woman whom I visited not long since in company with Seraphina, made many inquiries about our friends; and when Seraphina told her of mother, and how hard it was for her to give us up, and yet how willingly she did it, she seemed to appreciate it all, but added, 'If she only knew how much joy you give us every time we see your beloved faces, she would not be sorry that she gave you up.' We have on the whole great reason to bless God and take courage, — although the Holy Spirit is not poured out in as large measures as we could wish; yet, one after another comes in, hears, is led to inquire, to search the Scriptures to see if these things are so, and finally to become a firm, intelligent believer in the gospel. Our Sabbath school is attended by thirty or forty,

24*

half of whom are men in Mr. Everett's class. B. Hachadoor has a class of girls, and B. Hagop of women. There
is also a class of little boys. This Sabbath school is a
new thing for the congregation, and entirely separate
from the seminary. It is held at noon on the same plan
as our Sabbath schools in America.

"The day-school is increasing. A man came to-day
and applied for the admission of a boy twelve years old,
from one of the most respectable families in the village.
We rejoice over such, as it helps remove the barriers
from the coming of the multitudes. Many of the poor
are afraid of the priests, and can not come or send their
children on that account. One woman, who has lately
found her way to the chapel, and sent her little boys to
school, has been visited by the priests and threatened
with the anathemas of the Patriarch,— and told that she
would certainly go to hell, &c.

"She asked the priest if all these people—the Protestants — would go to hell. 'Certainly,' he replied.
'Well,' she said, 'if these people who preach the gospel,
and read the Bible, and lead holy lives, are going to hell,
I am willing to cast in my lot with theirs. I will go
along with them.' 'And are you going to take these
children to destruction too?' he asked.

"He also asked her what monthly reward she would
get for coming here. She told him that she got none;
she would not have either the Armenians or Protestants
think *that* her reason for coming. True, she was in debt
and trouble, but she would sell her house, or any thing
she had in her chests, to pay the debts; but she would
not be driven away from those people. She came herself, and begged a spelling-book, and took her first lesson
in reading. She keeps her book constantly by her, and
in a week could read three or four pages in the Tract
Primer quite well. Her case is remarkable. She says,
'Oh! we have got everything to learn,' and it seems as

though she wanted to *drink in* the knowledge in large draughts."

Mrs. Everett's last letter home.

"September 28, 1854.

"MY VERY DEAR PARENTS: How often in imagination I visit you in your new home, it is impossible for me to say; but if our Master's business were not urgent here, such visits would be attended with earnest longings once more to see you face to face, that I might express in words the gratitude due to my dear father and mother.

"It is long since we have heard directly from you. Mrs. I. G. Bliss, in a letter to her sister here, speaks of having taken tea with you, which she enjoyed very much. We want to hear particularly of dear M——, of you all. Where is your amanuensis, sister K——? Dear *mother* must write. . . .

"Our school is again in full operation. New scholars have taken the places of those who left, but the number of professedly pious ones has diminished. To-day is set apart for special prayer that the influences of the Holy Spirit may descend and abide with us. Oh! if we could be assured that your prayers mingled with our feeble petitions before the throne of Almighty grace, then would our faith be strengthened. Do pray for us always.

"We need a double portion of wisdom, grace, and strength. You will be glad to know that we are all in health. Sumner has recently made a visit to Nicomedia and Bachjejak; he left us on Saturday, and returned on the next Thursday. He went on an important errand, determined to know nothing but Christ and his cause. Our dear Susie was in a state to make us anxious, having a very severe cold. She has been delicate all summer, but is now constantly improving; and we call upon our souls to bless the Lord that we are spared the bitter cup that we feared was preparing for us. . .

"We have all been almost breathless for the last few

days to get news from the war. The great onset upon Sebastopol was to be made, and that it would be a terrible struggle none doubted. The cholera had made great ravages among the English and French. Before embarking for the Crimea, they were disheartened, but their courage revived on the way, and they disembarked in fine spirits, without opposition, within twenty miles of Sebastopol. Last Saturday morning a large French steamer, with four flags flying, passed down the Bosphorus. The salute was fired, and there was no thought but for *the news*, — what tidings! *Success*, of course; but oh, how dearly purchased, and the work yet incomplete! Still, great demonstrations were made. Guns and rockets poured forth until a late hour Saturday night. You will get a particular account of the battle by the papers, and I will only say that the heights back of the city were taken, but with a fearful slaughter. The Russians, of course, had every advantage of position and numbers, and the only marvel is, that the allied army was not entirely destroyed. A Russian officer said, they expected to fight *men*, not *demons ;* but the French and English rushed on with the fury of devils incarnate. The loss of life on both sides was immense ; eighteen hundred English, and fourteen or fifteen hundred French killed and wounded ; — some of their bravest officers fell. Steamers are bringing down the wounded, and the hospitals here will be filled. We confidently expect to hear that the city is taken, but it will be a terrible struggle. Oh, how much blood spilled! how many will rush into eternity! how awful! How many hearts are rent with grief by this destruction of human life ; but how much deeper the wail from the world of woe! If we could not feel that the Lord reigns, and that all this is permitted, that the day may hasten on when all shall feel and acknowledge his sway, we should despair.

" All is quietness here, save the cry of those who are

distressed for the necessaries of life; food of all kinds, and fuel, are nearly or quite double the usual price; consequently there is great distress, and only a prospect that it will increase as the season advances.

"Did M. in her last give you particulars in regard to our work? Last Sabbath our chapel was filled. Sumner feels that it must be enlarged, — some partitions must be knocked away. A few days since, Sumner was called to a house to meet some half-convinced Armenians, and spent two and a half hours in conversation on exclusively religious subjects. The truth is gaining ground in this village, and throughout the land. Mr. Dwight is fairly settled in the city proper; Henry Otis made quite a stir this week by raising his little American flag on the premises. Four or five cavasses came to inquire into the cause of such a demonstration, and gave some cautions. . . . Our families here are quite scattered. Three in Bebek, one alone in Pera, two in Hass Keuy, and one in the city proper. . . .

"My sheet is filling up, my lights are fading, the bell has rung for retiring, and I hear my husband at the door, returned from some Armenian visits. Here he comes, and says, 'Will you tell them that I am alive? It is a shame that I can not write them once in a year!' He writes very few letters. His hands are full of work, and his heart too. He is a genuine missionary. I do wish you could come and see us. We should be too happy to show you your grandchildren, and then your children — *three*. Are *you* not blessed; are not *we!* Our blessings are numberless. Rest and unalloyed happiness we must not look for here."

CHAPTER XXV.

In approaching the close of a life we have followed with so much interest, we would fain linger around the last weeks and months, and gather up their few fragmentary records. Her last letters to American friends were in September. Her health was not good at that time, and had not been for some time previous. In addition to her usual cares, she had felt much anxiety during the summer for her youngest child, who was suffering from teething; and this anxiety, with the weariness and confinement attendant on the nursing of a sick child, had caused her to look pale and worn, and oftener than usual sad. There are many little notes written by her during this period to Mrs. Hamlin, and another missionary sister, Mrs. Bliss, who was spending the summer in Constantinople with her family, for her own and her husband's health. These notes are full of her own kind heart, which always seemed more thoughtful of others' troubles than its own. To Mrs. Bliss, in Pera, she writes in the latter part of the spring: —

"My dear Sister: I hope none of you have been seriously affected by this chilly day, and that you are ready to try what country air and scenery, and donkey riding, and visiting with old friends, &c. will do for you. Your apartment awaits you. Will you not come on

Wednesday, bag and baggage? We will give you so warm a reception that you will not be disposed to *shake* for many a day."

To the same sister, in Bebek : —

"Can not you spare one of your Bebek songsters to bear a message over the hills to your deserted abode? We long to hear that you have been revived by the genial air and society of that quiet, charming village. It must have been a relief to you to get away from such a care-ruffled spirit as mine. I used to think I should always be light-hearted. But really, how are you all? Has the foe (intermittent fever) assaulted any of you? Have you commenced sea-bathing? We are very busy preparing for examination; pardon this hasty line. Will you not join us in commending our little flock to the care of the Good Shepherd?"

The latter part of the summer she was thrown from a horse, and had a very narrow escape from serious injury. She thus speaks of it in a note to Mrs. Bliss, then at one of the Prince's Islands : —

"My DEAR SISTER: In one word I must relieve your kind anxiety for me. It was indeed a wonderful escape in *great* peril; but I received no injury, save the jar and the fright, from which I recovered in one day. A new consecration of my unworthy life to my Master's service, is all the return I can make. How little we know what is before us when we rise in the morning, or lie down at night. 'My times are in thy hand.'

"It would give us all very great pleasure to visit you in your island retreat; but I fear *my* desire to do so will be disappointed. Your invitation shall be extended. We are *so* sorry that you are *in statu quo* as it regards health. When will the cloud pass from above you?"

To Mrs. Hamlin, as the summer vacation was closing, and the last school-term which she was to superintend was about to commence, she wrote : —

"How soon our vacation has passed! I must confess that I almost shrink from the care and toil before us. Oh, the responsibility too! Sometimes I wish to feel it more, sometimes less. Who is sufficient for these things?"

To Mrs. Bliss, a few days later:—

"You must have learned ere this to 'walk by faith,' and no doubt you find real peace in taking the hand of the Omniscient, and walking quietly on, despite the dark veil that is drawn before your own eyes.

"School has commenced; not all the pupils are yet here, but a good number. Do ask a blessing for us,—a large blessing, such as God is ready to grant.

"Susie dear is gaining. How good God is to us! The rest of us are quite well. Mr. E. goes to Nicomedia Saturday. Love—much—to each of you.

"Ever your sister,   S. H. EVERETT."

This was nearly the last of these little sisterly notes from her hand and heart. During the month of October, she had more than one attack of illness of a bilious character, causing her friends considerable anxiety; but she was most of the time about, caring for every thing in her large household as usual, until the sixth of November, when she gave birth to another daughter, her sixth child. After this she regained her strength, though not rapidly, as there were unfavorable symptoms about her from the first; but she was hopeful, and at the end of a fortnight was able to leave her room. The following note to Mrs. Hamlin is probably the last she ever wrote:—

"HASS KEUY, Nov. 27, 1854.

"MY VERY DEAR SISTER: It was a great disappointment not to see your face on Saturday, particularly as we can not hope for the privilege this week. How much could I tell you of God's goodness to unworthy me. Surely *with loving-kindness has he drawn me* to make a new consecration of my whole self and all mine to him. These *four little ones,*—will not the dear Jesus own them as his if we bring them in true confiding faith?

"Baby is in the regular succession of *model babies,*—very little care, and contributes her full measure of joy. You should see Susie perform over her. She informs every body that we '*in got a baby.*'

"This morning I got up before breakfast, (three weeks,) and I expect to take tea with the family in the study. Saturday I was drawn into the hall, and yesterday walked to sister's room. My progress has been steady, though a little slower than usual, owing to a troubled state of my stomach for some weeks previous to my confinement; but I have had no fever and no relapse, and received no injury from seeing my friends. Oh! my dear sister, I am called upon to begin life anew.

'Life is real; life is earnest!'

How unprofitably has mine been spent thus far; and I feel that I am growing old. What matter, if I am ripening for heaven?

"Pardon this note (the first) written with a trembling hand. We are so sorry you could not accept *our* invitation for the 30th. We shall imagine you all very happy, and we too shall hope to 'be very thankful in a quiet way,' tell Mrs. Hinsdale, with love. Please give my warmest love and thanks to Mrs. Schauffler and Mrs. Riggs, and assure them by this that I mean to write them. You have all been *very* kind. Adieu!

"SERAPHINA."

On Thanksgiving day, three days after the above was written, she joined the little party, consisting of her own and Dr. Goodell's family, in her parlor, and sat with them at table, though a very sore mouth prevented her partaking of the dinner. The next day she was taken alarmingly ill, and was brought so low that it was feared she would hardly survive through the night. But though, as appears from the above note, all her hopes and plans had been for life, this sudden approach of death gave her no alarm, nor did she manifest the least unwillingness to meet his summons. On the contrary, she received it joyfully, as if, while to stay longer here was very pleasant, and strong and tender ties bound her to the world, she felt that to depart and be with Christ was far better. The only moment in which the shadow of a doubt appeared to cross her mind, was when repeating with her husband the hymn commencing —

"When thou, my righteous judge, shalt come,"

she stopped at the line —

"What if my name should be left out."

"*If* — *if*," she repeated, — "oh, there is no *if*, — he will accept me, I *know* he will;" and turning to her husband she asked, "Do you not think he will receive me?" He replied — "Yes, he has promised, and he can not deny himself. He will receive you through Christ," and from that moment every doubt was set at rest for ever, and she longed to depart. On being asked by her husband if she did not wish to live to train up her dear children for God, and to labor a little longer for him, she replied, "Yes, if it is his will. Dear children! They are Christ's, *all* of them. Yes, I shall meet them again. He will keep them and you; *you* must train them for him." She then asked for them to be brought to her, embraced them, and committed them and her husband once more to the Saviour. Describing this scene after she was taken from him, her husband says: "I was silent with wonder to see how she loved the dear Saviour, and could thus calmly, yes, triumphantly, yield to the sundering of the sweetest of conjugal ties, and the deepest of maternal affections, *because he called*." She sent messages of love to the scholars,

and wished they should be told how her heart had yearned
for their salvation, and how she had been almost overwhelmed at times with longings for this, when praying
for them in the meeting they had been accustomed to
observe on Saturday evenings, in concert with the
Oroomiah and Beirut schools. "They *must* love Christ,"
she said, with strong emphasis.

She wished the Armenians to be told how much she
loved them, and to the sisters in the church she sent the
message, "to be *whole* Christians, wholly devoted to
Christ." To all friends in America, and to all her missionary friends, forgetting none, she sent farewell messages of love.

During all that night her husband read to her portions
of Scripture, as she was able to listen, and prayed with
her many times. So she continued, seemingly wrapped
up in the word of God and communion with him, until
daybreak, when she said, "I thought I should go before
the morning." But she was not to go quite so soon.
Her earthly work was not yet quite completed, and she
was brought back from the borders of heaven, to remain
a little longer with those who were hardly so ready to
give her up as she was to go. For some days her state
appeared critical, and then it was thought that the danger was past, and that her precious life was to be spared
to her family and to the missionary work. When she
first saw that she was probably to come back to the cares
of earth, she expressed some disappointment, but soon
said to her husband, "If it is the will of God I wish to
labor with you longer for the Armenians, and train up
our children for him," adding that if God should continue
her life, she would strive *to be more Christlike.* For two
weeks she gained strength, and with this new prospect of
life, revived all her plans for doing good.

On Friday, December 22, the school was to be dismissed for the Christmas vacation, and she wished to see

and speak with all the scholars before their departure. It
was a pleasant day, and she was removed into the parlor,
and reclined on the sofa, while one by one the girls came
in, and received each a few earnest words of counsel and
exhortation, and an affectionate farewell from the faithful
teacher and loving friend, who had so often counseled
and prayed for them, but who would never with her living voice address them again. She had gathered up,
perhaps unconsciously, all her strength for this last duty
to the dear school, to which she had for so many years
given the best energies of her large heart, and loving,
Christlike spirit. That night she was seized with a
violent chill, followed by a fearful fever ; then came wandering of mind, succeeded by heavy stupor, until, on the
morning of the 27th, she peacefully fell asleep in Jesus.

During those four days she had a few intervals in which
her mind appeared perfectly clear, and at such times she
expressed a full consciousness of her situation, and the
same readiness to leave the world that she had before
done. Once, seeing her eldest child enter the room, she
said, "Ellen, do you know mamma is going home, — is
going to die?" The evening before her death, she
awoke from a long, heavy sleep, exclaiming, "Bless the
Lord! Why don't you bless the Lord?" Soon after
she repeated, "Jesus! dear Jesus!" many times with
peculiar emphasis and tenderness. Later in the night she
requested those about her to sing, and Mrs. Hamlin and
Mr. Everett commenced —

"Jesus, lover of my soul,"

while she joined in singing parts of the hymn. She
wished to see her children once more, and when they
were brought, she kissed them tenderly, and said she left
them with perfect confidence in the hands of their heavenly Father. She missed the little one, and asked for
her, and seemed much affected as she embraced her. Dr.

Goodell said, "We will watch over and care for your dear children;" to which she replied, "I have given them all to the Lord." She afterwards called all the friends in the room by name, and said a kind word to each, and took a very affecting leave of her sister. "Christ has gone to prepare a place for me," she said. "He will come; he has promised; he *is* coming, and I will go." Those who were with her felt that they had never been in a dying chamber which seemed more bright with the Saviour's presence. She slept a little, and on waking, recognized her husband once more, and gave him a last embrace. This was about midnight. She then sunk into a state of unconsciousness, in which she continued until her spirit broke its earthly fetters, and soared upward into the unclouded light and blessedness of heaven.

25*

CHAPTER XXVI

It was December 27, 1854, that Mrs. Everett died. Early that morning a small company, consisting of two gentlemen and two ladies, might have been seen gliding in a caïque over the blue waters of the Bosphorus and Golden Horn towards that house of death. It was one of those beautiful mornings which so often light up that brilliant region, making palace, and tower, and dome, and gilded spire glitter with a magic glory, and seeming to the fancy of the beholder to realize all the images it had ever conceived of oriental beauty and magnificence. But on this morning that little missionary company were not thinking of the visible splendors around them, though these might have insensibly assisted them to realize more vividly the glories of another city, even a heavenly, to which their minds were directed, and the blessedness of that dear sister, who, they thought, and said to each other, might be, even then, just entering its pearly gates. Yet they hoped to find her still lingering on these mortal shores, and to catch one more glance of the eye, to receive one more pressure of the hand, and perhaps hear one more parting word from her ere she should go over the " narrow stream," and vanish from earthly vision and communion. As they landed and walked towards the dwelling where she had so often greeted them with her sweet smile of welcome, they became more silent and sad, their fears prevailing over their hopes. When they " drew nigh and beheld the house," their eyes turned immediately towards her apartment, and the opened window, letting in the light and air, and sounds of busy life, confirmed their fears, and they looked at each other with an expression which said, "It is all over!" Just at that moment Dr. Goodell opened the gate and came towards them, meeting them with the solemn words, "*She is gone!*" In silent sorrow they all walked on together, and entering the house, passed through the empty hall, and up the deserted stairs, to the study, where the stricken family were sitting with the few friends who had come in to weep with them. But what a hallowed chamber was that! Christ's presence was there, as really, almost as sensibly as with the mourning family in Bethany. The husband, from whom had just been taken the dearest object of his affections, looked as if he himself had been permitted to accompany her to her celestial home, and to look in at its gates unclosed, and see the golden streets and the crystal river, and catch glimpses of its blessed inhabitants, and snatches of the "wondrous song they sing," and as if his thoughts were still of that glory, rather than of his own heavy bereavement. And truly, he was not himself far from its blissful possession. There in that little mourning company were *four* who were not long to be denied the full sight and enjoyment of those heavenly scenes. The feet of one had come, even then, almost to the entrance of the holy city, though they knew it not. Just one month from that day Mr. Benjamin went to his rest and reward. Mr. Everett, Mrs. Hinsdale, and Mrs. Hamlin all followed before three years had elapsed. Sweet was the conversation in that little group, — blessed it was to be there. Before dispersing, the Rev. Mr. Thompson, of the Scotch Mission, offered a prayer, and then those who had not looked on the loved form of the departed, went into the apartment where it lay, — not a darkened chamber, but that one where they had seen the opened window; and the bright morning light, falling on the lovely features, revealed their placid expression, indicating the peacefulness with which the spirit had departed.

The following letter to one of the Secretaries of the Board at Boston beautifully expresses the impression left on those whose privilege it was to be with her in her last hours.

CONSTANTINOPLE, Dec. 27, 1855.

"An hour in heaven, what a glorious thought!" And a beautiful morning it is to go from earth to heaven, — a morning without clouds, — fit emblem of the clear sunshine that illumined the "privileged chamber," from which, at 9 o'clock this morning, our greatly beloved sister Everett took her peaceful departure. We sung sweet hymns around her dying pillow, and at her departure we fell upon our knees to give thanks unto him "who hath abolished death."

But the blow is a very heavy one to the bereaved family, to the Female Boarding School, to the little Protestant church and community here, and to all our families. And what else, or what better can we do, than "take up the body and bury it, and go and tell Jesus?"

Your brother in Christ,   W. GOODELL.

The funeral was attended the next day by a large number of people; Americans, English, Scotch, Armenians, and Greeks, and among them all were none who had not come as sincere mourners. Dr. Hamlin made remarks, and offered prayer, in English. Dr. Dwight did the same in Armenian, and at the grave, Dr. Schauffler enlarged with much feeling and beauty on the illustration of the resurrection made use of in 1 Cor. xv. 37, 38. The remains of Mrs. Everett were interred in the Protestant cemetery in Pera, where also lie those of many other precious members of the mission circle, — though only for a short rest, as the ground is appropriated by the government for other uses, and its slumbering tenants must soon be transferred to another resting-place. But they "sleep in Jesus," and no changes shall disturb their repose, till "the Lord himself shall descend from heaven," and shall call them forth from their graves, with the saints and martyrs whose dust has so long mingled with that hallowed soil.

"Asleep in Jesus. Far from thee
Thy kindred and their graves may be,
But thine is still a blessed sleep,
From which none ever wake to weep."

From the many letters written to the bereaved husband and other friends, testifying to Mrs. Everett's loveliness and usefulness as a missionary, and the high estimation in which she was held by all her missionary brethren and sisters, we can give only a few extracts. These are from the communications of three who knew her longest and most intimately.

From a letter written by Dr. Goodell to her parents.

"That was a bright day to us and to this mission, when she came to Constantinople. She brought with her all the vigor and freshness of youth, all the charms of a kind and benevolent heart, and all the fascinations of a cultivated intellect and cultivated manners, united with great buoyancy of spirit, and an unusual degree of liveliness and loveliness; and all these she consecrated entirely and cheerfully to the blessed cause of Christ. Her voice was sweet, whether in conversation or in song; sweet was her spirit, and sweet were all her ways. Her words were always words of sympathy and encouragement. The law of God was in her heart, the law of kindness on her tongue, and the love of Christ the great ruling motive of all her actions."

After speaking of her various labors, Dr. Goodell says :
"But her work is done, and *well* done. She came here
on purpose to work, (as she herself incidentally mentioned to Mrs. Goodell during her last illness,) and we
bear her witness that she *did* work, and at times far beyond her strength. She literally wore herself out. She
seemed, during the last year, to be under an extraordinary
excitement, and to be borne on by impulses not to be
controlled by ordinary considerations. Souls for whom
Christ died were perishing around her, and she felt all the
constrainings of his infinite love. We must occasionally
have grieved her tender spirit by our earnest entreaties
that she would spare herself; and while 'zeal for God's
house was consuming her,' she must have thought us to
be 'savoring not the things that be of God, but those
that be of men.'

"Oh, how precious is thy name, beloved sister, daughter, friend! All our recollections of thee are inexpres-
sibly tender. 'What have we done,' say the whole Protestant community, 'what sin have we committed against
God, that he should so soon remove thee from us?"

From an obituary notice, by Mr. Dwight.

"Besides the care of the boarding department of a
school of between thirty and forty scholars, she always
participated, to a greater or less extent, in the instruction
of the Armenian classes; and for four years she devoted
two hours a day to a class of Greek girls, carrying them
through several branches of study in their own language,
which she had taken pains to acquire for this special
purpose.

"It was always perfectly evident to all, however, that
her object was not the mental discipline of her pupils, nor
their advancement in human science, however important
these may be. Compared with the knowledge of God,
and reconciliation and obedience to him, they were as
'chaff to the wheat,' in her estimation. She never left

her native land, she never would have left it, merely to
propagate human science. Every thing she planned or
attempted had a direct bearing upon the spiritual and
eternal good of those for whom she had devoted her life.
She labored assiduously to bring and keep before the
minds of the pupils the great things of the eternal world;
exhorting them individually and collectively to give their
hearts to God; and who can wonder that the blessing of
God continually followed her labors, and the labors of
those who were associated with her?"

Speaking of the missionary work she performed in visiting among the Armenians, he says : —

"It is believed that hardly a native Protestant family
can be found in all Constantinople and its environs which
has not had the privilege of welcoming her within its
doors, most of them many times ; and all the families
upon whom she called, felt that she had left a blessing
behind her.

"She was eminently a friend of the poor and needy,
and was always planning to relieve their wants, chiefly
by finding work for them to do. Even during her last
illness, after her physician (an Englishman) had been
prescribing for her one day, she made arrangements to
procure, through him, some of the materials which had
been provided for under-garments for the English troops
in Scutari and the Crimea, in order that they might be
made up by some of the poor sisters of the church. They
were afterwards brought to her room, and she directed in
regard to the division of them among those who were to
do the work.

"Mrs. Everett had acquired great fluency in the use of
the Armenian language, and her uncommonly prepossess-
ing appearance, her sweetness of tone and manner, and
her wonderful facility in adapting herself to people of all
classes, gained an easy access for her to all circles and to
all hearts, while her intelligent and well-stored mind, her

clear apprehension of divine things, and her deep and
earnest piety, through God's blessing, sanctified every
visit and every conversation. Widely was she known
among the females of the Armenian race, and long and
most deeply will her loss be deplored. Her own pupils
are found in Broosa, Nicomedia, Trebizond, Tokat, Erzeroom, and other places, some as pastors' wives, some as
teachers, others occupying more private spheres; but all,
it is believed, imitating the bright example of their beloved teacher in striving *to do good;* and many a heart
will throb with emotion, and many a tear will fall, as the
tidings of her early departure are carried abroad over the
land."

Miss West, who succeeded Miss Lovell in the female
seminary, and resided two years in Mrs. Everett's family,
writes to the parents of Mrs. Everett.

"Never shall I forget the impression made upon my
mind when I first saw her lovely countenance, and received a sister's welcome. I had heard much of her previously, but I thought 'the half has not been told me.'
And as her character unfolded to my view, as days, weeks,
and months rolled by, I admired, wondered, and was
reproved by her bright example. I felt that her walk
was close with God, her life hid in Christ, and that impression deepened till the day of her departure. I have
often thought what I will now say, never did I see so
symmetrical a character; a mind better balanced, or
energies better directed, looking at the one great aim of
her existence. I have watched her under all circumstances, — those most calculated to bring out the weak
points in a person's character; and in *all* she was the
consistent Christian, the faithful missionary, the devoted
wife, mother, sister, friend. I have been amazed at the
amount of work she accomplished for the school, the
Armenian females, and the cause in general, combined
with the charge of her young family, and the warm hos-

pitality she extended to all. I shall ever be thankful that I was permitted to be connected with her during the last two years,—to take my first lessons of one so deeply imbued with the missionary spirit.

"What a glory was shed around her death-bed! Never, while memory lasts, shall we forget those scenes. During her second convalescence of nearly two weeks, it was my privilege to spend some hours each night and morning in her room. Those were precious hours, and the words she then dropped sank deep into my heart. If I failed to bring with me the verse for the day when I came early in the morning to relieve the watchers, she would say, 'What word hast thou for thy servant?' Would that I, or any one, could cause the last scene to pass before your mind's eye more vividly than words can do! Those partings with all her heart's treasures, calmly committing her little ones to the Great Shepherd's care, —the sweet recognition of her dear friends during her lucid intervals, and her calm resting on her Father's almighty arm,—the longings to be near and like him, and the strong faith which triumphed even in death,— *these* made that sick-room a holy place, 'quite on the verge of heaven.'"

Sleep peacefully, sister!
  Thy work is all done;
Thy conflict is ended,
  Thy bright crown is won;
Afar from earth's turmoil
  Now sweetly repose,
On that fair cloudless shore
  Where life's bright river flows.

Sleep peacefully, sister!
  Our tears can not come,
Our grief can not reach thee
  In thy blissful home;
Not thy husband's deep anguish,
  Thy babe's helpless cry,
Nor a sister's fond yearnings
  Can cause thee one sigh.

26

Sleep peacefully, sister!
  Though round thy cold bier
Armenia's sad daughters
  All weeping appear;
Though long be their wailing
  And bitter, that thee,
Their loved guide and teacher,
  They no more may see; —

Yet peacefully, sister,
  Enjoy thy repose;
No more need'st thou wake
  At the voice of their woes.
Ah! well hast thou finished
  Thy mission of love,
And priceless gems gained
  For thy bright crown above.

Sleep peacefully, sister,
  Wife, mother, and friend;
Oh, would thy bright mantle
  On us might descend!
Oh, would we might follow
  The path thou hast trod,
Till like thee we find rest
  In the bosom of God!

CHAPTER XXVII.

MRS. EVERETT was gone; but it was difficult to think of her as *dead*. The home which her presence had made so bright, did not seem, now that she was no longer visible there to the eye of sense, to be shrouded in the dark drapery of death. A life like hers leaves something of its brightness behind it, like the reflected light lingering in the west after the sun itself is shining on another hemisphere. She was missed everywhere; in the missionary circle, the school, the meetings, in all the scenes where she had for nine years moved with so much grace and sweetness; most of all in her own home was her absence an ever-felt reality; yet so pleasant were all the memories of her, of her daily life, her countenance ever lighted up with gentleness and benevolence, her voice always so sweet, her sick-room so peaceful, her last hours so triumphantly blessed, we could only think of her as living still more lovely than here, in another and more blessed "apartment of our Father's house." And so her bereaved husband appeared always to think of her. While his desolate heart yearned for her society, and while he felt his own and his children's loss to be irreparable, his countenance yet shone at times with the near communion he enjoyed with God, and the vivid apprehensions of his dear wife's blessedness, and that which was in reserve for himself when the remainder of his now lonely pilgrimage should be traveled. He had always been a devoted Christian and faithful missionary; but he seemed to all who knew him to grow rapidly in grace under this affliction, and to give himself with increased ardor to the work which remained for him to do. An anxious and tender father always, he redoubled his care and prayers for the little ones whom he now regarded as a legacy committed to his special trust by their dying mother. But his toils, and cares, and sorrows, were not long to continue. In a little more than a year he was called to leave them all, and join his beloved Seraphina in the rest and the bliss of the upper world.

Mr. Everett died of a malignant typhus, March 8, 1856. His disease was very rapid in its progress, seizing him while actively engaged in his work, and terminating in less than a week. But he was all ready, and his dying chamber, as that of his wife had been, was a scene of triumph over the last foe. With the same unfaltering trust, he left his four children in their heavenly Father's care, expressing the strong belief that he should see them all in heaven. The last words he was heard to utter were, "Fullness of hope! Fullness of joy! Fullness of glory!"

The last sermon he preached in English was in the mission chapel in Pera, the Sabbath before he was taken ill, from the words, 2 Tim. i. 10: *Who hath abolished death, and hath brought life and immortality to light through the gospel.* The following passage, describing the Christian's death, seems almost a prophetic picture of his own. After representing the death-bed of one unreconciled to God, he continues:—

"Now turn to the chamber where the good man meets the same messenger. No fear is in his heart. No dread of the approaching messenger disturbs the calm peace of his soul. His language is, 'I desire to depart; I wish to go. To die will be gain.' No love of earth, nor the dearest objects of earth, nor the closest ties that unite hearts here below; not wife, nor children, nor friends, can turn his thoughts from the glory about to be revealed. 'Jesus has gone to prepare a place for me. He has come, and I will go.' Where is the fear of death? where the dread of the grave? In their place there is triumph, there is fullness of joy; there is the end of faith, *eternal life realized.*

"And is not temporal death abolished also? The Christian does not fear him, but says to him with an assured countenance, 'Come when thou wilt, O Death, I desire no delay. It is a long time since I settled my affairs, and have been waiting for thee. The principal part of myself is not here, my heart is already ravished into heaven, where Christ awaits me with open arms. Therefore, notwithstanding the fearful darkness that surrounds thee, and the designs thou hast to destroy me, I will follow thee as courageously and with as much joy as Peter did the angel of light who threw open before him the gates of his prison.' To a soul thus stayed on Christ, there remaineth only life and immortality of bliss, brought to light through the gospel."

We make one more extract; the whole sermon is rich in spiritual thought and feeling.

"In view of this subject, well might the apostle, my beloved brethren, exclaim as in the context, 'For God hath not given us the spirit of fear, but of power, of love, and of a sound mind.' How full of meaning were these words in the mind of the apostle in view of this glorious truth revealed in the text! And now you, you who are called according to his purpose, may see and rest assured that there remaineth no more death. He 'hath abolished death, and brought life and immortality to light.' Brethren and sisters, keep in view the glorious triumph he hath won. Was it for himself or for you that he trod the winepress alone, in garments dyed in blood? Do you

26*

find it difficult to realize, amid the cares and sorrows and toils of this life, that there is no more death? Oh, it is because you are not yet sufficiently acquainted with this great conqueror of death! You are not familiar enough with his glorious character, with his infinite love, with the power of his resurrection, with the sin-killing power of his blood. 'It is a faithful saying, for if we be dead with him, we shall also live with him.' Yes, *now* we shall live with him a life that is a sure foretaste and beginning of eternal life."

HARK ! again the voice of wailing comes from Asia's distant strand!
EVERETT, the beloved and faithful, rests with the bright spirit band.

Fighting in the foremost combat, all his gospel armor on,
Joyfully he heard the summons, — " Faithful one, receive thy crown ! "

Weeping brethren gathered round him, — those he 'd loved and toiled with
    long, —
Tender babes, twice orphaned, clasped him, yet the Christian's heart was
    strong.

Friends so dear, yea, children dearer, could not here his heart detain;
Faith assured him he should meet them where is felt no parting pain.

Death's dark river could not daunt him, Christ's sweet presence at his
    side
Brightened, with celestial glory, all the darkly flowing tide.

Heaven, with all its radiant prospects, rose before his raptured eyes,
Sweet, familiar voices called him to his mansion in the skies.

Ask we, weeping, why so early he should lay his armor down?
Why, while veterans still are toiling, he should wear the victor's crown?

Jesus answers, — " What thou know'st not now, hereafter thou shalt know·
Patient wait; my wisdom, goodness, soon eternity will show."

Fast they 're falling, the true-hearted, valiant champions of the Cross;
Who will, with a like devotion, hasten to repair their loss?

Not Armenia 's seeking only, but the Orient nations all,
Waking from their ages' slumber, for the gospel earnest call.

E'en the haughty Moslem, casting pride and bigotry aside,
Seeks, of the once hated Christian, knowledge of the Crucified.

Oh for Godlike pity, moving all who bear the Saviour's name!
Then should none — barbarian, Moslem — for the gospel plead in vain.

CHAPTER XXVIII.

WE will now return to Mrs. Hamlin, the sole survivor of the little company who had sailed together in the Stamboul, in February, 1845. In order to complete the history of her too brief earthly course, we must go back a little, to where we left her about the time of the removal of the girls' seminary to Hass Keuy. Just before that event, and while Mrs. Everett was rejoicing over her fifth babe, the deep fountain of a mother's love was first unsealed in Mrs. Hamlin's heart, by the birth of a little daughter. Some of her feelings are thus expressed, in a letter to Mrs. Crane of Oroomiah, March 31, 1853.

"I have been wishing, for many days, to find time to congratulate you upon the happy event which *I* can now well believe has filled your heart with a joy such as you have never before experienced. A mother's joy over her first-born, — what is there like it? Is there any other joy like unto it? any other emotion to be compared with those which filled your heart when the form of the precious little *immortal* was first placed in your arms? when its voice first met your ear, and its eyes first opened upon its mother's face? . . . Have you heard that a mother's joy is mine? Our little Harriet Clara was born four weeks ago this morning."

To Mrs. Thayer, July 6, 1854.

"Oh, could I sit down by your side a moment, how

quickly would the stiff, unsociable pen be thrown aside, and the busy tongue find 'sweet employ.' No hesitation in the choice of subjects would cause a moment's loss of time; but past, present, and to come would be reviewed, with all the way by which the Lord has led, and is leading us, and the ten thousand mercies with which our cup has been filled, mingled, it is true, with some bitter drops, but still overflowing with goodness and mercy. I should show you my precious little Clara, and you would smile at the mother's fondness, and remember your own lost darling, — lost, yet *saved*. Our little pet is now running alone, and of course, running into all sorts of mischief, requiring some one to be continually running after her. I should love to show you too, my four elder daughters, and I should tell you, or try to tell you, how much I love them, and how I wish I could be to them *all* a mother should be.

"July 10. On Saturday last, we had, in our parlor, a farewell meeting with our dear brother and sister, Van Lennep. Forty persons were present, — all missionaries and their children. It was a deeply affecting season, especially so when Mr. H. reminded them that the last time we had thus assembled for a parting meeting, was in that same room, when we came together, to commend to the grace and mercy of a gracious Father, the beloved mistress of this house and her weeping family, as they were about to leave for Rhodes."*

Mrs. Hamlin felt deeply the many vacancies made by death in the Armenian and neighboring missions, during the last four or five years of her life, and sympathized tenderly with all the bereaved ones. There are many sweet letters, written to missionary sisters in affliction, expressive of the tenderest sympathy, and suggestive of sweet topics of consolation. She was especially affected

* See "Light on the Dark River: or Memorials of Mrs. H. A. L. Hamlin," page 215.

by the frequent visitations of death in her own more immediate circle, and none touched her so nearly as the removal of Mr. and Mrs. Everett, her earliest, and almost her dearest companions in the missionary work. Some of her letters referring to the loss of these dear friends, are so interesting that we insert them, though at the risk of involving a repetition of some of the circumstantial details. To Mrs. Crane, of Oroomiah, in whose repeated and severe afflictions she had manifested a sister's sympathy, she wrote, a few days after Mrs. Everett's death :—

"MY DEAR SISTER: We have heard of the new treasure which has been bestowed upon you, to gladden your bereaved heart, and lighten your desolate fireside, and I have wished, ever since the intelligence reached us, to tell you how much I rejoice in your joy, as I have wept in your sorrow. . . . You, dear sister, have, during the year just closing, been privileged to become, if I may so speak, an object of the special attention of our heavenly Father. He has not left you to yourself, but once and again has visited you, *not in wrath*, but with the tokens of his fatherly love, with chastenings which, though for the present not joyous, but grievous, are still the undoubted evidences of his love,—and yet again has he visited you with his healing balm. . . .

"My letter will, perhaps, be the first to communicate to you the painful bereavement which we as a mission, and I as a friend and missionary sister, have been called to sustain. You will weep with us when you learn that our dear sister Everett has ceased from her labors on earth, has closed her sweet eyes upon the world, and left us, to join the redeemed family above, to be with the 'dear Jesus' she so much loved. Ah, yes! she and your beloved husband have already met before the throne. I need not say her end was peace. It was my privilege to spend the last night of her life in her sick-room, and to be recognized by her with a sweet smile and a kiss, after it was thought she had ceased to recognize any one. She had, however, after this, several intervals of consciousness, when she spoke to her husband and sister, and Miss West, desired her children to be brought again, that she might kiss them, and often repeated the dear name of Jesus. Once she said: 'He has gone to prepare a place for me, and why should I stay? I *will* go,' repeating these words many times. . . .

"We earnestly pray that this severe affliction may be blessed and sanctified to us, as a mission, and especially to the school, where she has been such a blessing. And oh, how loudly does it speak to *me!* Ten years we have enjoyed together the sweetest intercourse, but *her* work is finished here, — 'She has done what she could.'

"I have only a small space left to say how much and often we speak and think of you, and how much I wish to hear from you of your present situation, and plans for the future. I intend to write to Mrs. Rhea, to accompany this. May her life be an ever-increasingly happy and useful one. Permit me to wish you a *happy* new year. It will not, I trust, seem out of time, or unsuitable. May God so richly make up to you, by the communications of his grace, for what he has removed from you, that the ensuing year may indeed prove, in the smiles of his love, a very happy one!"

To Mrs. Thayer, April 19, 1855.

"You have learned, perhaps, by the papers, of the sore bereavements which our mission has suffered during the last few months. The year closed over us darkly, as we bore to their last resting-place the ashes of our beloved sister Everett. To me it was and is a great loss, — like that of a *sister*. In just a month from the day of Mrs. Everett's death, Mr. Benjamin, a most beloved and useful missionary, was taken from us, and a few weeks after, their daughter Meta, by the same fever of which her father died. Who will be taken next? seems now to be the thought in the minds of all. Oh that these repeated admonitions may not be lost upon us, but lead us to be more watchful and more diligent in the service of our Master!

"You have heard, no doubt, also, of the earthquakes which have alarmed us, and laid in ruins the city of Broosa. The little Protestant community there are for the present dispersed, their new church, which was nearly completed, leveled to the ground, I believe, by the last earthquake. We have felt repeated shocks here, but none of them strong enough to do any injury, although they have given much alarm.

"Of the war you probably know as much, and learn it almost as soon, as we do. We have now in our neighborhood a large camp of French soldiers, preparing to go to the Crimea. Their neighborhood is anything but desirable, as they are continually disturbing the quiet of our little village, passing and repassing in search of wine shops. They have raised the price of everything so much too, that we almost dread a famine, besides cutting off the supplies of water from Pera, for their own accommodation. We have calls continually from them for Bibles and tracts, although there are but few Protestants, and we hope that in this way some seed may be sown, which may eventually spring up. Our hitherto very healthy village has been twice visited with the cholera. My husband is the *village physician !* and is called upon continually for medicines and attention. He has, I believe, been the means of saving many lives, and their gratitude, in these days of trial, seems unbounded, though at other times too many are ready to revile him as a *heretic.* He keeps cholera medicine constantly on our hall table, and we are almost constantly making arrow-root, &c., for the convalescent."

BEBEK, June 8, 1855.

"MY DEAR PRUDENCE: I had proceeded *thus* far in

my letter, when a pair of little pattering feet were heard
in the hall, and a soft voice at the door cries, 'Ope' e
door, ope' e door, mamma!' and then, 'Take me in mamma's lap,' and so ended my writing for a while. But now
the little one is tired of mamma's lap, and has consented
that I should take my pen again to write to 'Auntie.'
Dear little pet! I wish you could see her. And I wish
you could see *all* my pets, and that I could welcome you
for a few weeks or months to our home and hearts. In the
latter your place is secure and undisputed; but it would
be pleasant to *show* you your home in this far-off land.

"I have been searching in vain for your last letter,
received not long since. The date I have forgotten. I
felt like answering it immediately upon its arrival, but
having again a house full of company, I was obliged to
postpone the pleasant employment till after the annual
meeting, which has just closed its sessions, and most of
our friends are dispersed. There was a larger number of
delegates than usual, present,— Aintab, Arabkir, Cesarea,
Tokat, Marsooan, Trebizond, Salonica, and Smyrna, each
sending one or more, with their families. The meeting
continued more than two weeks, and some of the discus-
sions and reports were thrillingly interesting. Mrs. Goodell remarked, in relation to the meeting, when the reports
from some of the interior stations were read, and to the
day when we all united in celebrating a Saviour's dying
love, that none of the meetings of the Board in America
had, to her, surpassed in interest the meetings of this year
in Constantinople. These meetings were indeed saddened
by thoughts of the painful breaches made in our circle
since the last annual meeting. Pleasant voices, which
then mingled with ours, are now silent in the grave; and
active hands, ever ready to labor and aid in the blessed
work of building up the Redeemer's kingdom, are now
motionless and hidden from our sight. But these voices,
though to mortal ears silent, are yet, in sweeter tones than

27

ever here on earth, tuning a Saviour's praise, and those hands are still busy in the service of the Master they so loved when in this world. . . . Mr. Everett expects to move to Bebek next week, in order to assist Mr. Hamlin in the Seminary, and Miss West will be left alone with the care of the female school. I think it is quite too much for her to undertake, but it is her own wish, and there seems to be no limit to her ambition (in a *good* sense) and zeal.

"Miss West has just sent me a letter from her sister Sarah, announcing her intention to come to her aid. She is delighted and thankful, as well she may be. It is not many missionaries who enjoy the privilege of a mother's or a sister's aid and society."

"BEBEK, March 8, 1856.

"MY DEAR SISTER: Again the hand of the Lord is laid upon us, again our hearts are bleeding, while with tearful eyes we look up, and ask *why* is his chastising hand again thus laid upon us. But oh, what unutterable joy is to-day the portion of our *dear departed brother Everett*, as he again meets his Seraphina, his little ones, your dear husband, and above all, his precious Saviour, whom he so loved, and who enabled him to meet the last enemy so calmly and peacefully! Yes, dear sister, our dear brother Everett left us last evening at six o'clock for his home above, after a short illness of only seven days. Friday evening of last week he spent with us, *apparently* as well as usual. Saturday morning he did not feel quite well, but went over to Vizir Khan to the station meeting. In the evening as they were returning in the steamer, he complained of severe pain and suffering, and my husband saw that he was very ill. He told me afterward that it appeared to him then that the arrow of death had reached him. It is a pleasant thought that the messenger found him not slumbering, but *laboring*. He was engaged during the whole of the time on the steamer in religious conversation with an Armenian whom he found on board. The next morning he was unable to leave his bed, and never after arose. The physician gave scarcely any hope at any time. Mr. Hamlin often said, 'He is going just as dear brother Benjamin went, though more rapidly.' His peace and confidence were from the beginning unwavering. He calmly committed his little children to the Father of the fatherless. 'They are Christ's,—they have been given to him, and I have the firmest confidence that I shall meet them all in heaven.' Others will no doubt write you particulars which I have not time to-day to do. We are indeed brought low. Ah! why is such a dry branch as I spared, while such as he, as his beloved wife, and your dear husband, are taken? In mercy to *me*, I trust, that I may learn to be more faithful, and awake to more diligence, and surely in tender mercy to them, that they may enter upon rest. They were my fellow-passengers eleven years ago, and now only I am left. It is a day of storm and wind and snow, the gloomiest and severest we have had this year, so that to have the funeral to-day seemed almost out of the question."

"How like a dream does it all seem," she writes to another missionary sister, two months later, "the passing away in so short a time of all that dear family,—father and mother in heaven, and the orphan children now nearly arrived at their parents' home. All gone from among us, except their ever green and precious memories, and the blessed influence of their example and works."

Mrs. Hamlin was this spring called to a severe trial in sending from her their two eldest daughters to finish their school education in this country; and in parting from her husband, who accompanied his daughters for a short visit to his native land. For these daughters, as for all the five towards whom she had assumed the relation of mother, her affectionate heart cherished almost a mother's tenderness, and it was with much solicitude, and many earnest prayers, that she had for a year been anticipating the time when they must go far distant from parental care and guidance. Her letters make frequent reference to this, and occasionally also to the yearnings which the prospect of her husband and children visiting America, revived in her own heart to see once more her native shores, and the dear friends of her childhood and youth, after an absence of eleven years. But here, as always, she yielded cheerfully to the claims of duty, and prepared to remain behind, and take care of the four younger children. A little boy whom they called Alfred, had been added to the family group, a "great pet," as she writes, "being the first son after six daughters." He was now a "fat, rosy, laughing babe" of eight months. As Mr. and Mrs. Clark were to take charge of the seminary during Mrs. Hamlin's absence, it was thought best that Mrs. H. should remove to Hass Keuy, partly that she might in her loneliness be near Dr. Goodell's family, where she always felt as a daughter, and partly that the older children might enjoy the benefits of the little school for missionary children there, taught by one of Dr. Goodell's daughters. From this place she writes April 27th.

"I am writing this as you see, in my *new home*, — the first letter I have written from our new abode. We came here last week, and are as yet all in confusion, but I hope in a few days to get quietly settled, and enjoy *two or three* days of peaceful rest, before my husband and daughters leave for their long journey.

"May 12. Days of busy excitement have passed, while I have been unable to find a moment's time for writing, and hardly for thought. But now our dear ones are *gone*, and I am *alone* in a sense which I never realized before. Three days ago my husband and daughters started upon their long journey, and should Providence favor them, and carry them in safety, they will be in America by the last of June. They go by steam, visiting Paris, London, Edinburgh, &c., then by steam over the ocean. It was the wish of the Committee of the Board that my husband should visit these cities, and that his journey and absence should be as short as possible, — therefore he takes this course. It will be an interesting journey to the girls, and one I should much like to enjoy with them. Still more should I rejoice to be with them on their arrival in their father-land, to see them happily domesticated somewhere, and enjoy with them the refreshing society and communion of dear friends. But a 'wise Providence seems to have directed otherwise, and I try cheerfully to submit. But you can hardly imagine how desolate our house appears, how long the days are, though filled with business, and how every corner and every apartment seems to echo with the voices and footsteps of the departed ones. . . .

"I have not written half I wish and ought to say, and indeed I never do. But I am always hoping that a day of leisure will come when I may collect my thoughts, and for once write as I would like to do. I send you a *living epistle*, and you must question him, and draw from him all I would say were I with him. Introduce him to all our dear friends, but do not detain him long."

"BEBEK, February 20, 1857.

"You see I am again in Bebek, but not in our old, much-loved home. Mr. Clark, who took Mr. Hamlin's place during his absence, still remains, and we have taken a smaller house within speaking distance. It was thought best that my husband should take the theological department in the seminary, leaving the charge of the institution to Mr. C., and thus giving Mr. H. time and opportunity for more preaching and laboring among the people. He has just opened a new place of worship in a

27*

hitherto uncultivated part of the city, and has much to encourage him, and lead him to hope that a blessing will follow the undertaking. It takes him from home to a distant part of the city every Sabbath, which in severe winter or stormy weather is somewhat trying; but we trust we shall see cause to rejoice in the sacrifice of a little comfort for the cause of Christ. I often fear that he is assuming too many cares and duties, but while so much is to be done, and the laborers are so few, one can hardly stop to measure strength. And well it is that our strength is not in ourselves. I am not speaking of *myself*, for I often feel unworthy the name of missionary laborer. . . . The missionary work never seemed dearer to me, and perhaps was never more encouraging than now. Oh that the Spirit might be poured out from on high upon the youth of our beloved land, that they might in crowds be ready to consecrate themselves to the missionary work. There is much ground for encouragement, hope and faith in regard to the Mohammedans. Many, very many, are purchasing and reading the gospel, and already there are cases of hopeful conversion. How the matter will go on is known only to God. Whether others who come to a knowledge of the truth, will be suffered quietly to renounce Mohammed and confess Christ, remains to be seen. God reigns, and will bring his own cause off triumphant in the end, we know."

"March 13, 1857. Mary, are you going to give any or *all* of your children to the missionary work? Come and *see* us, — come and see this land and the people about us, and see if your heart is not touched, and you are not ready to consecrate *all* your loved ones to the blessed work of teaching these lost multitudes the way of life. Give them all my love, and tell little Sarah that '*Hats goosin*,' which means *they* wish bread, — the *bread of life*. If she will come here I will teach her more Armenian, and she shall be a little missionary."

To Mrs. Crane, May 10.

"You have doubtless heard of the wonderful movement, silent, as yet, but deep, among the Mohammedans. You probably know that several have been baptized, and many others are convinced of the truth. We are almost daily hearing of new and interesting cases. Since the commencement of Ramazan, we have heard of the imprisonment of four for adherence to the gospel, and for *breaking their fast.* How they will endure persecution for the name of Christ remains to be seen, but *one* of them seems, I hear, to be a most interesting and decided case.

"Our little home flock are all well. *Allie* is running about, and calling 'papa! dear papa!' The Misses West are visiting me, as it is now their vacation. Their school, *my* 'first love,' is very prosperous, — frequently visited with the gentle rain from on high. We are greatly rejoiced to hear that you are enjoying *showers* upon your field. I have not seen any letters from Oroomiah, but have been told that the seminaries were enjoying a precious revival. Oh that *we* too might be visited!"

The following letter describes some of the scenes of the last Annual Meeting in which she was to have a part: —

"BEBEK, May 30, 1857.

"MY VERY DEAR PRUDENCE: Your two precious letters of Feb. 18, and April 18, lie before me, and I wish I could hope to send you any thing half so good in return. I have been in such a whirl of business for the last two or three weeks, that I fear I shall hardly be able to write a connected and readable letter. It is the season of the annual meeting of our mission, and every house is full of guests. Yesterday the meetings were held in Bebek, and we determined, instead of entertaining our friends at our different houses, to lunch all together in the large hall of the Seminary building. *Forty-six* grown persons sat at a long table in the hall, while a merry and happy little company of twenty-one children sat at a table in an adjoining room, feasting upon strawberries, &c. It was a delightful interview; not alone the gathering around the social board, but more especially the meetings for religious intercourse and business which preceded and followed it. As our missionary field widens and *whitens*, these annual meetings become seasons of deeper and deeper interest, from the great and important questions and measures which are coming up before the Mission. And never since its commencement has there been a time of more interest than the present. I wish you could be here once at such a time; you would get a better idea of our work, its difficulties, its successes, its pleasures and trials, and above all of the magnitude of the work, than you could get in any other way. And you would have such an opportunity, too, of becoming acquainted with some of the choice spirits with whom it is our privilege to be associated, though not often meeting except on such occasions. I had the pleasure of entertaining, last week, Mrs. Van Lennep and her family, from Tokat. She is a precious sister. She and Mrs. Everett have always been peculiarly dear to me. While she was with me, her little boy, a very lovely child, was very ill, and as soon as he recovered, *my* little Alfred was seized in the same way. For two or three days I was very anxious about him; but God heard my prayers, and he recovered almost as rapidly as he became ill, and I now hear his happy little voice in another room, merry as ever.

"June 8. My letter has been unavoidably neglected for many days. I have just returned from attending the closing meeting of the annual session at Pera. It was a most interesting and affecting season; and I could not but wish that you, and other dear friends to whom I am indebted for letters, could have been present at this meeting, and listened to the recapitulation briefly made, of all

that has been done during the meeting, and of all that is
to be done and hoped for during the year to come.
Never before have I been so impressed with the magnitude of the work, and the *blessedness* of it.   Oh for
more entire consecration to it, and greater usefulness
in it!"

Mrs. Hamlin was now rapidly finishing up her life's
work.   All unconsciously to herself and to those about
her, she was fast approaching the end of her pilgrimage;
and as she drew near to that home of the blessed, into
which "nothing entereth that defileth," she became more
and more assimilated in spirit to its holy inhabitants.
Her husband and others remarked that during these last
months she was "more than ever spiritually minded."
In the prospect of removing into a new house which was
preparing for them, she more than once said to her husband that they might never all occupy it together, and
that they should have no desire for earthly rest, and
pleasant circumstances here, lest these should turn their
hearts from heaven.   A few more of the last written ex-
pressions of her love and tender interest for her dear
absent friends we may record.

To Mrs. Schauffler, then in the United States, she
wrote, Aug. 6, 1857 : —

"In the multitude of letters which will, I am sure, await
your arrival in Boston, I can hardly hope to be able to give
you any *news*, and yet I can not consent to be found
wanting among the multitude, though I should only
repeat what others tell you.   We received your notes
from Marseilles two or three days since, and were glad to
hear that you had been carried so far in safety.   Our
thoughts and prayers attend you from day to day, and
we trust the Good Shepherd also attends you, and will
make this journey and visit a great blessing to yourselves
and to the cause of Christ.   . . .

"You will hear from others that the Freemans* are at last safe in Bebek, and how they are disposed of. They will, I fear, miss you very much, for no one can be to them what you have been. But I trust they will be happy and useful. We will try to do for them what we can. Another time I will try to write something more worthy of so long a journey; this will merely serve to tell you how much we think of you, how much we miss you and long for your return, and that we will endeavor to do what we can for the dear boys you have left behind. You will of course hear from others of the political agitation just now. The French and Prussian arms taken down, and the French ambassador on board a steamer prepared to leave in three days. Can it be that the Lord will again permit war to desolate all Europe. *He* reigns.

"Kindest love to Mr. Schauffler. How much we miss him at all times, but especially on the Sabbath, we can not express. My dear husband is, if possible, busier than ever. Last Sabbath he organized a small church of seven members at Balat. He desires love to you and yours. I feel more like asking you to pardon this very hasty and imperfect note, than to answer it; but I do hope to hear from you. Love to *all* American friends, (mentioning many by name.) Good night!

"Your affectionate sister,   H. M. L. HAMLIN."

The following is her last letter to her mother. The brother of whom she speaks with such tender anxiety, and for whose spiritual welfare she had for many years been deeply solicitous, did not long survive his sister; but he left, for the consolation of his widowed mother, the hope that he had gone to meet her in heaven.

BEBEK, Oct. 5, 1857.

MY DEAR MOTHER: Miss West leaves here in a day or two for my own beloved home of former days. You

* A family of converted Turks.

will be surprised to see her, but a nervous illness has so weakened her as to render her unable to endure school labors and confinement, and her physician advises a visit *home.* I have stayed at home from meeting this evening, in order to hastily pen a few lines to you. From a letter which Maria received lately from Palmyra, I learn that you and Henry are in P., and he "quite low." I have most anxiously awaited every mail, hoping and yet dreading, to receive a letter from you; but none has reached me, and I am still indebted to second-hand letters for all the information I get of dear Henry's illness. I have not written to him, much as I have wished to do so, because I know so little of his feelings. I find it difficult to realize that he is a man, and I think of him as the beloved "little brother" I left twelve years ago. But I long to hear from you something of his state, — his bodily and spiritual state. We remember him daily in our prayers. Even little Clara, every night, of her own accord, prays that God would "please make dear uncle Henry well."

Our hearts are full of anxiety also in regard to our dear Susan, who is in very feeble health. We have written for her to return home if possible this fall. . . . And now what can I say through you to my beloved brother? Perhaps, before this reaches you, he may be beyond the reach of any message. But if not, oh tell him how his sister's heart yearns after him; how she longs to hear that he is not without a cheerful hope in Christ, and a cheerful submission to the will of God, whether it should be life or death, and that she longs to be able to cherish the joyful hope of meeting him in a better world, — and for this prays night and day.

My dear husband sends much love and earnest sympathy in your present care and anxiety, *perhaps* your deep affliction. God bless, and comfort, and sustain!

Ever your affectionate daughter,

MARTHA.

To Miss West she wrote the same evening: —

"MY DEAR MARIA: I have heard that you are probably to leave for Smyrna on Wednesday of this week! Is it possible that you are to go without coming again to Bebek? To go to *our* home, and I not see you again? I would gladly go to Hass Keuy, but I fear it will be impossible. Well, God go with you, carry you in safety, and grant you a happy meeting with all your dear friends! And then, after you have been refreshed and strengthened, may you be brought back again to the work which will so much need your presence and oversight. We trust God will look after the school in your absence, and give to your sister all the strength and aid she will require; but we shall all long for your return. And what shall I say, through you, to all the dear friends in Palmyra? When I begin to think of them one by one, I know not where to stop. Give my love to them *all*. Tell your mother that *I*, that all thank her for giving up two daughters to this good work."

After special messages to several very intimate friends, she says: —

"Tell them that, *perhaps*, at some future day, if God spares us all, we may meet in that goodly land; but if not, there is a better land; and there, I trust, a joyful meeting awaits us.

"Greetings to the dear church, of whom perhaps few now know me personally, and to any and all of my Sabbath-school class you may meet, all now grown to be women and mothers. . . .

"Finally and again, may God be with you, and give you the light of his presence, and grant you restored health and a happy visit. Ever truly and affectionately your sister,   MARTHA."

Mrs. Crane, one of the missionary sisters in Oroomiah, with whom she had maintained a regular and frequent correspondence, was also on her way to America, and was to sail from Smyrna in the same vessel with Miss West. To her Mrs. Hamlin wrote the following letter, to reach her in Smyrna: —

"Bebek, Oct. 13, 1857.

"My dear Sister: Our short interview, and sudden and hurried parting of yesterday, were so unlike what I had wished and hoped for, that I have felt quite unreconciled to letting you go thus. I hoped, when I heard you were on your way hither, that I should enjoy a good visit with you, though it must be a parting one; that we should together have reviewed the past, and recounted anew the dealings of the Lord with us, and together have enjoyed *once* more the sweet privilege of bowing before our Father's throne. But as all these have been denied, I can not deny myself the pleasure of snatching a few moments this evening, hoping that a line may still reach you in Smyrna. I want to thank you for all the good I think you have done me, by your sisterly affection, and precious letters. I need not ask you still to remember me, to pray for me and my children, and our work; I know you will do so, and sometimes will, when you can find a leisure hour and strength, write to me as of old. Can you not see my dear mother? She is now in Palmyra, with a sick, and perhaps dying brother, her only child, and 'she a widow.' And will it not be possible for you to see our daughters? . . . . "Our prayers will follow you through all your long voyage, and we earnestly pray that if it be the Lord's will, you may be greatly benefited by the journey, and yet live many years, — live to see your dear boy a minister of the gospel, a missionary, — live to see great and wonderful triumphs of the Redeemer's kingdom. I would write more, but can not. And now once more *farewell!* The blessing of the Lord, his unfailing, gracious presence be with you on your voyage, and evermore? We shall soon meet, — soon shall enjoy unbroken

28

intercourse with the loved ones gone before, with each
other, and, better than all, with him who will be our
soul's delight, the brightness and glory of heaven, — if
indeed one so unworthy, so full of sin and imperfection
as I, may hope to reach that holy place.

"Will you hand the enclosed note to sister Maria, some
pleasant morning after you have entered the Atlantic?

"Love to all your party, and to our dear friends in
Smyrna. Farewell!

"Your ever loving sister,   H. M. L. HAMLIN."

This is the note to be handed to Miss West — "sister
Maria" — after entering the Atlantic. On the envelope
is written: "Atlantic Ocean, morning of the 17th of November, 1857. Have just passed through the straits.
Eddie handed me this welcome letter."

"Good morning! Perhaps you will require that I should
give my name and *wherefrom.* You did not expect to
meet a stranger so far from *terra firma;* and indeed I *am*
no stranger. I flatter myself you have guessed me out
before this. I hope this morning's sun finds you cheerful
and happy, and free from that enemy of all comfort, —
seasickness. You have turned the *last corner,* although
a long journey still lies before you. May the divine hand
bear you safely and happily over the great sea, and fill
your soul with gratitude and adoration.

"It is late in the evening, — nearly every one has
retired. The time I had devoted to writing you a good
long note has been taken up by Master Alfred, who
seemed determined not to sleep when I most desired it.
But I have taken just enough paper to assure you of a
sister's love and sympathy, and also of her poor, unworthy
prayers that you may be strengthened, and speedily
brought back to the work so dear, I trust, to both our
hearts.

"We will try to do all we can to cheer your sister during your long absence, and hope she will frequently find a home with us for a night or two.

"My dear husband joins with me in love to you and all your homeward-bound fellow-travelers. We shall long to hear good tidings from you as soon as may be after your arrival. Pardon this little hasty note, hardly worthy so long a journey. It will be in vain, I suppose, to ask a reply immediate, as there is no ocean post, no carrier-pigeon, no telegraph at your command,—unless you can write your reply upon some passing cloud, or upon the moon's fair face.

"Good night, and good-by *for a little*.

"Ever your affectionate sister, MARTHA."

She to whom this note was addressed, little thought, while perusing it, that the hand that traced it, and the warm, loving heart that breathed through it, had been nearly two weeks still and cold in the grave.

Mrs. Hamlin's death was preceded by few of the usual antecedents of that solemn event. Not even a brief illness was given, to prepare herself and her friends for their long separation, and afford her an opportunity to leave her dying testimony to the power of that faith of which she had been so bright a living example. From an active participation in all the scenes and employments of this life, she was transferred, almost in a moment, to the scenes and employments of another and higher life. But so habituated was she to the contemplation of that life, so heavenly in her feelings and aspirations, it could hardly have surprised her greatly to find herself so suddenly ushered upon its scenes, and mingling in the joys of seraphs and redeemed ones around the throne of God.

On Thursday, the 5th of November, she was slightly unwell from what appeared to be a cold. That night she retired with a severe sick headache, such as she often suffered from, and during the night obtained little rest,

owing to the pain and sickness, accompanied with faintness. Between 5 and 6 o'clock in the morning she experienced a sudden loss of memory; then followed a terrible
convulsion, to which succeeded a state of lethargy. From
this, bleeding aroused her only for a moment, when she
turned on her husband one last look of love, and then
closed her eyes for ever on him and on all the scenes of
earth. A sweet, placid expression gradually spread over
her countenance, and at half past nine she quietly
breathed her last, Friday morning, Nov. 6, 1857.

"We had no time given us," writes her bereaved
husband, "for farewells, for tokens of dying love to children and friends, no last messages, no cheering words of
triumphant faith. But I have what is better than all
these combined, the testimony of a life of singular purity,
devotedness, and self-denial. Mr. Goodell, in a consola-
tory note, remarks: 'Your beloved partner, who made
your family so happy, and who has now gone to be with
the happy for ever, was certainly one of the most faultless persons I ever knew.' To God be all the glory! But
the same thing which makes my consolation to abound,
increases also my sense of bereavement and loss."

To his daughters in America, Mr. Hamlin wrote: "For
your dear mother herself we have no occasion to mourn.
Among all the servants of Christ whom I know, I can
not select one who I think had a more constant desire to
serve him, to do his work, to receive his approbation, and
to enjoy his presence and blessing in all the events of
life, and in all its duties. His word, his kingdom, his
cross, were precious to her. She was humble, devout,
affectionate, self-denying; always seeking others' good
rather than her own. Above all, she most earnestly
prayed that God would give her grace and wisdom to
guide this dear family to him. Has any one ever seen a
sign of her being to you, and Carrie, and Abbie, and the
little sainted Mary, a step-mother? I can testify to the

depth and earnestness of her love, and solicitude, and prayers for you all."

Extract from an obituary notice of Mrs. Hamlin, by Rev. Dr. Dwight.

"Mrs. Hamlin, then Miss Lovell, arrived at Constantinople, in the year 1845. She came expressly to take charge of a Female Boarding School, which had long been projected, but remained unopened for want of a suitable Superintendent. Testimonials of her moral worth, and of her general fitness to engage in such a work, were furnished to the Prudential Committee of the American Board, by her pastor, and copies of these testimonials reached Constantinople before she arrived. They were so strongly worded, that the missionaries were ready to ascribe them in part to the partiality of friendship, and we dared not hope that she would fully answer the description given; but we can truly say she did answer it, and even exceed it.

"The brother in whose family Miss Lovell resided during the first five years of the school, remarks of her, that during the whole of that period, in no word or action of hers, did he ever see any thing which he could have wished otherwise, so faultless was she in all her deportment. She was a person of delicate sensibilities, refined taste, and varied accomplishments, natural and acquired, which fitted her eminently for the place she occupied in this mission, and all that she possessed she cheerfully laid at the Saviour's feet.

"Her influence on the school, and through the school on the whole Protestant community in Turkey, can scarcely be overestimated. Within six years there were no less than four seasons of special religious awakening in the institution, during which there was the most striking evidence of the presence of the Holy Spirit, working with great power on the hearts of the pupils. . . . . We can all testify to the faithful earnestness with which

28*

our departed friend entered into these scenes, and to the great practical wisdom and tact she ever manifested in dealing with individual cases. The fact is, she was constant and fervent in prayer, and the Lord was faithful to his promise, and gave her the help that she so much needed in her deeply responsible position.

"After seven years of the most assiduous labor in that important sphere, she was called to assume other duties and responsibilities as the wife of our now afflicted brother, and the mother of his then motherless children; and great indeed were the light, and joy, and gladness she brought into that desolate household.

"The same unobtrusive zeal, diligence, perseverance, and Christian faithfulness that characterized her whole course in the Female Boarding School, she carried with her into the family, making a hearty, firm, and unfaltering consecration of herself, not simply to her appropriate household duties, but to the far higher and nobler work of the spiritual training of those intrusted to her care. Distrustful of herself, but keeping in view a high standard of maternal duty, she was led to seek help from God in frequent and earnest prayer; nor did she seek in vain.

"She had deep conviction and experience of the power of prayer, and often did she solicit Christian friends to unite with her in praying for objects in which she was interested. The last request she ever made of some of her dearest friends was, that they would pray for one in whose salvation she felt a special interest. Only a few days before her departure, while speaking with her husband of their youngest child, she expressed, in the strongest manner, the one desire of her heart, that he might live to preach the gospel of Christ; and remarked that she could truly say, '*he was a child of many prayers.*'

"Of Mrs. Hamlin it may be said, with eminent truth, that she was always 'diligent in business, fervent in spirit,

serving the Lord.' While she was eminently a praying
Christian, she was also a watchful Christian. She ever
exercised a holy jealousy over her own heart, and was
exceedingly afraid of the paralyzing influences of this
world." . . .

Referring to her sudden departure from this world, Dr.
Dwight says: " But none who knew her life will feel the
need of last words from her to satisfy them that she is
now a happy spirit, among the blessed around the throne
of God. . . . And never will she regret having made
the sacrifices she did, that she might lead the daughters
of Armenia to receive the truth as it is in Jesus. Some
of those who through her instrumentality were guided to
the Saviour, and have since been gathered to his upper
kingdom, we can not doubt, were ready, with rapturous
joy, to welcome her coming there; and we trust that
many others will yet join the happy company, who will
bless God for ever that he brought our beloved sister to
this land."

And she too sleeps in Jesus, — she, the last
Of the devoted three, who o'er the deep
Together took their way; forsaking home
And kindred for the love of him who died
For them. Faithful she toiled, nor counted dear
Time, talents, — yea, her all, if she might win,
From her benighted sisters of the East,
Some jewels for his crown; nor toiled in vain.
For many a priceless gem shall sparkle there,
By her meek counsels and her earnest prayers
Reclaimed from sin and death. But not alone
Do sad Armenia's daughters weep her loss,
For one is there, — chief of the mourning train, —
Who called her by the tender name of wife;
And children's woe, so passionate, though brief,
Breaks forth in piteous plaints for her who ne'er
With the warm promptings of a mother's love
Will soothe again their little griefs and pains.
Ay, verily to her has been fulfilled
The Saviour's promise of a hundred-fold,
To those who for his sake shall leave their home
And kindred, even in this present life.

> Not fathers, mothers, only had she found,
> Brothers and sisters, but a happy home
> Of wedded love.   And now her work complete,
> Her mission all fulfilled, and having well
> Performed each part, of teacher, sister, friend,
> Mother, and wife, her Master wills that she
> Shall go up higher.   All prepared was she,
> Though on her ear had rung no warning cry,—
> " Behold the Bridegroom cometh! "
>
> >   Shall we say
> She went too soon?   Too soon exchanged the pains,
> The weariness and sorrows of the way,
> For the sweet rest, the perfect bliss, of heaven?
> Oh, let us follow her in meekness, faith,
> And self-denying labors for our Lord;
> That we, like her, may to the paths of peace
> Allure some wandering souls, and leave, like her,
> The memory of a life filled up with deeds
> Of usefulness and love.

For those who have read through the preceding pages, a summary of character will hardly be necessary.   Yet it may not be unprofitable to consider briefly some of the more prominent traits which made these two Missionary Sisters so lovely and useful.

It has been remarked that in natural temperament they were quite dissimilar, and the reader will doubtless have noticed something of this dissimilarity in their letters. Mrs. Everett was of an ardent, impulsive nature, and very lively and social; Mrs. Hamlin serious, quiet, and reserved.   But the same grace modified both these temperaments, and from each wrought out beautiful and consistent Christian characters.   If Mrs. Everett's liveliness ever led her into lightness, as she intimates in some of her letters that it did, in her early years, the love of Christ, and a deep sympathy with him in his yearnings for the salvation of perishing souls, chastened that liveliness into a steady cheerfulness, which helped much to keep up her energies, and enable her to meet, with such unruffled sweetness, the varied and arduous duties of her missionary life. The same love for Christ and lost sinners, diverted Mrs. Hamlin's mind from all morbid tendencies, if it ever had any, and by keeping constantly before her a great object to pray, and labor, and hope for, made her also a cheerful as well as earnest Christian.

The reader may have noticed the coincidence in the time of their conversion. Both consecrated themselves to the Lord, and united with his people, at the age of fifteen. And not only did they both commence their Christian course early, but they commenced right. Their consecration to God was hearty and entire, and like Saul of Tarsus, their first question, and the question that seemed to be ever in their hearts was: "Lord, what wilt thou have me to do?" Yet they did not sit down in idle expectation of some great work being provided for them, but went at once to the performance of every duty, doing every thing, however small, "as unto the Lord." Mrs. Everett, in her school, sought constantly the spiritual good of her pupils, and both, earnestly and tenderly tried to persuade their unconverted brothers and sisters to come to Christ, and to bring all their Sabbath scholars into his fold. Their early letters, as well as the testimony of their friends, show that they were always prayerful, studious in the Scriptures, and active in doing good as they had opportunity. It is not strange that with this faithful discharge of duty, and earnest seeking after more knowledge and grace, they should have felt their hearts drawn towards the millions perishing for lack of knowledge in other lands, — that the "missionary spirit," as it is called, should have been early kindled in their souls. The missionary spirit, — why should this term be used in any peculiar sense? What is the missionary spirit but the Christian spirit? What but the love of Christ, constraining the Christian to love all for whom he died, and to be willing to go wherever he shall lead, and engage in any service he shall appoint? And why is one Christian to possess *this* spirit more than another, or why should there be a class to be distinguished as possessing the "missionary spirit?" These two young Christians thought of the love of Christ, and of all he had suffered for them, till their hearts burned to do more for him, — to make greater sacrifices in return for his infinite love. They thought of the condition of the greater part of the world, and the general indifference of Christians to the state of their benighted brethren and sisters, till they longed to go and tell some of them of the Saviour they so loved, — not because there were none to be guided to him in their own land, but that here there were enough to teach the ignorant and the sinful, while those distant ones were perishing for want of the teacher to tell them of the Saviour. That this was the outgushing of their love to Christ and the souls for whom he died, and not a mere enthusiastic impulse or desire for novelty, is evident from their entire willingness to go to any part of the world. To India or China Mrs. Everett at first expected to be sent; Mrs. Hamlin, when asked, said she would not raise a finger to decide the question as to where she should go; and this entire willingness to be guided by the Lord, this singleness of devotion to his cause and his will, gives us one clue to the secret of their uncommon usefulness.

There is another thing to be noticed, as showing how they accomplished so much, — their industry. It has been remarked by those who knew them most intimately, that they were never idle. Every little fragment of time was carefully gathered up by them; they seemed to keep ever before them that they were to "do with their might what their hands found to do." And habits of system and order helped them to do all they did without hurry or confusion.

Yet one other trait which was prominent in both, should not be overlooked, — their feminine delicacy, and nice sense of propriety. Their zeal for Christ, and desire for the salvation of the perishing, never led them to over step the proper limits of their position. In their own sphere they exerted all their energies to do good, and point the lost sinner to the Cross ; but the sweet womanly virtues of gentleness, meekness, and the most retiring modesty, were their crowning ornaments. And in nothing is their example more worthy of imitation than in the fidelity and grace with which they discharged every domestic duty. They had not " so learned Christ " as to believe that in following him they were to neglect their first and most sacred duties as wives and mothers, and heads of households, and it was in all the relations of home that their deep and earnest piety shone most beautifully.

Does the attainment of such elevation and symmetry of Christian character seem a difficult one ? It is not easy; but it is worth striving for. Through faith and patience, through much prayer and watchfulness, those missionary sisters acquired it, and by the same "looking unto Jesus," the same persevering effort to overcome every obstacle, we, who have traced their earnest, unfaltering progress, may follow in the same path, and find it, as they did, growing "brighter unto the perfect day."